THE DISTANCE

Also by Jeremy Robinson

Standalone Novels
The Didymus Contingency
Beneath
Kronos
Xom-B
Flood Rising
MirrorWorld
Apocalypse Machine
Unity
The Distance

Nemesis Saga Novels
Raising The Past
Island 731
Project Nemesis
Project Maigo
Project 731
Project Hyperion
Project Legion

The Antarktos Saga
The Last Hunter – Descent
The Last Hunter – Pursuit
Antarktos Rising
The Last Hunter – Ascent
The Last Hunter – Lament
The Last Hunter – Onslaught
The Last Hunter – Collected Edition

The Jack Sigler/Chess Team Thrillers
Prime
Pulse
Instinct
Threshold
Ragnarok
Omega
Savage
Cannibal
Empire

Cerberus Group Novels
Herculean

Jack Sigler Continuum Novels
Guardian
Patriot

Chesspocalypse Novellas
Callsign: King
Callsign: Queen
Callsign: Rook
Callsign: King 2 – Underworld
Callsign: Bishop
Callsign: Knight
Callsign: Deep Blue
Callsign: King 3 – Blackout

Chesspocalypse Novella Collections
Callsign: King – The Brainstorm Trilogy
Callsign – Tripleshot
Callsign – Doubleshot

SecondWorld Novels
SecondWorld
Nazi Hunter: Atlantis

Horror Novels (written as Jeremy Bishop)
Torment
The Sentinel
The Raven
Refuge

Post-Apocalyptic Sci-Fi Novels (written as Jeremiah Knight)
Hunger
Feast
Viking Tomorrow (2017)

THE
DISTANCE

JEREMY & HILAREE
ROBINSON

BREAKNECK MEDIA

For Hil, you've taken your first brave step.
Now it's time to run.

—Jeremy

To Jeremy, my husband of twenty-one adventurous, creative years,
and to my Dad, who when I was seventeen years old said he wanted
the first copy of my first book.

—Hilaree

GRIND

1

POE

I scream in pain, gripped by his loving-turned-violent hands. He drags me down the stairs, into the basement. My legs bounce over the steps, loose and rubbery, lacking motivation to fight or kick. I'm lost. Confused. She follows us down, her face twisted in an expression I can't understand beyond a single word: crazy.

They've gone mad.

My shin cracks into the corner of the railing's support post, snapping my mind into crystal clear focus for a moment that drags out, stretched like a rubber band. As I'm forced and shoved downward, time slows enough for me to wonder, *how did this happen?*

My mind flits back a few hours. I'm sitting on the living room couch, and for some reason, thinking about Todd.

I told him to leave. Actually, that's not true. I told him to hang himself from a coat rack and die, but the message was essentially the same: go away.

Why? I could give a long list of reasons. The usual trite bullshit that marks the end of every relationship. But the truth is, it's a long time trait. Probably genetic, skipping a generation, like baldness, but more surly and vocal.

As a short-for-my-age five year old, when adults, bending at the waist, infuriated me with the question of what I wanted to be when I grew up, I said in my tiny squeak, "A hermit on a mountaintop".

But that never stopped them from trying to pull more words out of me. What I wanted most was the uninterrupted benevolence of solitude. I wanted to draw. I wanted to read. I wanted to observe. I loved the furious insides of my own small head, the container for my big thoughts. Even then, total introversion's beautiful appeal gripped my imagination, and my self-image materialized as a small, capable pioneer. Alone, on purpose.

I wanted silence. I still do.

And now, wrapped in an ancient, granny-squared afghan in my parents' living room, feet up on the cracked leather hassock, sketchbook resting beside me, I know why I told the father of my child that he didn't need to stick around. Because there's nothing better than autonomy. Because my tiny frame, already showing the no-bigger-than-a-raspberry child, will do just fine on its own.

The crackling woodstove draws me up to a sitting position, heating the living room of the house I grew up in. Fire attracts me. I lift my hands toward the warmth. Dried blue paint clings around my cuticles. Scribbled notes tattoo the back of my left hand. Important things to remember or considerations for in-progress paintings. *Call gallery. Emphasize strength—red? Get prenatal vitamins.*

I'll raise that kid myself.

"Woodstoves smell like Frost's poetry sounds," my father says, coming in from the barn. The night is black and white behind him, through the open kitchen door; a blizzard swirls through New Hampshire's forested evening. He stamps his boots against the doorframe, freeing clumps of snow, and hangs his red parka on the hook near the stove.

My mother perches on the edge of a kitchen chair at the table, peeling squash. Quick little movements. Shards of peel fall orange around her feet, somehow missing the table, her mind several steps ahead of her present state. "How's our little calf?" she asks, not looking back to see if Dad is listening. "Can you get me two more butternuts from the cellar? We'll have to plant more this year, they grew so well. Maybe more potatoes, too." She peels, lightning fast. "What did we use for fertilizer this year? Straight manure, right? I was thinking we could try crab meal next year."

I take the seven steps it requires to reach the kitchen from the couch, and sit across from her at the table, afghan around my shoulders. "Mmm...maybe you could feed the entire town, Mom. That squash smells so weird." I lean over to sniff it. "Dad didn't hear you, he's down cellar already."

"Poe. You've got a little bun in the oven, honey. *Everything* will smell weird." She glances over her glasses at me. "And make you want to throw up."

My father emerges from the cellar and sets the squash down on the table. So he *did* hear her. Or read her mind, which is more likely. "Make you want to throw up...like being locked in a room, forced to watch reality TV." He looks off into the middle distance. "No. That doesn't quite work."

We stare at each other, thinking. "Like riding a roller coaster," he says. "In July." My father and I ponder in images, analyze and articulate with visual illustrations of our thoughts. We're cute together that way, and have formed careers out of our commonality—mine as a painter, his as a poet.

"Riding a roller coaster in July," I say, "next to a fat guy who smells of cheese dogs, spilled beer and mustard, and whose tight white T-shirt is soaked through with sweat."

"Perfect!" He ambles off to the living room, all elbows, knees and shoulders, smiling.

My mother, mentally filtering out our visual aid, continues where she left off. "Obviously we'll need more tomatoes, maybe more cherry. Those sweet ones you like, Poe. Can just pop them in your mouth." The endless provider of food tips her gray ponytailed head, thinking.

I grab a second peeler from the drawer and start in on squash number two, not because I'm helpful, or hungry, but because

I want the smell to go away, and that's not going to happen until these gourds are stripped naked, diced, boiled, buttered and consumed.

Toward the end of dinner, the inevitable.

"You really should consider just moving back here with us, Poesy," my father half mumbles, using my lifelong nickname, his mouth full of chicken they raised and butchered themselves. "With the little squirt. It doesn't matter how old you are. Who cares? The shit's going to hit the fan before you know it. We're under constant threat. Humanity is vulnerable, although we think we're not." He leans back in his chair, hands behind his head, arms creating huge triangle wings, convinced and casual about it.

Here we go, I think. During my late teenagehood, my parents began dabbling in all things supernatural and weird, whether it was crop circles, ghosts, or time travel. You name it. Aliens were the big topic. UFOs. Abductions. Crazy stuff, like those people on Unsolved Mysteries, but without the far off look in their eyes. That was always the difference. Despite the crazy, my parents always seemed lucid and thoughtful.

I went to college at MassArt in Boston, and was happy to leave them a few hours behind me, up north, getting embroiled in their 'research.' It affected their political leanings and their relationships with friends. Ten years later, their superstitions and concerns for humanity's well-being are causing them to seriously consider becoming survivalists. They bought the cow this past year. Of course, when I mention all this to friends, they say I'm lucky to have such sane parents. I can see their point. They're not angry. They hardly ever fight.

My mother fiddles with her burgundy prayer shawl, one her sister knitted for her, adjusting it over her thin frame. Wisps of gray hair are tucked behind her ears, girlish. She leans forward and extends her hand to me. I let her squeeze my fingers. "How many people have the Hochman's now? Poe? How many?"

I don't answer.

Not because I can't, but because the number numbs me. Over ten thousand cases of the disease worldwide, spread by a virus. Ten thousand, including the dead and dying. Compared to the flu, it still wasn't the world's number one killer virus, but it was the most deadly. While the very young and very old are at mortal risk from the flu, Hochman's kills everyone, even the healthiest of us. Here in New Hampshire, there hasn't been a single reported case. Yet. Massachusetts is up to thirty, so it probably won't be long before it crosses the border, a refugee looking for a new home, always looking for a new home. Each host dies within five days. But maybe our smaller and more spread out population will slow it down?

My mother continues, doom and gloom like mist in the air, thick. "You honestly think we're all going to be just fine?"

I want to get up and leave; I feel irritated, pregnant and tired. I want to go back to my quiet apartment and work on a painting, but one look outside, at the raging blizzard, reminds me why I came here tonight. My crappy apartment building, with its crumbling brick façade and old, drafty horsehair plaster walls insulated by centuries-old layers of wallpaper, will likely lose power. A heatless home in central NH, in February, gets too cold fast. My pipes will probably be frozen when I return.

My parents, of course, have a generator, with enough propane to blow up the state. And there's always the woodstove. Many chilly childhood nights, before the generator purchase, were spent camping in the living room, woodstove raging, a line of sleeping bags on the braided rug.

"I'm having a baby," I tell my mother, and stand up, clearing dishes and avoiding the sour subject. My mother understands. Any woman who has carried a baby would. A bleak future cannot be considered lightly, over a meal, while growing a soul that will have to deal with whatever hell awaits. She gives me a nimble pat on the back, freeing me from the conversation, and heads to her chair in the living room. Then she sits down and picks up her knitting, knowing I'll insist on doing all the dishes.

I watch my mother while rinsing dishes, the fork clanking loudly as I scrape clinging potatoes into the garbage disposal. I can see her from the kitchen sink, her legs folded beneath her on the chair. We sit the same way, our light, muscular frames always bent into pretzels. She's knitting socks, beautiful already, terra cotta orange yarn, flecks of green, her hands ever busy. She's tiny and energetic, like me. Our hands constantly create. This is what I'll look like thirty years from now, my child cleaning the dishes.

"Dad, you write anything new recently?" I run the hot water, filling the deep, white porcelain sink with bubbles. Five years ago, my father was nominated for the Pulitzer in poetry. He lost to a woman from Nigeria.

I shiver a little—it's cold in the kitchen, despite the crackling woodstove. I roll up my sweater sleeves and sink my arms deep into the water. "You guys should put some plastic up over these windows."

My father steps up beside me, eying the goodies on the stovetop. "Eh, we'll see. I've got a few pieces in the works. How about you? Is that gallery in Portsmouth showing your new series or some of your older stuff?" He helps himself to another piece of strawberry rhubarb pie, one of two featured pies at dinner. This one he baked himself, the strawberries and rhubarb from their prodigious garden, waiting in the freezer for a year.

The television in the living room comes on, my mother blinking at the bright screen. She's watching the news. I have to talk over it.

"The exhibit's next week, actually. My new stuff. You know, the really huge canvases. They want six of them, which is amazing. They'll take up the whole gallery."

A weatherman drones on, like we didn't already know about the snow. Been snowing all day. It'll continue heavily through the night. Storm of the year. Potential for three feet. I hear the channel change to some sitcom rerun. Seinfeld. An episode where Jerry finds out yet another new woman in his life is minutely flawed and runs the other way. *Screw you, Jerry,* I think. *Who needs you? I don't even watch your damn show.*

My father brings more plates to the sink. Pie crust crumbs cling to his short white beard. "You're a mess," I say, and I brush him off, my wet hand dripping water on his blue plaid flannel shirt. The shirt matches his eyes. He taps my nose once with his fingertip, and I turn back to the soapy water. Snow is beginning to stick to the kitchen window above the sink, a ring of white.

He leans against the counter and wipes the old dishes, stacking them dry on the table. "I think those are some of your best. The colors are so vivid. You're like a young Frida Kahlo. My little Poesy."

I feel shy. He's never complimented my painting in that way before. "But without the bushy unibrow." I hand him a rinsed plate.

He snorts. "Like Kahlo if she..." he starts, when my mother screams from the other room.

"Calvin! It's happening. I think it's happening!"

The plate slips from his fingers and drops to the oak floor. It shatters. Shards slide across the kitchen, under the table, under the refrigerator. He ignores them and crunches right over the pieces in his LL Bean moccasins, straight to my mother. She's standing in front of the television, her knitting needles in one hand, half-finished orange sock in the other.

I follow my father. "Dad, you broke a plate!"

He ignores me and stands there next to my mother, eyes wide, focused on their television.

I'm annoyed and confused. Waves of pixilation distort Jerry Seinfeld's face, like he's melting into squares. The storm. We'll lose power soon, if the dish on the roof is being affected—an indicator of snow accumulation and windy conditions.

"I can feel it," my mother says. "Can't you?"

My father nods, but it's non-committal.

I want to shake them. What's the big deal? We're a bunch of hardy old New Englanders.

"Okay, so...Dad, you want me to help hook up the generator? I'm gonna clean up that plate first, though." They ignore me. I'm invisible. I've seen them like this before, at the height of their UFO ramblings. But it's been years since they got this bad.

My mother picks up the remote and changes the channel to a live news report. Local, snowy, a woman in full blizzard gear reporting from the seacoast, twenty miles away.

"In addition to severe snow accumulations ranging from thirty to forty inches, the area is experiencing an audible phenomenon that is slowly increasing in volume..." The reporter flicks in and out of pixilation. And then I hear it. At first I think it's coming from the report, but no. The electricity flickers and a low grinding noise, like tires stuck on ice—a revving engine—tickles my ears. I head back into the kitchen, to the window, and peer out at the darkened driveway.

There's no one here, no car, no stuck snowplow. The grinding increases in volume, and I open the kitchen door, squinting into the yard. The barn's outline is visible through the swirling snow. Wind smacks me in the face, the temperature below zero. I stand there, already shivering, trying to figure out where the noise is coming from, when I hear my parents' urgent whispering from the other room.

I close the door. The grinding noise now fills the house. I crunch back over the broken plate, lights flickering like a horror movie and start to joke, "Guys, remember that creepy film with—"

My parents, who I would describe as slow, because they're never in a hurry, lurch toward me. My mother flings aside her knitting, Dad still holding the dishtowel. Their eyes are wide, scared animal eyes, foreheads furrowed upward. They each grab an arm and haul me back through the kitchen to the still open cellar door.

"It's happening fast. We need to get her down there *now!*" My father tugs me, hard, down the stairs. I am too shocked to say anything, to do anything. So I let them lead me down the staircase. My heart flips over and over, and I think, irrationally, *will they hurt me?* I'm about to burst into tears. Why didn't I see this coming? They're fucking nuts. I should have known. I should have noticed more. I shouldn't have ignored the signs. All this time, alone in the woods with their weird theories and their cow. Who wouldn't go crazy? When was the last time they left the house? When did they last talk to anyone other than me? I'm so used to their idiosyncrasies.

I'm small but I'm strong, my frame wiry from genetics, a slight marathon addiction and seasonal, vigorous gardening. But confusion weakens me. My mother breathes hard; she's panicked. Terrified. I've never seen her like this.

The grinding grows louder, like twin engines are revving in the basement. Right around the corner. Outside. Everywhere. But I see nothing. Just our normal New England basement with shelves and shelves of home-canned goods and dried jerkies. Bins of apples and potatoes. That's when I notice the upright coffin. Or, what looks like a coffin—from Star Trek. It's sleek, black and standing sentinel in the corner of the cellar, between the extra freezer and the washer and dryer.

"Honey," my mother says to me, opening the coffin door, smooth on new hinges. I'm crying now, so sad and scared that this is the end result of their beautiful lives. Their smart, loving selves, going crazy in a snowstorm in the woods. "You're going to have to go inside."

She points to the coffin. Its interior is plush, jewel green. I realize I hadn't been down to the basement in several months. The grinding increases, the velocity faster. I stare at her, then at my father, standing next to her. Tears pour down my cheeks. His hand clings to my forearm, his blue flannel cuff rolled up, just a bit, white hairs on his tan wrist.

"I don't...Mom. What do you think is happening? It's just the electricity. Because of the storm." I take a deep breath. "It'll be over soon. We're just as safe upstairs." I step toward the stairs but my Dad, still stronger than me, holds me fast. Only seconds have passed, but the abrasive noise keeps increasing, faster, louder.

"It's happening, Poesy, what we've always known would happen." He needs to shout, now, to be heard. "It's why we built it. The pod."

The pod.

Reality slams into me. A lifetime of classic sci-fi movies watched with my father on Saturday mornings has merged with his UFO obsession. This...pod...is for me.

He glances at the upright pod. "They told us to."

"I'm not getting into anything!" I shout, through choking sobs. Grinding, grinding, like a motor in my eardrum. They look at each other.

"We can't drug her," my mother yells, "she's pregnant!"

That's when I freak out. I yank away from my father and run up the stairs. He grabs my wrist, pinning it to the railing, and I trip, hitting my elbow on the step. I stand and look at him, one step higher. When I was a little girl, I would stand on a low stair, he on the floor, and I would say, "Daddy, am I going to be this big?" I would then step up another stair and ask again and again, until I was taller than him.

He wraps his arms around my waist and I fight him with all my might.

"I'm sorry, Poe! We have to! We love you so much! It's going to happen any second now! Get in!" He shoves me into the pod, and tries to shut the door, but I push against it. The grinding is deafening.

We reach a stalemate as my mother freezes, a strange frown on her face. Is the noise causing her to have a stroke? Or the stress? Then, her lined, lovely face turns pale and caves in on itself, like undercooked meringue, eyebrows meeting her chin. Her knees buckle. My father stops pushing the door, and staggers a few steps backward, losing a moccasin to the cement floor. His neck bends awkwardly forward, his head drops to his chest. Like erasing a chalkboard, top down, their bodies collapse into white powder.

Into dust.

I scream and slam the door shut.

2

AUGUST

Shaved coconut. It's the closest comparison I can think of for Maggie Chow's skin. Pale white. Peeling curls. Even the exposed flesh beneath the cracked dermis looks like it's been soaked in a bucket of bleach and left to dry in the hot Arizona sun. Without thinking, I lean closer and see that her form is little more than barely held together granules of powder, clinging to their original shape.

The elevator doors slide shut, sealing me inside once more, curtains at the end of a macabre opera. Without a floor button pushed—there are only two options, T for top and B for bottom—the elevator sits idle. I stare at the line where the two halves of the door meet, at my disfigured shape in the brushed metal surface. Despite being a fog of color, my reflection appears more human than the woman I just saw lying on the white linoleum tiles.

She's dead.

Maggie, my employer and friend, is dead.

Something hard and warm taps against my ear. I flinch away with a shout, all of my trapped anxiety bursting from my lungs. The elevator wall shudders from the impact of my flung body. The lights flicker. A searing pain shoots from my elbow to my fingers before bouncing back up my right arm. I've hit my funny-bone on the unyielding, flat metal railing.

"Damnit," I say, and reach around to cup the joint. Instead of the soft embrace of my left hand, I feel the impact of something hard. Looking down, I find my phone. I must have taken it out while looking at Maggie's body. The small screen displays a failed call. Claire. My daughter. Her photo fills the screen, covered by the text: *Call Failed. No Signal.*

I dialed?

This is what touched my ear, I realize. I was making the call on auto-pilot. But why?

Maggie.

I clench my eyes shut, squeezing them tight like Venus flytraps. The image of her corpse flashes into the darkness like a strobe, her white skin gleaming. I can't hide from the image. Not behind the closed doors of the elevator. Not behind my eyelids. Probably not in the laboratory a mile and a quarter beneath me, either.

The lights *tick,* like there's a fly inside the elevator. That should be impossible. The lab is a static free, clean environment. We don't allow dust in, let alone insects.

An image of Maggie's powdered flesh flaking away and disrupting the lab's delicate measurements comes unbidden to my mind. She wasn't wearing a clean suit. *Why wasn't she wearing a clean suit?* The light blue suits cover our bodies, head to toe. Unlike biohazard suits, they don't keep contaminants from getting in, they keep them from getting out. Skin cells. Moisture. Even passed gas. The human body sheds an untold number of particles every minute of the day. The clean suit contains it all. But Maggie wasn't wearing one. She would never do that.

That's when I realize that I've removed my hood. I vaguely remember feeling trapped upon first finding Maggie's barely held together form. I must have yanked the hood free. Maggie's solid white face resolves in my mind's eye, a mannequin of clinging particles.

I try crushing the image away, but with my eyes shut, there's nothing else on which to focus. Nothing else that matters as much.

Not the ordinary concerns of everyday life. Not the dark matter we've been searching for. Maggie's powdered form threatens to consume me. My eyelids flutter open. I turn toward the ceiling, looking for the fly.

The ceiling is gone. As are the walls and floor.

The lights are as dead as Maggie.

There is no fly. Never was. It was the power going out.

I'm trapped. For a moment, I feel relief. If I can't open the doors, I don't need to see the body again. Whoever comes to set me free will remove her first. They have to.

Then I remember that the hole beneath me descends for more than a mile. It's the deepest man-made tunnel in the world, and it ends at one of the world's most sophisticated laboratories. The place is nicknamed 'Desert,' in part because of its location in Arizona, but also because its true title, Deep Space Research and Technology (DSRT) is just missing a few vowels. The descent takes fifteen minutes. But in a free fall, that time would be closer to one. And at the end of that drop, I would look even less human than Maggie.

But won't the brakes hold? I have no idea. As an astrophysicist, my expertise—if I'm honest—revolves around subjects that might not actually be real. I live in a world of theories and math, of decimals and numbers, keyboards and sensors. I've been holed away in a subterranean lab, watching a screen—my only company—in search of dark matter particles. I haven't seen the sun in a week. Like most people, I exist in the macroscopic, but my mind is sharply focused on the subatomic or the far reaches of space. I have no idea how elevators work. Or if the brakes will eventually fail without power.

My fear of a violent death trumps my anxiety over seeing Maggie's withered form again, and I reach for the doors. I shake out my still tingling arm, reach out into the dark and take a step. My hand finds the cool metal wall, but not the doors. I must have turned around in the dark.

Sliding to the side, I move left to the next wall. Still no doors. I repeat the process, feeling entirely helpless in the dark. I find the line where the two doors meet, the line that just a moment ago had bisected my blurry form. My shaking fingers slip into the layer of rubber that cushions the inner door. I pull on the large metal rectangles, but they resist. Feeling trapped, I grit my teeth and yank. They split apart, but my muscles, unaccustomed to anything more physical than pushing a button, ache in a way that reminds me of childhood. I can feel the fibers in my arm stretching and snapping. The sharp pain focuses me. If I don't open these doors now, I never will. I'll starve before the sinews heal.

I shout out, putting the last of my strength into pulling the doors apart. My arms shake. My chest knots. I hope someone will hear my howl, but when I see the absolute darkness on the other side of the doors, I know no one will be coming. Not any time soon. The whole facility has lost power. The revelation saps the determination from my fingertips and they slip free.

The door, open just a foot, remains still. Shaking my arms, I sigh with relief. Then I thrust myself into the gap and squeeze through. The rubber seals cling to my chest and stomach, holding me in place. I start to shake as a rising panic takes hold of me before I even know why.

The elevator.

The brakes!

If it fell now, I would be crushed. Or severed in half lengthwise. Ignoring the pain in my compressed chest and pinched belly, I shove my way through, inch by crushing inch, expelling the air from my body.

Then I'm free. Out of the elevator. And flailing. I've tripped over my own leg. I twist around as I topple forward, landing on my backside. My hands slap against the cool floor, stinging madly. Momentum and gravity pull me back, slamming my head on the linoleum.

Spots of light dance in my vision. For a moment, I think I'm looking through a telescope, watching some kind of interstellar light show. But the lights fade and the darkness of the hallway, along with my full understanding of my situation, returns. Despite the lump forming on the back of my head and the jolts of pain wreaking havoc with my nervous system, I smile. I'm free of the elevator. I'm—

A series of hacking coughs wrack my body. I convulse and sit up. Dust. Despite being blind, I can feel the cloud of dust surrounding me. It tickles my skin. The malformed tears in my eyes turn to paste. The flavor of the stuff fills my mouth as I take a breath.

Like uncooked instant oats.

Remembering my dry suit, I reach over my head and yank the clear plastic mask over my face. Magnetic strips seal the hood in place, and I breathe filtered air once again. While I'm not breathing in any more particles, I can still smell and taste them. The gooey grit they created clings to my teeth.

Before I can worry about contamination, a loud click spins me around.

Light!

Distant and dull.

Then a second click and a fresh blossom of light, closer this time.

The battery operated emergency lights are coming on.

The bulbs just outside the clean lab's foyer click on. I wait patiently, knowing the next set of lights will be inside the clean lab.

Click.

The lab glows dull and yellow. I can see.

Everything.

Including the white flakes beneath and around me. I fell atop Maggie Chow's body and it crumbled apart like loosely packed chalk. Like it was ash. My stomach lurches. Maggie Chow's body is in my eyes, nose and mouth. I *breathed* her!

I reach up for the clean suit hood, but I'm too late. I pitch forward and vomit into the clear mask, heaving three times until my stomach is emptied. Then I slip my fingers inside the magnetic seal, peel it away and let the bile slide atop Maggie's remains. A desecration. But it can't be helped.

Lost and confused, I stand and run. My first few steps are uncertain, as my boots are coated with speckles of dried flesh, slippery on the smooth floor. But then I hit the lab doors and shove into the foyer. The doors don't seal. And the giant vacuums inside the wall, meant to suck away every last piece of dust, don't activate. I want them to. So badly. But the air remains still and quiet.

I burst through the second set of doors and sprint down the long hallway, lit every fifty feet by emergency lights. I reach my top speed, which is probably close to a jog for most people, and I feel a cool breeze coming from the hallway ahead. I round the corner and spot the research facility's front doors. They're wide open. Just thirty feet away. But the three human sized lumps of white on the floor keep me locked in place. Their identities are hidden. Exposed to the open air, their facial features have eroded into mannequin flatness. But their clothing and I.D. tags reveal my co-workers. Scientists. Engineers. *Friends*. All dead. Like Chow.

I note that I've already started disassociating. Maggie is now Chow. Soon, she might not have a name. But I'm not going to judge my psychological defenses, because I'm starting to feel very lucky to be alive. Something horrible happened here.

Wind slips inside the hall, generated by the rapidly cooling desert outside. A vortex forms at the end of the hall. White and horrible. My dead friends sift into the air, pulled aloft by the wind and thrust down the hallway. But I don't run away. I can't. I need to get out, and that means I need to go through the ashes.

Screaming, I run forward, straight into the undulating wall of white, dead dust. It collects on the outside of my mask and I nearly collide with a wall before wiping it away. It's like snow on a windshield, but dry, and lifeless, and lacking even a hint of beauty.

Then I'm free.

And outside.

I tumble down the five concrete steps, staying upright thanks to a metal railing. Reaching the pavement, I fall to my knees, yank the mask from my head and take a deep breath of cool night air. The Arizona desert will be an inferno when the sun rises again, but for now, I consider it a blessing.

Until I feel the dust.

I turn my head toward the full moon above. It's an obscure white sphere casting a halo of light. Curtains of white slide through the sky, propelled by high winds. My first thoughts are: *clouds* and *fog*, but there isn't a trace of moisture in the air.

It's dust.

The same dust birthed by Maggie Chow's corpse. But there is so much of it, flowing out of the West. *From Phoenix*, I think. As I stare up at the night sky, breathing in the dead, I wonder just how many people it would take to form a cloud of ash that big.

All of Phoenix, I decide, which is troubling, because that large a number of people would also include my daughter.

3

POE

The darkness is total inside the upright pod. Crushing me, the thunderous roar grinds faster, the fluctuations combining into a single flat note that drowns out all thought of my parents.

I'm going to lose my hearing.

I'm going to die.

My baby.

I curve one protective arm around my middle, but need to shield my ears. I turn my abdomen to the cushioned wall; flatten my ears with my hands. I slowly slide to my knees. The ground rumbles and shakes, teetering the pod. I stretch my arms out, steadying, and immediately regret it, the noise needle-sharp in my ears. *It's an earthquake,* I think, and my small prison wobbles like it's in the back of a pickup truck. I curl my entire body onto the floor, hugging my knees to my chest. The top of my head presses against one side; I just fit. Despite my clenched shut eyelids, red and pink swirl across my vision.

My whole body vibrates.

Like a finger lifted from a keyboard, the roar stops. The box totters another few seconds, slowing, a coin returning to stasis on a table. Everything is silent. I release the breath I've been holding, but I stay curled on the tiny floor, twin to my fetus.

Relieved that the noise has stopped, I lie silently, my cheek cooling against the metallic floor. I open my eyes and then close them, seeing only uniform darkness. My ears ring in rhythm with my pulse, *stab, stab, stab*. I slide a hand across my barely convex belly, feeling around for any sign of...anything.

Nausea churns through me, threatening, as I adjust my position. *I can't throw up in here.* I squeeze the bridge of my nose, rub my temples, try to steady my breathing. *In through the nose, out through the mouth.*

They're dead.

I cradle my head in one arm and my abdomen with the other. *What the hell happened?* They turned to powder. To dust!

Panic seizes my chest as the image of my mother's face folding in on itself flashes into my mind's eye, a horrible painting, fully realized, impossible to forget.

I stand up and feel all around on the walls, hands shaking, involuntarily patting the padded fabric. My breathing shallows. Stars flicker around the outskirts of my sightless vision. I need to sit down, but before I do, my fingers find a small hole in one wall, a pucker in the cushioned fabric. I hold my quaking hand near it. A gentle whiff tickles my skin. An air vent.

Why did my parents build this? How did they know what was happening? I think back, rubbing my temples. *My Dad said something about being told to build this.*

Shit, they're dead.

I can't cry. I really want to. But I just stand, shaking, until my legs lower me back to the floor.

Hours pass. I think. I'm both parched and in need of a toilet. The vent delivers air to breathe, so that's not a concern, although I hyperventilate off and on, when I allow my thoughts to focus on my parents.

How long will I be able to breathe in here?

How long should I stay?

Without warning, light blinds me, my pupils so dilated from the long darkness. I gasp and cover my eyes. As they start to adjust behind my hand, I peek out, squinting.

Green fabric surrounds me, silky and quilted, designed for comfort. My very own padded room. I stand, knees stiff. With my elbows bent, I can touch both sides at the same time. Some kind of lock keeps the door closed, sealed against whatever happened on the other side. The light shines from a line of LEDs along the walls. I glance up. Two words are printed on the ceiling. I stare at the words, but see only letters, my mind lost in a haze, unable to make sense of the casual, out of place scrawl. I stand on my tippy toes, like proximity to the words will help, when a loud buzzer, like the grinding chime of a security door being unlocked, sounds out. I flinch away from the grating sound, slamming into the back wall with a shout of surprise.

I hesitate, listening to my breathing. I have to pee. The buzzer chimes again. This time it's comforting, a sound everyone knows. *Maybe I'm dreaming. Maybe that's my alarm clock and I'm about to wake up.*

It buzzes again and this time the deadbolt snaps open, erasing any doubt as to the sound's meaning. *The door is unlocked*, I think, *I get it. But why open on the third buzz? Why not the first? Is it counting down something?*

I count, timing the gap between buzzes, occupying my mind.

Fifty-seven, fifty-eight, fifty...there it is again. Telling me to leave.

I reach for the lock, a simple, undersized brass knob. My hands slicken with sweat, quaking, and I can't get a good grip. I try to swallow but I'm spitless, my tongue like dust.

Dust.

I take a micro-step backward, pat my belly and then squeeze my fingers into fists. I wipe my palms on my jeans.

With shaking hands, I twist the knob, and the door swings open to the cellar.

4

AUGUST

Pebbles grind against my knee caps, hurting more than anything so small has a right to. My chest aches as I stretch out my arm, twisting it at an odd angle, reaching beneath my SUV, a Toyota Highlander—hybrid, of course. This simple movement is almost too much for me. All that time spent in a chair, staring at a screen, and not enough time moving, hasn't helped my physical condition. Simple tasks like prying open an elevator door or retrieving a hidden key are almost beyond my ability. It's the future I've dreamed of since childhood. Man evolved beyond the need for physical labor. Robots. Cyborg implants. Life made easy through immobility. But a mind set free to roam the cosmos, I now know, has trouble completing the simplest physical tasks.

The *shhhhh* of windblown white flakes sifting over my body and masked head doesn't help. This act of retrieving a key, to start my vehicle, roots my mind. A mental checklist organizes my thoughts, creates order and keeps me from slipping into a panic-fueled despair. I can feel the abyss lapping at my toes. So I focus on the steps in front of me and try, desperately, to ignore the night-mare surrounding me.

Shhhhhh.

When my fingers graze the small plastic case, it feels like a victory. Then my shoulder cramps, and I have to fight through a wave of pain just to clutch the thing. Pulling it free feels like I'm being drawn and quartered by a sadistic medieval executioner. Then, with a sudden pop, the case is free. I slide out from beneath the SUV, my shoulder still throbbing, and manually unlock the door.

But I don't climb in. Instead, I open the door, push the 'unlock all' lever and slam the door closed once more. I move to the vehicle's rear and lift the hatch, stepping beneath it and out of the storm of petrified life. A pocket, free of the shifting dust, forms around me as the wind moves from the SUV's front, to its rear and beyond.

The mask lifts free, releasing me from the scent of bile. I quickly shed the clean suit, sitting on the vehicle's bumper. My clothing is slick with vomit, so I shed it, too, down to my boxers, never once fearing that someone will spot me, gleaming white, basketball belly, swirling hair fringed in gray. I know they're all dead.

I lean forward, away from the open hatch, and I shake my fingers through my hair. White flakes flutter free, some dropping to the ground, some carried away by the breeze. I move my fingers through my beard, brushing Maggie Chow out. Each twitch of my hand moves faster, becoming frantic, stopping only when the sting of scratched flesh grows unbearable. My fingers come away with a thin coat of blood. Normally, the sight of blood, especially my own, would set me to swooning, but I simply marvel at it now. Living stuff. My only company.

I keep a change of clothes in the back. I'm prone to spills and random acts of clumsiness. Door frames are my nemesis. I pull the jeans on, followed by a fresh NASA logo T-shirt. I pick up the new, XXL button down, but put it back. There is no one to look nice for. The contents of my stomach didn't reach my feet inside the clean suit, so I slide my feet back in my shoes—black slip-on Skechers that look far more hip than I am, but they're comfortable.

I step over the discarded clothing, pulling the hatch down around me. My pulled muscles strain against the door until the vehicle's sensors detect the movement and hidden gears start spinning. I didn't bother buying the push button starter upgrade, but heavy doors that opened and closed on their own felt like a necessity. Before today, the automatic hatch made me feel confident. A display of my evolved state. Now I just feel weak.

I *am* weak.

Evolution, with its survival of the fittest, somehow overlooked me tonight.

I'm not yet sure if I should be grateful.

The door whirs closed, sealing me inside a dark tomb with perfect, flake free air. In the absolute silence that follows, I become aware of my breathing, uneven and quick. *Slow down*, I think, but I've never been an athlete. I have no experience slowing my breath or calming my body. This flesh and blood machine has always been a vessel for my mind. Nothing more.

In through the nose, out through the mouth. That's what coaches say. I try it, pulling a long breath through my nostrils, smelling the car's interior—leather and fabric, warmed and cooled repeatedly over the past week. I feel no attachment to the Highlander. My DNA is decidedly un-macho. This is the reason my wife, Carly, left me. Over time, my lack of primal, testosterone-fueled toughness did me in. Brawn sometimes wins over brains when it comes to the heart. Her second husband looks like a silverback gorilla. A mechanic with dirty nails, no savings and few ambitions. But they are happy. Hunter-gatherers forming a tribe. Last I heard, they were up to five children. I'm glad for her and often envious of her husband, but I can't change my nature.

Before leaving, Carly gave me a gift. A tribe of my own. A daughter. Claire. Precious and frail. Smart like her father. Now twenty years old and a college graduate, ready to begin her master's program with a focus on biology, she is the love of my life. The solitary concern of my heart.

My thumb slides over the glowing phone's smooth surface and pushes too hard on the 'Call' icon. My daughter's face appears on the screen. Her light brown eyes are surrounded by tan skin inherited from her mother, and smooth, straight auburn hair inherited from me.

"Please pick up."

My voice is dry, and the movement shakes free a granule of Maggie Chow, wedged between my cheek and upper gums. I spit, suddenly aware that I can still taste the dead inside my mouth. Can still feel the slick grit, like a dentist's polishing paste, slipping toward the back of my throat. With the last of my unbroken thoughts, I switch the phone to speaker mode and crawl over the divider, into the back seat. The interior is spotless, free from the detritus gathered by people who transport family or friends. But my salvation rests between the front bucket seats, held reverently by the cup holder, like an ancient idol nestled on a pedestal. I reach for it, and pluck the Styrofoam cup from its resting place.

I pry the plastic top off and look inside. The cover and sides are slick with moisture, evaporating during the day and dripping back down during the cool nights. A contained ecosystem. But there is no life in this liquid terrarium. The week-old black coffee, sealed in a man-made container, lacks any trace of mold. I pour the mouthful of cold, dark liquid into my mouth. The bitter flavor explodes against my taste buds, the flavor rancid and beautiful. I swish it around, willing it to cleanse every nook and crack, a staining oral baptism that will leave me feeling clean.

Not wanting to open the door again, I spit the fluid back into the cup. A cloud of white particles spins in the darkness. For a moment, I see the Milky Way galaxy from afar, spinning within my grasp. A dream come true. And then, I just see Maggie Chow, spit out.

"Hey," Claire says. "If you're a human, leave a message. If you're a robot, screw off." The phone beeps and I smile. Claire has a sarcastic wit that I appreciate, but can't duplicate. In addition to being a poor specimen of masculinity, I'm also not that funny.

It's unusual for Claire to ignore my calls. Two rings, tops. I look at my watch. Its 2:34...AM. But she keeps the ringer on. She'd still pick up, maybe even faster since late-night calls like this are usually bad news. So I leave my message with a barely hidden quiver in my voice. "Hey, honey. If you're there, please call me back. Something... horrible has happened, and I want to know you're okay." I nearly vomit again. Her apartment is in Phoenix. It's just an hour drive from here, but... I look up at the sky. Moon-lit death scours the black curtain. "Just call me back." I feel no shame over the cracking in my voice. I would endure the tortures of hell to know she was all right.

I would drive straight through them, too.

Before I do, I think about the time. It's not uncommon for me to work late nights. Given Desert's focus, most of the team, who prefer the view of stars to blue sky, stay late into the night. But 2AM is extreme, especially for Maggie, who has kids. Whatever happened, it took place earlier. Maggie's location is the giveaway. When I'm working in the subterranean lab for extended periods, she makes a daily visit via the elevator to make sure I haven't gone insane, despite knowing that I prefer the warm whir of electronics to human conversation. She was on her way to see me when it happened, which places the event's timing around 6pm...eight hours ago. It took that long for me to realize Maggie hadn't come down to see me, and when I called up, no one answered, which is unusual, even at this time of night. Even if the science team had all gone home, the security team would have answered.

After covering the Chow flavored coffee and placing the cup in a back-seat holder, I contort my aching, 6'2" body, climb into the front and slide behind the wheel. The car starts with a gentle purr, the headlights automatically cutting through the darkness, turning black to static white and illuminating the swirling white parking lot.

The radio, left on, hisses at me. I reach out to turn it off, but pause, tapping the 'Scan' button instead. The digital numbers scroll swiftly, like the altimeter of a plummeting aircraft—both warnings of impending doom. There aren't many stations available in this empty swath of Arizona desert, but three or four come in clearly and another dozen flicker in and out. Tonight, the airwaves are silent. No one is talking. The numbers finish their first lap, and tirelessly begin a second. I reach for the power button, but a sudden, blaring sound stops me in place.

I curse. Of all the stations that could have come in, it had to be the one playing Bon Jovi's *Bad Medicine*. I clutch the steering wheel, letting the song play out, trying to avoid an 80s flashback. I fail. The song transports me back to my parents living room. I'm lip syncing the song with my friend. We're playing air guitar and drums, making fools of ourselves for the girls seated on the couch. When the song finally ends, I realize I've been tapping out the beat on the steering wheel. *God, I hate that song.*

I hold my breath, waiting for the DJ to chime in, but the radio plays only silence. No static. No voices. But then, a commercial. Two minutes of commercials. Silence follows them. Then, again, music. INXS, *Devil Inside*. The station is on auto-pilot, playing preprogrammed music and ads, but the DJ, whose voice should be filling the gaps, isn't there.

I hammer the power button.

Phone still on speaker, I dial 911, and place it on the passenger's seat. While the phone rings, I put the SUV in drive and head for the lot's exit. The white dust filling the air makes it hard to see, but the reflective red circles on the gate help me find the way out. Upon reaching the gate, I stop. I'm not getting out to lift the wooden rectangle, so I ease forward. The red and white striped plank is no match for the beastly vehicle. It cracks and falls away.

I pull through, keeping my eyes on the double yellow line a few feet in front of the Highlander. Other than white, the lines are about all I can see, and like Dorothy's yellow brick road, I'm going to follow the guiding color through this strange land, hoping that this Tin Woodman will find his heart intact.

I drive through the night. The phone beside me, reaching out for help, never stops ringing.

5

POE

My parents' clothing lies in two heaps on the cellar floor, a mere five feet from me, like dirty laundry waiting to be washed. The familiar fabrics are intermingled with small piles of dust. I step out of the box, and stand motionless, stupid with fear.

I hold my breath. *What if the air isn't breathable?* Hand still on the door, I consider stepping back inside it, and just staying there for a while.

Indecision will kill me. The air in my lungs threatens to expel. My chest constricts. My throat cramps. Beads of sweat erupt on my upper lip, across my forehead. I peek around the back of the pod and notice the air tank. Three of them. I can see the pressure gauge. It's nearly spent. My lungs feel crumpled. I have to decide.

I allow one tiny gulp to escape, hoping to trick my body into thinking it has captured a breath. My vision blurs and the hissing air behind me stops, a spent balloon, stilled on the floor. The decision has been made for me. Last words fill me, the final thoughts of a death row walk, before the hanging. *Thank you, thank you, for this life. It has been beautiful.*

Also, almost imperceptible, *Please, I'm not ready.*

Energy permeating my cells, attempting peace, I close my eyes and breathe.

Taking several deep choking breaths, my vision evens. I pat my body all over, gasping. Still alive. The air smells metallic, like pennies or blood. But there's no blood. I step once toward the piles of clothing, where my parents stood just hours ago. Two lumps. His blue flannel shirt, her prayer shawl, his moccasins, two pairs of pants. Blood rushes to my head, my heart flips over. Some unfrequented corner inside me splinters, and I start to cry. I nudge his shirt with my toe. White powder puffs out from it; some sticks to my wool sock.

I wail, hovering with my foot in the air, unsure what to do. *That's my father.* Nauseated, deep grief and revulsion wash over me, and with gagging sobs, I gently tug my sock off with only two fingers, from the ankle, careful not to touch any of the powder, and I place it on the floor.

I'm going to throw up. I run up the basement stairs in my lone sock, taking two steps at a time. I make it to the kitchen sink and vomit all over the unfinished, dirty dishes. Then again.

I rinse my mouth with icy cold well water, the tap like a natural spring. Then I splash my face. The chilling wetness constricts my skin and sharpens my thoughts, shocking me back to the present and survival. Water dripping from my nose and lips, I glance right.

The phone on the wall is within reach, their ancient, beige, rotary telephone. After a quick pat dry, I take the phone in hand. Each rotation of the disc clicks painfully slow, ticking around as I literally dial 911. Ringing. I slide down to the floor, with my back against the counter. The clock above the stove reads 3:42. Sunrise is still four hours away. I was in that thing for over six hours. *Why aren't they picking up?* I let it ring for five more minutes. Dust bunnies spin in the corner, propelled by a draft. I stand up and pace around the kitchen, the phone cord tangling on the kitchen chairs.

Five minutes gone, I wait five more. No one answers. I hang up and dig in my parka pocket for my cell. I only hesitate a second before I tap his name. It's the middle of the night, but still. Rings and rings.

"Hey, you've reached Todd, leave me a message, thanks."

"It's me," I say, and I start to cry again. "There's been an...accident at my parents' house. I'm snowed in. I don't know what to do. Can you please call me back?"

I call friends. I call relatives. I call a wrong number. I call the operator. No one, no one, no one answers. I spend the next hour leaving twenty-six messages. I open the kitchen door to the blizzard, and snow swirls in. I call him back again, and leave another message. *Why isn't anyone waking up to my call?*

I take a deep breath, go outside of myself a little bit, and try to think objectively. If I were a person who knew what to do in emergency situations, what would I do? The smell of my recent expulsion fills the room, so I turn on the tap and spray the dishes, rinsing them cleanish. Feeling the nausea still, I sit at the table and put my forehead down.

I am very alone. So I let it happen—I cry myself dry, I sob, I shriek. What else can I do? I walk around the house, crying, my arms tucked around my belly. I stop in doorways, clinging to the solid wood frame for comfort. In the living room, the TV is still on, the Brady Bunch, of all things. The episode where Marsha gets hit in the nose with the football, and its replayed over and over again. My mother's partially knitted orange sock and knitting needles lie on the braided rug. I don't go upstairs; it feels too far away from them. Instead, I pick up the sock, disentangle it from the needles, and lie down on the couch with it pressed to my cheek, to my nose. The orange alpaca wool smells like vegetables, her work and also patchouli—her scent.

I need to wait this storm out. Something's wrong with the phones. My parents are dead. They're not coming back. Afghan pulled over me, sketchbook kicked to the floor, I fall asleep.

Radiance streams from the windows surrounding me. Morning, and with it, an end to the tempest. Dizzy with exhaustion, my head killing me, I sit up and don't even entertain the thought that perhaps I was dreaming.

I know I wasn't.

In the kitchen, I try the calls again, 911, everyone I know, numbers I don't know, the operator. Again, ringing or answering machines, and again I leave a ridiculous amount of messages. Struck with the irony that I can still taste vomit on my tongue, and that my stomach is growling, I get myself a glass of water and swish it around before spitting it over the dishes in the sink. *God, those dishes.*

Famished, I sit with the leftover pie and a clean fork, and eat the remaining strawberry, juicy half, delicious and perfect. I refill my water glass with raw milk from the fridge, amazed we didn't lose power. We.

"Me and you, little one," I whisper, patting my belly.

Resisting the urge to peek into the basement, I head to the kitchen door and pull on my Bogs boots, which reach almost to my knees. I hesitate in front of our line of parkas, mine tiny to fit my five foot two frame, army green with faux brown fur hood, my mother's pale blue, my father's bright red, size extra-large. I grab the red, slide my arms through, and let it engulf me before stepping outside.

There must be at least thirty inches of snowfall, glistening quiet, smooth like bleached Saharan sands. I can hear my parents' cow in the barn, forty feet away, mooing in irritation. Her little calf is separate from her, to keep him from draining her milk supply. So she's waiting for my father to milk her.

"It'll have to wait, Sylvia!" I holler. Named after Sylvia Plath, of course. My father was still tossing around her calf's name—a tie between Alfred, after Lord Tennyson, and James, after Joyce. I voted for James. I guess it's my choice, now. It's good—he looks like a James.

The need to escape my environment overwhelms me. The nearest house is a half mile away, if I use the snow-covered dirt road. Shorter if I cut through the woods in the back. I head for the woods.

The snow between the trees is deep, each small breeze freeing more from the branches above, the storm's last throes. I sink through the fresh powder with each step and occasionally break through the firmer, old snow, up to my thighs. A clunky, inconvenient way to travel. I should have taken the road; at least it had been plowed before this snowstorm. And, as I reach the old white farmhouse, I remember my parents have snowshoes. *Idiot. They raised me better than this.*

I tramp up to the neighbors' front door and knock. A lion-headed golden retriever pops into view at the window to the left of the door, paws up on the sill, barking, panting, happy to see me.

Snow melts inside my boots. It's freezing out here, definitely below zero. The wind picks up. Snow flings from the roof, the ground, whirling around me, picking at my skin. My nose hairs are frozen. I go to the window on the right and peer into the house. The dog again pops up into view, paws on the sill, enormous fluffy red head, and tongue to the side. He's nearly as tall as I am, and I press my ungloved, reddening fingers to the glass to shade the view into the house above his head. I can't see much, a living room, typical New England fare.

In classic, private New Hampshire style, living in the woods, my parents and I rarely associated with our neighbors. Once or twice a year felt like enough, like neighborly. Not that there were many neighbors to begin with, and all at least a half mile away. I think I've talked with these people—a young couple with maybe one or two children—twice. Both times, years ago.

They're not answering. The beautiful dog barks wildly, and I decide to try the door. It opens easily and immediately a tongue laps my face, two heavy paws on either shoulder, the dog as desperate for company as I am. I glance at the driveway. A car sits, heaped in snow. The dog is alone...but not.

Like me. Pushing past my fears and this frenetic, spinning ball of red fur, I step inside.

6

AUGUST

Snow in Phoenix. It doesn't happen often, but winter occasionally vacations in the arid South long enough to leave a white residue. *It's not snow*, I think, not allowing myself false hope. The thin coating of white, covering the ground and buildings, isn't melting under the glow of the morning sun, or sixty degree temperature. *At least it's not in the air anymore.* The trip to Phoenix took four hours instead of the usual one. Poor visibility and abandoned, still running vehicles, not to mention a few pile-ups, slowed my progress. As the sun returned to the sky, the winds died down and the dead dust slipped from the cloudless sky.

I'm stopped in the middle of Route 60. The freeway is mostly empty, but enough vehicles dot the road to make speeding a dangerous prospect. The buildings' windows gleam in the bright, orange light, dulled slightly by the white dust clinging to the surfaces.

I look at my front windshield. It's coated in a thin film of white. *Static,* I think, and turn on the wipers, spraying the glass with cleaning fluid the color of a tropical ocean. The dead smear back and forth across the glass until the view becomes clear. I turn the wipers off and watch the last of the white run down the sides of the windshield.

My phone chimes, sending me sprawling away from it. I recover from the violent flinch and descend on the phone like a peregrine falcon. Is it a text? A voicemail? I fumble with the device, nearly drop it, and then clutch it tight, pressing the power button. The screen flicks on, displaying a thin red power indicator and the message, '20% battery life remaining.'

"Damnit!" I shout and drop the phone before I can smash it into the floor.

The near contact spurs me onward. I throw the SUV into 'Drive' and speed around a yellow VW bug. Old school. Pot leaf bumper stickers on the back. Typical Phoenix youth. Not Claire, though. She'd been straight-laced and focused on achieving her goals. She could have picked any path and excelled. Her mind is a laser, precise, powerful and sharp. She's a perfect creation, and while I don't really believe in God, if there *is* a creator, erasing Claire from the world would be like Michelangelo setting fire to the Sistine Chapel. If God does exist, and spared me, why not her?

It's a thin argument, especially given my beliefs, but I'm grasping. Desperate for hope.

Phoenix passes in a blur. Claire lives on the north side of the city in a nice apartment building that I help pay for. Manicured grounds, a gym, a shimmering pool and an interior that would cost a fortune in other parts of the country, all painted in hues of warm brown and adobe red. Southwest city living at its best.

The streets are far from empty. I'm not sure what time this... whatever it is...happened, but it couldn't have been past midnight. The number of vehicles littering the streets hints at an active night. Clogged intersections force me onto the barren sidewalks as I work my way through a section of town housing more than a few clubs. But in some spots, even the sidewalks are blocked. Cars on the move when things went to hell continued forward, crashing into each other, store fronts and in one case, a fire hydrant. While the skyborne torrent of water—the only thing moving besides me— holds my attention for a moment, it's the crashed vehicles that fascinate me. Although the front ends are crushed, there's no evidence to suggest a violent end to the vehicle's occupants. No shattered windshields. No blood. And certainly no corpses. Just still vehicles and flaccid airbags.

As I close in on Claire's neighborhood, my stomach starts to seize, cramping tightly. My first thought is that I'm dehydrated. It's been a while since I drank anything. But my other symptoms—sweaty hands, nervous jitters and short breathing—reveal nerves frayed like old corduroys. I'm terrified by what I'll find.

Relief comes in the form of distraction when I catch the scent of a burning fire, chemical and acrid—burning city, not woods. That the city, or part of it, is burning, heightens my sense of urgency. In Arizona, fires can get out of control even with half the nation's fire departments chipping in. Without a fire department or even a single firefighter, the entire city might burn—and then take half the state.

As I round the corner onto North 7th Street, the fire comes into view, a few blocks east of Trillius West, the posh name for Claire's apartment complex. The slick black sign is straight ahead, the gates closed. I take one last look at the blaze. It must have started recently, perhaps from a stove left on or a candle left burning. I didn't see smoke from outside the city. But the blaze is already large, sliding through neighborhoods like stop motion mold over fruit. A slight breeze carries a cloud of white dust west.

It's coming this way.

I slow to a stop, staring at the gate. It's steel, two halves joining in the middle. A guard house sits off to the side. I've visited enough that the guards just buzz me through, but no one sits behind the security glass. A flicker of orange pulls my attention to the West. A store front, four blocks away, erupts in flame.

Conjuring every ounce of fuck-it manliness I can manage, I cram the gas pedal down. The monstrous Highlander roars and charges forward. To my surprise, the gate is far more flimsy than it looks, and it folds inward, granting me passage to the complex with only a metallic shriek for resistance.

Tires squeal as I push the SUV through the clear parking lot, racing toward the far end, where Claire's ground floor apartment awaits. The heavy vehicle skids to a stop across three parking spaces. I spill from the driver's side door, nearly slipping on the dust covered pavement. Outside, the scent of smoke is overpowering. I'm coughing before I reach the door. I try the knob. Locked.

I reach into my pocket for the keys, but find it empty. I didn't recover my keys. They're in my coat, hanging in my office. The only key I have is inside the still running Highlander.

"Claire!" I bang on the door, first with my fists, and when that hurts, with my feet. The jarring impact of each kick confirms that I won't be kicking my way past the lime green-painted metal door.

I look around for something to throw at the large bay window beside the door, but find only plants, woodchips and parked cars. Then I spot a brown paper grocery bag on the walkway leading to the neighbor's apartment. I met her once, the neighbor. She was nice. Late thirties. A single mother. Claire told me to ask her out. Thought we'd be a good match. All of this is fresh in my mind as I crouch by the bag and peer at the woman's groceries, doing my best to ignore the flower pattern skirt and tank top lying beside it.

She's dead.

The thought slips through my mind, an unwelcome intruder. Fighting tears, I stand, shout in anger and kick over the bag. Green apples roll free, followed by a package of sausage and two boxes of kid's macaroni and cheese. Amid the tumbling food there is a *clink* of glass striking concrete.

Wiping away tears, I crouch and look in the bag again. A bottle of wine sits at the bottom. I grasp the bottle's neck and carry it back to Claire's apartment. Without ceremony or pause, I hurl the bottle into the window. The shattering glass feels like an explosion, and for the first time, I'm aware of the absolute silence surrounding me. I stand still, holding my breath. In the near perfect silence I hear the crackle of distant fire.

I kick away the few shards of glass still in the window and carefully hoist myself up and over the sill, using a living room chair on the other side for balance. Sliding out from under the curtain, I get my first look at the apartment beyond. It's fairly Spartan, decorated with funky, brightly colored furniture that reveals Claire's artistic side. Compared to my house, this is like a modern art museum. An entire wall of her dining room is a print of cut limes, matching the front door.

"Claire!" I shout, despite feeling certain I won't get a reply. "Claire!" My voice cracks as I begin weeping, and I clumsily run from the living room to the kitchen. It's pristine. No dirty dishes. No food left out.

No dust.

I check the dining room.

The bathroom.

And finally the bedroom. I pause in front of the open door, steeling myself for the most likely scenario: loose blankets covering a pile of dust. I step inside, primed to fall down, wailing in despair, and I find a made bed. I wander around the room, looking for signs of my daughter's passing, but find nothing.

Feeling more confused than hopeful, I head for the guest room where I sometimes stay, and find it equally pristine.

She wasn't here.

I wander back to the living room, feeling denied.

Sometime during the drive here, I came to terms with what I would find. Claire is gone. Along with everyone else. Some kind of cosmic event has reduced life to dust, and I, being more than a mile below the ground, had been spared. It was a crazy theory, but as a scientist, I couldn't ignore the evidence. I knew she was gone, but had to complete the journey anyway. If I couldn't have Claire, at least I could have closure.

But now...she is just absent, perhaps part of the dust cloud last night, or coating a building, or scattered—her dehydrated cells as distant from each other as the stars in the sky. I would have collected her remains. Would have buried them, or spread them out at the ocean. Something to say goodbye.

I sit on the couch. The leather squeaks under my weight. I feel empty and emotionless, primed to implode, but denied the catalyst.

What now?

I search the room and stop on a framed photo of Claire and me. She's fifteen in the photo and I'm about fifteen pounds lighter. There's a lake in the background. I'm holding a fishing rod. She's holding the line where a hooked sunfish dangles. Neither of us was good at fishing, but that wasn't the point of fishing. Not for the average person who doesn't catch fish to eat, or care about landing the largest bass. That quiet time spent with a loved one is about the best feeling on the planet. Bonds can be forged without ever sharing a word.

I stand from the couch, take the photo from the wall and carefully undo the backing. With the image free from the frame, I peer at it, into it, trying to live in that moment in time, but I fail.

Motion from outside the broken window spins me around. Smoke, black and violent, rises into the air, on the far side of the adjoining apartment building. Time's up. I pocket the photo.

Despite my despair and loneliness, burning alive isn't a fate I'm willing to resign myself to. I hurry back to the guest room and retrieve Claire's backpack from the closet. The bottom drawer of the room's dresser is filled with two sets of my clothing. I stuff both into the bag and head for Claire's bedroom.

At first I'm not sure why I've come to the room again. She's not here. But then I spot something intimately familiar and realization dawns. I hurry across the room and pluck the baseball cap from the bed post where it hangs. Claire is a Red Sox fan. I'm not sure why. She grew up in Arizona and I've never been into sports. But I took her to a game once, Red Sox and the Diamondbacks, when she was ten. Bought her that hat. She was the only one in the stadium wearing a cap with a bright red B on it, but she didn't notice. Or didn't care. At the game's conclusion, she stood solitary, cheering for her victorious team. It's why I came back to her room; a memento to accompany the photo in my pocket. I place the hat atop my head and make for the kitchen.

Seeing the fridge, my empty stomach rumbles. I've missed two meals and at least two hefty snacks. I open the fridge and take four water bottles, two cans of soda and a quarter gallon of milk. I raid the cabinets next, taking a box of protein bars, four apples and a bag of trail mix. It's not exactly meal material, but it's also not going to go bad. I'm not sure why I'm taking so much food and water. I don't live too far from the office. I can be there in four hours. Something about the end of all life in Phoenix has turned me into a hoarder. *No*, I think, *I'm just preparing for the worst...like it can get any worse.* Stuffing everything but the milk into the back pack, I take a step toward the door, but pause, remembering the freezer's contents. After opening the freezer door and retrieving a single box, the view outside the living room window turns orange.

The building on the far side of the parking lot has just gone up in flames. Windows shatter and fire roars. A hot breeze flows through the apartment, carrying smoke and white flakes that could be people, or ashes, but is most likely both. With wide eyes and full arms, I run toward the blaze.

7

POE

"Aren't you a good boy? Who's a good boy?" He's gigantic, his dark red fur gorgeous. At my heaviest, I'm a strapping one hundred and fifteen pounds, and he's probably not much less than that. He whirls around me as I step past the threshold, around and between my legs, slapping me with his tail. I rub his sides and he stands, paws balanced on my shoulders, tongue cleaning my face. My eyes tear up with the recognition that I was badly in need of connection. His loving attention overwhelms me. If he wasn't so huge, I'd pick him up and carry him over my shoulder like a baby, nuzzling.

"Where is everybody, big guy?" He drops down from his position on my shoulders with a thud and leads me into the house.

"Hello?" I call down the hallway. The walls are covered in family photographs and old, floral wallpaper. Lamps glow from the living room as I pass into the kitchen, following his wagging behind. A static sound, maybe an untuned radio station, emanates from somewhere in the house. The beautiful, wide plank oak floors creak. The corridor opens into the spacious kitchen, which smells chocolatey.

Following the dog, I walk around the huge farm table and stop short, in front of the oven. An uncooked pan of brownies sits on the stovetop. He lies down, paws extended, whining, his nose buried under a crumpled pair of jeans and a brown wool sweater. From the pile, between his teeth, he gently lifts a gray slipper, wrinkled striped sock still tucked into the toes, and he rises to his feet. As he turns toward me, a puff of white powder wafts into the air, swirls around his paws and clings to the fur on his nose and his red limbs.

I scream, and yank him away by the collar. He sneezes, drops the slipper, and shakes all over like he just went for a swim, his tags jingling. I step away as white powder drifts between us and across the linoleum, like flour patted, baking bread.

"No! C'mere, boy." Rising nausea fills my throat, my stomach seizing. They were people. Now, like my parents: dust. I scan the room for a landline telephone and see nothing. A cell phone rests on the counter and I pick it up, try 911 while holding his collar. Like at my parents' house, the phone rings and rings. Shaking now—again—I try a few more numbers, and get only voicemail or ringing. It strikes me that I keep attempting the same thing, with the same effect, and that exacerbates my helplessness. *Why should making calls from a neighbor's house be any different than from my parents? It wouldn't.*

The dog and I stare at each other. I've got him by the collar, and he sits down, pawing my leg and whining.

"Do you need to go out? God, you poor thing." He barks and wags his tail. Still trembling, I follow him to the back kitchen door, open it and let him bound out into the snow, realizing too late that I maybe should have leashed him.

But, no. Quickly finished, he bounces through the snow back inside, just as the kitchen goes eerily quiet. I wonder what's different and realize the refrigerator has stopped running. The digital clock on the stove is black.

I run into the living room, dog at my hip. The lamps are off, so I'm pretty sure the electricity is out. Stepping toward a lamp to give the switch a futile try, I notice another clothing pile on the braided rug. No, two piles. I step closer, holding the dog's collar again, and see navy blue sweatpants and a sweatshirt. And, footy pajamas, yellow and white striped, tiny. The now recognizable, pasty white powder piles. The loss of children, possibly many, multiplies the event's cost in an exponential equation I can't comprehend, and can't face. But my artist's mind gives me no choice, conjuring images of a child at play, and then, folding down on itself. Dad disintegrating, too, his last thought worry over what was happening to his child.

"Damnit." Unable to endure another second, I run down the hallway, leaving a stunned dog behind. Then I'm out of the house, stumbling down the porch stairs into the front yard's deep snow. It's a blinding sun-brightened tundra. Fierce wind pings my cheeks with drifting, icy flakes. Gigantic, ancient maples in the front yard shake loose a new blizzard. I can't escape white powder.

It was the wind, I think about the power outage, taxing a snow laden branch until it broke. I'll need to get the generator going. I take the road this time, running, shambling, tripping through the nearly three feet of fresh snow, clutching the red parka closed, feeling crazed. As I jog through the drifts, my fingers and cheeks numbing, I feel sharp pangs in my lungs. It's too cold for this kind of thing. Then I have the sudden thought, *how many people are dead?*

The question numbs my mind with countless possibilities. Without an answer, I can't think of anything else until I find myself standing in front of a familiar street-side mailbox.

Broken from my trance-like state, I head around the house to the back door, still following my mother's rules about wet boots. I'll leave them by the door, on the mat, where they can dry without soaking the hard wood floors.

In the back yard, Sylvia greets me with her plaintive mooing. Her voice is muffled, but resounds from the barn.

I want to shout to her again, to tell her I'll be right there. But she's a cow. She won't understand a word of it, and it won't make me feel any better. So what's the point?

After quickly confirming that the power is out here, too, I retrieve a pair of gloves and trundle the generator out of the barn, struggling with it in the deep snow. Each heave moves it only a foot, and my shoulders ache by the time I reach the back of the house, where the generator's power runs inside and to the breaker box. Knowing I'm close to the right spot, I stop, turn around and look for the hookup. It's nowhere in sight, buried beneath several feet of snow.

A thousand curses flit in and out of my brain, clogging the freeway of self-expression with so much angst that I fail to verbalize it. Instead, I get a shovel from the barn and dig. At first, with tired, slow hands. Then with the crazed frenzy of a lunatic. And finally, when the small gray outlet box emerges, I heave with the slow, steady pull of a New Englander at work, ignoring the pain, doing what needs doing.

With the outlet box exposed, I turn to the generator and grunt. It's now several feet above the outlet. Logistically, it's not a big deal, because the cable that attaches the generator to the house is ten feet long. But the generator runs hot. The snow beneath it will melt. Inside an hour of running, it could be submerged in a puddle of melt water.

Why am I bothering? I wonder. The wood stove will heat the living room. I can put the food outside.

A hot shower, I think, and feel the sweat dripping inside my clothes. *A long, hot shower.*

Digging resumes.

Snow cleared, cable connected, I attach the large propane tank, stationed beside the electric hook up, to the generator and twist the valve open. After making sure all the switches and knobs are in their starting positions, I yank the starter cord. With a cough, the generator roars to life. It's used several times a year and is always reliable. I picture my next steps, inside the house, to the basement and the circuit breakers which will direct the flow of electricity into the house from the power grid to the generator.

No, not the basement.

I make it part way before stopping in the kitchen, listening to Sylvia moo and the generator hum, hesitating at the top of the cellar stairs. I run my fingers through my hair, rub my temples. Delay action however I can.

Locked in place at the top of the basement stairs, I can smell the air that is still cooler than the first floor. It smells of the sweet things canned by my parents, and of oil, but not of them. Of their remains.

I need to do this.

To know that it will work. I'm not just living now. I'm not simply existing. It's not even about surviving. It's about growing a life. Protecting that life. And that means taking care of myself. As rugged as I can be, and have been, the life inside me is fragile. If I'm going to stay healthy, I need to be rested, and clean. And that means power.

I run down the cellar stairs, straight to the gray metal box on the wall. The small door opens with a clang. Hand written instructions for the generator's operation are taped inside, my father's scribble, but I don't need them. I've done this before. After shutting off the main breaker and all the rest, I switch the incoming line from the main, to the generator. Then, one by one, I turn the necessary breakers back on—fridge, stove, water pump, water heater, kitchen, living room, bed room. I leave off the rest of the house, including the washer, dryer and microwave. But, is it working? To find out, I switch on the basement breaker. The lights shine bright. A loud buzz spins me around, a scream on my lips, my heart pounding. The pod is on again, buzzing at me, pulling my eyes toward the limp forms on the floor.

I run from the basement, skirting around my parents and dashing up the staircase, hands on the steps like I did when I was a kid. At the top of the stairs, I'm desperate for something normal. For something I know. I head into the bathroom, close the door, drop my pants and sit on the toilet.

When I'm done, and calmer, I turn toward the bathroom mirror, but stop. I know what I'll see. Black bangs with a single blue streak, wet and stuck to my forehead. My father's brown eyes, ringed and swollen from crying. Red cheeks and a redder parka, which I'm still wearing. I'll look pitiful. My image will suck away my lingering strength.

I grip the sides of the sink, staring down at the drain, listening to Sylvia's bellow. "You're okay. Stop being such a pussy. Now go take care of that stupid cow." I storm out of the bathroom, wet socks leaving damp, rule-breaking footprints through the house, into the kitchen.

Then I scream.

8

AUGUST

A wave of searing air almost sends me back into Claire's apartment, but the ring of fire reaching around the parking lot leaves little doubt that the building will soon be ablaze. I hurry to my SUV's driver's side door, yank it open and climb inside. With the door ajar, I put the still open and overflowing backpack in the passenger's seat and wedge the milk in next to it.

I glance in the rearview. Not for any good reason. It's just habit. But the reflection makes me shout. Flames roil over the parking lot, consuming vehicles just thirty feet behind me. They quickly catch fire, their tires billowing dark black smoke. A gust of wind forces the flames toward me.

With another shout, I reach for the door, feel the heat cooking my skin, and yank it closed. With shaking, nervous fingers, I turn the key and the engine shrieks at me. *It's not going to start!* I think, consumed by panic as the fire threatens to turn me into dust as well. I turn the key again and am greeted by the same grating sound.

This makes no sense! The Highlander is only a year old and is in perfect condition. My muscles tense as I prepare to turn the key again, but then I catch sight of the dash. The numbers glow orange. I tap the gas pedal with my foot. The RPM needle snaps up.

I left it running!

Shifting the big vehicle into drive, I realize I'll have to do a U-turn through the flames to leave the lot. So I shift into reverse, twist around in my seat and hit the gas.

I've never been much of a driver. Sure, my record is spotless. I've never been in an accident. But that has less to do with my skills and everything to do with my hyper defensive driving style. I never speed. Never drive closer than a hundred feet behind another vehicle. I even use my turn signals when no one else is on the road. So when I hit 20 mph in reverse, I'm breaking all kinds of new ground.

But I barely notice. A wall of violent orange races across the parking lot, consuming vehicles. Looking back, I groan as the security building catches fire. The heat is so intense that the time between first contact and being engulfed is just seconds.

At the far end of the lot, in front of Claire's apartment, the first cars that caught fire explode. Fiery debris leaps across the macadam and lands in the wood chips, bushes and Claire's living room, sailing straight through the broken windows.

"Goodbye, baby," I whisper as the building's façade blooms brightly.

Then I'm looking back, gritting my teeth and aiming for the gate, which has bounced back into a closed position and is partially concealed by flames. I squint as the SUV's rear end approaches the gates. Despite the ease with which I plowed through them the first time, I tense in dread expectation of the impact. Violence of any sort is out of character for me.

Once again, the gates, struck by my goliath vehicle, burst open like the eager arms of a grandmother's embrace, but not without cost. The rear windshield cracks in a spider-web pattern and then folds inward. Smoke slides over the ceiling, a living thing seeking me out, showing the way for the flames that will surely follow.

But then I'm through the blaze, in the street and barreling toward a storefront. I slam the brakes, partly because I don't want to crash into the store, partly because the store is also on fire. In fact, I'm surrounded by flames on three sides.

I speed forward, swerving around empty vehicles and racing against the fast moving, wind-driven flames. For a moment, it seems like the fire will win, that it will overtake and consume me. But when I hit 40 mph, I break free from the inferno—and nearly crash headlong into a commuter bus jutting into the road. I swerve hard to the right, grinding the Highlander's pristine gray side against the bus, losing my side mirror in the process.

When the road ahead opens up, I slow and check the rear view. A wall of flame, like some giant, glowing sandworm from the *Dune* movie slides across the cityscape.

Phoenix is going to burn. The whole city.

So I don't bother staying, and I don't look back again. I didn't find Claire's remains or say goodbye, but retrieving the photo and her hat at least gives me something to remember her by. Something to hold on to. It's a little bit pitiful, but this Red Sox hat is just about the last thing in the world I really care about.

I leave the city the same way I came, tracing my steps back through the empty streets and sidewalks, dodging wrecks and that lone spraying fire hydrant that won't be able to stop the city from turning to ash. Back on Route 60, I put on my blinker, pull to the shoulder and stop. I realize I could have just stopped in the middle of the freeway—there's no one else around, maybe anywhere. But I'm not in a rush to disregard all my safe driving habits in a single day.

Free of the city and the threat of burning, I reach for the box resting atop the open backpack. I open the SUV door, step out into the warm late morning sun, only vaguely aware of the white powder filling every crack in the pavement, and climb onto the vehicle's roof via the severely scratched up hood. I sit down cross-legged, like some kind of Australian aboriginal guru. All I need is a bullroarer and a loincloth. While I don't have any of that, I do have a box of melting ice cream sandwiches.

It's only been fifteen minutes since I left Claire's but the sandwiches have about five more minutes before they reach an inedible sludgy state.

As I watch a column of widening smoke rise up over the city, chased by licks of bright orange, I drown my sorrow in a hundred grams of sugar. The first two bars help. A surge of energy spins my mood in a less depressed direction. The third bar undoes all that progress. My stomach twists. Not from the junk food. I could live on it. It's the reality of what I'm seeing.

The north end of Phoenix is on fire. I can't see the flames, but the amount of smoke drifting off to the west says it all. I'm south of the black cloud, but if the wind shifts, the air will quickly become impossible to breathe.

But it's not even the city's destruction that has me feeling sick. It's the emptiness. An American city is being destroyed, and I'm the only one here to see it. Millions of people are dead, including my daughter. My ex-wife, too, probably, and the silverback and their children. Not to mention the millions of people I don't know. The families. The children. The babies born yesterday, only to be dust today.

What happened?

What the fuck happened?

How is any of this even possible?

I've spent a lifetime studying the world and the vast space beyond it, and all of my scientific knowledge and degrees are no help.

My eyes sting, trying to weep, but there's nothing left. I'm not dehydrated, I'm just...empty.

Like the city.

Like...*how far does this extend?*

Has this happened everywhere?

I was so consumed with the idea of finding Claire that I haven't considered the scope of this tragedy. The lack of help, of planes in the air, or helicopters arriving from outside the event radius, suggests this is bigger than Phoenix.

But how much bigger?

I toss the half-eaten ice cream sandwich to the roadside. The box follows it. Then I'm tossing two wrapped and uneaten sandwiches into the scrub brush just beyond the guard rail. I shake the drippings from my fingers and slide over the SUV's side. My ankles and knees grind when I land, the pain reminding me that I belong in an office chair, not racing through cities or leaping from the roofs of cars. Not that I leapt. It was more of a controlled slide and a three foot drop. Even more pitiful.

Back in the Highlander, I open a bottle of water and down it, hoping the liquid will help dilute the sugary sludge settling in my gut. Once again, my rising despair is being held at bay by direction. The next step is simple: make a phone call.

I don't have any other family left, but I do have colleagues all around the world, working in laboratories, at telescopes and at various space agencies—in the U.S., Europe, Japan and Russia. If one of them answers, I'll know this is local, and that, at least, will be some comfort.

I pick up my phone and scroll through my contacts and tap on a name, starting with a U.S. colleague in New York. "C'mon, Tyson, pick up." My leg shakes back and forth. Each ring increases my desperation. On the fourth ring, I get his voicemail. Tyson's voice is deep and cheerful, as always, but his chipper message frustrates me. I hang up and open my contact list. I decide to go intercontinental, dialing Victor Danshov, an astrophysicist with Roscosmos, the Russian Federal Space Agency. We spent a summer together at the Very Large Array in New Mexico, searching for pulsars. We were young, and did more drinking than hard science, but our friendship lasted through the years since. After a moment's delay, the call connects and rings. Six rings and an answering machine. Victor's heavy Russian message is impossible for me to understand. His English isn't much better. But the message is clear. No one is home. Maybe not even alive.

As Victor's voice continues, it's suddenly cut short. I pull the phone away from my ear and look at the screen.

Dead.

Like everyone else.

Don't go there, I think. The dark thought is what I fear, but I'm still not sure it's true. How could such a thing happen? My scientific mind quickly posits a theory: something exotic, some kind of radiation, slipped through Earth's magnetic field. Something we don't fully understand yet. Dark matter, for example. What happens when a planet moves through a dense patch of the stuff? *Not this*, I think, knowing that my monitoring equipment would have detected such an occurrence, and I would have been equally affected, even underground. The one thing of which I'm sure, is that I'm going to figure out what caused the people of Phoenix—and my daughter—to turn to dust. An image of Claire's birth comes to mind. The first time I held her. Impossible fragility. *My girl is gone...* My head lowers to the steering wheel. I just want to sleep. To pretend it's not real.

A loud squawk snaps my head up. I turn and look out of my open door. On the side of the road, a raven, its black feathers fluffed up, wrestles with a second, a single wrapped ice cream bar held in both beaks.

"There's two," I say, and then I realize what I'm seeing.

Life.

The birds survived.

Maybe other people did, too?

I close the door and start driving. Destination: home. There's no real strategy to the location aside from comfort, but it's a direction. Something to focus on. That and the birds. If there are birds, there could be other animals, and if that's true, then there have to be people. I tell myself this, over and over, throughout the long drive through the desert, during which I don't see another living thing.

9

POE

The big, neighbor dog peers at me sideways, front paws on a kitchen chair. He commits three more vigorous, slurping licks to the leftovers and then arcs joyfully down from his meal, to my side. He barks once, sits and wags his tail.

"I guess I didn't shut the door very tight," I say to him, and bend down, rubbing him behind his ears. I sigh and check his tags. Pulse returning to normal, I recognize how soothing this animal's presence is to me.

"Luke, huh? As in Skywalker?"

He barks and licks my face. Sylvia continues to bellow, ready to burst if she isn't milked soon. I think I'll put James in with her...after I collect some milk for myself. Luke and I can't possibly drink as much milk as she produces.

All these animals, suddenly mine. I sigh again, more of a groan this time. My parents raised me with farm animals, and I understand them, but like many people's childhood constants, they're something I tolerated as normalcy, but didn't choose for my own independent existence. Animals annoy me with their routine neediness. They keep you at home, and attached.

Luke and I head out to the barn, the familiar tang of hay, manure and warm mammal bodies so consoling I nearly lie down. Surprising, this sudden sense of home.

After cleaning a teat with an antimicrobial wipe, I sit on the milking stool and go to work on Sylvia, her udder tight and bloated. Luke keeps trying to stick his nose in the pail, and I shove him gently away with my bent leg. James, Sylvia's calf, a fraction of her size with adorably large eyes, would probably like to have a go, too, but my parents keep them separate so she'll produce milk. Continuing the practice seems like a good idea, given the circumstances. The chickens poke around, clucking, feminine.

All these animals, so ridiculous.

All these animals. All alive and unharmed. Whatever happened to my parents and the neighbors didn't affect the animals. They all seem fine, vigorous and healthy. How did they escape the same fate?

Finished, I give Sylvia and James a few pats, their furry coats soft due to my father's frequent brushing and care. His hands were here, so many times. I need to watch the frequency of these thoughts. My eyes start to blur, teary. After pouring the steaming raw milk through a strainer, from one pail to another, I set it on the counter to chill and look around for a clean spot and sit down on the hay. Luke plops next to me, his head in my lap. Sylvia shuffles heavily, nudging my head with her snout and knocking my hood backward. James shoves his snout through the slats looking for more attention, or maybe just reminding me to put him in with his mother.

All these creatures to care for. What the hell am I going to do?

I feel a slight whirl of nausea and realize that in my overwhelmed state of mind I have forgotten the most important creature of them all.

"Sorry, Squirt," I whisper, my hands across my belly.

I stand up and look at the dog.

"Time to pull our shit together." I move James in with his mother and he assaults her udder, nudging with his nose and then drinking. Steaming bucket of milk in hand, I walk back to the house, imagining what it will be like to do this thirty pounds heavier, most of it in the front.

Luke bounds through the snow beside me, eager for a drink, ignorant to the changes going on inside me. "Things are going to get harder," I tell the dog. "But we can handle it."

He continues vaulting about, burying his head in the cold snow. If only both of us could be so joyously oblivious.

"We can handle it."

Before taking stock of the food stored in the house, I turn the television on, hoping there will be a live news reporter filling the screen, explaining the strange event that took my parents and neighbors. The first station is static. I switch to a second and flinch away from the screen. Big Bird and Cookie Monster are singing. I pause on the channel for a moment, feeling hope. I know the episode was recorded thirty something years ago. I recognize the song. But the voices and animated movements feel like life. Human life. Maybe it's simply that something—anything—is still on TV, but it gives me hope.

The third channel confuses me. The camera angle is slightly askew, but I can make out something long and wooden, finished, like a piece of furniture. *It's a news desk.* Empty. Devoid of anchors, and apparently, camera operators. I switch to another station, and this time, a clearer and closer shot appears. A news desk sits solitary in front of what should be a busy news room, but is just empty space and glowing computer screens. I check the station logo in bottom right. CNN. National news out of New York. Five hours away by car. The news ticker at the bottom shows snippets of news, now a day old:

President signs immigration bill into law despite vocal opposition...

Hochman's patients have gone missing in Memphis, Chicago and Boston...

Severe Winter Storm Warning for Northeast Coast. Power outages expected. Whiteout conditions...

"No kidding," I say and glance away from the text. That's when I see them.

Two people.

What's left of them, anyway.

Two small piles of white powder sit atop the news desk. One is mixed with a necklace and framed by earrings. The other mingles with an ear bud. I can picture the two news anchors, discussing who knows what, sitting in their chairs, elbows on the desk, maybe joking, maybe reporting on the storm, or the Hochman's outbreak, and then...what? Did they react on camera? Did viewers see them disintegrate? Or did no one see the spectacle because they were too busy dying?

I sit down hard on the braided rug and scoot back toward the couch, clutching my knees to my chest. I stare at the TV.

How many people?

Luke trundles in, belly full of leftovers, and schlumps down next to me, tail thumping. My mind is blank. I feel empty, eye of the storm calm. I reach behind me, tug the afghan down from the couch and pull it over my head, like I used to as a child—instant fort. Luke noses his way under, one eyebrow raised in curiosity. We sit there breathing, the three of us, for a long time, spots of light between the knitted knots. I pick up the remote and switch the channel back to Sesame Street, peering out through the holes in the blanket, my fingers clutching the spaces between. Bert is doing the pigeon dance.

An hour later, I investigate my parents' house. Stocked fridge, generator running, we're good for at least one week, or several if I first eat what will expire soonest. Kitchen cabinets reveal a variety of canned goods, dry perishables like Honey Nut Cheerios and my favorite, cinnamon graham crackers, purchased by my parents specifically for my visits. So, we're not going to go hungry any time soon.

There is also a freezer in the cellar, filled with my dad's pies and frosty, slaughtered, vacuum-packed chickens. *It's a good thing I turned on the basement breaker*, I realize. Along with the equipped freezer, home-canned soups, jams, spaghetti sauce and pickles line the shelves along two walls in the basement—mostly my mother's work, her garden ever-generous. But if I can avoid going down there for a while, I will.

I wash all the dishes, the well-pump still functioning with the generator's assistance. And then I sit at the table, my head in my hands.

My mother's face, crumpling inward. The look on my dad's face, his voice, 'Poesy,' his hand on my arm. With my fingertips I graze the spot on my arm where he last touched me, between my wrist and elbow. It's a little tender still. He held on hard. My mom had patted my back, right here in the kitchen, her thin frame a tiny shift in the air. Her wispy self, right behind me, draped knit shawl. I can't help it, I turn and look.

Hopelessness bends my body down until I am lying on the kitchen floor, my cheek against the frigid, old linoleum. I feel a little bit like I want to die, too, and maybe I will just welcome the darkness. I've faced depression before, but nothing like this. This is drowning. An inescapable depth. Sinking, rocks in my pockets.

Luke canters over and licks my face, tasting salty tears. He goes to the kitchen door and paws at it, whining. I've never owned a dog before. It's an unceasing chore, but his constant needs are like a hand reached over a precipice, keeping me from falling.

"I'm coming," I groan from the floor.

I sit up, hands on my bent knees. I feel dizzy with confusion and sadness. These creatures, dependent on me, Squirt, Luke, the cows, the chickens. They will propel me to move off the floor, even though I don't want to. I want to just lie here, halfway under the table, and go to sleep.

I wobble to my feet, though, and let the dog out. It's freezing outside, and I lean against the doorframe, allowing my body to experience the frigid air, letting my brain flip over and away from the murky pond it was in a minute ago, there on the floor.

Just because my parents, the neighbors and the newscasters on CNN are now dust, it doesn't mean that I'm alone. There could be other survivors. Somewhere in the world. Maybe even here in town.

I have trouble believing that my small parents, with their strange ways, were the only ones who knew or prepared for what was coming. There was nothing extraordinary about them. Nothing that set them apart, at least not from other UFO-fascinated survivalists, of which there are many. What happened to me could have happened to others.

They're out there, I decide. There have to be at least a few. I just need to find them.

A shiver rumbles through my body, involuntary and cold. "Luke!" The dog's head lifts out of a snow drift he's mistaken for a snack. "C'mere, boy!"

He springs to life and runs to the door, waiting until he's inside to shake the snow balls from his fur. "Mom would have serious issues with you."

His reply—laying down on the antique braided rug in the living room, soaking it with his thawing wetness—says he doesn't care. I turn back to the open door and the coldness beyond. I feel beckoned. Called to find another survivor. My conscious mind says this is unwise. Outside is freezing. Maybe dangerous. My subconscious supplies the impetus to embrace bold action.

Prenatal vitamins.

My parents didn't believe in vitamins, their feeling that humans receive everything they need from locally grown, nutritious food. I, however, am a bit less crunchy, and I will ingest things from bottles if I feel they're necessary. Or fun. Or delicious. Squirt and I need more support than jarred produce can provide. If I had known I would be here longer than a single night, I would have brought my supplements. But who could have predicted this fate?

No one, I think, and then correct myself. *My parents.*

I decide to leave the generator on, to keep the fridge and freezer cold, and the heat running, and head out to the barn to locate the snowshoes. The grocery store is two miles away, an easy walk for me...when there isn't three feet of snow. On the way back to the house from the barn, the arctic air shoots straight through me.

Back inside, I wrap in layers—my mother's fleece balaclava, Gore-Tex gloves, long underwear taken from her upstairs bureau drawer and my dad's red coat, which comforts me. Snowshoes clipped on, I look like some kind of weird refugee from the frozen badlands of a sci-fi movie. I head out into the gleaming white world, the snowshoes doing their job, dispersing my weight and allowing me to walk (mostly) on top of the snow. Luke follows me out, his paws sinking, each step a leap. "It's a long walk, buddy. You sure?"

He watches me with eager eyes, tail never tiring.

"Suit yourself."

I walk out past my buried car, snow drifts looming taller than me. I wouldn't be able to drive five feet without getting stuck. I consider taking my parents' truck, but my car is in front of it. I feel like I want the walk, anyhow. Something to do.

The long, tiring snowshoe walk down my parents' road, where the snowplows hadn't begun to clean, takes over an hour. After exiting the wooded street, we pass a car, off the road, still running. I peek inside, tiny butterfly of hope in my gut, and am greeted with several heaps of clothing, white powder swirling around the interior, slipping across the dashboard and the seats, propelled by the car's heating vents. I decide not to open the door.

Twenty awkward, snowshoe steps ahead is a big, red, Chevy truck, its hood bisected by a pine tree, engine quiet. Again, inexplicably, the little flicker of hope. Maybe, this time, someone? And then a second thought, maybe someone who's legitimately hurt, not powder, and in need of help after an accident?

As Luke and I approach, a hefty, black German Shepherd pops into view, just as Luke did earlier at the neighbor's house, giving me a weird sense of déjà vu. He eyes us for a quiet moment, looking from me, and then to Luke. When he sees the dog, the shepherd becomes unhinged. It barks savagely at Luke and I think, for a moment, that this shepherd might just be afraid of other dogs, but then it turns toward me and intensifies. A strand of drool slaps against the glass. Sticks. Smears as the dog grinds its teeth, lips and snout against the window.

Startled, I tip over backward onto the partially snow-covered street. I'm still wearing the snowshoes, which I could have removed on this sort of cleared street, and I twist my ankle. The pain is sharp, but not in the grinding, broken bone way.

Luke is unsure what to do with this vicious creature and stands, head down, tail between his legs. He's not a fighter, that's for sure.

I remove the snowshoes and the boot on my right foot, then peel down my sock to inspect my hurt ankle. Throbbing, starting to swell. *No,* I think. *No, not now, not here.*

Snow soaks through my backside, freezing my legs and bottom. The dog keeps snarling at us, his scratching paws beating out a steady staccato beat on the glass, trying to break through the window.

"Asshole!" I yell at him and scrape up a mittenful of snow from the pavement, hurling it at the window.

I have now managed to enrage the dog more, and I watch his anger escalate, a weird, throaty, growling-wheezing combination. Intimidating as hell. But he's got me pissed. At him. At everyone for dying. For leaving me alone. At whatever kind of God could allow something like this to happen. I stand to my feet, the pain fueling my anger. "Fuck you," I tell the dog, the words flowing out low and sinister, but in a way a dog can't understand. So I shout, barking the words, "Fuck! You!" And I punch the glass.

The dog flinches back, stumbling and falling into the door on the far side. But before I can feel good about establishing my dominance, he returns, unleashing his fury on the driver's seat headrest, tearing it apart in seconds, and then striking the window so hard I hear a crack. Blood flows from the dog's mouth, mixing with frothy saliva, as he continues his barrage on the glass.

I suddenly realize he might be able to break a window, and neither I, nor Luke, would be able to protect Squirt from that monster.

"I hope you rot," I tell the dog, and I limp away, snowshoes tucked under my arm. I'm freezing, my butt is soaked and violent death is trapped in the car behind me, fighting to get out. *That dog is just fighting to survive,* I think and I look down at Luke by my side. *Like us. But doomed.*

10

POE

Crap, my ankle hurts.

As we walk, I examine my feelings. Limp, step, limp, step. Strange how the terror of that dog brought out my rage and steeled my fortitude a little. *Fuck you, dog! Rot to death!* I grin, just a small one. I can make choices. I am still in charge. I've got Luke and Squirt, and we're walking to the store. The normalcy of it gives me peace. I notice the trees, heavy with melting snow, bending down as though in reverence to my passing. A single branch vaults up as the snow slides away, snapping a salute. I give the maple a nod and carry on. Limp, step, limp, step.

I grow accustomed to the pain, and the reality of what I've just done floats to the surface. *I just left a dog to die a slow and painful death. It will starve. No, it will die of dehydration before that happens. Both are horrible deaths.* It feels...evil.

No, he would have killed Luke and bit your face off.

He was covered in powder.

Somehow, my brain short-circuited that part and saw only his black fur, but now, picturing it again, I realize he was covered in the white powder. Of course he was. But I still can't let him out of the truck.

Maybe if I were alone. If Luke had stayed home and I'd never become pregnant and the world hadn't ended so that the emergency room could sew my face back up. But here? Now? I can't let that dog out, any more than I could put a gun to my head.

Sobered a bit by these thoughts, my heart softens for the animal the further I walk away from him. It strikes me, a punch in the gut, that there are probably many, many unattended pets and farm animals that will be in need of care. Parakeets in cages. Unmilked cows. Thousands of dogs, cats and guinea pigs, trapped in their homes, covering the interior spaces in poop and urine. Some escape and go feral; some just waste away. Sheep and goats, trapped in their foodless fencing. How many? Once again, I can't fathom it. How many? Were other countries affected, too? I imagine wild creatures—lions and elephants—slowly taking over the savannahs once again. The reforesting of the temporal forests. Great apes. The flourishing of eco-systems. I push it further: tuna, whales, unfished oceans. The short run tragedy of humanity's—and their pets— decimation are a long term win for the planet.

That's so screwed up, I think, shaking my head.

I look down at Luke, trotting beside me. He's adjusted his speed to accommodate my limping gait. I feel a bit like Noah, after the ark. But at least he had his wife and children.

As we travel further along the main road, several more cars sit motionless, some running, heated and clear of snow. Some are dead and covered over. I don't have the resolve to look inside them. If I see one more pile of dust, or one more savage pet, I might go home and never come out again.

My ignorance-is-bliss tactic works, and we reach Hannaford, the local grocery store chain, fifteen minutes later. The vast parking lot is covered in three feet of smooth white snow, undulating where it rises up over bushes and a few cars. I stop and listen. The world is quiet. No hum of humanity. No birds. All I can hear is the impossibly small sound of loose, wind-driven snowflakes ticking over the frozen lot. The emptiness of this vast silence leaves me drained, so I start walking again and take comfort in the jingling of Luke's dog tags.

We weave through the few empty cars in the parking lot and I hear one of them still running, nearly silent. I glance into a few of the cars, where the snow has fallen away from the smooth glass windows. Most are empty, but a few hold the now-standard powder clothing piles, of people waiting in the car while their loved one went to grab a few things to weather the storm—gallons of milk, bread, snacks. I find the still running car, a small hybrid, clear of snow, heated from within. With the frigid temperature, the heat would need to be on in the car for someone waiting. I find I'm surprised by the length of time a car can continue to idle. Full gas tanks? Super efficiency? The mystery is weirdly comforting and offers a nice distraction.

Luke and I stop in front of the automatic doors for a few beats until I realize they're not going to open—the electricity is off here, too. And no one was around to make sure the generator was operating. Unsure about what to do next, I shiver and watch Luke pee into a snow bank.

I didn't come all this way to be stopped by a lack of convenience, I decide.

Pushing one of the doors open, cool, dark, quiet greets me. Luke pushes past me, thrilled, and he bounds down an aisle before I can stop him. All this rule-breaking I'm about to do, when I stop to consider it, is disconcerting. Breaking in—although technically the doors are unlocked, allowing a dog to run free through a grocery store and looting are all new experiences. It feels wrong, even though I know there's no one here to care.

This grocery store is considered by many rural New Hampshirites to be too fancy and expensive, with its aisle of specialty food items displayed on wooden shelves and all-natural cleaners and beauty care products. Shiny floors, sushi samples and organic pears from Chile. We're used to cheaper, generally tax-free living than our neighbors to the south in Massachusetts, and usually we pride ourselves on our Yankee ingenuity. But I love this shiny store, which has always carried everything I need.

Inside the door, chaos. I step over several powdery clothing lumps, next to a full, dripping grocery cart and two tipped over shopping baskets. A half-gallon of Breyer's chocolate ice cream has melted onto the floor, mixing with the white powder, creating a white-specked brown puddle, like tree pollen after a rain. My presence and the cold wind behind me stirs the air, lifting some of the nearby powder. Granny Smith apples lie scattered a few feet away. Luke jogs his return to me, paws slipping on the waxed floor, a chunk of plastic-wrapped cheddar cheese between his teeth. He drops it at my feet, lies down and starts gnawing, oblivious to the white beneath him, or perhaps seeing it as snow.

The store feels dead. There's no electrical hum of cooling units, no music or announcements. The bustle of people, voices and squeaky carriages is missing. Children should be negotiating for snacks, babies fussing. Old ladies with coupons, taking forever at checkout. A profound sense of aloneness shivers through me, like the onset of a fever.

The initial reason for our trek dawns again on me—to find survivors, people like me. And prenatal vitamins. So far, I've been disappointed by a man-eating dog and too many powder piles. I had hoped that this store and the lure of supplies it provides might draw other survivors out, but I am clearly the first visitor to arrive.

Luke follows me, cheese in mouth, to the stationery aisle, his clicking nails the only sound aside from my wet squeaky boots and the metallic rattle of the wind on the roof. It's surprisingly dark in here. The windows at the front of the store provide the only light, already diffused because of the gray sky. In the stationery aisle, I select a black, spiral-bound pocket notebook and a package of Sharpie pens. I put the notebook back and pick up a green, instead. I need some color, some cheer. I break open the package, uncap the pen and write, 'Pens and mini notebook.' When—if—things return to normal, I'll be able to pay for everything I take. I'm about to add Luke's cheese to the list, but my hand won't move. I try to force it, but only manage to scribble a jagged line. Some part of me is resisting the fantasy that life will return to normal again. That I will have to pay for what I take. That anyone will care.

A teardrop taps against the paper, absorbing and turning the white sheet transparent, revealing the blue lines of the next page.

A second tear falls, tapping the page and snapping me fully out of the fantasy. "Damnit!" I yell and throw the notebook into the display, launching boxes of Bic pens and Crayola Markers into the aisle.

I stand there, arms crossed, ignoring the tears and squelching the sobs building in my chest. I'm too angry to cry. I bend down and pick up a package of markers, then stare at it. The bright primary colors mock me. I turn and throw the box over the aisles. Centrifugal force pulls the markers from the box as it spins, showering the floor. Making a mess. I grin and look down at Luke. "Whatever you want boy. Go to town."

He just stares back, waiting to follow my lead. I head to a nearly empty shopping cart, skirting the pile of dust that's mostly covered up by a heap of winter clothing. I take the birthday card, roll of wrapping paper and candles out of the cart and drop them on the floor. Then I replace them with pens, pencils, markers, crayons and a few watercolor sets. Several pads of paper go next. It could be argued that I don't need any of this to survive, but I would argue that I need it to exist. Art is how I process, and I have a lifetime of processing to do before Squirt is born. With enough art supplies to last me a month or two, I put my hand on Luke's ever present head. "Let's go."

Before I make it to the end of the aisle, I shiver. It's freezing in here, not sub-zero like it is outside, but the stillness of the air feels like a chilled blanket. I'm used to overheating in stores, and usually I drape my coat over the cart. Now I can see my breath. Despite the fact that I'm dressed for an Arctic excursion, the shaking gets worse, but is it the bitter cold, or nerves?

That's when I notice the smell, and the shaking gets worse.

Nerves. Great.

The usual scent of an enclosed, heated, public place is missing. There are no perfumed bodies, unwashed armpits of people fresh from their workouts, smokers unaware or uncaring about the tangy nicotine trail left behind them or the generic, icy, breadcrumb smell of frozen food items encased in cardboard. No warming rotisserie chicken. Today the store smells of pennies, and thawed meat; the aroma of fresh road kill when it wafts through an open car window in the spring, wet with a hint of decay.

I gag, but contain it. I've now experienced worse.

Luke and I wander the store, starting at the pharmacy aisles, where I read the labels on the prenatal vitamin bottles and glance at the actual pharmacy, with all those medications, only to be dispensed with prescriptions. I realize I could grab anything. Should I pilfer through there? Plan on the possibility of getting sick? I feel overwhelmed with the need for planning, and want to ignore the compulsion to foresee the future.

For a moment, I entertain the possibility of killing myself. I could find a sleeping pill. Something serious. Like Ambien. Take the whole bottle. I picture it, the calm. The ease, no more pain. I'll drift off, mind numbed to the pain of death. And then I picture Luke, alone, his tail between his legs, lying beside my still form. And then Squirt. Dead inside me.

I gasp my way out of the vision. One hand to my mouth, the other clutching the prenatals.

I'm sorry I considered it, Squirt.

I walk away from the pharmacy and the sinister opportunities it offers, focusing on what to take. Should I bother with perishables? Have they already perished? How many hours has the electricity been out, here? Is Luke going to get sick from that cheese? I decide to avoid the fresh meat and dairy. The rest is fair game.

I limp through the aisles, taking boxes of food that won't go bad any time soon, canned goods and entire boxes of dark chocolate bars—the expensive kind I normally can't afford. As I round a back aisle, headed for the produce, a splash beneath my foot stops me. A salty, warm fish smell fills the air. In the very dim light, I look down to find a puddle, swirled with white powder. Ice from the fish coolers has melted and overflowed, mixing with the dead. I limp away and lean my back against the now-cold rotisserie chicken counter. The fish smell reminds me of the ocean. The beach. I see my mother's long brown hair, her thin, girlish body in her size-small, blue bathing suit, bending over my sand castle with me. She's digging the moat. My father sits under an umbrella, reading and grinning at us.

I flinch when Luke suddenly puts a paw on my leg. I didn't hear him walk up. The wind is picking up outside. The metal roof rattles, the poor man's thunder sound effect. The fish freezers drip, a constant plop on the puddle-soaked floor. The darkness of the store closes in on me, adding weight. *I'm too far back,* I think. *I should have stayed near the windows. Near the light.* Strange, this primal fear of the dark. I now know there are much worse things in the world.

Beckoned by the scent of still-fresh fruit and vegetables, I enter the produce section. I envision myself gorging on apples, pears and grapes, eating it all before it goes bad, but then I wonder how I'll carry all of this two miles through the snow, while wearing snowshoes with a swollen ankle. My first step is to transfer what I've taken into two canvas bags, the kinds people buy to assuage their guilt over using plastic and save the planet. The two bags are nearly full when I turn my attention back to the fruit. I pick through the organic apples. Luke, tuckered out, lies down next to me on the cold floor.

A particular red apple, shiny and new, lacking any bruising, calls out to be eaten. My mother would ream me out for not washing it first, would remind me that even organic fruit can be sprayed with pesticides for transportation, but I'm hungry. I wipe the apple on my pant leg and take a bite. The crunch echoes through the empty store. The flavor takes me to a hundred different orchard visits. I take a second bite. The crunch sounded wrong, like part of the noise came from the far side of the store. I chew slowly. Silently. Listening until the half chewed fruit rests still in my mouth. I'm about to resume chewing when, somewhere in the store, the distinct sound of a can falling to the floor and rolling away roars through the air like an approaching tidal wave.

I lean forward and push the apple from my mouth with my tongue, unwilling to make a sound. I glance up into the mirror above my head. *Why do grocery stores have mirrors above their produce?* I bend a little, trying to see behind me, but only fruit and shadows fill the view.

Something scuffs, still distant. Luke raises his head, ears perked. This noise is different, like it had a cause. Cans, off balance, can fall. I wasn't exactly careful when I went through the aisles. But loose food doesn't scuff.

We aren't alone.

My instinct, in my loneliness, is to call out. I open my mouth to shout, 'Hello,' but I'm silenced by Luke's low growl. My heart patters wildly, hummingbird wings, and I grab him by the collar. He breaks away from me, running through produce and around the corner, down another aisle. The hair on the back of my neck rises. *Like a horror movie*, I think.

In seconds, Luke scampers back to me, whimpering, tail between his legs, ears flattened. He's drooling. He paws at me and I bend down to hug him.

"It's okay," I whisper, but the words have an unusual bump in the middle of them.

We crouch quietly in front of the apples for a minute, both of us with ears perked. To our left now, perhaps an aisle over, I hear a dragging sound, like heavy fabric being pulled across the floor.

Luke whimpers and pees, right there.

We're definitely not alone. And Luke is terrified.

Quaking all over, I take this as a hint that we need to hide. I hold him by the collar, heft my two heavy bags onto one shoulder—unwilling to give up my hard-foraged supplies—and we head in the opposite direction from the noise, past the bakery and the deli, back to the gross, sloppy-floored fish section. We step lightly through the rancid puddles, thick with fish oil and white powder, and crouch behind one of the freezers. Luke sits down, right in the liquid, and I cringe. He's trembling.

The smell is overwhelming. My eyes water and I try to breathe through my mouth.

I hear the dragging sound again, a repetitious shushing. It's coming closer. *Following.*

I tuck my head down and cling to Luke. Both arms wrapped around his girth, fingers laced under his collar. My heartbeat clobbers my ribcage.

The sound is right in front of us, a heavy noise, like someone dragging a mile long, deflated, hot air balloon through the store. Water gurgles, pushed by something. Small waves wrap around the counter, lapping against my boots.

And then it passes. Moving on.

As the sound fades, the fish smell is momentarily masked by the loveliness of roses. *What?* I haven't seen the sound's source, but the way it terrified Luke, I would have expected it to smell foul. But flowers? The wafting, rose-scented breeze lingers for several minutes, and it brings tears to my eyes. It's so beautiful. Different from roses. Better. *What is happening?*

A distant clunk accompanied by a rising and falling brightness tells me that some door on the other side of the store has just opened and closed. Daring to rise up a bit from my crouched position, my hamstrings suffering in the half-squat on my hurt ankle, I peek through the dripping fish freezer. I don't see anything. I wait a full five minutes. I don't hear anything.

Luke rises to his feet as well, his furry butt and tail dripping with the foul-smelling liquid. Bits of wet powder cling to his fur.

We need to get the hell out of here. I realize that I had already come to believe that there were no other survivors. *So what the hell was that? I should have looked.*

I shake my head at the idea. Whatever it was, it wasn't good. There's enough instinct in the reptilian part of my brain, and Luke's, to know that much.

I wait five minutes more, and when again nothing happens, I take a step around the freezer corner.

"Stay, Luke. Good boy. Stay."

I scan the store, looking down the back aisle. The rear of the store is lit in stripes of dim light filtering past the tall aisles. I see nothing but rows of food. Then, a rolling marker, spins at the end of an aisle, drawing my eyes. Still, nothing, but there is something wrong with my vision. The chip display at the end cap is blurry. I blink, thinking there must be some residual tears turned to eye goop in my eyes, but it doesn't help.

Then the chips move.

No, not the chips.

Something *in front* of the chips.

The indistinct shape slides forward, into the light, still unseen, but now shimmering, bending the light. It's...huge. Seven feet tall, maybe. Half as wide.

A ghost, I think. The planet must be populated by them now, billions of people cut down before they were ready, like that *Torment* novel. The words on the bags blend with the colors, a mushy melting effect, refracting light bright enough to illuminate the surrounding area. I hear the dragging sound before it stops.

Luke's dog tags jingle and I look down at him, wondering if he will charge to my rescue or abandon me and flee. But he's as stuck as me. Then his head tilts in that funny way all confused dogs do. I look up, expecting to see the shimmer sliding toward me, revealing its true ghastly self.

Instead, the shimmering light is gone, disappeared.

"Like a ghost."

11

AUGUST

The trip home is much faster than the journey to Phoenix. The sun is high in the cloudless, deep blue Arizona sky, and the white dust has settled to the ground, much of it now mingling with the desert. Despite the improved air quality, a swirling cloud of the dead spins into the air behind the Highlander, kicked up in the vehicle's wake. Working my way past the empty vehicles and large wrecks is far easier. Moving slowly, I maneuver between rows of vehicles, viewing them as oversized gravestones marking the final resting places of countless travelers. Not that their bodies are here.

Nearly all the vehicles on the road and in the city, not to mention the surrounding suburban houses and city apartments, all have one thing in common: open windows. The event took place, I believe, at 6:30 PM on a Friday evening. The weather forecast, which I check every morning, even when I've sequestered myself in Desert's underground lab, predicted an unseasonably warm 75 degree weather and high winds from the West. Not cold enough for heat, or hot enough for AC, but perfect for open windows. That's how the cloud of human dust has grown so large. People's loose remains were sucked out of their homes and cars—not to mention the hundreds of thousands outside enjoying the evening—and were carried over the desert.

I arrive in Superior, a small Arizona town fifteen miles from the lab and just inside the southern fringe of the Tonto National Forest, at 11AM. It's kind of a ramshackle place that's frozen in the early 70s, populated by adobe mobile homes, scrub brush, endless dirt and a smattering of short trees in constant need of moisture. Many of the buildings are vacant and falling apart. It's basically a depressing craphole, but the familiar roads and epic vistas surrounding the town begin to ease my tension.

The community I settled in five years ago, Nebula Estates, was built shortly after Desert's research facility, named to attract the bevy of astro-scientists relocating to the area. And it worked. Most of my neighbors are also coworkers. As I turn off the empty Route 60 and onto what appears to be an unassuming side street, I hit the brakes, squealing to a stop.

A mountain lion, massive and defiant, stands in the road, its head cocked toward the vehicle. Its eyes pierce the windshield to find my face. There are three predators in this part of the world that pose a threat to people: rattlesnakes, coyotes and mountain lions. The snakes will stand their ground, but they won't pursue a person. There's nothing to be gained. A coyote will only attack if cornered. They know well enough to fear mankind. But mountain lions... Although people aren't normally their preferred prey, they *will* stalk and kill a person. In fact, they're the only predator in the world that will move *toward* the sound of human activity, rather than away from it. That I'm the last person on Earth might make me an irresistible treat to the predator. *I'm an ice cream sandwich*, I think, *but wrapped in a metal shell. Safe.*

I honk the horn defiantly. The cat doesn't flinch. It just stares for ten more seconds and then seems to lose interest. As it strolls away, it looks back one last time, meeting my eyes, as if to say, 'I know where you live.'

Despite the big cat's disconcerting appearance, it's another living thing, and that's encouraging. My list of survivors has grown to four: two ravens, a mountain lion and me. But are there more?

There have to be.

The black gate, an ornate iron affair, appears ahead. There's no guard shack. The heavy gates detect the windshield-mounted sensor and open automatically. *The power is still on here,* I think, and I chide myself for not considering the possibility of it being off. I stop, waiting for the gates to open enough for me to fit, and then I speed in, worried that the cat will follow the vehicle inside. The community is surrounded by a gleaming white, eight-foot-tall fence, so once the gate is shut, the mountain lion won't be a concern. Or will it? Can they jump that high? Feeling a little paranoid, I stop on the far side of the gate and watch it close.

No lion in sight.

The dark pavement and bright yellow lines dividing it are free of white residue and vehicles. The event must have taken place when no one was coming or going. *Unless,* I think, *there are survivors.* I roll down the windows and slow to five mph, honking my horn, hoping that a familiar face will run from one of the McMansions lining the sides of the curving road. The neighborhood is pristine. Automatic lawn sprinklers have sprung up in several yards, their *tck, tck, tck, shhhh,* a strange comfort; it's a sign of life, if only artificial. But nothing else moves.

I pull up to my home, a long beige ranch with a two-story, two-car garage, above which is my office. Unlike my neighbors, who elected to have green lawns and acacia trees in the middle of a desert, I went with stones and cacti. It's not exactly a welcoming sight, but I don't have to care for it, which is important, since I'm so rarely home.

I pull into the garage and cut the engine. Silence greets me. In general, the desert is a quiet place, especially during the day. But here, close to town, the pulse of human activity drones in the background, white noise that I hadn't really noticed until now. The silence is like a pressure on my ears. I hit the garage door button, more eager to drown out the silence than to protect the vehicle. Who's left to steal it?

Inside, I put my keys and wallet atop a small table, just inside the garage entrance. The silence inside the house is more bearable, probably because I'm used to it. The solid construction and triple-paned windows keep the outside world...outside.

Of course, right now, all I really want is some kind of confirmation that the outside world still exists. I head for the kitchen, which is dressed in chrome, shiny black granite and richly stained brown wood. Any respectable chef could make a feast in this kitchen. I mostly make Captain Crunch and microwavable pot pies, but I'm not here to eat. The iPad resting on the bar is my destination. I left it plugged in and on, so I'm online with a button push, screen swipe and double tap.

My first destination is the BBC news app I check every morning I'm home. I don't have cable TV, or get a newspaper, so my one source of news is the Internet, and I've found the BBC the best source of global news that isn't full of American political strife. The app loads as usual, lingers on the updating screen a little longer than usual, but then pops up a stream of stories from around the world.

Relief floods into my body as I scroll through the horizontal thumbnails in the Top Stories track. But my grip on the device tightens when I reach the end and see nothing about Phoenix. Or Arizona. In fact, only one of the top stories is in the U.S., the murder trial of a pop star. I tap the pop star story and note the date and time: yesterday at 5pm. I go back and check three other stories with similar results. The most recent story, about the mystery virus known as Hochman's, named for the man who discovered it and then perished from it, was posted yesterday at 5:30pm. Despite my urgency to find signs of human activity, I linger on the Hochman's article.

I'd been following the virus's progress before heading into the lab for the week. The virus spreads quickly, via the coughing and sneezing present in the first day of infection. The first case was recorded in China, but it had already spread around the world, taking advantage of a defect in the genetic code present in nearly everyone—if not everyone—on the planet. Researchers were rushing to find a patch for the human genome, and had begun looking for survivors, but thus far, the survival rate was zero. Absolute zero. Contracting the virus was a death sentence. Over the course of a week, the infected human body would simply fall apart, like a well-cooked roast. Quarantine zones had been set up in major port cities where cases had appeared—Los Angeles, San Francisco and New York in the U.S., and thus far, the virus had remained under control, but a catastrophic pandemic was feared. The end of human civilization hadn't seemed as possible since the Cold War.

Too bad no one even saw the real threat.

You don't know everything yet, I tell myself, and I switch from the BBC app to Facebook. I don't have a lot of Facebook friends, just 54, and like most people, only a handful of them are actual friends. The timeline pops up, filling with posts. Photos and videos of people I know or vaguely know fill the screen, mixed with advertisements and pop culture memes I don't understand. All dated for yesterday. Facebook is still up, but no one is posting. I switch to my Twitter account, where I'm following just twenty people, but they're twenty different people, and some post frequently. The story is the same.

I broaden my search to the rest of the Internet as a whole, visiting news sites first. Like the BBC, the news is silent about Phoenix and dated for yesterday. My final stop is Reddit, which even during the apocalypse, would be filled with conversation. I find the last post is dated yesterday, time-stamped for 8:30 EST. It reads, "Does anyone else hear that freaky noise? I'm in New York."

There are four replies, time-stamped a minute later.

"Hear it. Cali."

"Hellz yes. Toronto."

"WTF. YES!!! London."

The fourth reply is in Japanese script, but the location is in English. Tokyo.

If this mystery sound, heard around the world, has something to do with the event that turned everyone to dust...

My worst fears are starting to resolve.

Shaking my head, I reach out. The motion is without thought, but when my fingers wrap around the neck of a Jack Daniel's bottle, I quickly unscrew the cap, tip the bottle to my lips and suck down a burning gulp. Then another. And another, until the words, *I'm alone,* fade from my mind.

12

POE

I don't hesitate. I pull each bag of food over my shoulders, and step out of the fish water. I know that Luke will stay with me now. I'm trusting in that.

I sneak out from behind the freezers and move along the walls, like I know how to do this sneaking thing, like cops do it in the movies, eyes darting, movements smooth. Except that I'm limping with heavy bags and a big red dog. I leave wet footprints and a fishy trail. Easy to follow. But, strangely, I'm the one doing the following, taking the same idiotic path toward the dangerous unknown as the morons in horror movies. But curiosity, the desire for answers, pulls me like gravity. We make it to the dairy freezers, and I peer around the corner, only my forehead and half an eyeball visible.

The shimmering is there, moving away from us, passing by bread shelves.

It's like looking through water. The background is still visible, but blurry and warped. A loaf of bread, put back sloppily, hanging off the shelf, spins and falls to the floor as the thing passes, giving the loaf no heed. *It's solid,* I think, *not a ghost or spirit or something intangible.* My next thought is, *It's looking for us.* But I quickly discount that. *It already found us. Saw us. And now...what? It's leaving? Just a quick, how do you do, neighbor, sorry about wiping out the human race?*

I have no real knowledge that this thing is responsible, but what else could it be? That said, why would an entity responsible for the deaths of billions stop by a grocery store just to pay me a visit?

The thing moves around the corner, out of sight, bringing its dragging sound and rose scent with it. I wait, listening, breath held, fingers cramping around Luke's collar. He presses his head against my leg.

The dragging sound fades, moving steadily away from us.

I should run.

What the hell is that thing?

I listen, ears straining, balancing heavy on one foot, just toes on the other, until I can't hear the dragging anymore. And then I limp my way as fast as I can down the bread and dairy aisle, hoping it's not waiting in silence for us, right there, when I round the corner. Yogurt, cheese, bagels, loaves, peanut butter at the end...

The front door is so close, just have to turn this corner. I flatten against the endcap and look, frantic. I see nothing, then full out run, limp, run. Luke is way ahead of me. He beats me out the door. I scurry through the self-serve register, my bags falling to my elbows. I should leave them. But can I ever return here? I glance back, around, nearing the doors. I forget the mess at the entrance and slip on the melted ice cream and the dissolved people. I skid and let out a moan of pain.

My ankle. Liquid, chocolate ice cream splashes onto my pant leg.

Then I'm at the exit door, shoving it through loose snow, packing it to the side just enough for me to slip through.

Outside, the wind has picked up again. I'm still wet through from my earlier fall, my ankle is throbbing and an unearthly presence is scuffing through the grocery store on the other side of these walls.

Luke rolls around in the snow, excited to be outside, away from the powder piles and the *God-only-knows-what-that-thing-was.* Underneath my layers, a veneer of panic sweat transforms into goosebumps and I shiver violently. *Keep moving,* I think. *Get away.*

Life suddenly feels like a recurring dream I used to have as a child, trapped in a house that was sometimes a school, pursued by something unseen. I knew that house like it was my own, the same familiarity with which I know this store. And now, that same unknown something, is looking for me...for real. So I do what I did in those dreams. I run. We round the corner of the grocery store, my ankle throbbing.

I can't walk all the way back like this. I'm going to do long term damage. I lean against the brick wall of the store, lifting my foot, eyes darting all around. *Is that thing going to come outside?* I need to move. *Run!*

Maybe I could drive part of the way, up to our unplowed road? I could use one of these cars, maybe? I limp quickly across the parking lot, reach a car and place my mitten on the handle. I stop. Can't do it. Two piles of powder mixed with clothing. One in the passenger seat— with knitting. Someone was knitting a warm, blue hat while they waited. And in the backseat, small, red mittens, a parka, overalls, boots. I don't open the door. What would I do with their remains? Besides that, would the car have any gas? They wouldn't have been waiting out here in the frigid evening without the car running to keep the heat on. I look for the small hybrid. It's silent now.

I can't keep hesitating. I'm getting cold, and I think I'm being watched. Across the street, several houses sit silently. Glancing backward at the storefront reveals nothing—I can't see inside. It's too blindingly white out here and too dark in there. Even if I could, I'd look right through it.

It's watching us, I think, even now weighing the worth of this confused, pitiful survivor. I head for the houses, not looking back, and not knowing what I'm looking for.

I reach the first ancient Colonial two minutes later, Luke by my side every second, and I find the door locked. My thoughts spin. I'm starting to feel panicky. I limp around the front of the house and come face to face with a shiny red snowmobile, backed out of an open two-car garage that is filled with not only two cars, but boxes, hunting gear, skis, bicycles and skateboards. You name it. If not for my ankle, I would take the skis, and if not for the snow, the skateboard, but instead, I eye the snowmobile.

The key is in the ignition. I glance around, and notice a two-tone snowsuit that has blown away into a nearby shrub, helmet on the ground. The owner had just backed it out of the garage when the event occurred, and maybe sat waiting for a friend to arrive. Snowmobiling with friends anytime, even during a blizzard, is a fairly common, rural New Hampshire activity, but not usually my cup of tea.

I try the snowmobile key, it just clicks and nothing happens. *Gas*, I think. It was idling here all night. In the garage, I find several full portable tanks, and I lug one back to the snowmobile. I feel inept and ridiculous, exhausted with anxiety and the pain in my ankle. One of the two canvas bags filled with food tips over on the snowy walk and a bag of oranges rolls out. Luke picks it up in his jaws and runs off with it.

I want to cry. I don't know where the stupid gas tank is and I feel on the verge of some kind of precipice. Teetering. Anxiety swirls through my body to my fingertips. I'm freezing. I allow myself to cry a little while I finally locate the tank and pour the gas inside.

When I open up the enormous hatch on the back of the snowmobile, four partially frozen Sam Adams six-packs await. *Nice. Drunk snowmobiling, good for everyone involved.* I consider getting plastered on alcoholic slushies and falling over into a snowbank, allowing nature to decide my fate. When I realize that nature, or something, has *already* decided my fate and left me as the sole survivor of some kind of apocalyptic event, I remove the frozen beer and stuff my canvas bags inside, without the beautiful oranges.

"Luke!" He jogs back to me, snowy, bag of fruit still in his jaws. Weird dog. "You're gonna have to walk. Come on, boy." Misunderstanding, or perhaps outthinking me, Luke climbs up over the snowmobile and lies across my lap. *He's done this before.*

The engine roars to life, and I ease out of the driveway, moving carefully, but then I remember the roads are empty, and that there is a shimmering thing haunting the grocery store across the street. *If it's even still there.* It could be ten feet away and standing still. The thought propels me, and the snowmobile, toward home.

13

AUGUST

"Show me the way to go home," I bellow, standing above my open and smoking barbeque. I've thrown on a steak and nothing else. Alone at the end of the world, I've decided to eat like a man, or at least how I think tough men eat. Because that's what I am, right? A tough man. The last man in the world! "I'm tired and I want to go to bed!"

The lyrics come out slurred, sloppy and unsure. I only know the song from watching *Jaws* at least two dozen times in my life. It's been a few years, but the song is part of my favorite scene from the movie. The camaraderie of that celluloid moment feels like a dream. I want buddies to sing with! I want Richard Dreyfuss to help me figure out what's going on, to impress me with his wit and the breadth of his knowledge. That's the kind of guy I need to be, and I think with a crooked grin, that I at least have the look down...with a few extra pounds.

The sun has fallen behind the mesa to the West. After a day spent drinking, I'd witnessed the most vivid sunset I'd ever seen. At first, I thought it was the alcohol, but then realized it was probably because of all the human dust drifting around in the atmosphere. That, and smoke from Phoenix. Neither of them helped my mood, so I hit the bottle a little harder and decided that cooking with gas was a good idea. I haven't set myself on fire yet, but the night is still young, and I still have a quarter bottle of whiskey to go.

My head suddenly feels heavy, and I lean back, eyes on the deep purple sky, mouth hanging slack. The stars are out. Not all of them, of course. The Milky Way won't be visible for another few hours, and even then the full moon on the horizon might be bright enough to drown it out. But it will be a spectacle, either way. Maybe I'll lie outside tonight. Watch the satellites zip past.

A flicker of motion tracking across the sky catches my attention. *Speaking of satellites.* It's rare to see the glowing hull of a passing satellite this early in the night. But this one is bright. And a little larger than most. *Is it the space station? No, it's moving too fast.* In fact, it's moving a little too fast for *any* functional satellite.

Perhaps, without control from people on Earth, some of the satellites will start falling to Earth? I shake my head. That will happen eventually, but not in a single day. Most of the satellites orbiting the planet will continue to function, powered by the infinite sun, waiting to transmit signals to no one, until long after I'm dead. I watch the bright speck glide across the violet curtain of fading day, and then, it's gone. But not. My vision has moved beyond it. I track back, expecting the moving point of light to slip back into view, but I only find a stationary star.

What star is that?

I find Polaris, the North Star, at the tail end of Ursa Minor, orienting myself to the night sky. I move back to the star in question and even in my hazy drunken state, I know that it is not a star at all. It's the satellite—stopped, in between the constellations Cepheus and Draco.

How does a satellite orbiting the Earth suddenly stop?

Someone is controlling it, I think. But at the speed it was moving, coming to a full stop would have taken a few revolutions around the planet. The sudden, jarring stop performed by the satellite would have torn it apart.

And then, it does the impossible again, reversing direction and accelerating. "What...the..." I gasp. The satellite disappears.

Maybe someone *is* controlling it, and just pushed it beyond its stress limits, breaking it into pieces?

Fat drips from the steak. Flames sizzle up. I stumble back a step, laughing as a wave of dizziness swirls through my body and dots of light swirl in my vision for a moment. I have had far too much to drink. Or not enough. I take a swig, put my arms around two imaginary chums, and sing, "I had a little drink about an hour ago, and it went right to my head!"

I bump against a chair and slump into it. "Man, I want to watch that movie." I slowly come to the conclusion that I cannot watch *Jaws*. My copy is VHS, but I no longer have a VCR. *Who does? Nobody, that's who.* But my neighbor, Phil, who is kind of a jackass, has a home theater and an ungodly number of DVDs and Blue Ray movies. He showed me once, the day I moved in. I haven't been back over since. Phil is an aberration in the neighborhood. He doesn't work at Desert. He's not a scientist. He's not even intelligent. He's a local who won the lottery. A millionaire. And instead of moving someplace nice, he decided to stay in Superior and build a superior home, twice the size as the rest of the Nebula houses. He's got a four car garage, a pool, a guest house, a maid, a gardener, my jealousy and no family to share it with. His only redeeming quality is a massive HAM radio antenna, rising up from the back of his property.

And now...he's gone.

My drunk eyes widen in time with my slowly puckering lips. I raise the bottle of whiskey toward the three story home blocking my view of the sweeping mesa. "What's yours is mine, buddy!"

I lean forward and half-stand three times before managing to get back to my feet. "What's yours is mine," I say again, trying to convince myself that the blurry plan hatching in my head is morally solid. He's dead and gone, after all. I can stake my claim on pretty much anything, right?

"Fucking right."

I point at the steak on the grill. "You! Keep cooking. I'll be back." I laugh and repeat the words with my best Schwarzenegger impression. "I'll be back." The trip to the backyard fence gate is just fifteen feet over a level cobblestone walkway, but it feels like an obstacle course. The gate supports my weight as I lean on it, letting it guide me around toward Phil's backyard. I negotiate his fence's gate and stumble toward his deck, which is big enough to land a plane on. I stagger to a stop, ten feet from the sliding doors blocking my way into the kitchen.

I look down at the nearly empty bottle in my hands and shrug. It worked before. After a quick swig, I pitch the bottle forward, nearly throwing myself to the deck. The bottle sails forward, on target despite my inebriation. And then, like some kind of supernatural being, the bottle sails straight through the window without shattering it. I reel back and gasp. Is the world still changing around me? Have the laws of physics been altered along with the human race?

Somewhere inside the house, the bottle shatters.

"I'm not cleaning it up." The words come from some deep recess where my adolescent self still resides. The current me, who is lost in the sauce, remains focused on the window, which somehow became immaterial. I move toward the door, eyeing the clear space. There's something odd about the glass.

There's no reflection, I think, waving my hand. I reach out for the strange glass and pass straight through. I yank my hand back. But shock turns to uproarious laughter when the simple truth of the situation filters through the haze and reaches whatever still functional part of my mind struggles to keep me upright. The door is open. I lean on the frame, gripping it with both hands, unleashing a torrent of laughter at the floor.

I glance back at the deck, and understanding sobers me, a little. Stops me from laughing, at least. A pair of shorts and a T-shirt lie on the deck, just shy of the grill, which is twice the size of mine. The clothing is speckled in white, but the rest of Phil has been carried away by the winds. Beyond the clothing are an empty plate and a pair of tongs. There's no meat around, but if birds survived the end, then scavengers probably stole the dead man's meal. Phil was outside when the end came.

I give his empty clothing a two fingered salute, despite the fact that neither of us served in the military, and that no one actually salutes like that, except in movies.

Right, I think. *That's why I'm here. The movie.*

Humming the *Jaws* theme song, I step inside the house, which is surprisingly tidy. I half expected the place to look like Phil hadn't forgotten his trailer park roots, which I realize now is a horrible thing to think. Not all people who live in trailer parks are cocaine snorting, cheap-beer-swilling slobs. But since no one is around to judge me, I can think whatever the hell I want. So, screw Phil. The place is only clean because he had a maid.

Everything inside is as fancy as the outside, gleaming from a recent polish. Even the hardwood floors in which I can see my reflection. A clicking sound stops me in my tracks.

Something is in here with me.

Oh god, that mountain lion found a way inside!

Run, I think. *Hide!* But I know any sudden movement will only result in me kissing the floor. So I stand still.

The clicking grows louder and a long, gray muzzle slides into view from the foyer at the front of the house. It's not the lion, but it's still deadly to a pudgy, defenseless, far from sober man like myself. A coyote. It stalks toward me slowly, nose to the floor, eyes on mine. But it's not growling. Do coyotes growl? I heard they hiss, but it's not doing that either.

The desert predator pauses in the hallway, sniffing the wet floor and the shards of glass where the bottle landed. It takes a single lick, does the closest thing I've ever seen to a canine wincing and continues forward, straight toward me.

It stops beside me, but looks away, raises his nose to the air and sniffs. Once. Twice. And then, without so much as a look back, it strides out the door and down the steps.

"Thanks, Wile E," I call out, and I close the slider while my racing heart slows.

Hand on the wall for balance, I move down the hall to the front of the house, where the basement stairs are located. Most homes in Arizona don't have basements, simply because they're not required. There's no frost line to worry about. But the subterranean level is naturally cool, and gives Phil an extra thousand square feet for his hobbies, including the home theater, and the HAM radio setup. It's not a traditional basement, hidden behind a rarely opened door. The staircase leading down is as grand as the one leading up, carpeted in noble maroon runners. With a firm grip on the railing, I descend into the basement hallway. Framed movie posters line the walls, mostly 80s comedies, and not the good ones. The theater is at the far end, so I open the first room, flick on the light and find a storage room, full of well-organized accumulation. I move to the next room and find the HAM radio. I point at it, squinting, trying to think something.

"I'll come back to you," I say, and I continue down the hall, focused on my mission like James Bond. I raise my fingers into a pretend gun, sliding against the wall while I walk, aiming and shooting at imaginary enemies. I'm a badass. A drunk badass.

I run into the door at the end of the hall and nearly sprawl to the floor. The doorknob clutched in my hand, holds me upright. I twist the handle and bumble into the room. The home theater has six leather recliners with cup holders on three levels. Genuine stadium seating. The far wall is white and fifteen feet across, ready to receive the projected image. But my destination is the back wall, where, on either side of the door, Phil's collection of DVDs awaits.

The lines of colorful text are a blurry mess. I lean closer to read them and fail to stop, mashing my face against the collection. I close my eyes, take two weary breaths and lift my head. Directly in front of me is a great white shark, rising through the water toward a swimming woman.

"Thank you, God," I say. First, I survive the apocalypse and now I find *Jaws* without having to read a thousand different titles. Someone is looking out for me. I pluck the case from the wall, kiss it and head for the door.

I slide against the wall again, this time just trying to stay vertical. When I reach the HAM radio room, I lean in the door and take another look. Knowledge finds its way through the fog of my mind. HAM radios use long radio waves, bouncing them off the ionosphere, then back to the ground and back up again, ping-ponging the signal around the world. Hard core HAM radio operators can even do a moon bounce, using the celestial object to ricochet signals to various locations around the globe.

The chair by the radio looks comfortable and more used than the theater seats. The boxy transceiver sitting atop the desk is sleek, black and very expensive looking. It's surrounded by sticky notes and photographs. Intrigued, I flop down into the chair and look at the detritus. The sticky notes have names, callsigns, frequencies and locations. Beneath each is a photo. All women. All lookers. Phil was using his expensive HAM radio to pick up women around the world? I start to chuckle when the realization finally dawns on me that this device can contact people, and emergency services, around the globe.

I turn it on, and a pair of table top speakers crackle to life. He's got an old school desktop microphone on a stand. I pick it up, hold down the call button and say, "Uhh, hello? Is anyone there?"

I release the button and listen to dead air.

My understanding of how HAM radios work is spot on. Unfortunately, my practical experience with operating one is absolute zero. And while I'm confident I could figure it out in less than five minutes— while sober—in my current state, luck will play a part.

I turn the knob, switching frequencies. "Hellooooo. Yoohoo. Anyone there?"

I listen to more dead air. I could do this all night. And for what? Further confirmation that to survive the mystery event that wiped out humanity you either had to be a desert scavenger or more than a mile below ground? No thanks. Instead, how about some fun? I hold down the call button, clear my throat and belt out the first song that comes to mind.

"Gina works the diner all day!"

By the time I get to the chorus, I'm lost in alcoholic bliss, my own voice sounding like the siren song of Jon Bon Jovi himself. "Whoaaa, we're half way they-ah..." I stand to my feet, victoriously pumping my fist in the air. "Whoa-ahh!" My head spins from the sudden change in thin blood flow. I spill backward, landing in the chair, which leans back to cradle me and then keeps going. When the wheels roll out, I'm propelled to the floor like a returning space capsule, except my head doesn't land in the water, it slams into concrete. I see the ceiling above me shrink and fade to black like an old cartoon. Then I giggle my way into unconsciousness.

14

POE

Luke and I limp inside the house and collapse in the living room. The dog, usually a blur of motion, matches my bone tired state. I lay on my back on the braided rug, wet dog curled up beside me. I think about the shimmering object. Object? Being? Energy? I remember Luke's terror. Dogs peeing in fear always seem so pitiful. Not that it wasn't justified. Whatever that was, it felt...wrong. Unnatural. And I'm pretty sure it had something to do with the extermination of humanity. What else could it be?

I should have killed it, I think, and then I realize that attacking something so unknown and potentially dangerous wouldn't have been much different from taking a bottle of Ambien. Staying alive is going to mean staying smart. Or at least not stupid.

I sniff and realize I stink. Sweat mixed with dried ice cream on my pants, and the debris of the dead. Fish water, soaked in, frozen and now thawing. Even in crises, bodies need care. But I can't move.

Entropy continues. It's so quiet.

Did I imagine the shimmer?

My parents' old farmhouse wraps me up, a womb. I let myself feel safe, even if just for a few minutes. I am too tired to do otherwise, to fight and panic nonstop. With a smooth gradient I fail to notice, my thoughts become dreams.

I wake up feeling stiff. My short black and blue hair has dried in crazy spikes, which cheers me a bit. The room is darker than when I got home. How long did I sleep? I get to my feet and look at Luke. His eyes are half open, looking at me, eyebrows twitching with indecision, asking if we're staying or going. "Stay," I say, and lean on a window sill, watching the orange streaked sky turn red through the endless pine woods. I lean my forehead against the icy glass, roll it back and forth, my skin burning, nose tip grazing the glass. My breath fogs the surface.

The cold numbs my skin, but can't work its way any deeper, no matter how much I want it to.

I am trying to decide what to do with my parents' remains.

I straighten, then trace a spiral with my fingertip on the fogged glass. *They're dead, Poe. What would you do if they had died of more natural causes? Like a heart attack while asleep in bed, or a long illness? You would honor them somehow. You would bury them, scatter their ashes someplace lovely. There would be services, people who loved them. Things would be said.*

I realize at that moment that my parents had actually requested at one point to be cremated upon their deaths. We had never quite gotten to the discussion of what to do after that. I walk into the kitchen and stand at the top of the cellar stairs. It feels like all of this happened years ago, or just a minute ago, but not yesterday. Everything seems warped. Out of body.

They're down there.

If I bend a bit and crane my neck from the top stair, I can see the piles of powder and their clothing on the cement floor. Luke, back on his feet, tries to push past me and investigate the basement, but I block him with my leg, step down and close the door behind me.

I have to do this alone.

Alone forever.

My heart plunks heavy and rapid. Chills run through me and my intestines rumble uncomfortably. I leave the cellar, closing the door behind me, and let Luke follow me into the bathroom.

I'm breathing heavily, near hyperventilating.

I can't do this.

I am all alone.

My hands wrap around my belly. Not completely alone. In time, there will be another voice. A friend for Luke. A companion that I will one day leave alone, too. Will the baby be strong enough to survive on her own? Will I?

I sense a new darkness lurking on the outskirts of my thoughts. I imagine a paper thin wall, a dam, holding back the murkiness like tons of gallons of water. My drowning inevitable, and soon. Tiny leaks spring from cracks in the wall. I need to stop thinking like an artist. Stop imagining.

Back to the cellar.

I can't just leave them there.

I find myself standing next to the piles on the concrete floor without remembering walking down the stairs. My mere presence stirs up the light powder. My body starts to shake when I realize that no matter how I deal with their remains, I'm going to get some of the powder on me.

First, their clothing. Leaning over, I gently lift my father's flannel shirt with just my thumb and forefinger. My body quivers with shock and anxiety. A cloud of powder puffs out from his shirt as I dangle it from one sleeve, at arm's length. Tears stream down my cheeks. My nose is running.

I need some kind of receptacle. Like an urn. I look around. The only thing I see is a bright orange five gallon bucket in which my father keeps their pipe snake for unclogging the toilet. *No fucking way.*

The depth of my loneliness crashes over me again, threatening. *I can give up. I can just give it all up. I don't need to do this.* I picture Squirt, and I almost don't care.

I need help.

With that thought, standing in my stocking feet on the cold cement floor, desperation a musty pit opening up in my brain, my dead parents all around me, I suddenly feel like I can breathe a bit. The shaking slows.

I gently place his shirt back down, and walk around the chilly basement, looking at the shelves, trying to figure out what can hold their remains. I find a small broom and dustpan near the washing machine and return to the piles. *I can collect them now, and find something after.*

No matter how gently I sweep, the brushing motion causes the powder to fluff into the air, near my face, repelling me. "Damnit!" I shout. Luke whines and paws at the door.

Driven by anger at my parents' remains, as stubborn in death as they could be in life, I make a decision. I head back up to the kitchen utility closet and roll out the vacuum cleaner, the comforting bump of its old wheels like company. I realize that the bag is probably full, or at least soiled, with everyday detritus, dust, farm soil, spilled things. Considering what I'm about to do, this seems at the very least indecent, and at the worst, profane and sacrilegious. After replacing the HEPA filter bag, I put on a pair of bright yellow rubber gloves, from beneath the sink, and pick up a black trash bag.

Back in the basement, I try again to lift my dad's shirt but the powder poofs out once more. *Vacuum first*, I decide, and I attach the soft brush to the hose end. I flick the switch to on. Gently, like bathing an infant, I pick up my father's shirt for the third time and cradle it in my left arm. I'm not shaking anymore. It's difficult to squat with my strained ankle, so I sit right down on the hard, cold floor. My father's signature sawdust and hay scent lingers along with that stale vacuum smell, which this time includes balsam needles from their Christmas tree, still nestled somewhere in the hose. Before I realize it, a twist of anticipation burbles through my belly, *Christmas!* Memories have a mind of their own, residing in our cells, beckoned to the present through the weirdest means. The powder smells of pennies. Copper, iron?

I kneel on the cement and carefully massage the shirt with the brush, removing all traces of powder. Then, the same with everything else of his, and next, the remaining white on the floor. I fold and place his belongings into the trash bag as I go.

I give a once over to my own clothing, and move on to my mother. The shaking returns a bit as I start on her violet shawl, the one with the prayers of her sister woven into each intricate knit and purl. My mother explained to me once that during the creation of prayer shawls, the craftsperson always uses a multiple of three to determine how many stitches the shawl will have, three being representative of the Holy Trinity. I've always had mixed feelings about God and the supernatural. Sometimes, in my past, during quiet moments, I've thought I could sense God: a friendly, but still wild predator, sneaking up on me, hunting me, but not to harm me. Like spying, checking out what I'm doing. Or reverse the roles, and I could sense my hope of capturing something elusive, a baby grabbing a toy for the first time, all the elements finally coordinated, relief as five fingers hold tight, even if just for seconds. For that matter, where does all my artwork come from? My mind briefly scatters back to the shimmer in the grocery store. I catalog these thoughts for later. I focus on my task.

I panic when the shawl, so feather light and soft, gets sucked up into the hose. I reach over and click off the vacuum, then tug the shawl out. My heart beats irregularly, the hummingbird returned, a few loud thumps. I take a deep breath and resume, stretching the shawl along the floor with my knees, and I vacuum it clean from one side to the other. The imperfection, messiness and weirdness of this process saddens me more.

Finished with her clothing, her slippers and the floor, I again swipe the brush over my own body. Then I shut off the vacuum and look around the basement. I wish I could open the bulkhead, let in some air, but a winter's worth of New Hampshire snow prevents me.

I limp back upstairs, my ankle throbbing from all this up and down. But then I get another trash bag, head back down and place the new, recently filled vacuum bag inside it, softly pulling the plastic ties tight. Not very beautiful, or ceremonial. But they're together, at least. I'll have to look around the house for something to put it all in. Maybe there will be a lovely chest in the attic or the barn, an heirloom I've forgotten. In the Spring, I'll dig into the thawed earth and bury them.

For now, I tuck the two bags onto a bottom shelf, under the glowing pink, canned lines of strawberry-rhubarb jam. Not a totally inappropriate spot for my parents. They both loved strawberries.

The task done, the floor clean and the basement once more accessible, a slight weight lifts and allows my mind to return to the present. Where my body aches. And smells.

The water heater kicks on, a throaty roar, making me jump. I follow the ticking water pipes across the ceiling, imagining them stretching throughout the house, heating every room...including the bathroom...and the tap. Just the thought of a hot bath makes my muscles sag. I place my hand on the bag holding my parents remains. "I won't leave you here forever," I say, and then head up the stairs.

15

POE

After turning on the bathtub tap, I slide out of my clothing, step on my parents' scale, and am shocked to see that I've actually lost four pounds. I'm usually skin and bones at 115 pounds, but the scale reads 111. Shouldn't I be gaining weight by now? Isn't Squirt growing?

I close the bathroom door to observe myself in the full length mirror hung on the back of it. Tiny, naked me, muscle tone still intact, brown eyes round like Oreo cookies, my snow white belly a tight paunch, and not big enough. I run my fingers through my short hair, making it stand on end. I need a shampoo, some scrubbing. My legs need shaving. Pits, too. The combination of musty barn, layers of sweat and dog dander odors coming from my body are ripe. I spread my fingers across my middle, my thumbs at my waist, and I visualize my baby, small peapod, my only human companion.

Luke barges through the door and flops down on top of my feet. I reclose the door and take a good, long look at my body in the mirror. Our three bodies in the mirror.

"I'm going to try to do better from now on."

I close my eyes and send my attention away from my anxious brain, my stuttering lungs, down, down, to my uterus, where things are warm, red and liquid. I imagine my heartbeat, my child's company. I imagine my baby in comfort, gently floating, cells dividing, limbs changing every day. I imagine nourishment flowing from me, to her.

I imagine *her*.

A little girl, then.

"Please forgive me for not paying attention. May you grow healthy and strong. May you have a beautiful brain and a feisty spirit. I love you. I will always take care of you. No matter what." It's the closest I've ever come to a prayer. And it's all I can manage. My body cries out for hot water. I slip into the bath, close my eyes and drift.

My thoughts ramble through the past few days—the event, finding Luke, my journey to the grocery store and my encounter with the...thing. The frantic race home and my parents... When it all starts to overwhelm me, I turn my attention to the future. A game plan. It's just me now. There's no one else to rely on, so I can't spend a single moment of a single day not preparing for the future. For the inevitable birth. *I'll need more than food,* I think, and mentally I walk through my parents' house, taking stock of what is there and thinking I need to tour the place again. I see the upstairs in my mind, head toward their bedroom and stop beside a door to my right. When I was little, this is where my toys were. Now it's my Dad's office. Laptop, bookshelves...

My eyes snap open and I push myself up into a sitting position, the sudden movement lifting Luke's head off the floor.

I can't believe I forgot.

Just one room over, behind the creaking, closed door, sits an amateur Ham radio setup. I stand from the tub, grab a towel, wrap it around me and head out the door, leaving a trail of water that my mother would cluck at, and then dutifully wipe. I open the door and find the radio, which I've never seen without my father sitting in front of it, playing with knobs, listening to strangers around the world.

I plop into the dusty, rolling desk chair, hope zinging out of each hair follicle, down my arms and legs, blushing like a fever, my skin overly sensitive. Or maybe just cold from still being wet. I give the setup a once over. I find the microphone and plug it into the jack labeled, *mic.* Something is already plugged into the jack labeled, *phones.* I follow the cable, expecting to find a headset. Instead, I find speakers. *Works for me,* I think, and I turn my attention back to the microphone. Does it need batteries, or does it draw power from the receiver? Why wasn't I paying more attention to this hobby of his?

He once described, to my mother and me, his connections with other amateur radio users in Humboldt County, California, in Vancouver, even all the way to mainland China. The conversation was short. Shame and regret roll over me for the past self who ignored what I considered my father's dorky habits. I had the Internet, and a phone. Who needed this cute, prehistoric method, useless as Braille to the sighted? I have no idea how this thing works. Modern technology barely needs the user.

I almost don't want to try turning it on, the desire to connect is so potent, the possibility of not connecting unthinkable. The window blind next to the table harbors several cobwebs, and since I see no actual, intricate spider designs, I open the blind, letting the moonlight in. On a normal night, even the full moon wouldn't add much light to the room, but the world outside is white, reflecting and somehow amplifying the moon's glow. It's bright enough outside to read by. Magical, if not for the end of the human race. *How much of that white is actually dust?*

I push the receiver's power button.

Luke noses his head under my resting hand.

I hear nothing. A quick glance around the boxy equipment, dials and meters. What am I supposed to do? I notice a volume knob. Turn it. Static. That's a start.

Should I say something? Am I connected and broadcasting?

I lean into the microphone, hold down the button. The static goes silent, so I assume the microphone is working.

"Hello? This is..." I remember that my Dad had some number, a call sign or handler identification or something, his legal way of broadcasting to the world, but I don't know what it was. I suddenly want to have a southern accent and say things into the microphone like, 'Ten-four, good buddy.'

"My name is Poe MacDowell. I'm in Barrington, New Hampshire. In the United States. Um. East Coast. We've had some kind of..." My voice trails off and my finger lifts from the button. How exactly am I supposed to describe what has happened? *Everyone is dead. Everyone is powder. Except for me. Please help me. Please find me.*

"We've had some kind of apocalyptic event. There's no one left. We've got a lot of snow, and I can't get anywhere. Can anyone hear me? Hello? Is anyone there?"

I wait, lean back, giving someone a chance to answer. I wait minutes; I wait for eternity, petting Luke, my hand repeating the path from his forehead down to mid-back, over and over.

I repeat my message several times, never really varying the words, because the shaking is starting again, and the repeated words are a strange anchor to not crying. I take an hour, repeating. Repeating.

When a bone jarring shiver runs through my body, I realize I'm still sitting in a damp towel. The house is beginning to cool around me and I don't want to crank up the heat, taxing the generator, for which I will eventually have to get more propane. Moving fast, I get some fresh clothes—jeans, T-shirt, hoodie sweatshirt and thick socks—from my backpack, dress and return. The few minutes of moving clears my mind, and when I sit back down at the radio, my mind feels sharper.

I don't just have to speak and listen on this one frequency. There are other options available. I look at a digital number display, which I'm assuming shows radio frequencies. *Like a car radio,* I think, and I smile when I see a button labeled 'Scan.' I press it and the numbers leap to life, scrolling quickly.

This is turning out to be pretty self-explanatory. A small buoyancy of mood makes me sit up straighter. My chin finds its way to my entwined fingers, elbows on the desk, watching the digital red numbers scroll, like waiting and watching on the dock end of a fishing line.

How long can it scan? How many frequencies are there? I've forgotten where I started from. I stand up, getting pissed. Am I using it wrong? I'm so frustrated; I kick the desk chair across the floor. It tips over when it catches on the braided rug and clatters down. Luke runs out of the room.

And then, the numbers stop. I hold my breath, looking at the frequency: 162.450. "A winter storm warning is in effect. Snow accumulations up to twenty-four inches are expected in...Rockingham County, Strafford County..."

I tune out the rest. I've heard it before. The NOAA severe storm warning played during the drive to my parents' house. Like other forms of automated broadcasts, there isn't anyone around to shut it off. *Where does this broadcast from?* I remember. *Gray, Maine. Must still be power there.*

Feeling frustrated by the robotic feminine tease, I hit the scan button again. The numbers scroll once more, stopping five more times to play the various NOAA messages for all of Maine and New Hampshire. I tap the scan button until I'm past them.

The scanner continues to do its thing, the sound of nothing but fuzz through the speakers. I pace around the office, looking at bookshelves, which cover the walls, with the exception of an acrylic painting on canvas. I gave it to him back when I was a budding artist, in high school. It's a reproduction of a photo of the two of us. He's tall and dark-haired, dressed in faded 80s jeans, holding my tiny two year old, then blonde self, balanced on a petting zoo fence. Dusty ground, goat nearby. We're grinning ear to ear, squinting in the sun, our spring jackets matching navy blue. I'm wearing red sneakers. In real life, my mother took this picture right before a cow walked up behind me and started eating my then hay colored hair. It's one of our favorite family stories.

Stacks of books teeter all over the small antique settee in the corner, nowhere for a human to sit. Several of them are open to places my Dad was researching or reading. Multiple copies of his most recently published poetry book, *Inferno Return*, sit in neat piles in a cardboard box under the window.

As I bend over to pick one up, a flash of shadow against the snow outside catches my attention. I freeze, moving only my eyes toward the glass and the bright snow beyond. Movement makes me blink. I press my palms against the glass, staring. Just beyond the barn, where the cow fence meets the endless woods. I watch, not believing. *Did I just see someone?* I bang on the glass, and then feel startled by my own stupidity. I jump back inside the room, ducking, remembering the grocery store shimmer.

Who is out there?

What is out there?

I peek again and see nothing. Just the familiar, blue-lit, snow-covered backyard farm. I don't even see footprints.

I twist the lock open on the top of the window and gently tug the sticking, old wood upward, trying to stay to the side, out of view. I want to hear, I want to sniff.

For what?

For roses.

I want to be closer but not be known about. I want to spy, not be spied upon. The antique frame creaks a little and I stand like a statue. I realize I may be making the wrong decisions. Even if it is another person, and not the shimmer, why are they standing outside my house in the woods, at night, all creepy like?

The shadow shifts, lengthens, behind another tree.

I hold my breath.

There's no denying it. Something is there.

A bear, I think. *No. Hibernating. A deer, then.* That makes sense. There are more than thirty thousand deer in New Hampshire, and it's not uncommon to see them in the back, picking at the crab apple tree.

The radio cackles to life, and I yelp in fright, falling down hard on the floor.

A voice booms in the room.

A man.

Singing.

"Halfway there, uuuuhhhoohhhh! Livin' on a praaaaaayer!"

I reach up, yank the window closed, and cringing, I stand, exposed for a moment before pulling down the shade. Too fast. The shade snaps back up, spinning, slapping against the wood. I fumble with it, control the pull, until it's back in place, hiding me from the presence outside that absolutely now knows I'm here. But I barely think about that as I lunge back to the desk and the voice of a potentially drunk man.

"Take my han', make it, I swear, uhhhhhhohhh, livin' on a praaaayer!" The vocal sounds of guitar riffing follows.

Definitely drunk, and singing Bon Jovi.

I depress the button on the microphone and yell, "Hello? Hello! Can you hear me?" Then I release it.

"...used to work on the docks, union's been on strike, he's down on his luck," and then a quiet pause. I listen, my finger above the microphone button, but he was just catching his breath.

"Ooooohhhhhhh, halfway there, uuuhohh! Livin' on a prayer!" and more vocal guitar sounds. I'm also assuming air guitar at this point.

I try the microphone again. "Hello? Maybe you could stop singing long enough to hear me? The song can't last forever. I'll just keep talking for a bit and maybe you'll stay on this frequency and hear me. My name is Poe MacDowell. I'm in New Hampshire, in the United States. I am alone. Sort of alone. I've got a dog and all these...fucking animals, and some weird shimmery thing is lurking at the grocery store. I just saw something creeping around out in the woods, and I don't know what to do." I release the button.

"...workin' for the man, she brings home her pay for looooove, oooh, foooor loooove..."

I speak into the microphone again. "And you sound like you've had a few too many, huh, pal? Yeah. And everyone here is dead."

"Livin' on a prayer!"

"And. I've got a baby growing inside of me. I think it's a girl." Warm tears run silently down my cheeks. "Her name is Squirt. For now."

I release the button, listening to him sing. He hasn't stopped yet. He hasn't heard me. I have been talking to myself, in my father's office. I turn up the volume on the speakers and lean back in my chair. From the sounds of it, he's careening around the room, bumping into things. I imagine him holding the microphone almost lovingly, really performing, you know? Really getting into it. Swaying, dancing. I wonder what he looks like. I wonder where in the world he is. A laugh burbles up, unbidden, through my tears. He's not the worst drunk singer I've ever heard, and I admit to having heard many. I let myself listen to this other human, this person that is not me. Such a relief, like a fever breaking, these other, not-alone sounds. His voice is deep, a little scratchy.

God, he's ridiculous.

Suddenly, the man's 'wooaah,' sounds like genuine surprise, and the song is cut short by a loud thump. Static follows. I jump from the chair, shout into the microphone.

"Hey, you there? You still there? Can you hear me?" I wait and listen.

Static.

"Hey, pal, you there? Fuck, did you pass out?" *Where did he go?* I look at the frequency on the dial, dig around in the desk drawer for a pen, find one, and scrawl the numbers on the back of my left hand on top of the other, fading notes. Just in case.

Both hands pull at my hair. "No, no, no, no, no. You still there? Hey!"

I pace the room, sweating terror and irrationality roiling over me, a tidal wave, unavoidable. I picture him passed out drunk in his man cave, right across from his model rockets or whatever the hell. His long, greasy hair strewn across his face. He's wearing sweatpants and his fat rolls over the waistband. Now I hate him, now that he's probably passed out in a puddle of his own puke, never having heard me. Before, he was singing to me. Just me. Now I know he was singing to himself, his stupid self. Before, he was my friend, and we could have gotten along.

I imagine him waking up on the floor tomorrow morning, laughing about the bender he went on, going about his business wherever it is that people are still alive and well, popping an aspirin for his hangover headache, eating a bowl of cereal, drinking coffee out of his favorite mug. Heading off to work. If there are that many people still alive, if working is still happening somewhere. My brain somersaults.

I will never reach him again. My imagination knows this. I perch on the edge of the chair. I look at my hands.

I've always felt big in the world. Despite my relative smallness, my tiny stature and lower than average body-weight, I usually experience my physical presence on the planet as substantial, a confident taker of space, needing few things. I produce art, my gestures expansive. Wherever I go, in a crowd, on my own, I feel solid. I exude strength. I can take care of myself.

But now, I feel vulnerable, ant-sized. I picture the whirling Earth, viewed from outer space, only it's spinning wildly. When I zoom in, through the layers, stratosphere, cloud cover, sky, treetops: there's me, barely visible. A speck in the entire universe, my movements so minute they don't even matter. I could be squashed and lifted from this spot like an unnoticed insect on the bottom of a shoe, my voice ridiculous and squeaky small. I am tiny and lost, blanketed claustrophobic and oppressed by the rest of the planet. I am less than a detail.

I am miniscule, but not alone in the world. Not yet. Fighting this confusing mash of conflicting emotion, I press the button and speak, "Hello, please respond," calling out to this strange man in some unknown part of the world, intent on continuing until the generator's propane runs out.

16

AUGUST

"Hello," a voice says, creeping into my emerging consciousness, an audible light cutting fog. "Please be there."

"Claire?" My voice sounds funny. The C enunciated sharply. The rest like I'm speaking through a mouthful of soup. *What happened?* I fell. My head throbs. Have I so severely injured myself that my speech is screwed up? I try to sit up and the room spins. Concussion?

"Come back," the voice says, feminine, but *not* Claire. "Where are you? Answer me, damn it!"

The woman's sudden anger makes me flinch, both from the volume of her voice and the commanding nature. This is not a woman to be—a woman! A speaking, living, breathing woman!

I roll to the side and off the back side of the rolling chair, flopping against the hard floor, Pinocchio with cut strings. Focusing all my efforts into my arms, I push myself up. "Hello! I'm here!"

"Please," the woman says. "Please answer me."

She can't hear me.

She—the HAM radio.

Her voice is coming from the speakers. With renewed energy and determination, I get my feet under me and stand. A gravitational force, which seems to only affect me, pulls me hard to the side and slams me into the wall. I lean there, breathing, drunk out of my mind, injured, but fighting it. "I'm coming."

"I heard you," the woman says. "I know you're there. Please, you have to reply. You *have* to. There's no one else."

The woman's desperation matches my own. Somehow, like me, she's survived the unthinkable and is now desperate for human contact, reaching out across the globe. And she found me...she found me, but she'll never know it if I don't make it to the radio. One flick of the frequency and I might never reach her again.

I turn my eyes to the device. It sits atop a desk on the far side of the room. It's just ten feet away. The chair lies on the floor, blocking a direct path. In my current state, the chair might as well be the Great Wall of China. But I have to try. I'd surmount any obstacle on Earth just to reach this woman. I don't know her, but I know she is important, that she will save me, and if she is equally alone, I might save her, too. "Coming," I say and set my jaw. I map out a route across the room, circumventing the tipped chair. I can cover the distance in five steps and then use the table for balance.

Pain blossoms in my skull, opening from the back and unfurling through the inner space behind my eyes. I place my hand on the back of my head, smothering the sharpest pain. My hair is damp. Warm. Tacky. My hand flinches away and comes back red. I'm bleeding.

What are the signs of a concussion? I can't remember, but they're probably similar to being drunk, so I don't bother with the assessment. I just assume I'm drunk *and* concussed, so making it across the room without cracking my head on the table is probably a good idea.

"You're not coming back, are you?" the woman says. "You're either gone, dead, or don't give a damn that you're the only other person on the planet."

She's really getting angry. I'm about to lose her.

A deep breath fills my lungs, but does nothing to restore balance or clear my thoughts. I focus on the imaginary path and strike out with the boldness of Magellan, reaching for what seems an impossible and impassible distance. Three steps in and I'm doing fine. But I'm listing to the side. The arced path that would have taken me around the chair becomes a straight line. The chair rears up, an iceberg set to sink my efforts. I stretch out, my gait matching that of Sasquatch, and I step forward. Front foot planted firmly on the floor, I lift my rear foot and bring it up, missing the chair but clipping my leg. My knee pops forward and I sprawl out, reaching, grasping.

The table top greets me unkindly, driving its edge into my ribs. With nothing solid to grasp, I slide to the side and fall. As I lose sight of the table's surface, I reach out and take hold of something solid. Instead of slowing or stopping my fall, the clutched prize comes with me.

An act of mercy by whatever cosmic being might have created the universe and destroyed mankind spares my head from a second impact. I land on my side, the blow knocking the air from my lungs and sending a jolt of pain from my elbow to my shoulder. But I'm conscious, and looking up at the table's edge, a skyscraper's height above me. An unattainable goal.

"Whoever you are, or were, goodbye." A click sounds as the woman removes her finger from the transmit button. I can see her in my mind's eye, angry and alone, reaching for the power button, or frequency dial. I reach for the table's edge, desperate. But my hand isn't empty. I'm holding the microphone, its cable stretching up and over the table, still plugged in!

I push the button, and with the little air left in my lungs whisper out a raspy, "Wait." It's all I can manage for the moment. I remove my finger, and focus on breathing, on replenishing the oxygen to my lungs, hoping my thinned blood will carry enough to restore a measure of lucidity.

"Oh my god." The woman's voice returns like an angel riding a beam of light from the clouds. "Are you there? Was that you?"

A click signifies that she's released the button. She understands how the HAM radio works. I push the transmit button, and after a deep breath, manage to say, "Catching...my breath. Hold...on." Then, to make sure we're not cutting each other off, I add, "Over," and release the button.

"Uh, copy?" she says, unaccustomed to the awkward radio talk lingo. She understands the radio, but isn't used to it. "I'm just glad you're there. And alive. Is there anyone else with you? How far does this reach? Where are you?" I hear her breathing for a moment, and she adds, "Over."

Her barrage of questions fades as I focus on the one thing that really fills me with hope, her breathing. The fast-paced in and out sigh of a living person's lungs. A loose smile slides onto my face as I lean my head against the cool concrete and press the transmit button. "Let's start with names. I'm August. Over."

"Poe," she says. A literary name. "Where are you? Over."

"Arizona. An hour outside Phoenix. You? Over."

I catch the tail end of a curse, which tells me she's far away before she confirms it. "New Hampshire. Is it the same where you are? Over."

"You mean, is everyone dust? Then, yes. And I'm alone. And before you ask, yes, I'm drunk. And I think I have a concussion. Over."

"I heard the singing," she says. "I knew you were drunk, but even still, Bon Jovi? Really? Over."

She's got a sense of humor despite the circumstances. I smile. "The song seemed appropriate. And, I might add, my prayers have been answered. Over."

"You prayed for the world to end? Over."

"For you," I say. "In a non-specific, mostly drunk way. Over."

After a brief pause, her voice returns. "So, August from Arizona, what are we going to do? The way I see it, we're partners now. Over."

She's right about that. The question is, "How do we do this? Should we meet halfway? Over."

Her response comes fast. "You need to come to me." A moment later. "Over."

The quick and firm reply feels strange. Like a demand. But I'm not totally opposed to it. I can make the drive in just a few days, if I drive flat out without sleeping much. I've had enough sleepless nights at work to know I can handle it. And it's not like there's any traffic to slow me down, other than empty cars, and there are no police to enforce speed limits. If only I knew how to fly a plane, I could be there tomorrow. Of course, I need to sober up before I drive anywhere. Still, her fervent reply strikes me as odd. "Why? Why not meet?" I leave out the 'over,' but she understands the natural break.

"I can't leave," she says, sounding a little desperate, but then clarifies. "I'm—I'm pregnant. And there's at least three feet of unplowed snow outside. I couldn't leave if I wanted to."

If she wanted to. Despite the conditions preventing her from leaving, it's clear she also doesn't *want* to leave. A sudden fear for her wellbeing slips out of my mouth. "Are you okay? I mean...you know, mentally? Emotionally? You must have lost people."

"I'm..." I hear a sniff of tears. "I vacuumed my parents today."

Holy. Shit.

While Claire is gone, I didn't have to endure that kind of personal, mind-bending horror.

"Who did you lose?" she asks.

"My daughter," I say. "Your voice sounds a little like hers. She was twenty. Still a kid in my eyes. I couldn't find her...remains, and her apartment burned down, along with the rest of Phoenix."

Silence follows. There're no apologies or condolences. We've both lost everything.

The small mental connection between Claire and Poe is enough to kick my fatherly instincts into gear. I'm not much of a Silverback, but that doesn't mean I don't have the desire to protect my girl—or in this case, someone who reminds me of her. Poe lost her parents. I lost a daughter. Maybe we can salve those wounds for each other?

I push the call button again, "I'll be there as soon as I can be." I put as much confidence into the words as I can muster. If New Hampshire is under three feet of snow, despite the unseasonable warmth in the Southwest, then I'm going to have to deal with that problem when I get there. Maybe it will melt? Maybe I can requisition a snow plow and carve my own path North? Problems for the future. Right now, she needs to know I'm coming. But there's no way I'm going to cross the country without a way to get in touch. "Can I call you? On the phone?"

"Power's out," she says. "There's no cell service."

"Landline?"

"Hold on."

I picture her leaving the HAM radio in search of whatever landline phone she might have. Maybe she has to dig the thing out of a closet? How many people still use landlines? I haven't had one for two years now, which is probably foolish, but I'm a slave to modern technology, for better or worse. While she's gone I manage to right the chair and hoist myself into it. The cushion feels like Heaven, smothering me in a hug, tending my bruised body.

My eyes drift across the table, past photos of exotic women with creative nicknames: China Doll, Lima's Got Legs, Russian Roulette. My slow visual tour of the desk stops next to Good God Geisha, a Japanese beauty who is now most likely dust. Sitting next to the woman's smiling face is a phone. But it's no ordinary phone, it's a satellite phone, capable of calling anywhere on Earth via satellites that will continue functioning when the cell towers and land lines fail, and there is no power to fuel HAM radios. I pick up the phone and reach for the microphone's call button. Poe beats me to it.

"No luck," she says, her voice surprising me. I nearly drop the sat phone, but cling to it. "No dial tone. The power outage must be wide enough to affect the phone lines now. Any ideas?"

I look at the phone in my hands. "I don't suppose you have a sat phone?"

"A what?"

"Satellite phone."

"I'm at my parents' house," she says. "I doubt they'd have one."

She's right. Most people have no use for a sat phone. Phil, on the other hand, must have used it for transcontinental dirty talk. What a strange guy.

"You can get one," I say. "But not at a RadioShack or anything like that. It needs to have a service plan in place, a satellite to connect to. If you can find that, we can stay in touch. And if the power goes out, there are solar chargers. And those you *can* get at RadioShack."

"Where am I going to find a satellite phone?" she asks.

"Emergency services. Hospital maybe. Police station. Fire station. They might have them to stay in touch if the phones go down."

"Might," she says. "You're not sure."

"I'm not sure of anything anymore, except that I'm coming to you. Today. Once I'm sober enough to drive."

I hear her chuckling on the other end. Then, "Better give me your number so I can call you when I find a phone. And in case I can't reach you again, I'm in Barrington, New Hampshire. 40 Stinson Lane."

After scrawling down the address, I power up the sat phone and read her the number. Rather than hang up, we spend the next two hours sharing bits and pieces of our lives, talking about what happened, what it means and how I'm going to reach her. Neither of us has any understanding of what has happened, and she skirts the story of how she survived in such a way that it's clear she's not comfortable talking about it. Probably still too raw.

That she's still functioning is a testament to her internal fortitude. While I emerged from the underground to find everyone turned to dust, she witnessed her own parents crumble and fall apart. I can't begin to imagine what that felt like. We talk for just two hours, but I feel like I know her now. Like we're close friends. And maybe we are. We've skipped past the small talk that typically fills conversations and got right down to it, maybe trying to prove our worth to each other. After all, why were we spared and not everyone else? What makes us worth saving? When I've sobered up enough to drive, I finish the conversation with, "It's time for me to go."

"I don't want you to go," she says.

"The sooner I leave, the sooner I can reach you."

There's a pause, and then, "Drive fast, but safe. You need to make it here, but slow and alive is preferable to fast and dead."

"I will," I say. "There is nothing in this universe that could stop me." *Not a God-damned thing.* "I'm going to pack and leave inside the hour. By this time tomorrow, I'll be half way there."

"Okay," she says. "Okay. August?"

"Yeah?"

"Thank you."

"For what?"

"For not being dead."

"Any time," I say. "Over...and out."

"Over and out," she says, her voice quiet and afraid once more.

I feel a tug on my heart. Stay and talk, it says. Don't leave that voice. By the time I reach the door, steady on my feet now, the tug has changed. Instead of being pulled back, I'm propelled forward, a spacecraft slung around the moon back toward Earth, toward home.

Toward Poe.

JOURNEY

17

AUGUST

It's three in the morning and I'm still wide awake. Normally, this might be a nuisance, but tonight's foray into the sleepless dark is purposeful and fueled by hope and horrible-tasting caffeine drinks pillaged from a corner store. After taking several smaller roads north from Superior, I've reached Interstate 40, which will take me clear across the country. The highway is almost completely empty, mostly because the world came to an end on a Friday evening and few people would have good reason to be on this barren stretch of road. It would be a commute to nowhere.

There are a few cars on the road. Some dark, a few still running, idling on one side of the road or the other, their lights acting as beacons in the otherwise pitch black night, attracting swarms of desert insects that assault my SUV's high beams as I pass. In a day, any still-running vehicles will run dry and cough their last, never to run again. All around the world, the last vestiges of the human race, left running and unattended, will begin to break down, overheat or run out of fuel. And yet, the satellites above will function for decades.

My thoughts turn to Poe and her quest for a satellite phone. I've looked at my sat phone, resting on the seat beside me, powered up and plugged into the cigarette outlet at least once a minute, hoping to see the digital screen light up with an incoming call. My intellect knows there won't be a call. Poe, locked in the frozen North, can't go in search of the device until the sun is up and some of the chill has been sapped from the air. She's also got a sore ankle and a baby on the way.

On the surface, she's not exactly the best person with whom to share the end of the world. The child she carries will not only sap nutrients from her body, slowing her down and making her less physically able, but it will also distract her from the realities she has to face. But maybe that's a good thing, and if I'm honest, she probably has a far worse opinion of my survivability. I'm a subterranean-dwelling scientist with his mind on the outer reaches of space and the physical capabilities of a jellyfish...a jellyfish with a skeleton. Not that I told her that. I didn't think sapping her hope would be a good start to our relationship.

Beneath the surface, Poe is strong. Stronger than she believes and probably stronger than me. I'm not sure what would have happened to me had I found Claire's remains. I might have just let the flames take me, turn me to ashes with the rest of them. But Poe...she *vacuumed* her parents. Is saving them to give them proper send offs. That kind of internal fortitude is what you need to survive the end of the world. What do I have? The ability to think problems out, and as Poe knows, to get plastered.

After leaving Phil's house, two hours and twenty minutes after entering, I found my grill burned out and holding a crusty steak husk. I'm lucky the house didn't burn down. Not that I care about the house. I haven't felt truly at home anywhere since I was a kid. But I was glad to have my clothing, travel supplies and personal items. After packing for a one way trip, and filling a box with personal items, mostly related to Claire, I donned the Red Sox cap and struck out for Home Depot. I took as many five gallon gas tanks as I could, filled them at a nearby gas station and stacked them in the back of the SUV. The vehicle might be a gas guzzler, but it's also rugged enough to handle a lot of weather, off-road travel if necessary, and it can hold a lot of gas in the back. I might have to ditch it for another vehicle later on, but for now it's home.

Feeling the weight of the darkness around me, I try the radio. There probably isn't much to listen to in this part of the world on a normal night, but tonight there's nothing. Whatever stations that continued broadcasting playlists are either out of range or just off the air, which seems likely.

I hum, but still have Bon Jovi stuck in my head, so I resort to tapping out a beat on the steering wheel. I make a mental note to find CDs. There aren't many stores in this part of the world, and I'm definitely not opening a dust-filled vehicle to find music. But I'm an hour outside Albuquerque, New Mexico. I'm sure the roads will be more congested in the city, maybe even impassible, but if I'm lucky, there might be a Walmart near an exit.

But can I do that? Can I walk through an empty, dust-filled and possibly dark mega-store just to find traveling music?

No, I decide, but then I think about what else I might be able to find, making a mental checklist.

Food. Canned goods. Some perishables if the power is still on.

A propane cooking set for campers.

Plastic utensils.

Every meal will be a picnic.

Guns.

I flinch at the thought. What would I need a gun for? Some long dormant hunter-gatherer whispers from the depths of my mind. *You're going to have to learn how to hunt.* Canned food isn't going to last forever. This is long term. This is reality. I'm going to have to hunt for food. That means killing, bleeding out, skinning and hacking up animals. I'll need a rifle, ammunition, a sharp knife and a fair amount of resilience. I used to think that searching for dark matter, perhaps the most elusive substance in the universe, took fortitude, but the idea of surviving without modern technology and infrastructure horrifies me. My life before was easy. Externally, it still is. I'm *driving* across the country. But that will be impossible soon enough. Images of slaughtering animals fills my mind again.

My stomach sours. If I can reach Poe, maybe we can head south to warmer climates and be vegetarians?

A surge of caffeine kicks in, and my bladder fills like a water balloon held to a faucet. "Geez," I say, noticing that my own voice sounds strange. I haven't heard a human being talk, myself included, since I left the HAM radio behind. With the urge to pee nearly overwhelming me, I pull to the side of the road, illuminating a stack of railroad ties, the only landmark for miles in either direction. A large white banner hangs from the ties, reading, "Railroad ties! Cheap!" and then a phone number. Why would anyone think to sell, and/or buy railroad ties in the middle of the New Mexican desert?

Leaving the SUV running and the high beams blazing, I hustle to the side of the road, undoing my belt. As the pants loosen, I round the railroad ties to the back, instantly feeling stupid for hiding myself. I could have opened the door and pissed on the road. No one would have seen me. No one would have cared. But what's done is done, and I'm not about to step back into the open just to prove I'm not ridiculous. And who's around to call me ridiculous? Who's going to see me hiding from no one?

No one. That's who.

The sound of my pee striking the hard-packed desert surface is loud. "The sound of relief," I say to myself, thinking of a commercial tagline. What was it for? Rolaids? Alka Seltzer. "Plop, plop. Fizz, fizz."

With a quasi-punch drunk smile on my face, I look up at the stars. The night sky is a vivid and powerful picture. My mouth slowly opens. As an astrophysicist, I've sought out the lightless places in the world, in search of views like this. Most people live and die without ever seeing a natural night sky. It's breathtaking, and I stand there, pants loose and business out, staring at the sky, for a full minute, no longer peeing.

Satellites crisscross the sky, pin points of mobile light, sometimes getting lost in the brightness of the stars that are light years in the background. I watch them while my subconscious mind puts my pants back together. I'm probably standing in a puddle of my own urine, but I don't care. The view above is so captivating. The human race might be dead...but out there...out there is life. Countless and strange. I've known it since I was a kid, long before Earth-like planets were discovered and the Drake equation calculated the possibility of life beyond our small pinpoint of existence. I reach my hand up toward the sky, extending my index finger, seeing only a silhouette against the Milky Way, I trace out the equation: $N = R^* f_p \times n_e \times f_l \times$—

My night sky calculation is cut short by the appearance of another satellite. It's moving faster than the others, in a way that is familiar. I've seen something like it before...something...when I was grilling the steak! But had I really seen that? Or was it the booze? I'm not drunk now, so I watch the distant bright light trace a path across the sky, a white *Etch A Sketch* fleck with no trailing line. Unlike the other satellites, I have no trouble keeping track of this one. And then, just like before, it stops. The jarring cessation should have torn it to pieces, but it just hangs there, motionless.

"What the hell are you?" I ask the sky, taking a step forward like it will help close the distance.

I'm so entranced by the stationary satellite that I don't hear the approaching car until it's nearly passed me, which is surprising given how loud it is. The vehicle's engine roars, and the speaker system pumps Metallica's *Enter Sandman* through the open windows and into the otherwise silent desert night. I run toward the side of the railroad ties, waving my arms and shouting, but the car zooms past on the far side without slowing, the Doppler Effect hum of its tires on the pavement quickly fading.

18

AUGUST

I run into the road, frantic. My arms wave with the fervency of a chick's first flight. "Hey! Hey!"

The driver hasn't seen me. I'm probably visible, a black splotch surrounded by the bright light of my SUV's high beams, but the driver has no reason to look back. There's no one else on the road and my SUV is just another empty, still running vehicle. If anything, the high beams will prevent him from looking back, unless... I hurry back to the SUV, intent on flashing my lights. In the dark night, that should get my fellow survivor's attention. If not, I'll drive like a maniac, catch up and get his attention.

And then, somehow, I do.

The car's red brake lights cut through the dark. The vehicle slows, pulling over to the shoulder. I'm not the only one still obeying the rules.

I hold my breath as the driver's side door opens and a young man climbs out. He's lit by the small interior bulb, but I can see enough. He's slender, maybe early twenties. Has a sharp look about him. Intelligent, but physical. A good person to survive the end of the world with.

"Hey!" I yell again, but the guy hasn't turned off the music...and he's not looking my way.

He's looking up.

I follow his turned up head to the blazing sky. At first I see nothing but the endless universe. Then I see an aberration.

The satellite.

It's doubled in size. Closer.

Which tells me something I should have already deduced: *it's not a satellite.*

I stand still, just one hundred yards from another survivor, and watch the light in the sky. It's motionless now, but must have moved. Or grown. Which seems even more unlikely. But it's stationary again, and I need this guy to know he's not alone.

I hurry behind my still open door, reach inside and flick my high beams on and off. It takes a moment, but the man cranes his head in my direction, his eyes following a moment later. Confusion adds wrinkles to his youthful face. The light in the sky combined with the flickering lights must seem otherworldly. He still can't see me. I'm lost behind the brightness of the SUV's illumination. I shut the front lights off, allowing the interior dome light to illuminate me.

I wave to him, a ridiculous smile on my face that I think probably mirrors his own. He dives into the car, and the blaring music falls silent. He reemerges a moment later, ready to shout something, but doesn't. Instead, his eyes are tugged skyward again.

The 'satellite' is growing, its brightness nearly illuminating the ground now. Before I can ponder what it could be, it disappears. The stranger and I turn to each other at the same time, both befuddled. He raises his arms in a slow-motion shrug.

Whatever the light is, we can talk about it in person instead of long distance gestures. I slide behind the steering wheel, ready to speed across the distance and greet my new friend. Before I can put the headlights back on, or shift into Drive, the road ahead explodes with light. From above.

I squint away from the bright light until my eyes adjust. Then I look out and see the impossible. The bright light from high up in the sky now hovers just fifty feet above the young man, illuminating him and his Ford Mustang in a cone of white illumination.

Looking at the light stings my eyes and provides no clue as to what I'm seeing. If there is something physical projecting the light, it's hidden by the brightness.

The young survivor holds a hand over his eyes, and gazes up.

My stomach churns. The hairs on my arm defy gravity.

This isn't right.

This is...

Puzzle pieces snap together. The human race turned to dust. Almost everyone, everywhere, while animals and plants were spared. It's an extinction so odd and species-specific that the only real way to describe it is otherworldly.

Alien.

Damn it.

I slam the SUV into drive and crush the gas pedal to the floor. I'm pressed back into the driver's seat, while my still open door slams shut. The first twenty-five yards flash past, my charge punctuated by the squeal of tires.

And then, nothing.

The SUV sputters, the engine silent. Lights flicker and die. The vehicle falls still and mute. I see the same thing happen to the Mustang, its rear lights fading. The young man doesn't seem to notice. He's locked on target, unable to look away from the light. Is he entranced? I've never believed the UFO abduction reports, but this seems like a classic example.

And then it isn't.

The man isn't pulled up into the sky, riding on a beam of light. He simply stares up, mesmerized by the...whatever it is, above him, oblivious to the shape moving behind him. It's a vague visual distortion, like heat rising from the road, but condensed into a moving form, indistinct, but solid. Present. And real. And the way it's sliding up behind the man leaves little doubt about its intentions.

"No!" I shout, shoving open the SUV door and running on foot. I'm out of shape. My legs burn by the fifth stride. My lungs follow shortly after. But I don't slow. I can't. I have a duty to this man, this other survivor, one of the last people on Earth. If the shimmering figure moving through the light plans to harm the man, I can't let it.

"Look out!" I try to shout the words, but they come out at half volume, constricted by breathless lungs. The man either doesn't hear me, or is too distracted by the light above him, which is as silent as it is luminous. I attempt a second shout, but I'm too out of breath and still have twenty-five yards to cover.

The thing slides up behind him, this man that could be my friend and traveling companion. While Poe represents a future hope, this man is present and providing immediate hope. If only he could make me brave enough to do more than shout. I find myself shuffling instead of running, slowing my pace and shrinking my stride. Violence outrages me, but not enough to propel me into it. The best I can do is shout from a safe distance.

As I open my mouth to cry out again, my hope is blotted out, as something unseen punctures the man's back and comes out his chest covered in red. It's a thin spike. My first thought is that it's a spear tip, but then I notice the joints, bending and probing before being drawn back.

As the man falls to the pavement beside the Mustang, a new emotion bolsters my charge: rage. It drowns my fear and makes me feel like someone else. Someone stronger.

A high-pitched scream, a battle cry tinged with terror, rises from the depths of my body and announces my berserker attack. My mother's father was a large Nordic man and somewhere inside me, some ancient Viking DNA asserts itself. For a moment.

The wavering energy spins in my direction. I see a shape. A hunched body, cloaked in warbling light. I see the neck, and head, turning toward me, resolving out of the bright light. And then, like an explosion of darkness, I see it—really see it—for the first time.

Its long, black face, craggy, angular and sinister, while horrible, is nothing compared to the eyes, swirling with oil. They're almost lifeless, blank, uncaring and yet leveled right at me. I see the horrible visage for just a flash, but the face is etched into my visual memory like the filament of a too-long-stared-at light bulb. The snapshot hits me like a bowling ball to the gut and stumbles my charge, churning my insides.

But even this ugly thing can't stop physics, and this object in motion, which is my body, stays in motion until it collides with an opposing force—the shimmering form. With disastrous results.

19

AUGUST

It's hard to describe what happens next. The jolt of impact, and the pain it brings, is poignant, but only vaguely familiar as something previously experienced during my childhood. I feel what I think are limbs. And a body. Fabric of some kind. And then the pavement below, which ceases our downward momentum and erases the skin from one of my elbows. The stinging scent of ammonia assaults my nose. Wincing from the wound and the ammonia stench, my panicked mind shrieks, *you're on top of it!*

Move! Get away!

Before I can act, I find myself floating, as though weightless. And then not. My stomach lurches as gravity takes hold and tugs me back toward the bright blue earth, which isn't earth at all. It's the Mustang. The realization that I've been flung off the strange being is knocked from my mind, scattered, along with my senses, by a collision with the car's hood. The flat metal surface buckles, transferring some of the impact's energy out through the hood, but most of the punishment vibrates through my body. It's repeated a moment later when momentum keeps me moving, rolling off the side of the car and falling into the desert soil on the far side.

Sucking dusty air into my desperate lungs, I turn my head to the side, looking under the car. To the left I see the man, a puddle of blood, bright red in the intense light, surrounding his body. But his chest continues to rise and fall. He's alive, but for how long?

Shimmering movement to the right snaps my eyes toward the visual aberration I tackled. It's recovered from the attack and is sliding toward the man, each step dragging some unseen fabric over the pavement. *Shhh, shhh, shhh.*

A sob of fright hiccups from my mouth. I look around for someplace to run. To hide. An overwhelming instinct telling me that flight is the only option fills me with guilt. I would abandon this man if I could. But a small fragment of my mind considers finding a weapon of some kind. Maybe there's something in the car. But there isn't time for that. Or to hide. The creature...or whatever, is just feet from the young man's defenseless form.

My fingers scrape against something smooth and hard. There's a softball-sized stone partially buried in the dry roadside. I scrape my fingernails around the hard edges, bending my nails back and chipping away hard-packed dirt that hasn't seen moisture in a long time. The rock lifts free, its weight increased tenfold by the nerves shaking my limbs.

Do it, I tell myself. *What good will I be to Poe if I die here, too? What good will I be if I can't bring myself to defend a human life?*

I'm sure the way I spring up from the far side of the car looks comical, like some kind of human whack-a-mole. My voice cracks as I shout, but it's still surprisingly commanding. "Hey!"

The thing reels around toward me, its wooden face snapping into clarity for just a moment as our eyes meet. The dead eyes horrify me, but also give me something to aim at. I throw the stone with all the force I can muster, wrenching my elbow in the process, and send the rock sailing over the car. The thing turns away, its face winking out, concealed within the shimmer once more. But the hurled stone must find its mark...or something equally solid, because the primitive weapon bounces off an unseen surface and elicits a shriek that sounds more angry than pain-fueled.

I hit it, I think, surprised.

Whatever force repulsed me has limits. Maybe it needs to recharge, or maybe it needs to be triggered manually? Perhaps both. Either way, I definitely caught it off guard. It was just a glancing blow, but the result is satisfactory. There's a strange shuffling, a barely audible hum and then I can no longer see the shimmering distortion that marks the being's presence. The light from above flickers three times, each flash accompanied by a deep, resounding *whump* I can feel in my chest. Then the light, and the UFO—God, I hate that term—are gone. I search the sky for some sign of its retreat, but if it's up there, I can't see it. I search the night sky for missing stars, which would indicate an object blocking out part of the sky, but the night is clear. And quiet. Until the mustang and my SUV both roar back to life. I shout, jumping from the sudden noise, and then hurry around the car, limping with each step.

I fall to my knees beside the man, lost about what to do. The wound on his chest is a thumb-sized hole that I know reaches all the way through and out the other side. There is nothing I can do to save him.

"Can you hear me?" I ask, voice wavering.

His eyelids flutter.

"You're not alone," I tell him. It's not much, but from one last living man to another, they're the words I would want to hear. I take his loose hand in mine, noting the stream of blood flowing down my right arm. "You're not alone."

His eyes open. Blue and pale. They search the darkness and find my face, lit by the car's interior light. "What...happened?" The words are a whisper, barely audible over the throaty, chugging V8 engine.

I don't really want to talk about that. If he can't remember what left him in this condition, there's a small chance his exit from this world to the next will be peaceful. "What's your name?"

He licks his lips, painting them red with blood. "Steve Manke..."

"Steve," I say. "I'm very happy to meet you. I'm August."

His eyes widen like he's just realized he's going to die. In fact, I think that's exactly what has happened until he smiles and says. "August. Find August." His smile broadens. "I found you."

He dies like that, the smile on his face, strange relief in his eyes. All because of my name. What did he mean? Technically, I found him, but my name seemed to mean something to him. Could he know me somehow? While August isn't a common name, I don't recognize the man, or his name. He's a stranger, but the way he looked at me. The way he reacted to my name...

I let go of his hand and step back.

Who was this man?

More than that, what the hell was the thing that killed him? I know the answer to that question, at least in part: it was one of *them*. The unknown them that somehow turned the human race to powder and is now seeking out and killing stragglers.

Except for me. Why did it let me live? It can't just be because I hurt it, *if* the stone hurt it at all. It flung me away like I was a toy. I suppose it's possible the stone wounded it, but it doesn't feel right. It *let* me live.

Maybe it's just saving me for later? Prolonging my death. Plotting out some horrible ending because I managed to catch it off guard. That alone surprises me. I'm not a fighter. If you'd asked me an hour ago, I would have told you flat out that I am a coward. In fact, I still am. But I felt a flicker of something stronger in me. Something that will take action sooner than later next time. If there *is* a next time. *God, I hope not.*

"Should I bury you?" I ask the dead man. It's what a noble person would do, right? The problem is that I don't have a shovel, I'm wounded and can feel body parts starting to swell. The time it would take me to find a shovel and dig a proper grave could put me an entire day behind...probably more.

My body tenses as I'm struck by a thought.

Steve was moving through the dark night, bright and loud. Obvious to anyone, or anything, above. Was it his car that attracted the creature's attention. Will mine?

Staying in this desert without transportation, while wounded, will be a death sentence. I quickly make up my mind to finish the drive to Albuquerque, but after that...a car might be too obvious a calling card. The idea of traveling cross country without a vehicle is nearly as horrifying as being attacked by aliens, but I owe it to Poe to not get killed. I can't leave her—and her child—alone.

Feeling guilty about not burying Steve, I decide to check his car for a shovel. The front seat is a mess of junk food wrappers. It looks like he raided a snack machine. The back seat holds loose piles of clothing, food, water and a sleeping bag. I check the trunk last. Gas cans. No shovel. Still, I can't just leave him here, exposed, food for the vultures.

Steeling myself with a deep breath, I lift him up by his armpits. His dead weight is surprising and strains my fresh injuries, but I manage to slide him onto the seat and tuck his legs up under the steering wheel. He slumps over, head smacking the console between the seats. Avoiding the tacky blood covering his torso, I pull him back up and buckle him in place. The car is already running, so when I hit the radio's Play button, Metallica booms from the speakers once more. I roll up the windows and close the door, muffling the noise. I didn't know Steve, but I suspect this is the best mausoleum I can provide for him. "Thanks for making it this far," I say. "You gave me hope that there might be others."

Two firm pats on the car's roof and I start the long walk back to my SUV. Each step is harder than the last. By the time I'm behind the wheel and closing the door, I'm desperate for painkillers. But right now, I need to drive, reach someplace safe and try not to advertise my presence to the watchful eyes above. I shut off the SUV's lights, wait for my eyes to adjust and then drive by the light of the cosmos and the moon, hoping that Poe will call soon, so I can tell her our meeting is going to be delayed, by weeks, if not months. As my sore muscles ache and turn rigid, I fear that reaching Poe will be as impossible as saving Steve Manke's life.

20

POE

Six hours since I talked with August, but it feels like much more time has passed. Tender, intellectual August, not at all what I imagined when I heard his passionate karaoke. I don't know what he looks like. Never asked, but I picture him as being large in a stoic kind of way, but that might not be true. It's his stalwart insistence that he can and will reach me that has me picturing some kind of modern Odysseus. But he's also an astrophysicist, so he's smart, and he spends a lot of time on his butt, in a chair. Maybe big, but not in shape. I definitely don't see him as fat, though. I think I would have heard it in his voice. I see him in glasses, kind eyes shrunk to half their true size.

But how kind is he? Despite being drunk, we had a deep conversation. But what's he like sober? He's a good man, I tell myself, the kind of man who, at the world's end, risks being burned alive in search of his daughter. The kind of man who then gets drunk to dull the pain. I don't see the alcohol as a weakness, though. Were it not for Squirt, I would have gotten plastered, too. Instead, I see his drunken state as a testament to how bad it hurt. I heard it in his voice, too, when he spoke of Claire. His pain mirrors my own.

August said he was coming, and I believe him. I don't have any other choice. Right now, the no-expectations-hope-in-a-stranger feels like the most beautiful of prospects. It'll take him awhile, once he nears the East Coast and its three feet of unplowed snow. What does the Midwest look like right now? How far will he actually be able to drive? Will he be able to access gas stations? I shake my head. There are too many potential variables and roadblocks to consider. I won't sleep until he arrives if I think about them all.

I've decided to ignore my fear and venture out in search of a satellite phone. After a quick breakfast of fresh eggs from the chickens, of which there will always be too many, I stretch out my joints. My ankle is feeling better, just a slight stiffness now, an uncomfortable twinge.

Part of me wishes it was worse. That the pain was horrible enough to justify putting off this errand. I'm terrified of going out again. I can wait, I tell myself. He could be here in a few days.

Or he could get lost.

Or hurt.

Or worse. What if there are other shadowy shimmers in the world?

I should have told him, I think. I'm not alone. Not really. There's a shadow in the woods and a...shimmering thing, that feels like a figment of my imagination, in the grocery store. But how do you tell someone that and not sound like a loony, to be avoided at all costs? If I was crazy, would he still come? Is he *that* good of a person? Am I?

But I didn't tell him, so the answer doesn't matter. He doesn't know about the shimmer, or the shadow, or my parents' advanced knowledge or the fact that I was thrown into a God-damned apocalypse-protection pod. And I didn't tell him about the two-word note, though Squirt and the weather made that omission the most natural of them.

I'm glad I didn't tell him, I decide. Because he's coming. A living, breathing human being is on his way to find me, and if I'd told him everything, maybe he wouldn't be.

My lifelong desire to be alone has been fulfilled, and all I want is for him to get here. To end this aloneness. The childlike, probably childish, fantasy looked like painting and dreaming and wonderment about the world around me. Now it looks just the opposite. My expressive self has been shocked mute. The world is frightening. But not all of it. Not now. Not with August. I feel so grateful that out of all the possible connections the radio could have made, I was given someone who sounds halfway normal.

But is he still okay? Is he on his way? I have no way to know.

I stand, dressed for winter, at the back door. The cold morning air swirls around me, stiffening my nostrils and seeking out the pores in my clothing, exposing the weak points. I close my eyes, picturing the small town. There's a walk-in clinic on the far side of town. A police station a little closer. But the fire station is the nearest of the public services that might have a satellite phone. It's a little further than the grocery store, but I've got the snowmobile with a full tank. I'm not too keen on going anywhere near the grocery store, but I made it out of there with a dog, and a limp, so zooming past on a snowmobile should be doable.

A long list of doubts slips into my thoughts, but I ignore them as staunchly as I did Todd's litany of relationship complaints. Bossy. Inflexible. Emotionally unavailable. The truth I never admitted is that he was right. I'd give anything to have Todd with me now. He wasn't a bad guy. It was me. I was...unkind. Another secret to keep from August.

"Luke, be a good boy. I'll be right back." I lean over in my puffy parka and snowpants and hug his heavy body, burrowing my face in his neck fluff. He lays down and turns over on his back, wanting a belly rub, which I grant. "Wish me luck," I say, and before he realizes I'm leaving him behind, I close the door.

Stepping from the doorway, course plotted and self-deprecation completed, I take a moment to service the animals—feed for the chickens, fresh hay for the cows—and head for the snowmobile. I think about going back and locking the door, but then remember that my parents haven't locked their door in over fifteen years. This neighborhood, along with most of the state, is safe enough to—

My feet crunch to a stop in the deep snow. New Hampshire, and the larger world as a whole, is no longer the same place. The rules, if there are any, are different now. With a shadow and a shimmer on the loose, I'd prefer not to come home and find something waiting for me inside the house. I head back inside, take my father's overflowing key ring from the hook beside the door, say a second goodbye to Luke and twist the deadbolt home with a snap. The sound drives me back with a gasp, my imagination launched back into the pod, its deadbolt popping open.

But I'm on the outside now. In control. Or, at least, pretending to be. And I'm free to walk away. Which I do. Quickly.

The snowmobile starts without a fuss, and I putter out of the yard. I feel both like I don't want to draw attention to myself by zooming, but that if I move too slow, something might catch me. The specter in the grocery store didn't seem fast, but that's like seeing a car roll for the first time and assuming there isn't an engine hidden beneath the hood. Who knows what the unknown is capable of. Isn't that why people always fear it? Unlimited potential includes an infinite number of horrible outcomes. So I compromise and drive the speed limit.

I follow the same path as before, down our unplowed snowy road that leads to the more recently plowed but still snowy Route 202. I can still see my deep footprints from before, despite the wind's efforts to erase them, running alongside the snowmobile tracks from my return trip. The snowmobile's path acts as a road, and I follow it dutifully, keeping the footprints to my left. Imaginary double yellow lines. I've always been a safe driver.

My eyes tear up from the cold wind rushing past. As I blink them from my blurring eyes, I can feel the moisture evaporating from my face, leaving stiff paths of salt. *I need ski goggles*, I think, and I imagine myself scrawling a reminder on the back of my hand. Despite the urge to turn my head down, away from the wind, I keep my eyes on course, blurry, but less likely to run into a deer or moose. Through my bent vision, I see the path ahead, winding around now dead cars, following the same path as my footprints.

But then not.

A quarter mile ahead, cloaked in the shadow of an overhanging, leaf-barren oak, is an aberration. For a moment, I wonder if the line cutting through the snow is a shadow, distorted by my blurry vision, but quickly realize that's not the case. The line is broken and even, Morse code dashes, transmitting a message that even I can read: you are not alone.

I slow to a stop beside the line deep footprints, more than a little stunned. Ahead, there is one set of footprints, for as far as I can see. Then, a second set veers off across the road and into the woods. I know I didn't make them, and the treads—rough, wavy lines around a L.L. Bean logo—don't match my boots, though the size seems similar. *A woman*, I think. Or a short man. Either way, this person followed me, and rather than taking the path that led directly to my front door, he or she opted for the stealthy route through the woods that stretches all the way to the backside of my parent's farmhouse.

The hair on the back of my neck rises, a deep, mammalian instinct I am experiencing more and more often. The snowmobile idles as I take a few steps forward, part of me wanting to follow the stranger's path. I shiver in the middle of the silent, white street.

I scratch at my eyebrows with my mittens. Twist my lips. Bounce up and down. But I don't move forward or backward.

I recognize that I am not doing well, that a small psychological fissure has opened in my head, just a tiny cleft, but large enough to notice.

Who is this person? What do they want? Unlike August, he or she is a stranger. Unknown and not trusted.

I need a second brain. A consensus of the living. August is still new to me, but known and invited.

I get back on the snowmobile, and my course set for the fire station. For August.

As the engine revs louder and I start moving again, I'm relieved that someone doesn't run out of the woods and attack me. Then I'm back at full speed, feeling safer, but only for a moment. Impending doom rears up and makes me nervous. I smile when I realize why. That stupid asshole dog is up ahead.

But is he alive still? Would he have frozen overnight? I can't believe I did that to a living thing...

Guilt draws my eyes downward, and I don't actually see the car until I'm nearly beside it. The first thing I notice are two sets of human footprints, mine and the stranger's, along with the flattened snow where I fell. But it's the third set of non-human footprints that seize my stomach, the muscles tightening to form a protective wall.

The door is open.

Someone let the dog out.

The four-legged tracks head back toward town for fifty feet before turning off into the woods. It could be anywhere.

My belly flips over and I twist the throttle, picturing those alligator jaws, the long snarling snout, the black eyes. I don't stop the snowmobile again, driving the rest of the way to the fire station like a bat out of hell. I suddenly don't care who or what hears me, the fissure in my brain making the bridge from panic to wisdom problematic. Does having the knowledge that this crack exists prevent any true losing of my mind? I certainly hope so. For now, I can watch over the space for signs of mental health decline, symptoms of crazy—a benevolent, nonpartisan gatekeeper.

The fire station in sight, I realize I've been holding my breath, and I breathe with a shudder and a few hiccups. The snowmobile's engine grows louder as the sound reflects off the station's brick façade, announcing my arrival to anything with ears. I turn the vehicle off and listen for a reply. I'm alone with the wind, whispering its haunting tales through empty tree branches and shifting grains of snow.

The door looms ahead, red and solid. I prepare myself for what I know I'll find inside—if I can get in, that is. Do firemen lock their doors at night? I imagine some Norman Rockwell scene: white T-shirts, cigarettes, poker. Dalmatian under the table. Apparently my knowledge of firefighter habits is stuck in the 1950s. I take it as a good sign that my artist mind, always speaking to me in images, is still in good functioning order. Although under the circumstances, it's now relying on tired clichés. I imagine a checklist.

Image production, check.

As I crunch and sink through the snow to the door, I hear something and stop.

A low growl.

Behind me.

The snowmobile's loud cry *has* been answered.

I pivot just my head, one shoulder, my eyes. The massive German shepherd that I sentenced to death stands colossal and angry, twenty feet away. Instead of him stalking me, I've delivered myself to the dog, still warm and ready to eat.

21

POE

The black Shepherd's growl rumbles, his throat clicking.

He barks once, drool spiraling away.

There was no blood by the car he'd been trapped inside, and his prints moved in the opposite direction, so whoever walked in my tracks and let him out, did so unmolested. Dogs, while not exactly smart, have good memories—at least for people. *He remembers me*, I think, *the woman who saved another dog, but left him to freeze or starve.*

While I want to just dive for the door and throw myself inside, I know the sudden movement will set the dog off. And I don't know if the door is unlocked. I could slam into the thick wood and fall back into the dog's jaws. Moving a slow step at a time, I walk toward the door sideways, facing the dog, keeping my gaze fixed on his, our battle for dominance all in the eyes. At least, for the moment.

I reach for the handle, and the dog's eyes flick toward it. He's a modern dog. Understands what doors are. That they can be passed through and slammed in his face.

He licks the side of his drooling mouth and lowers his head, hackles rising up, leaving little doubt about his intentions. I twist my hand over the knob, but it doesn't spin. My insides seize. Holding my ground, I remove the mitten from my hand, take hold of the knob once more, the freezing metal burning my skin. I apply clockwise pressure.

It turns.

The dog moves forward, one cautious step at a time, closing the distance to just ten feet.

When the handle stops turning, I tense, and then move. I push my shoulder into the wood, prepared for the familiar swing of an opening door. But I find only resistance.

A savage bark and the sound of huffing breath propel me forward. The door, frozen shut at its base, gives way and snaps open. The handle shudders in my grip, slipping free and removing its contribution to my balance. I spill forward over the threshold, making it inside the firehouse.

Devil dog makes it through, right after me, his long snout catching my leg. He bites down, lower jaw on my calf, upper on my shin, the teeth grinding with intense pressure. If not for the malleable calf muscle taking most of the crushing force, I think the bone would have broken already. He gives his head a shake. The teeth on my calf, large and sharp, cut through my snow pants, my jeans, to my white, soft skin, and tear. The sudden tug removes the rest of my faltering balance and I fall forward, crying out.

I land two feet away from a pile of clothing mixed with white powder. He's as big as I am, this monster animal, and I claw at the cold firehouse floor, my fingers probing the linoleum for a crack or imperfection, anything to grip and pull away. But there's nothing— the seams are smooth and perfect. My fingers squeak over the floor, and then slip, coated in white. He shakes my leg, tearing my clothing and skin, but reduces the pressure for a moment to adjust his bite. When he clamps back down a little lower, I feel the first trickle of warm wetness sliding over my leg. I'm bleeding. And helpless. I'm just his squeaky chew toy, an amusement, an outlet for his canine rage.

He holds on, pulling me backward, as my fingers burn with friction, grasping. His feet slip on the linoleum, and from my belly

I manage to push myself up on my arms, bend my free knee and kick him in the side of his head, reinjuring my ankle.

The blow surprises the dog, and he releases me with a yelp. But he shakes it off like a prize fighter, and lunges at the same time I do. I make it just a few feet before he catches my leg again, this time, mercifully, just the snow suit. But I land on my stomach, helpless once more.

My hands clench to fists, ready for a final battle. But the digits of my right hand squeeze over something dry. I glance. The hand lies atop the flakey fireman remains. I don't think about what I do next. It's as instinctual as it is horrible. Clutching a fist full of the dead man, I twist around, sit up and throw the dust into the dog's face.

It winces back, releases me once more, and after a quick inhalation, sneezes. And then again. By the third sneeze, I'm moving and trying not to vomit as the reality of what I've just done sinks in. I scramble and crawl across the floor. My legs feel useless. They might not be, but I'm afraid to try them. If I can't walk, I won't survive. And neither will my baby.

I imagine August, on his way. I flash ahead, weirdly, to a life with him and my child. A strange last family—daughter, mother, grandfather—three generations of survivors. The last of humanity. But that dream is currently slipping away...

Unless I stand. Stand!

I scramble to my feet, slipping in dust, and run into the window-lit firehouse. For a moment, the place falls silent, which unnerves me. I'm not sure why until I realize that it's the dog. It's not sneezing. Then I hear it again. Closer. The dog's nails click against the floor behind me, its heavy breath ragged with the promise of more pain. I emerge from the front office and into the engine garage, its two trucks still housed there. I don't make it far.

The dog leaps at me again, snagging the back of my parka. His jaws close on it, snarling and yanking me backward. Blood dribbles down my calf, filling my sock and the interior of my layers.

Tripping backward, I unzip my coat and shimmy out of it, leaving the dog to rip it to shreds, his paws holding it steady while he tugs and rips long strips into the air. *Who keeps a dog like this?* I shamble as fast as I can on two injured legs, moving around the garage until I spot the axe on the side of one truck.

Don't do it, dog. Don't come at me again.

I grip the axe handle and pull. It remains stuck in place. In my panicked haze I missed the safety latch. What good would an axe be if it could fall away with every bumpy road? I unlatch the axe and lift it from the truck. The weight of its head surprises me. Weighs me down. But it also bolsters me. I hold the heavy blade upright in both hands, ready to swing, but moving steadily away. I need to find the satellite phone, if there is one.

Stay there, dog. Enjoy my coat.

He's right by the door into the office space. I shift the axe over my shoulder, right hand above left, baseball bat style. I played baseball in middle school. That's right, baseball, not softball. I was swift like a tiny mosquito. Base stealing. No one could believe the power in my small frame. The balls would sail over surprised faces, every at-bat. I quit when the boys grew to twice my size. So I ran track, cruising past my opponents with the invisibility and silence of a flea. But I always missed the smack of the bat, the moment of jarring, arm-rattling impact.

Don't do it, dog, I think, when I see his eyes move from the shredded coat, up to me, one eyebrow cocking up higher than the other. Its head goes still, the jaw now jittering, loosening its grip on the jacket.

"Don't fucking do it."

With a powerful bark, the dog leaps. Jaws open. Toward my belly.

I can't run away.

There's no avoiding violence.

My baby.

I've got this, Squirt.

I swing the axe, the heaviness at the end like a weighted bat. I twist my frame, using every muscle in my body, transferring as much force as I can to the axe head.

And miss.

But not entirely. While the blade has missed the dog, the axe handle strikes the dog's head, connecting with a hollow *thunk*. The stunned dog lands on its feet, turning on me, tendrils of drool twisting toward the floor as I raise the axe up once more, my arms still burning.

The attack is announced by snarling lips and a throaty growl. Movement triggers an automatic response, my arms swinging around. *Eyes on the ball,* I hear some past coach shouting. Eyes open, I bring the axe around as the dog rises up again, once more reaching for my belly. Anger fuels the swing, propelling the blade until contact is made. The heavy blade's arc is tugged slower for just a moment, and then it's past the resistance, as I follow through.

There's a sharp cry and a meaty, wet thunk.

Not being eaten, I know I've done the job, and I turn to inspect the damage.

A severed limb lies still at my feet.

The dog, gushing blood, is out of its mind, trying to run on its side, but it only manages to smear a circle of blood on the floor, each revolution deepening the color.

I take a slow step back, the axe sliding through my loose grip until it falls free to the floor. I follow it, dropping to my knees, hands over my mouth, tears in my eyes.

I can't believe what I've just done.

Amidst all my artwork, all the emotional depths I've plumbed, the scrutinized images, never have I experienced this. What was I trying to say, all these years? My simple artist life, the erasing, the redrawing, the painting over, the final products equaled a body of work unaffected by true loss. In a life defending no one but my own strong self, I searched for meaning where there was none.

But now. I am killing this dog, brutally, to protect my child. Not exactly where I thought I would end up when I went to my parents' house. But the moment is far more profound than any image I have ever, or will likely ever conjure. The animal lies bleeding into the floor before me. I sit down next to him, so tired. I'll have to take care of my own leg soon.

Deep welling mercy overcomes me, as the dog's revolutions slow to a stop. It's still alive, eyes wide and confused, panting as its life slowly drains away. I reach out a tentative hand to stroke his side. He snaps at me, just missing my forearm. The action seems to ignite a new fire in the dog. He sits up, bounds to his feet with a fresh, bloody snarl and runs at my face. But he still doesn't understand his leg is missing, and when he tries to step on it, gravity pulls him over. He slides to a stop beside me, close enough to bite me, but he just lays still, the last of his vitriol leaking out on the floor.

Put him out of his misery, some part of me thinks. But what am I supposed to do? Hack him to bits like a psychopath?

With the recognition that I can hurt him no more, I crawl away, out of the garage to let him die. Alone once more.

"I'm sorry," I say to him, crying. I leave him there, his black side stuttering with labored breath.

Inside the office, I lean against the desk and sob. I scream curses at the ceiling. Blood continues to dribble out of the dog's bite on my leg. Wracked with pain and anguish for another life lost, I want to escape, to cease feeling, and maybe even living.

The fissure inside my mind widens, opening slowly, like an earthquake's sinkhole, letting in more and more darkness, the depth cavernous. No light can reach in there.

That poor dog. I think for a minute, imagining the kind of hateful person that could raise such a pet. I watch the hatred spread, the evil that loves violence, wicked, malicious intent, a human widening his own malevolent reach through his trained animal. Is that evil in me now? Because I was violent in return? This feels like a loss I cannot recover from.

But no. I think about Squirt, the knitting together of her little parts, and how she saved both of us. I wouldn't have had the strength to fight back if she wasn't around. I would have given in. And then where would that leave Luke? Sweet, lovable Luke? And Sylvia, my cow, and the other animals, dependent on me?

I summon the last of my artistic powers and imagine the fissure in my brain as a sinkhole in a dirt road. It's closing, just a bit. Two mighty hands are pushing and pressing the sides. Stiff clay, rocks and roots tumbling from the ground, until the two sides crash together like thunder, a cloud of brown dust filling the air. Fissure healed. We can now pass through here. The road is smooth again, the cleft mended. I imagine sunshine and birdsong.

I can do this.

Squirt has made the choice for us.

New life insists.

I find the firemen's bathroom on the second floor, above the garage, near the overnight quarters, and I strip down to investigate my bleeding leg. Not the most terrible wound, due to the padding of my winter layers, but enough to worry about and to tend. While the cuts aren't as bad as I imagined, the bites are already bruising, turning deep purple. *I'll put snow on it later*, I decide, and I prop my leg up on the sink, my ankle protesting as it takes all my weight. With the cut under the faucet, I turn the tap clockwise. Ice cold water streams over the wound. I squirt antibacterial soap over my leg and rub it in, screaming as the wound burns. But it's better than an infection. Still soapy, the water starts to gurgle and cough. *The power is out*, I think. *Stupid!* The water flowing from the tap is propelled by the pressure remaining in the line, and that will run out soon. Ignoring the pain, I scrub fast, clearing the rest of the soap away.

After patting the wound dry with a towel and holding it in place until the bleeding stops, I hop to the closet, open it and sigh with relief. A first aid kit sits on the shelf. After using all the gauze to wrap my leg, and cinching it tight with tape, I stand slowly, testing my weight. Both limbs complain, but the pain is manageable. Briefly, I wonder about rabies. I remember the jangle of his tags and think, no, just a dog raised in violence, responding to the frightening unknown the only way he knew how. There's nothing I can do about it if he was rabid, anyway. I wouldn't even know which medication to take, being pregnant, and there's no way in hell I'm going back to the grocery store's pharmacy.

Three steps toward the door, exhausted and thinking of bed, I remember the reason I came all this way in the first place: the satellite phone. I have no idea what one looks like. I think back to movies, stuff

I've seen on TV, people in the military, shouting into things. Maybe kind of like a walkie talkie/cell phone combination?

A quick look around reveals nothing obvious. If August is right, sat phones aren't common, and would really only be needed in a dire emergency, when cell networks, landlines and radio weren't working. So where would a fire station keep something like that? My eyes land on a closed door, and I realize I'm asking the wrong question. Not where, but who. The label on the door reads, 'Chief Dreyling.'

I head for the door. Locked. I try to shove it open, slamming my body into the solid wood, but I'm greeted by immediate pain from head to toe. That's not going to work. I look around for keys, but finding the right keys could take all day, and without my parka, the cold is starting to seep in.

The solution rears its ugly head and pulls a groan from my throat. Despite how uncomfortable it makes me, I don't waste time debating. Instead, I head down the stairs, propping as much of my weight on the railing as I can. When I step inside the garage again, I half expect the dog to be back on its immortal feet, ready to devour me. But it lays still, surrounded by blood, no longer breathing. The axe becomes my solitary focus and I pick it up. Its weight now feels like an impossible burden. But I carry it back up the stairs, one slow step at a time, until I'm standing in front of Chief Dreyling's office once more.

After a long, deep breath, I raise the blade up—eyes on the ball— and bring it down hard. The impact sends a jarring tingle up my arms, freeing the axe from my grip. But the racket of falling metal doesn't belong to just the axe. The knob has broken free. I hear a dull thunk on the other side, as the knob falls apart. The door gives way to my knee, granting access.

And then I see it, cradled in a charging station atop a black filing cabinet. The phone looks like an oversized, old school Nokia, but with a thick antenna. While I couldn't picture the Sat-phone, now that I'm seeing it, I recognize it for what it is and snatch it from the charger.

I push the power button, so nervous that I feel like I have to pee.

Nothing happens. I lift my finger again, and push the button. Still nothing. The phone is dead.

I turn my attention back to the charger and follow its cord down to the outlet, where it dangles free, not plugged in. Useless. "Smart thinking, Captain Dreyling," I grumble, and take the charger along with the phone and head, as quickly as I can manage, for the exit.

Outside, the cold assaults me. Without my jacket, atop a snow-mobile, I'm going to freeze.

Take a fire engine, I think. The heavy vehicle will be undaunted by the snow. I nearly turn back to the station door when I see a better solution parked across the street. A smile slips onto my face, as I read the word PROPANE stenciled on the side of a large tank. While my parents have a large supply of propane for heating and running the generator, it's not going to last forever . But this...this will get me through the winter and then some.

I cross the street, rolling my eyes as I look both ways. Aside from my snowmobile tracks and the dog's footprints, the layer of snow is perfectly smooth and undisturbed. I open the driver's side door without thinking and unleash a swirl of white powder. I step back, waving my hands in the air, holding my breath.

I consider giving up on the truck, but it solves too many problems to ignore. *He's not your parents*, I tell myself. *You already threw a fireman's remains. You can do this. It's just dust.*

Setting my jaw, and covering my mouth with my scarf, I step up to the side of the truck, place my forearm on the dust and clothing covered seat and brush the whole mass out into the snow. I still hold my breath and close my eyes, but the job is done quickly. I climb up in the cab and close the door, and put the sat-phone and charger in the passenger's seat. Then I look to the ignition. No keys. It's disappointing, but also a good sign. The truck wasn't left running. I glance around and find the keys on the floor, below the ignition. The driver must have been about to start the vehicle, making late night mid-winter deliveries before the weekend.

The truck roars to life. I turn up the heat and bathe in it for a moment, pin pricks of pain flowing over my chilled skin. Then

I throw the big vehicle into gear and pull away. There is a moment of resistance from the snow, and I worry that I'm stuck, but the truck's massive weight crushes the snow and pulls away. I take it slow and steady, making wide turns, but never stopping.

The drive home is uneventful, my head heavy with exhaustion. A mental checklist starts to form in my mind. The propane isn't a concern yet. So figuring out how to attach the truck to the home's tank can wait. But many other things can't. I'll feed Luke, check on the other animals and eat lunch, take a prenatal vitamin and wash it down with farm milk. Then I'll lie down. Sleep for days. My life has been reduced to a list of survival necessities. First this, then that. This is new for me, my brain more used to the divergent spontaneity of art-making, living for myself and the expression of that self.

As I near my parents' white farmhouse, two colorful figures move in the front yard. One is Luke, his red leaping unmistakable.

I pull into the driveway, snow blustering around the windshield. The other figure tromps through the snow to me as I open the door and step out. She lobs a tennis ball with her one good arm—the other hangs loose, like her arm is pulled up inside the jacket...or missing mid-bicep. Luke chases the ball down. He frisks through the snow, then digs under to find it.

I stand there, stupefied.

"Hi," she says. "I'm Leila."

22

POE

"Um," I say, still standing beside the big truck, its engine crackling as the engine cools. The wind whips our cheeks red. She's like an apparition, a slightly askew normalcy, a shift in perception. A woman throwing a ball to a dog. That happens every day.

But not anymore.

"Are you real?" I ask her. I can't help but feel I've gone insane, that the fissure has reopened without my knowing. But why would I hallucinate an unfinished woman? I've never even met an amputee before.

In response to my question the woman smiles and plucks the tennis ball from Luke's mouth as he returns it. She throws it again and Luke is off and running. First of all, hallucinations can't throw balls. Second, Luke was in the house—behind locked doors.

Granted, I've let myself into a house, a grocery store, a fire station and this propane truck, but this feels different. Why my house? It's unremarkable. No different than a thousand more in the area.

The footprints.

She knew I was here.

But I need to give her the benefit of the doubt. She's a *survivor.* A real and present human being. Who cares if she followed my footprints, waited for me to leave the house and then broke in to play with my dog? The old world me cares. A lot. But this isn't the old world. Everything is different. She might have been afraid of me. Maybe she was snooping? Trying to find out more about me and then found Luke and decided that anyone with a golden retriever couldn't be bad? But I'm the same person who left the German shepherd locked up, and she knows it. I'm also the person who lopped off that dog's leg and let it bleed to death. But she doesn't need to know that. No one does. And, I decide, she doesn't need to know about August. Not yet. Not until I really trust her.

"Sorry," I say. "I—I just wasn't... I didn't think there were any other survivors in this area. It's really, really good to meet you, Leila."

I extend my hand, though I almost want to hug her. For a moment, she just looks at my mitten and I realize my mistake. Her right arm is missing.

Oh, God, I think, *I'm an asshole.*

The woman—Leila—puts me at ease a moment later, chuckling and taking my right hand in her left. "It's nice to meet you..."

"Poe," I say. "Like Edgar Allan."

With a speed matching that of the angry German shepherd, Leila wraps me in a one armed bear hug. I'm not much of a hugger with people I know, never mind with a suddenly appeared stranger on my front lawn after a cataclysmic event. I'd much rather give people a friendly punch on the shoulder, a little harder for the close ones—the ones I know can take it. But I lean in and embrace back. We're in this together. I'm dwarfed by her. She has to lean down to hug me.

Her warmth makes me shiver.

"Poor thing," she says. "What happened to your jacket?"

When I don't answer, she pats me heartily, once, twice, pulls back and smiles at me. "I'm sorry I was lurking in the woods yesterday." She laughs, big, hearty and out of place. As an artist, I'm intuitive. I observe everything. Her gray eyes, framed by crow's feet from many years of smiling, don't blink enough. She's staring at me. It was *her* in the woods.

"That was you?" I force out a chuckle, part forced, part real, and wave away my discomfort. She was just checking me out. Like me, she's probably terrified and alone. "It's cool. Things are...strange now."

I walk past her, toward the house. Luke follows me. I feel badly about this sense of foreboding I'm experiencing around this woman. Who knows what she's seen?

"*Very* strange. Talk about an understatement!" She laughs her exuberant laugh again, and I find myself smiling back. So nice, another human, other emotions besides fear, depression and anxiety.

I let my worry go, just like that, like dropping a snowball into a warm puddle. Watch it melt away. "Do you want to come inside? It's ridiculous out here." I open the door, forgetting that she may have already been inside, when she let Luke out. *How did she get past the lock?* I think, but don't ask. There's probably an unlocked window somewhere. Maybe the bulkhead. I'll have to check later.

Move on, Poe. She's a survivor, like you. That's what matters.

We head into the kitchen, shed our gloves, boots, all our winter gear. I put the kettle on, bustle around as best I can getting tea supplies, honey, cups, spoons. I plop a box of crackers on the table. Leila sits quietly, looking at her hand. Graying hair and shallow wrinkles suggest she's in her fifties, fit, maybe an athlete. The sleeve on the side of her missing arm dangles loose. I wonder why she doesn't tuck it in or something.

"So, what do you do, Leila?" I'm terrible at small talk. I usually just launch into philosophy, art and books, but over the years I've picked up the social cues that other, more adept people use, and I figure now's as good a time as any to put someone at ease. I know I don't feel like talking about what's happened, and perhaps she doesn't either. I just want some normal.

She looks up, bright smile, nodding her head. "I'm a climber. C and C."

I squint. The only C and C I know of is C&C Music Factory, and I doubt she's an 80s pop singer.

She notes my confusion and says, "Caves and cliffs."

I turn around from the cabinets, lean against the sink.

"Oh, I see." But I don't see. How could a woman with one arm be a rock climber?

"I play the piano, too," she says. "For fun."

My ankle and bitten leg are both throbbing, calling out for pain meds. But I resist the urge to dull the pain. Anything that puts Squirt at risk, even just a little, is no longer acceptable.

I focus past the pain, on my guest. I want to be present for this woman. I want to know her. I want to feel hopeful.

She doesn't offer any more information, and like I said, I'm terrible at small talk, so I sit down with the tea stuff, open the cracker box, slide it toward her.

"I'm a painter. I play guitar, so I guess we're both daydream musicians."

Leila smiles and prepares her own tea and eats some crackers. The grinding crunch of her teeth on the crackers feels unbearable, like the grinding that signified my parents' deconstruction. The weirdness of this situation overwhelms me. But who is more uncomfortable, me or her? What is expected of us?

Leila wipes her face with a napkin, scouring crumbs from the corners of her cracked lips. Finished, she folds the paper square twice, halving its size, and then stands. With an aristocratic air, tea cup in hand, she heads for the living room like she knows her way around—she might—and pulls the bench out from under the piano with her foot. She places her tea on a coaster atop the piano, sits down on the bench and opens the fallboard protecting the keys. She gasps slightly and says, "Oh my. Ivory keys."

I like to think I'm observant, but I never knew the piano had ivory keys. I always assumed they were plastic. That my romantic father would have an instrument built with pieces of a poached animal surprises me. But it's just as likely that he had no idea the secondhand instrument was made with elephant tusks.

With her one hand, she flickers a few notes from the piano. I can tell she's good. *How long since the injury,* I wonder? *It was recent,* I decide. How could this woman have been a rock climber and pianist with just one hand?

I lean to the side, watching her sit, look at the keys, and then with a flourish of energy, play.

There's a tune to it. A melody.

The sound, so alive, draws me to my feet. I walk into the living room, slight upward curve to my lips, trying to identify the piece. But it's incomplete.

And once I'm in the living room, watching, I realize why. Whatever this song is, it requires two hands. But Leila seems to not notice. In fact, the way her head is moving, the slight pauses in the music where there should be high notes, and the awkward twitch of her nubby right arm, make me think she's not only hearing a complete song, but believes she's playing it with both hands.

Who am I to judge? If she comforts herself by playing one handed music, who cares? *I really am an asshole*, I think, but have trouble believing it. The amputated arm, twitching, insect-like, freaks me out.

My mind flees from the image of the woman's arms and invisible piano-playing fingers, and I suddenly remember August. I need to call him. But first, I need to plug in the phone. Let it charge. "Leila, I need to grab some stuff from the truck. I'll just be a few minutes. Make yourself at home."

After throwing on my boots, I head outside and squeeze my arms across my chest. It's a short walk to the propane truck, but my skin stings from the cold and I feel more awake. More aware.

Leila, despite being a fellow survivor, hasn't given me much hope. She's a broken person, requiring care, physical and probably mental. A fresh addition to my personal island of misfit toys.

I retrieve the phone and its charger from the truck and head back toward the house. In past years, my father and I would make bonfires in the backyard. When I was a kid, we'd roast marshmallows. When I got older, my father, the former hippie turned poet would smoke pot through a long pipe, like he was Gandalf. I joined him, of course, warming by the fire, trying our best to make smoke rings, but never quite succeeding. Mom never partook, but she didn't know it was pot, either. Our little secret.

Like August.

As I sneak back inside, I close the door with one hand and position the phone and charger behind me with the other. I'm not ready to share this yet. I feel relieved when I make it to the stairs without being spotted, and breathe easier when I reach the second floor. I head to my father's office and put the charger down beside the Ham radio. On hands and aching knees, I find a free outlet and plug in the charger. Without standing, I take the phone and snap it in place, waiting a moment. Nothing happens. *It will take time,* I tell myself, remembering that some devices won't work until they're fully charged, or at least until they've reached a minimum charge. I'll come back later and check.

I climb to my feet and suddenly feel an odd trepidation. I turn around to find Luke sitting behind me. When our eyes meet, his tail wags. Sneaky, but no. That's when I realize the one-handed piano playing has stopped. I take the stairs one creaking step at a time, moving slowly, more because of the pain than caution. But there is nothing to worry about. I find Leila standing in the living room, looking at the books on the bookshelves.

"What was that you were playing?" I ask with a smile. "It sounded familiar."

"What were you doing?" She asks, sliding a book back onto the shelf.

I'm taken aback. *None of your business.* But then, I think, she doesn't know me. She has no reason to trust me. Why are we both survivors? She is suspicious of me for good reason. But I know myself, know that I'm trustworthy, and don't know her. Again I am struck by the complications of survival. Life before the end was easier, despite sharing the planet with seven billion people.

"I went outside for some...toilet paper. I was going to the bathroom. Upstairs." It's a horrible lie, but who is going to ask for proof of such a thing. So much for trustworthy.

She turns and stares at me. "Didn't hear you flush."

"If it's yellow, let it mellow," I say with a half-smile, limping over to the couch and sitting down. My father's acoustic guitar, a fire pit companion, rests to my left, in its open case.

"Uh-huh," she says, and points to the guitar. "Pick it up."

An order, not a request. But I oblige her and lift the old guitar onto my lap.

"What kind of music do you play?" she asks, settling herself at the piano again. "You really do play the guitar, right?"

"Just about anything, none of it very good. I just like to mess around." I strum a little. "Do you know any U2?"

"Mmm...not really. What about Dylan?" She plays a few bars of *The Times They Are a Changin'*, with the one hand, the tune recognizable despite lacking half the notes, a fact of which I'm still pretty sure she's not aware.

Hoping the music will pull this woman out of whatever mire has claimed her mind, I do my best to join in. I hunt for chords, but keep up. And then, at once, I'm struck by the ridiculousness of what we're doing. It's crazy. We need to be preparing. Plotting. Rationing. Something. Winter is still upon us and will be for another few months. But we're just going to sit around playing horrible sounding rock songs?

Freed from the music's allure, but still playing along, I suddenly feel like I'm being watched. The sense is so strong, I stop playing with an abrupt wrong strum and turn around, looking out the window behind me.

The piano falls silent. "What's wrong?" Leila asks, her voice an odd sing-song melody, continuing the music. I realize that before, when I felt watched, it was her in the woods, and I involuntarily shiver. But it's not her now. Someone else then? Or some*thing*? That's one secret I will have to share with Leila, but not until I'm sure she can handle it.

"I'm just getting this feeling like we're being watched," I say. *No harm in being honest*, I decide. In what I now recognize as something Leila does, like a quirk or habit, she stares at me, unblinking. I decide to stare back. *My house, honey*. Luke seems to feel the uncertainty in the room and walks over to me, schlumps into my lap, knocking the guitar to the side.

Leila, without blinking, wearing a bright smile, says, "I'm hungry. Time for another snack?"

So much for feeling watched. She either lacks the weird sixth sense or really just doesn't feel it, which I suppose is possible, since she didn't see the thing in the grocery store and wasn't attacked by the German shepherd. Maybe I have a few more reasons to feel paranoid?

But it needs to stop at some point. Weird or not, we're in this together.

I need to either trust and befriend her, because she might be all I have, or to not trust her and kick her ass to the curb. But I don't see that ending well. Images of the dog's severed leg and spinning body flit through my mind. *No more conflict*, I decide. August is on his way. Will be here in days. I can handle her until then, and we can figure this out together.

"Fine," Leila says, lifting her good arm and stubby arm to slam them down, one hitting the piano bench, the other swinging through empty air. "I'll just help myself." She pushes herself up with her one arm, but spills to the side, clearly expecting her weight to be held by the missing limb.

Images of the dog return to my mind. How much like the dog is she? Is that why the dog spared her? Kindred spirits? When the woman growls, I suspect that's the case.

23

POE

"Ahh!" Leila shouts, and I clench my fists for a fight. But she doesn't come at me, she's just frustrated by her stumble. She looks around for the cause of it and finds nothing. She shakes out her arms, the rotating stub ridiculous. "Sorry. I've been such a klutz lately. Dropping things. I'm not sure what the problem is."

With a final huff of expelled aggravation, she heads for the kitchen, really making herself at home. It's funny, that expression, how uncomfortable it would be if someone really made themselves at home, helping themselves to everything. What's yours is mine. Maybe it's because this is my parent's house, not mine, that her comfortable cupboard rummaging feels off.

But it also gives me the chance to slip away, to check on the charging phone. I excuse myself again, rubbing my arms. "I'm a little chilly. Going to grab a sweater."

I take the stairs two at a time, alone, but feeling pursued. Upstairs, I lean over the satellite phone in my father's office. No change. The screen is blank. There are no small lights to reveal a charge. Feeling impatient, I snatch the phone from its cradle and push the power button. Nothing. *No*, I think. I give it a little shake, like that will help. I want to slap it. Then it hits me—I plugged it into an outlet that works only when the light switch on the wall is turned on. All this wasted time. It wasn't even charging.

I flip the wall switch up and the phone blinks, alive but not charged, and it won't be for a while longer, I'm assuming. Leila is going to get suspicious if I keep sneaking away, but can I wait until tonight to call him?

And what's the big deal if she finds out?

Why do I feel like I need to keep August and this phone to myself?

I pull up my sleeve and look at August's number scrawled safely on my wrist. I write the numbers on a wrinkled piece of paper and tuck it away. The ink on my skin will eventually fade. Still impatient, I try the phone. It blinks at me, still too weak to call anyone. *Hours*, I think. *Give it a few hours.* I sigh and run my fingers through my hair, and leave the room. Then I gently close the door behind me before going back downstairs.

I really don't want Leila to know about the phone. Is this just my old extreme need for privacy kicking in? One person in my life, and I'm ready to be rid of them? Could I really prefer the horrible solitude? I'm not sure. As I walk down the stairs, I make the quick decision to just talk to her, find out about how she survived. What her story is. What am I waiting for? The elephant in the room is stinking up the place.

She's sitting at the piano again, a cookie in her mouth. She bites a piece off, clutching the rest of the cookie with her lips while she chews. When she sees me coming, she flips the rest of the cookie into her mouth and quickly devours it.

"Not cold after all?" she asks, looking down.

I involuntarily look down at myself, caught in a lie, unable to look her in the eyes. "No, I just decided to turn the heat up instead."

If she buys the lie, I can't tell. She looks lost now. Her one hand rests on the keys, not playing. A puzzled look twists her face. She looks up at me with a frown.

Before I can ask her anything, she says, "How's the baby, Poe?"

I stop in place. Did I already tell her about Squirt?

My few and recent memories of Leila start to replay.

"She's doing fine," I say, keeping the peace. "I guess. Hard to tell. You know. Luke's not exactly an obstetrician." We both look down at Luke, who raises his head and thumps his tail at the sound of his name. I am wracking my brain, remembering our conversation in the kitchen, every word we've said since meeting outside.

Did I tell her about the baby?

"Good, good. So how do you know she's a girl?" Leila plays a few chords, soft and slow, but they're not fluid, like a melody. They're discordant. They don't match—like walking in one stiletto heel and one Birkenstock. The sound matches the confusion I'm feeling.

"I mean, I guess I don't really know. I just sort of have a feeling. Helps to assign a gender. Visualizing, or something." I remain still, frozen by the breadth of this woman's knowledge. How long did she watch me? Listen to my conversations with Luke? Could she hear me talking to August last night? Does she know I'm hiding him from her?

I didn't tell her. Maybe I'm showing more than I thought?

But would that explain everything she knows?

"How far along are you?"

I don't blame her for spying or snooping. I get it. But she could at least pretend not to know all this about me. But I see what she's doing now. I get it. This is girl talk. We're harkening back to a time that existed before the event, when women would gather and bond over their periods, procreation and comfortable-yet-supportive bra choices. In other words, a few days ago. Except that I never quite fit into that time, either. My boobs have always been too small, my discussion ideas too large.

"Three months," I say.

Some mental math slides through my mind like unbidden flash cards.

Six months.

I will give birth to another human being in *six* months. There will be no physician, no nurse or midwife. No hypno-birthing classes, birth ball or birth tub. Who will help me? Even if I could Google this stuff, how many people give birth on their own?

August. He had a daughter. Didn't strike me as the kind of person who would be absent at the birth. He's a smart guy, too, so maybe he remembers some of the details. When to push. When to breathe. The kind of information my own parents would have conveyed when the time came. But what if he doesn't make it? What if he fainted when his daughter was born and doesn't remember it?

I can't do this alone. I'm not that strong.

I start to get lost in this foreboding, when I notice Leila is scratching incessantly at her shoulder, her legs jiggling up and down, up and down. She's moving nonstop. And then she plays another few chords, again unattached to each other, then returns to digging at her shoulder, pulling at her clothes.

The playing stops suddenly. Leila turns to me with a crooked smile. "So tell me how you've been feeling. Healthy? Morning sickness?"

She scratches the shoulder again, rapid fire, like a rodent limb. The buttons of her blouse pop free. The shirt opens. I see an arch of black skin beneath, a fraction of what could be a broad circle on her chest, like some kind of horrible infection. My mind runs through the symptoms of various plagues I know precious little about. The black death sounds right, but I don't think it looked like this. Ebola...no. Small Pox would be bumpy. Even the latest plague to strike mankind, Hochman's, didn't turn skin black. Those people just fell apart. I glance at Leila's missing arm and dismiss it. If she had Hochman's, she wouldn't be up and about. She'd be dead.

I stand up. "Leila? Are you...okay?"

She cocks her head to the side, my question unheard. "Is everything gestating properly? Have you been monitoring your temperature? How many millimeters is your uterus currently measuring?"

I stare at her. The line of detailed questioning confuses me. "I'm sorry, what? *Gestating?*"

She starts to ask another question, interspersed with the piano chords and the itching. I interrupt her.

"Enough about me," I say, forcing cheer into my voice and casually waving my hand. "I'm really interested in hearing your story. How you survived the...event." I lean back on the chair arm, not comfortable with the idea of fully sitting, a vulnerable position.

"Well, I don't know if... Huh." She looks down at her hand, rubs the top of her thigh, as if trying to warm herself up. She's nervous, too. But, I don't try to comfort her. I want to know what happened. Maybe within her story is some key to finding out what we need to do? What really happened? And why. So, I wait, feeling done with the weird line of pregnancy questioning. I glance down at my still mostly flat middle.

No way she could see I was pregnant.

"I was at home when it happened," she says, not looking at me. She plunks a couple of keys on the piano, then a chord, C E G. It's like she's adding a soundtrack to her talking. She plays another chord; jiggles both legs up and down. The scratching above her missing arm resumes.

"So, you were at home? I was here when it happened. I...lost my parents."

She glances around the room, swinging her head wide, like suddenly my lost parents will appear, like they were hiding this whole time. "Have you *looked* for them?"

There's a negative shift in the room's energy, moving toward instability. My muscles tense. The fissure in my brain cracks open a bit, a little rift in a dry lake bed. A tangent.

Leila stands abruptly, knocking over the piano bench. She steps around it, leaving it tipped over on the braided rug, my mother's collection of music books spilled out. She scratches again. "But...but your baby. She's fine. She's healthy." She's stuttering and pacing the room. "Right? I need to know. I need...I need..."

It's her arm, I think. She's in denial, focusing on the baby so that she won't have to acknowledge that she lost the arm. Which means it's recent.

Overcome with sudden mercy, I stand and walk calmly toward her. "Leila, you're safe now. You survived. We both did. But you need to move past it now. Because I need you—the baby needs you— to get better." I'm no psychologist, but I'm pretty sure burying crap like this is the wrong way to go about it. Better to deal with it and move on. I think. That could just be the Yankee in me.

"Leila, were you underground?" I ask, remembering August's story. "During the event? Did you lose your...um...arm when, you know...the dust?"

I can practically see her arm raised up, maybe holding on to something, maybe reaching, turning to powder before her eyes, breaking her mind. It must be what happened.

"My what?" Leila stops in the middle of the room. We're a few feet apart. She stares down at me, reminding me that I'm short.

I'm not entirely sure what to say, so I ramble. "Your arm, Leila. I'm sorry to bring it up. But you have to face it. I've heard that some people can still feel missing limbs. Severed limb syndrome, I think. If it hurts we can probably get something strong from the pharmacy. It's not like we need a prescription." I take a step toward her, wanting to comfort her, wanting now to connect, finally. I feel very tired.

"My arm?" She looks at the open air where her limb should be, but isn't. Then she stares at me, her large gray eyes unblinking. "What. The. Hell. Are. You. Talking. About?"

24

POE

"Your arm, Leila," I say, quiet, stepping closer toward her. I gesture to the space where her arm should be, was, is now not. She looks at the empty space, seeing what only she can, before turning back to me, like I'm the one who is crazy. Her gaze intimidates me, partly for the wild look in her eyes, but also because they guide her body, which is twice my size. Easily.

I once worked as an art therapist at SafeHaven, a treatment facility for adults with disabilities. Sometimes the older guys, the ones who used to live in the institution before it closed down, who were most mistreated—beaten, hosed off for showers, electrocuted—would explode, throwing chairs, or people, unable to speak or express what they wanted to tell us. Their anguish. The room would clear, and they would call me in, the short artist, weighing a third of their weight. I never tried to figure out what they needed, because I don't think they even knew. I respected them enough to know I couldn't read their minds. So I would just allow my quietude to fill the room. I would extend gentleness to them, like a single flower in my hand. I would be gentle enough for both of us. I would be their calm. It worked every time. And then I would whisper their interests to them, remind them who they were. A little bit of emotional redirecting, a sleight of hand.

Leila is like them. Not well.

Her breath comes in gasps, gray eyes savage. I respect her enough to know that I cannot read her mind. I slow my breathing, way, way down.

"Never mind," I say. "I'm just tired. Probably the baby."

Leila stands still, listening, but the mania is still bubbling at the surface.

"Who taught you how to play?" I motion to the piano.

Her eyes dilate slightly. She leans back, bringing her upright again. I hadn't even realized she was leaning over me.

"You seem like a natural," I say.

She turns her eyes to the piano. "My mother taught me. It was supposed to be a lesson in discipline. I think she was disappointed I liked it so much." She smiles and laughs to herself, lost in a memory. She holds up her hand, looking back and forth between it and the missing one. Her fingers are powerful and callused. "If not for these hands, I might have done something with it. But the speedy tempos..." She wiggles her fingers. "I'm just not fast enough."

Feeling a fresh downward spiral en route, I redirect again. "You said you were hungry. Let's see what we can find in the kitchen."

I don't touch her, but walk with total confidence right past her, through the living room into the kitchen, expressing my trust. But it's a charade. As much as I loved those damaged men at SafeHaven, I never really trusted them. My heart patters around. I am alone with this woman.

I ache to hear August's voice.

I start taking boxes of things from the cupboards, a bit of bustle in my step, trying to act normal. What would my mother do? What food is a peace offering? Something friends would eat. My eyes are drawn to a box of chocolate chip cookies, but my mind is elsewhere. *Does she really not know her arm is missing?*

Leila steps into the kitchen, forehead channeled into several deep rivers. I see her as a woman gripped by some kind of amnesia, or an out-of-body experience. She looks like she's climbed from a car wreck, physically shaken but mentally incomplete.

Is this what I looked like when I left the pod?

No, I decide, and I put the open cookie box on the table, all smiles. It's her eyes that throw me, that make me think she's missing something else, something deeper. Beyond my understanding, but still somehow detectable.

"Cookies again," she says, the words a critique, and an accurate one. It seems that my default snack is cookies. I could have offered pie. There are enough of them. But she's already digging into the box. "At least there's some chocolate in them this time."

I need to be alone. Away from her for a few minutes. I'm not seeing things clearly. Not seeing her clearly. I lean against the counter, watching her gingerly sit on a chair. My arms encircle my little body, wrapping around to grab each poking elbow.

It's okay, Squirt.

August, get here, like yesterday.

We nibble for a few minutes.

She remains eerily silent the whole time, squinting hard while she eats, small rabbit bites, her cheeks up near her eyes. I dare not disturb whatever stasis I've created. I won't be mentioning the arm again, at least not today. The stairs beckon me, drawing my eyes every few seconds. I want to run up them, lock myself in my father's office and call August. I need a father's perspective. A second brain. At the very least, a sympathetic ear.

But how to get up there again without drawing attention? And will the phone even be charged enough?

Leila leans back in her chair, looks like she's about to say something. I interrupt.

"Leila, did you know I have some animals? In the barn?"

Her eyebrows rise in time with her slowly turning head. "Oh?"

"The chickens need to be fed, if you'd like the honors." It's not true, but chickens can always eat. "I'm sure they'd be happy to meet you. I think they're sick of me already."

"Probably," she agrees, and the knots in my back spring to life.

I show no reaction to the jab. "The feed is in the bucket, just to the right of the barn door. Just sprinkle some around to them. They'll love it."

At least my powers with people have not faded. She nods, still frowning, and walks to the kitchen door. She slips on her boots and heads out to the barn. No coat. Oblivious to the cold now curling into the kitchen through the left open door. She won't last long out there without a coat, but I'll take it. In my current state, my own fallible brain malfunctioning, I can't maintain the emotional sleight of hand for long.

I watch to make sure she enters the barn, and then I close the kitchen door and lock the deadbolt. Hesitation roots me in place. Should I lock it?

Will she believe I could have done so by accident?

Do I even care? I know nothing about her except, if I'm honest, that she frightens me. I don't want to let her back in at all. But is there a choice? She's not a dog I can just leave to die, and look how well that turned out. She'd probably just turn on me like the dog did. And it's not like the house is Fort Knox. Getting inside would be as easy as breaking a window, and then I'd be in real trouble. What if she broke all the windows? Would I have to leave the house?

Too many questions. Too many potential outcomes.

But I need to talk to August, and I need to do it alone.

The door remains locked. There is more chocolate in the house I can use as a peace offering.

I run upstairs to my father's office and close the door behind me, no lock on this one. I hover above the phone. Something looks different. And then I realize the change. A small green light on the top of the phone is glowing. I shake a bit as I lift the phone and punch the numbers written on my wrist. I end up dialing what I'm hoping is the wrong number first, because nobody answers.

I try again, carefully depressing each number. The slowness of it feels like a man's fingers around my throat.

It rings.

Again.

On the third ring, "Poe?"

"It's me," I say, melting with relief, but then realize he didn't sound right. "Are you okay?"

He tells me that the phone surprised him, that he's in a Walmart, of all places, and now that I have him on the phone, I just want him to talk at me. I just want to hear him breathe, listen to his movements through the phone, imagine his physicality and gestures. Pretend to know his face. Leila fades away.

He's telling me something about shopping. I'm listening to the texture of his deep voice. He will laugh from his toes. He will give great bear hugs. He'll have that distracted, over thinking presence of the geniusly smart. I slide down to the floor.

"Poe," August says, his voice serious, snapping my thoughts back to the here and now. He says something else, but I miss it, focusing instead on the sound of creaking floorboards just outside the door.

The office door opens slowly and Leila steps in. *I forgot to lock the front door.* I look up at her, confused by her clothing, which looks darker, stained dark red, and moist. Was she painting in the barn? Did I leave some old art supplies out there? Red spots speckle her face. Is that a rash?

Something in my mind clicks. The black skin. A rash. Hochman's or some other disease? Do *I* have it now?

"Who are you talking to?" she says, standing above me. Then the smell hits me, a corrosive, rusty stench.

It's blood.

She's covered in blood.

25

AUGUST

Warmth on my cheek rouses me from unintended sleep. The air is stale. My lungs feel dry. The morning sun sends its rays through the SUV's windows, which trap the infrared spectrum inside, warming the interior. I only vaguely remember my pell-mell drive to Albuquerque, fearing the whole way that I would be hunted down by the strange alien being. But I made it without incident, only slowing for the empty cars littering the highway. When I arrived in the city, the lights were still on. I spotted the Walmart sign from the highway, just two blocks away. As though my arrival were a trigger, the power winked out and the city plunged into darkness just minutes after I'd put the SUV in park between a hulking RV and a cherry red Corvette. Sandwiched between midlife crisis and late life acceptance, I fell asleep, escaping the pain shrouding my body.

I'd considered going into the mega-store while the power was still on, but once things got dark... Not a chance. I'd rather sleep in the SUV and have wheels beneath me than be caught in the pitch black, dusty-floored aisles with an invisible hunter-killer.

Now that the sun has risen, its orange glow strikes the storefront, and its windows, head on. If it gets much later, the sun's light won't penetrate the store's depths. Even now, most of the light will be filtered out by the tall aisles and stacks of smiley-faced sale displays. If there were any other path, I'd take it, but everything I need to start my cross country trek, sans locomotion, is inside that building.

I lift my arm and take hold of the steering wheel. The muscles in my shoulder, bicep and forearm painfully declare their resistance to the movement. I haven't felt this stiff...ever. At least my hand is pain-free, and my grip on the wheel solid. With my left hand, I toggle the seat back, which is fully reclined. I sit up, lifting with my gut and pulling with my arm. If there were anyone alive within a five mile radius, I'd be embarrassed by the way my stomach muscles jitter and struggle with the half sit-up. Hell, I'm embarrassed for myself. Of all the people left on Earth to cross the country in search of another survivor, I'm probably the least likely candidate to succeed. All I really have going for me is commitment. And it moves me, first outside the SUV and then one aching, lumbering step at a time, to the front entrance of Walmart.

The night before, with the power still on, the automatic doors would have slid open for me. I stand before the doors, thinking. They're not locked, but they don't look light. And I'm not sure I can lift, heft or move anything beyond my own body. The standstill draws my attention back to the sharper pain points. Left leg. Right elbow. The leg is bruised, and there is nothing I can do about that now, but the elbow is gashed pretty good, and stings every time I bend the joint, cracking the fragile scab and adding more blood to the tacky coating covering my arm.

With my fingers hooked around the side of the door, I pull. It resists and then slides for a half inch before catching and my fingers slip free. I stumble back and land against a large window.

"Screw it," I say, and look for an alternate mode of ingress. I find it lying beside two bundles of loose clothing. Without thinking, I head for the bat and bend down to take it. As my fingers wrap around the aluminum bat's rubber-wrapped handle, I spot the flecks of dust clinging to the clothes—a dress, sweater and heels to the right, a pair of child-sized cargo pants and long sleeve shirt to the left. The bat rests between the mother and son's remains.

I pause for just a moment, silently apologizing to the pair for my desecration. Then I lift the bat away, keenly aware that the grit beneath my fingers is likely the remains of the boy's hand.

The door mocks me. I hear it laughing at the bat in my hands. It has a metal push bar in the middle, which will make hitting it close to center a difficult and potentially painful job. Just beyond it, a second pair of doors await. I don't have the strength to do this more than once.

I extend my middle finger toward the door and approach the window instead. It's four feet off the ground, and huge, but I'm going to hit glass no matter where I swing, and there's only one pane of glass—albeit, thick glass.

The bat feels heavy in my weary hands, but its weight can only help. I consider swinging the thing baseball style, but the window is four feet off the ground and I haven't swung a baseball bat since I was a kid. I'm as likely to strike the wall as I am the window, so I opt for lumberjack style and raise the bat over my head. A primal scream, like I'm a caveman out on a hunt, erupts from my mouth, and I bring the bat down.

A painful vibration slams up my arms, explodes in my elbows and clutches my shoulders. When I open my eyes, I expect to see the window now mocking me, along with the door. Instead, it's got a long, vertical gash where the bat punctured it, and cut a rough, downward path to the sill. The glass yielded to my strike, but the thin plastic safety coating has prevented the whole thing from shattering. I take a step to the side, brace myself for the zinging pain and swing again. Pins and needles rocket from my hands to my elbows, but I get the same result. Using the bat like a chisel, I pound out the lower window between the two gashes. Once I've knocked it all loose, I push. The already spider-webbed glass resists for just a moment before cracking at the seam and opening inward like a doggy door.

After brushing the glass away, I slide through, noting that this is the second time in two days that I've climbed through a window I've broken. I don't think it will be the last. The daylight filtering through the windows is diffused by a copious amount of tinting I couldn't see well from the outside. It casts the inside in twilight-like gloom. But not pitch black.

When my eyes adjust, I search the area around me. A line of checkouts stretches toward the far side of the store, most covered in not-yet paid for goods and white dust. Heaps of clothing, mingled with the powdered dead, fill the gaps between the counters. To the far right, just beyond the produce section of the massive store is a McDonalds. I haven't eaten fast food in a long time, but the sign sets my stomach to grumbling. It's been a while since I ate.

Moving slowly, I head for an empty checkout lane and scour the impulse items. I find what I'm looking for hanging beside a box of Baby Ruth bars. After tearing open the mini-LED flashlight package, and doing the same to a Baby Ruth, I make my way into the depths of the store, led by a pitiful, light blue beam of light. But it guides me around the dead and toward the darker back wall, where most of what I'm looking for is on display.

Stop number one, flashlights. The selection is surprisingly large, and I take two small, but crazy bright Maglites along with a headlamp. I pocket the two Maglites and strap the headlamp on over my head and Claire's Red Sox hat, allowing my hands to be free. For a moment, I think about getting a cart, but then remember I can only take what I can carry in my pockets and Claire's backpack. I stand still for a moment, realizing that Claire's backpack, while sentimental, might not be the best choice.

My next stop is the camping section. The backpacks here dwarf Claire's and have sleeping bags attached, more pockets than you can count, and metal frames to help support it all. I tear open a box and slide the pack over my shoulder. Fits my body better, too. With a sigh, I head for the neighboring Sports & Outdoors display case, which I've kind of been dreading.

An array of rifles lie just beneath the glass counter top. Behind the counter is a wall of glass-door shelves, lined with boxes of ammunition. I know nothing about guns, but a rifle quickly catches my eyes. It's also the most expensive weapon in the case, so I take that as a good sign. The label says that it's a Marlin Model 336SS, which means nothing to me, but the little pictures of a deer and a bear, both with crosshairs over them, tell me it's powerful. Some of the other labels just show deer. Some show ducks. But this is the heavy hitter. I quickly scan the rest of the label and discover that it takes 30/30 Win. ammunition. Again, this means nothing, but at least now I know what to get. I break the glass with the baseball bat and lift the rifle up, revealing a manual tucked beneath it. I take the manual, too, and slip it into my pocket for later reading. Two more broken cases later, I have a strap for the rifle, which now hangs over my shoulder and six boxes of soft-tipped 30/30 ammo, twenty rounds to a box. I'm not planning to fight an army of those shimmering things, but I will need to learn how to shoot, and eventually, hunt. Canned food won't last forever.

I add portable food to my mental list of aisles to visit. My next stop will be first aid. I need to clean and patch up the elbow. Surviving the end of the world to die from infection would just be stupid. I also need traveling clothes, rugged with lots of pockets and some boxer briefs to cut down on the inner thigh chaffing I get every time I try a treadmill. Then food. High calorie stuff that doesn't require cooking and won't go bad. Traveling light means losing the camping stove, though I have several lighters for making fires. Last on my list, a bike. A car might attract too much attention, but I don't think a bike will be any different than walking.

The weight of the seven-pound rifle over my shoulder is annoying, but its presence and lever-style, cowboy feel gives me a boost of confidence. Once I figure out how to load and shoot it, I'll be a regular John Wayne...riding on his faithful Huffy. I smile at the mental image, and then bark out a scream when the sat phone clipped to my belt sends a shrill chime echoing through the store. I tear the phone from my belt and answer it before the second ring finishes.

Out of breath from surprise, I gasp once before saying, "Poe?"

"It's me," she says, her pleasant voice tinged with tension. She's speaking quietly, like someone might hear her. "Are you okay?"

"The phone surprised me," I explain. "I'm in the back of a dark Walmart."

"Walmart?" she asks.

"Where else can you find a rifle and a bike in one trip? Granted, it's all made in China, so I don't think the bike will last the trip, and it weighs an ungodly amount, but it's a start." I ask, smiling as relief takes hold. Poe's voice has a calming effect, but it doesn't last long. When I remember that Poe doesn't know about what happened last night, about the creature and Steve Manke's death, I'm gripped by crushing seriousness. "Poe," I say, "Listen to me. We're not—"

"Who are you talking to?" a new voice asks. I look around me, but realize the voice came from the phone. Poe is not alone. Whatever hope this brings me is dashed a moment later, when the voice turns angry and shouts, "Who the fuck are you talking to?"

"Poe!" I say, but I get no reply. "Poe!"

If Poe heard me and responded, I can't hear it over the screaming woman's verbal assault. But one thing does come through, Poe's frightened voice asking, "Why do you have a knife?"

26

POE

I slowly stand up, my mouth open, the phone, still connected, in my hand, against my ear. White tufts cling to her shirt and pants. Chicken feathers.

"Who the fuck are you talking to?" She towers above me, filling the doorway. The smells of blood and chicken shit and something else, something meaty, like raw steak, fresh from the cellophane wrapper, fill me with nausea. I gag and stagger back to the far wall.

Leila raises her hand. She's holding a large knife, slick with blood. I recognize the large, rusty blade, kept in the barn for cutting rope or twine, or tape. She holds the blade in her only hand, like she's fresh from chopping vegetables, just pausing. Casual. She wipes her forehead with her sleeve, the knife close to her face. Her arm leaves a red smear.

She's standing in the doorway. I can't get by.

August is saying my name, his voice close in my ear. He's an angel on my shoulder, keeping the crack in my brain from opening up again and embracing the insanity.

I ask the only question I can think of. "Why do you have a knife?"

She holds it across her mid-section, and smiles at me. I think it's the first time I've seen her smile. She has beautiful teeth, white and clean. I'm trapped in a horror movie, but this is real. I can smell the blood. Films and nightmares smell like nothing.

The phone remains at my ear. Leila steps into the office and closes the door behind her. I walk behind the desk, and then regret it. Now I'm trapped. Still smiling, she asks again, "Who are you talking to, Poe?"

Without disconnecting, I gently put the phone down on my dad's desk, next to the radio equipment. My desire to protect August and his identity overwhelm me. I try to exude the old calm confidence, that manipulation of emotions, working the room. The coppery smell makes me gag, and my voice shakes. I need to get out of this tiny office, now. But there's no way I can overpower her.

"Let's go back downstairs, okay?" I stand still, a stone, hating being unsure of what to do. Squirt appears in my mind, a little spiral, tiny limbs. I wrap my arms around my torso and glance at the window to my right. Could I jump?

"Not going to tell me," she says. "Keeping secrets." She waggles the knife back and forth in time with her next words. "Dirty little secrets. Daddy kept secrets too, but mommy knew. The metronome drowned them out. Tick, Tick, Tick."

She looks at me, eyes large. "Isn't that right? You knew. You *still* know. About them. About the owls. They took me, you know. And brought me here. Here! I'm from Seattle!"

Leila calms in a sinister way and glances down at her missing arm. "The black desires your baby. You know that, too, don't you? Such a know it all. Such a *fucking* know it all."

With two large steps she lunges across the desk, knife swinging sideways. She screams and cries. "What did you do to my arm, Poe?"

I lean back, dodging the knife, and bash my head on the bookcase behind me. A swirl of stars fills my vision. I'm dizzy with nausea. There's no space to move. In a flash of recognition, a surge of awareness, I understand where the blood is from. The animals, in the barn, where I sent her.

Luke.

She steps around the desk and in that millisecond I see my chance. My tininess might save me. I dive under the desk and through it to the other side, shoving the desk chair out and into Leila's gut. She tries to stop it, but reaches with her missing arm and the chair knocks her off balance. I stand and launch for the door.

The doorknob starts to turn in my hand. Each asymmetrical wood grain line on the door materializes in my vision as solid hope. I could count the lines, find imaginary facial features; the door is taking that long to open.

I'm too slow. Leila smashes into me, crushing my body between hers and the door, which closes with a bang. My cheek flattens against the wood.

I scream and flail, punching the sides of her head, out of control, unsteady. She backs up just enough for me to fall over sideways. My fingers curl as I fall, grasping her blouse, tearing it open. I land on my back and look up. Her braless chest is laid bare, the black skin exposed. There are two dark rings of skin emanating from what looks like a fresh puncture wound over her heart. It's the size of a nickel, thick with rumpled scar tissue. The unbuttoned shirt slips off her nubby arm, also covered in boils of scar tissue and loose, dangling skin that flaps with each twist of the non-existent limb.

I kick at her legs. The third strike finds her kneecap, knocking it straight, nearly inverting it.

With a cry of pain, Leila falls to her knees, the knife still in her hand. I back away toward another book-cased wall, when she slashes through my pants and strikes my shin, slicing through the many layers of gauze already there and the skin beneath.

I scream, the pain rolling over my body like a hundred bee stings. I inch backward on my elbows, across the ancient rug, my dad's books above my head. Leila scoots forward on her knees. I grab her arm with both hands, trying to pry the knife away from her. She slashes again and again, my grabbing making her movements erratic. Vague pain radiates from my core. Luke paws at the door, barking and barking.

As I think, *Oh, thank God, he's safe,* Leila and I both look down. My lower abdomen was exposed from the thrashing, my turtleneck untucked and rumpled up. A thin, long, red liquid line burbles against my pale, convex belly skin.

Some sort of strange animal moan escapes my lips. Pain, emotional as much as physical, blinds me. Rage tightens my grip on her arm. If she had two, I would be dead already. But I'm still unable to overpower her.

We're wrestling like this, the knife huge between us, filling the air, filling the whole room, when I notice something subtle. Like a shift in the atmosphere. The sound propels my memory back to the living room. The reporter on TV, talking about the grinding sound a moment before I heard it myself. That night. *It's happening again!*

"Stop!" I scream, at Leila and whatever strange power might control the grind. "My baby!"

"The baby!" Leila shouts. Mocking. "The baby! Everyone wants the—"

The grinding slams into us, a physical force, the revolutions faster and faster. Leila drops the knife next to me and we both cover our ears. This is it. The moment of my death, and like my parents, I know it's coming. But there is nothing I can do to save my baby.

I'm sorry, Squirt.

In seconds, like a time-lapse melting snowman, Leila's body turns to powder. The particles of her being cling to one another, a loose network of dust still in the form of her body. But the weight of her clothing becomes too much, and the whole thing collapses down. I close my eyes and mouth, afraid of the flaky powder, despite the knowledge that I'm next. I turn my cheek to the braided rug, as the dusty white lands on me, a huge flour sack suddenly split open and dropped from above.

Flat on my back, I scream through closed lips, and keep screaming until the sound of my voice is the only thing I can hear.

My scream fades.

And then, silence.

I've been spared. Again.

"Poe!" The small voice makes me jump. "Poe! Can you hear me!"

August.

He's still on the line.

Probably freaking out, which isn't unjustified.

His voice draws me up into a sitting position. I'm surrounded by, and covered in, Leila's remains. I'm numb to it, but not August's voice. I find the phone on the floor, a few feet away. The powder covering the screen blows cleanly away.

"I'm here," I say, breathless. "I'm okay." The words come out before I'm really sure. I look down at my belly, half expecting to see the womb sliding out of me. But it's still just a thin red line. I press it with my finger, eliciting a sharp sting, but nothing more. The wound is superficial, like a long paper cut.

But nearly more.

I want to cry, to scream about the powder covering me, but I've done enough of that. So I tamp down my panic and shock and try to sound composed, for myself as much as August. "I met a survivor," I tell him. "Leila."

"I heard her," he says, "but..."

"She tried to kill me." I think of the animals and stand.

"Oh, god. Are you sure you're okay? Is she—"

"Dead," I say, opening the door to a very relieved and happy Luke, bounding around in circles. I lower a hand to him while heading downstairs. "Yes. But it wasn't me. I didn't kill her."

"Is there someone else?" His voice is barely contained panic.

"No," I say, slipping my feet into my boots and unlocking the back door. Like Leila, I step out into the cold without a jacket, the frigid air mercifully numbing me. "It was them."

He's quiet for a moment, and all I can hear are my boots in the snow, tracing previous footprints down a now worn path, polka dotted red.

"Them...who?"

"The ones that did this. Killed everyone. Just like the first time, they turned her to powder. But not me." I stand before the barn door.

"Are you sure you're okay?" he asks again, and I can't blame him.

"Fine," I say, doing my best to sound composed. "Really. I'm just...a little numb. Emotionally. But I'm alive. Squirt's alive. That's what matters, right?"

"Right," he says, sounding relieved, but apprehensive. "Listen...I had a similar experience."

My hand freezes on the wooden door handle.

"I met a survivor, too," he says. "He wasn't like Leila. Wasn't dangerous. But...they killed him."

"And let you live?"

"No," he says. "I mean, yes. But they didn't turn him to dust. They stabbed him. Murdered him in a very human way. I tried to fight it, but—"

"You saw one? The shimmering things?"

He's quiet for a moment.

"You didn't tell me you had seen one," he says.

"I didn't want you to think I was crazy." I look at my hand, still on the handle, refusing to pull. "I didn't want you to not come."

"I'm coming," he says. "But we have a lot to talk about. And I'm sorry."

"For what."

"That the survivor you found is dead."

I open the barn. The chickens cover the walls, heads lopped off and thrashed about the room. I can see their bodies still kicking and flailing as she spun them in circles, coating the walls and ceiling in blood, a brown and red Jackson Pollock painting. James lays at my feet, just inside the door. His body has been stabbed multiple times, his tongue hangs out the side, his eyes open wide in odd animal disbelief. And then there is Sylvia, the only one of them who really stood a chance. Leila must have started with her, slitting the big cow's throat, letting her bleed out, while she unleashed her insanity on the other animals before coming for me.

"She deserved it," I say, and close the door.

SURVIVORS

27

AUGUST

The bike's brakes squeal as I slow to a stop, the rubber having worn away to metal. I've been riding the thing daily for a month now, slowly traversing New Mexico, the Texas panhandle—which still smells of cow urine—and into Oklahoma. The first two weeks were torturous, and I made very little ground. Never mind that my body ached from head to toe, and that my fitness level rivaled that of Grimace, the McDonald's mascot, the bicycle seat caused me intense pain in my backside the likes of which I'd never before experienced.

I've grown accustomed to it, though. I'm not sure if there is scar tissue, or the nerves have gone numb, but after a day's ride, I'm only mildly sore. My legs and lungs are another issue. They burn in unison, collaborating against my efforts. I've lost at least thirty pounds and am surprisingly toned, but I still struggle with hills, which have been few and far between thankfully. I take frequent breaks for food and water. Despite the relatively cool weather, I seem to seep sweat with each pedal forward.

Most nights, I've been lucky enough to find shelter. Homes. A gas station. Even a mattress store. But there were nights in New

Mexico, stuck in the endless desert, where I camped beneath the stars, protected by a small tent and wrapped in a sleeping bag that barely kept out the frigid night air. Those were the longest nights, waiting for a bright light to shine through the tent's thin gray fabric, or a coyote to tug on the zipped up entrance. But I was left alone. Aside from the pain wrought by endless travel, the continual hunt for supplies and the one time I fired the rifle, the journey has been uneventful.

That single rifle shot came two days after my encounter with the strange creature and Steve Manke. I spent an early morning hour reading the manual and loading the rifle. Its operation was fairly simple, once I figured out how to load the six bullets it can hold. Pull the lever to eject a spent round and chamber a new one, aim and shoot. I used a high-powered BB gun once, when my parents shipped a far younger me off to summer camp. I'd had to pump that thing twenty times, and when I pulled that trigger, the surprising kick sent the scope into the skin between my eyes. The crescent-shaped scar is still there. Maybe it's just because I'm bigger and stronger, but the rifle felt easier.

And louder.

That rifle's report rolled across the flat, packed desert, bounced off a distant mesa and rolled right on back past me. Anything human, animal or alien within miles could have heard it. So I haven't fired another shot. But if I have to, I'll know how, though my aim might not be the best.

While I still loathe physical activity of any kind, and have to battle against my relentless desire to stop, relax and never move again, every uncomfortable moment of this long trip has been worth it. I check in with Poe twice a day. Because of the time difference, I call her when I wake, and she calls me before bed, joking that it's time for me to tuck her in. We're slowly falling into the roles of adoptive father and daughter, despite having never met. But our conversations, long and without boundaries, have made our relationship one of the closest I've ever had. Battery life hasn't been an issue for either of us, yet. Her propane generator still churns out power, and will for as long as the propane truck she found can refill the tank. And I have a solar charger.

That said, I've encouraged her to not use the generator, or at least to use it sparingly. It's loud and could attract attention. We've argued about the safety issues...about *them*...several times, but we have different views on that subject. While I spend my nights hoping to never see them, she believes they already know exactly where she is. And it doesn't frighten her.

While I saw one of the Blur—Poe's name for them—kill a man, brutal and raw—she was saved from CL, short for 'Crazy Lady,' my term for the one-armed Leila. Whatever weapon they used to turn the human race to dust was used to kill CL, saving Poe, who was for some mysterious reason, spared.

Just like me.

We've compared stories multiple times, and the differences are stark. Steve Manke wasn't crazy, at least as far as I could tell. He was killed in a physical, personal kind of way. And the Blur I encountered smelled strongly of ammonia, where Poe's grocery store close encounter smelled of roses. But it's the similarities of our accounts that really interest us, primarily that we were spared.

Despite hours of conversation, we haven't been able to find any real commonality between us for why we would be spared and the rest of humanity destroyed. There is nothing that links us other than the fact that she lost a father and I lost a daughter. We've begun to fill those roles for each other, but there is nothing else that connects us. Not taste in music, books, movies or TV. Not geography, schooling, family trees or distant heritage.

Despite the possibility that we've been purposefully spared, I haven't even considered using another vehicle. The memory of Steve's violent death is still fresh and keeping the sandman at bay. I'm pretty sure the only reason I can sleep at all is because I'm so physically exhausted all the time. If there is even an ounce of energy left in me at the end of the day, my mind runs wild, imagining worst case scenarios. The morning after such nights, I'm tired, but I manage to pedal faster, spurred by fear.

As the bike comes to a full stop, I slide off the seat and place my feet on the ground. For the first time since I set out on the bike, the road ahead is blocked. There have been times when I've been forced off the road, walking the bike around a car accident, but this... This is an obstacle the bike won't make it past.

To my right is a large green sign reading Lake Eufaula. I've never heard of the water body, but its flat surface stretches to the north and south of my location, for as far as I can see. Three miles to the horizon, meaning this lake is, bare minimum, six miles long. I'm on a long, narrow stretch of land, cutting into the water, no doubt put here by a work crew and fleet of dump trucks. The highway behind me is dense with cars, but passable. The road ahead is a wall of twisted metal. Cars, trucks and an assortment of eighteen wheelers have crashed violently, their occupants probably turned to dust before impact. Most of the vehicles are skeletal, charred heaps, like some mythological dragon swooped overhead and laid waste to the highway.

Off the bike, I step to the side, into the grass, where I would normally circumvent such an obstacle. But that's not possible here. The swath of land on either side of the highway is just ten feet across and steeply sloped into the water. To make matters worse, a lot of the wreckage has either punched through the guardrail or rolled over it, fully blocking the way ahead. The source of the blazing fire is revealed, a ruptured gas tanker that somehow ignited and probably exploded, spewing fiery gasoline on the collection of cars.

I look at the bike. "Looks like this is where we part ways."

The front reflector stares back at me, indifferent and unresponsive.

"Yeah, I'm not really going to miss you either. You've been a literal pain in my ass." I chuckle at the horrible joke, and then a bit more at the realization that I'm talking to my bike. I'm not really sad to see it go. I don't know how to replace brake pads, so I knew I'd be getting a new bike sooner or later. But I would have preferred to not have to walk until I find a suitable replacement.

"Burnt out jungle gym or take a swim," I say, holding my thumb up to gauge the distance between me and the far side of the wreckage. I'm not the best swimmer, and the idea of finishing the day's journey sopping wet, and cold, holds no appeal. But the sharp metal and glass remains littering the road look like a death trap.

To better calculate the distance, I climb atop a nearby, not burned truck. I have a better view from here and start drawing out the math, whispering the equation to myself. With little in the way of scientific thinking, I've begun calculating everything, even when it doesn't matter. Like now, the distance doesn't really matter. My course is already set.

With an open palm, I erase the finger scrawled numbers from the imaginary white board. As I watch my open fingers slide back and forth, something strange catches my attention. At first, I think it's just the movement of my hand, creating an optical illusion. But when I lower the hand and still see the aberration far in the distance, I know it's real. But what is it?

I shrug the heavy backpack off my shoulders and suddenly feel like gravity has let go of me. The funny thing is, with the twenty-five pound pack over my shoulders, I'm still five pounds lighter than I was a month ago. The rifle balances things out, though. I lay the weapon down next to the bag and retrieve a pair of binoculars taken from Walmart, but rarely used thus far.

I find the object again, dark and shifting slightly, in the road far ahead. It's close to sliding over the horizon line. *Three miles away*, I think, and then I calculate. 15840 feet. 406 feet per minute at a quick, sustained walk. 39 minutes to get from here to there... but that's if the road were clear.

I raise the binoculars to my eyes, find the road and then scan upward to the horizon. The binoculars are powerful, but not quite strong enough for me to clearly see the object. Though I now know it's definitely moving, warbling back and forth. Or is that heat rising from the sun soaked pavement?

Then the thing pauses, and I know it's not just the rising heat. The color and size remind me of a bear, but it would have to be walking on its hind legs, and bears don't do that often. Do they? My knowledge of bears doesn't extend much beyond Yogi.

An arm reaches up and wipes across the head. In my mind's eye, I see a man, wiping sweat away from his eyes. Definitely human.

A shout bursts from my mouth. "Hey! Hey! Over here!"

I watch the figure through the binoculars. There's no change. He can't hear me. I look down at the rifle. He'd hear that...but he might not be the only one who hears it, and I don't want to risk this man sharing the same fate as Steve Manke.

I'm going to have to catch him.

Twenty-five pound backpack over my shoulders, seven pound rifle in my hands, I charge down the grassy slope and slide into the chilling waters of Lake Eufaula, never once considering that the phone might get wet, that my photo of Claire might be ruined or that I might sink like a stone.

28

AUGUST

The cold water reaches my crotch, seeps through the fabric of my worn jeans and paralyzes my body, so that all I can do is gasp and croak. "Holy...holy..." The sharp temperature shift retrieves my intellect from the emotional prison created by the discovery of another living person, just out of reach. I twist my head around and see the bottom of the backpack dipping into the water.

I step closer to land, pulling the pack out of the water. This works for the moment, but the front end of an eighteen wheeler blocks the path ahead.

Soft, lake-sodden earth wraps around my feet with each step. I think I probably should have removed my sneakers before entering the water—I'm going to get blisters once I'm free of the lake—but walking through this sludge barefoot... My body shudders at the thought, shoulders bouncing back and forth like a shimmying stripper.

I stop in front of the eighteen wheeler. The front end is submerged. The long trailer is a burned out husk of sharp metal. Holding the backpack and rifle over my head, I slip into deeper water, planning to circumvent the obstacle. The water reaches my shoulders when I've still got several feet to go, but if I take one more step, I'll be swimming. The only path left is up and over. Still holding everything over my head, I step up onto the truck's submerged rail, find my balance and then stretch my right foot up onto the wheel well. After bouncing twice, I spring up. My newly toned legs lift me up onto the water-covered hood.

The thrill of victory lasts just a moment. The heavy pack still over my head carries me forward. My feet squeak and slip out from under me.

I've heard about people getting in accidents, or being in dangerous situations and sensing time moving slowly. That's not true, obviously. Time is inexorable. But I think it's possible, in those moments of adrenaline focus, for the mind to move quicker. And for a moment, mine does. I see myself falling forward, my arms instinctively shifting down to brace the fall, bringing the pack and rifle toward the water. Without conscious thought, my mind assesses the situation and deems physical pain more advantageous than losing the contents of my backpack. My muscles move in unison, propelling me around so that I land, flat on my back atop the truck's hood, knocking the air from my lungs and sparing my gear, and the things most precious to me—the Sat phone and Claire's photo—from a watery fate.

My body on the other hand...

I lay there atop the slanted hood, in three inches of water, gasping for air, wondering if I've broken my back, if I should call Poe and tell her I'll be making the rest of the trip on my elbows, or a wheelchair if I can find one. Relief comes from the oxygen reaching my lungs and filtering out through my body. When I sit up two minutes later, I'm sore, but unscathed.

Having wasted enough time with this single obstacle, I roll to the side of the hood, lift my gear up over my head and hop down into the three foot deep water on the other side. My feet plunge through the water and continue moving through the foot of muck below. I feel the suction of it wrap around my legs. Thinking speed will set me free, I lift my right leg and feel a tug on my knee cap.

Impatience blooms like a nuclear blast. "Shit!" I shout, and then knowing no one will hear me, scream as loud as I can. "Shhhit!"

I heave the backpack and rifle to the shore and twist back and forth. When that doesn't work, I scream, "Shit!" again, and drive my elbows into the truck cab behind me. "Shit, shit, shit!"

Still clutched in a rapturous rage, I reach up, take hold of the large side mirror and yank on it. But instead of pulling it down, or reaching a stalemate, I shift upward. Clarity snaps into my mind like I've just been awakened by smelling salts. I pull harder on the mirror, wiggling my feet and sliding upward, freeing one foot and then, with a gurgling slurp, the other. I stand on the truck's rail, clinging to the mirror, and vent the last of my anger at the lake. I point toward the mud swirled water and shout, "Fuck you!"

Back on solid ground and ten minutes behind schedule, I recover my gear and jog to where the grassy slope ends and the land bridge gives way to an actual bridge, stretching over a narrow passage connecting one side of the lake to the other. It's a hundred and fifty feet across. A simple enough swim, without the backpack and rifle to keep dry. But there is no other way across.

He's getting away, I tell myself, and I step into the water, the chill of it not bothering me as much now that I know what to expect. I'm fifteen feet out when the water reaches my shoulders. If the grade on the far side is similar, I won't actually have to swim far. Gear hefted over my head, I turn around and lean back into the water and push off. With my legs dangling and the weight in my arms pushing down, I sink. When my feet touch bottom, the surface water wrapping around my elbows, I push off, bobbing up. Ancient swim lessons return and I kick like hell, pumping at the water with my legs. One of my sneakers slides off. Then the other. But I don't stop kicking, and now shoeless, do an even better job. Moving at the speed of an old dog, coughing and sputtering, I move across the water, kicking and grunting until my toes strike mud.

I put my legs under me and nearly fall. My legs have become Twizzlers, wobbling back and forth, the muscles beyond spent. I make it to shore on the far side and collapse to my knees. My sopping wet socks quickly annoy me and I peel them off, wringing them out as my energy slowly returns.

Elation that I've beaten this impassable challenge obscures the pain in my legs and draws a laugh. Without thought, I reach into the backpack, take out the phone and speed dial the only programmed number. I'm still a little giggly when Poe answers the phone.

"What's wrong?" she asks, worried. "What happened? Are you laughing? Oh my God, you scared me."

I quickly realize my mistake. Calls outside the designated times are for emergencies only. "Sorry," I say. "Sorry. I just...I swam across this lake."

"You swam across *a lake?*"

I look back at the short distance. If I explain, I'm going to seem like an idiot for calling. If I don't, I'm going to seem like an idiot for swimming across a lake. So I summarize. "A small part of it. The bridge wasn't passable."

"Still," she says. "You could have drowned. You need to—"

"I saw someone."

She's silent on the other end. Waiting.

"At least I think I did. He...or she was on the horizon, on the far side. I couldn't go around."

"Did you find them? Who is it?"

"I just crawled out of the water," I say. "I just had to tell—"

"What are you doing calling me?" she says, excited and impatient for more news than I've given her.

"My legs are Jell-O," I say.

"Man up, August!" she says, sounding almost chipper. Long quiet days with Luke have helped her heal from the dog, from Leila and everything else. She's proven to be resilient, and her good nature seems to be increasing in time with her waist size. She's showing now. Not that I've seen. These phones don't take photos. But I picture her as best I can. Poe, the pregnant. Poe, the strong. "You said you're in better shape than ever. Get a move on!"

Poe, the slave driver.

Without realizing it, I've gotten back to my feet, her words spurring me onward. "I'm going," I say, and grunt as I lift the pack and sling it over my shoulder.

"Call me when you find him...or her. No matter what time it is. You call me. But...be careful. Make sure they're not, you know—"

"Crazy Lady," I say.

"Yeah."

"I'm on it." I start up the incline and return my feet to the pavement. The warmth of it beneath my feet reminds me that I've got no shoes. *Damn.* "What about our regular check in?"

"Let's call this the check in. You find that person, August. Don't call me until you do."

"I will. Hanging up now."

"Okay."

"See ya."

"Bye."

The last exchange has become our traditional hang-up. This isn't the movies where we simply make a declarative statement and then hang up, leaving the other person to wonder if they lost a signal. We're clinging to each other with each call, neither of us really wanting to say goodbye, even now, with a potential new survivor just miles ahead of me.

The pavement is hot beneath my soles, but the sting keeps my feet moving quickly and the terrain on the side of the road, while grassy, is uneven and mired by stones, broken glass and who knows what else. I could pillage shoes from the dusty dead, trapped in their cars, but I don't want their shoes. Don't want their dead particles on my feet. I keep my pace even, walking in the shade of stopped cars whenever possible, hiding my eyes from the descending sun by donning a pair of sunglasses and lowering the bill of Claire's Red Sox cap. I walk this way for hours, scattered homes, endless foliage, and not a single living thing, other than the occasional distant bird. When night falls, I don't bother looking for shelter or setting up my tent. I keep right on moving, knowing that if I'm going to catch the stranger, it will only be when he stops.

I walk through the dark for two hours, headlamp mounted to my head, a mobile lighthouse, sweeping back and forth in search of life in the darkness. But it's not my eyes that finally detect the survivor, it's my nose.

Something is burning.

I quicken my pace, jogging up the road, my bare feet slapping and stinging. There's nothing chemical about the scent. It's wood. And when my mouth starts salivating, I realize there's another odor wafting through the night—cooking meat. My stomach rumbles, but I pay it, and the promise of a hot cooked meal with a fellow survivor, no heed.

My jog becomes a run.

I see the light ahead, off the side of the highway in a clearing by the trees. A campfire.

"Hey!" I shout. "Hey!"

"What the—holy shit!" a man says. "Who's there? Where are you?"

I see the man, bearded, but young, standing on the far side of the fire, flickering orange.

"Put it out!" I say. "Put the fire out!"

"What? Why would I—"

I leap the guard rail and charge toward the camp fire in a way that must look aggressive because the young man stumbles back, raising his hands. "Whoa, man!"

I kick dirt on the fire and when it's obvious that's not going to work, I tear my sleeping bag off the back pack, unfurl it, fold it in half and throw it atop the fire, following it with my body, smothering the flames beneath my weight. When I feel the heat reaching through the fabric, I roll away, pulling the sleeping bag back before it can catch fire, too.

When I stop and look back, the campfire is mostly out, reduced to bright orange coals. I get to my feet, hurry back and stomp on the single branch that's still burning. "Gah!" I shout, pulling back my bare, singed foot.

"What the hell, dude?"

"They're going to see it!" I say with enough urgency to get his attention.

"Who?"

"Just put it out!"

My earnest fear is enough to propel him into motion. He crushes the small flame and glowing embers beneath his booted feet until it falls dark. I switch off my head lamp and the night swallows us up. I turn my eyes to the sky, searching the stars for signs of movement.

"What are you looking for?" the man whispers.

"What's your name?" I ask.

"Mark Corotan."

"Well, Mark, I'm looking for anything strange, like a—"

"Like that?" he says.

"Where?"

"Behind you. Looks like a star, but growing."

29

AUGUST

"Run!" I shout, shoving Mark toward the nearby woods. But he resists. I might be another living human being, but I'm still a stranger, and in his experience thus far, a little bit crazy.

"Who is it?" he asks, looking at the brightening light while holding me at bay, arm raised between us. "Looks like a helicopter."

"A heli—do you *hear* any noise?" I'm still borderline freaking out, but I can't think of any other way to act with that light dropping down from the sky. "Anything at all?"

He listens for only a second, before I say, "You don't! Because it's *not* a helicopter. It's the...things that did this. That killed everyone. That turned the human race to dust."

His eyes widen, turn upward and then toward the woods.

While he's distracted, I close the distance between us and clutch his shoulders. "Please. I don't want to lose another survivor."

"There are others?" he asks.

"I know of three others," I say. "Now one. Because of them." I look back at the light. It's descending straight toward us and will arrive in seconds, which is a blessing because I know it could have dropped down in a wink. *They're looking for us*, I think.

Mark takes a step toward the woods. "My gear."

"We'll come back," I say, and drop my backpack. "We need to move, now!"

His glacial resistance cracks and falls away, setting him free to move. And he does, faster than me.

Before the light reaches us, he's in the woods, bunny hopping through the brush and making a racket. I charge after him, but lack his natural agility—not to mention shoes—and fall behind. I'm in the trees before the light drops above the camp's embers, illuminating the smoldering campsite with the brightness of the noonday sun on Mercury.

When I'm a hundred feet beyond the tree line, I slow and listen. My heart pounds despite my new level of fitness, the tempo set by fear, rather than a need for oxygen. Hearing no trace of Mark, I whisper, "Mark, where are you?"

"Over here," he replies, just twenty feet beyond me, peering out from behind a tree. Though the craft's bright light is filtered by the trees, there is still enough to see by. A sliver of bright white cuts across Mark's startled face, but slides away as he leans back to give me room behind the wide tree.

"The hell is that, dude?"

"I don't know."

"Where'd it come from?"

"Best guess," I say, and point upward, to a star-filled clearing in the foliage above.

"Seriously? Aliens?"

"That's probably the best word for them, yeah."

"So this is like, what, an invasion?"

I've considered this question many times since my first encounter. I have yet to come to any kind of conclusion, but I've ruled out invasion. "If this were an invasion, there would be more of them. I haven't seen any of them setting up shop, have you?"

He shakes his head. "Naw, dude."

"Then this is something else."

"Extermination," he says.

I don't agree out loud, but this is my leading theory as well. For some reason, the human race is being wiped out, while every other species has been left alone. After a month of travel, I've seen a large enough assortment of wildlife to know that only humanity was turned to dust. Best guess, these aliens are some kind of interstellar environmentalists. Maybe life is so rare in the universe, so precious, that after discovering Earth and finding the environment in dire threat thanks to human activity, they're exterminating the vermin, like we would termites. The theory still feels wrong—mostly because Poe and I were spared, but it's in the lead.

I peek around the tree, thinking, go *away. Just leave. We're not here.* But unless these are the stupidest extraterrestrials in the multiverse, they'll know what the still warm embers and strewn gear signify: they just missed us. That they didn't simply blink to life over our heads, tear us into the air in a beam of light and aren't tracking us from above, through the trees, means that there are limits to their technology, that they are still slaves to physics, to some extent.

We still have a chance, I think, and then I have my hopes dashed.

The light flickers for a moment, accompanied by a pulsating hum that I recognize. The last time I heard it was when the Blur fled the scene of Steve Manke's murder.

I grasp Mark's forearm. "It's coming."

"What is?"

"The Blur," I say. "One of the aliens. Maybe more."

"Shit," he whispers. "Should we split up? Leave two paths? He points southwest. "You go that way." Shifts his finger northwest. "I'll head that way. Go like a quarter mile and turn back in. Maybe we'll meet up again in the middle."

I appreciate his quick thinking effort, but I'm not sure—

Crack! A branch snaps behind us. It's like a gunshot at the start of a race. We both take off, me running in his planned path and him taking mine. Doesn't really matter I suppose, but as my legs carry me through the woods, I start to feel heavy. Emotionally more than physically, but the crushing weight saps my strength just the same. Then I realize why.

I'm never going to see him again.

Why? some part of my intellect asks. *That doesn't make sense.*

I run another fifty feet before the answer comes.

Because they're not here for me. They're here for Mark.

I stop, breathing hard, hands on knees. It's hard to hear anything over the sound of my gasping. I can feel fright creeping up on me, tingling in my fingers and toes, and I recognize it as the force that kept me from acting to save Steve Manke. I probably would have failed, maybe died, but there's also a chance the man would still be alive now if I had beaten my fear.

Without another thought, I shift the direction of my sprint, heading southeast at an angle I hope will bring me back to Mark sooner than planned.

The further I get from the craft's bright light, the harder it is to navigate the woods. It's hard to hear much beyond the sound of my own footsteps, crushing brush and snapping twigs that stab my bare feet, coupled with the heave of my panicked breathing, but there are sounds in the forest that don't belong to me. And a scent. Metallic.

Like pennies.

Like blood.

And ammonia.

They've found him already, I think. *Mark is dead.*

And then, he's not. But the pitch of his scream says he soon will be. The shout came from the northwest. I'd already crossed his path in the dark, but he's deeper in the woods. I change direction and run with abandon, risking a collision with trees and low hanging branches, knowing that if I don't, Mark will face the unknown and unseen, on his own.

I consider shouting to Mark, telling him to watch for the shimmer, but decide to not announce my approach any more than the sound of my feet are already doing.

"The hell," I hear Mark say, his voice near and terrified.

He's seen it, I think, *but doesn't know what he's seen.*

The trees clear and I see Mark ahead of me. He's on the ground, shuffling backward on his butt, looking at something I can't see, but evidently, he can. His face is twisted up in fear, the kind you might see before the downward cut of a guillotine blade. He's looking into his own certain death.

At least, that's what I think his face looks like. It's actually hard to tell. The air between us is distorted. Shifting. It's right there. I'm seeing Mark *through* it.

Making fists feels unnatural, but I manage it, first squeezing my thumbs beneath my fingers, and then moving them to the outside. It's not until I'm within striking distance that I remember I've got the rifle, its seven pound weight slapping against my back in a futile attempt to get my attention. *I'm here*, it says, *use me!* But I'm committed, angry and desperate.

I shout something like a battle cry just before the moment of impact. It's like a high-pitched roar, unnatural and frightening, to me at least. But the Blur, it just turns. I can't see its body or face, so if my dramatic arrival triggered any kind of surprise, I'll never know. The reaction I do experience not only argues the contrary, that it was *not* surprised, but also says that my arrival and attack was anticipated.

An invisible force, the same that flung me off the Blur's back a month ago, lifts me off the ground and propels me upward. My own forward momentum carries me over the creature. It has parried my attack with almost no effort. Before landing, I see the shimmer turn back toward Mark, shifting as a long, dark finger, a black icicle, rises from the light-bending cloak. *It's going to stab him*, I think, as I slam into the forest floor, strike my head and am absorbed into the emptiness of unconsciousness.

30

AUGUST

Mark's scream pulls me back from the abyss. For a moment, I think I'm still not able to see, but the prickly limbs of dry leaf litter poking my face tell me I'm lying face down. With a grunt, I roll through what feels like thick pudding, but is really just thick, humid air. Spring has come early to the South.

The sounds of struggle push adrenaline into my veins. It strengthens me and polishes my thoughts, but does nothing for the resounding pain pulsing through my head. If anything, the pain has intensified, but perhaps that's simply because I'm more aware of it. I lean up and get my elbows under me. I must have only been unconscious for seconds because the scene hasn't changed much. Mark is still on his back. The Blur looms above him. But the confrontation has evolved and nearly reached its conclusion.

The creature's dagger finger is just inches above Mark's chest. The only thing stopping it from impaling the young man are his hands, wrapped around the digit, holding it back. But not for long. His arms shake from the effort, and the sharp tip slides forward, an unavoidable fate.

Unless I can stop it.

Remembering the rifle, I slide it over my head and off my shoulder. The weapon is loaded, but I haven't chambered the first round for fear I'd accidentally shoot myself. I'm afraid the Blur will hear me and take action, but I have no choice. And it could work. It's already repulsed me once. It could still be recharging. Or maybe I just need to catch it off guard. Surely, a bullet can move faster than these things can think and trigger their defenses.

Mark screams as the fingertip pierces the skin of his chest, directly over his heart. His grip weakens for a moment, but then he grits his teeth and growls, shoving hard, pushing the tip back out. He's a fighter. I can't let this man die. I need him. The world needs him. Poe needs him.

I pull the rifle lever down and back up, sliding the first round into the chamber. I raise the weapon to my shoulder and aim toward what looks like empty space distorted by rising heat. The barrel of the weapon is all over the place, propelled by the chaotic shaking of my arms. I slip my finger around the trigger and then—

The shimmering mass spins, and a long, wooden face emerges, dead, oily eyes focused on me. I'm not sure if the sudden, fear-inspiring stare was intended to startle me into submission, but the opposite happens. With a terrified shout, I flinch back, my fingers squeezing, pulling the trigger.

The weapon kicks hard, the rifle butt slamming into my shoulder with unprepared-for force. It knocks me back and around, the rifle falling from my grip. But I'm awake now, and the pain in my head and arm are forgotten as I roll back around, grasp the rifle once more, snap the lever down and take aim, looking over the shaking sights.

But there's nothing to shoot at, aside from Mark, whose heaving chest reveals a still-living man. I climb up to my feet, disregarding a wave of dizziness, and hurry to his side.

He flinches back as I fall to my knees beside him. When I reach for his chest, he shouts and slaps at me with his hands.

"Stop it," I say. He's lost in panic, blind to who it is reaching for him. I catch his wrists and hold them still. "Stop! I just want to see how badly you're hurt."

His eyes find mine and his arms go slack, but then he's lost again—and not looking at me.

He's looking behind me.

I dive to the side and attempt to roll away, but just end up sprawling onto my gut, which has shrunken considerably over the past month. Despite my lack of grace, I avoid being struck. I can't see the attack, but I can hear the whoosh of something sailing past me, and feel the breeze it kicked up. I roll to my back, lift the rifle and somehow pull the trigger with my ring finger.

The bullet cuts through empty space and then punches through the branches above. There's nothing there. No ugly face. No concealed form. But I can hear it moving, sliding through the brush.

I crawl to Mark. We're both freaking out, there's no denying that. As much as I'm sure we would both like to handle the situation with the calm confidence of James Bond, we're more like twin rabbits trapped by a wolf. Well, if rabbits carried rifles.

"Tell me if you see it," I say.

"See it?" The quiver in Mark's voice makes him hard to understand. "I can't see anything, man."

"Just tell me if you know where it—"

"There!" he says, pointing behind me. I turn and pull the trigger. Nothing happens.

I forgot to chamber the next round.

A warbling shriek—the creature's battle cry—rips through the night, drawing shouts from me and Mark. I pull down on the lever, pointing the rifle toward the sound. The spent round pops out of the chamber, allowing the next to take its place. As the lever snaps back up, completing the half-second action, a face slides out of the gloom, focused on me. That horrible face. Its bark-like crags. Its oily, blank eyes. It scowls at me. *It loathes me*, I think.

No...its annoyed by me, but...indifferent. I am nothing in its eyes, and it is nothing in mine until it focuses its attention in my direction, which it does now with painful results.

I feel the pain before I see the attack. Agony explodes in my shoulder, and my eyes turn toward the source. The Blur's long finger has punched through the meat of my shoulder, slipping inside my body and striking bone, etching grooves.

A scream builds and then erupts from my lips.

The Blur's face remains unmoving.

"Oh my god!" Mark shouts, kicking away from the monster. "Oh my god!"

The Blur whips its head toward him. The face disappears.

What the f—

The face slams back into focus as the creature turns back to me. There's a swelling pressure inside my shoulder, and then the Blur yanks its finger out. The sudden jolt sends a spasm through my body, clutching one set of muscles after another, spreading from my torso out through my arms and down to my hands, which clench shut and pull the rifle's trigger.

The weapon fires into the Blur at point blank range. An earsplitting shriek so horrid that it brings tears to my eyes is followed by the sound of snapping limbs. For a moment, I think the thing has torn into Mark, but the crunching sound isn't bones. It's branches, and it's fading.

I hit it.

I *shot* it!

Accidentally, but still. It's something.

I roll toward Mark and grab his arm. "Are you okay?"

He's got a squirrely look in his eyes, like he's not okay, but when he turns to me, focus comes back like the shifting colors of a slowly changing mood ring. A smile emerges. "Dude, you were badass. Were you in the military or something?"

His question staggers me. I'm not sure which part of my clumsy, fear-filled, nearly botched assault fell into the badass category, but I decide not to argue. The kid has clearly not seen a single 80s action movie.

The UFO's bright light flickers in time with a loud hum, pulsing three times. In a blink, the light slips into the sky, taking its place among the stars, once again unseen in plain sight.

Feeling victorious, but beaten, I grunt as I stand and offer my hand to Mark. He takes it, and I pull him to his feet. But he doesn't let go of my hand. Instead he shakes it, thanking me and then saying, "You never told me your name."

"August," I say, and the word hits him like a sucker punch to the gut.

My hand flings free from his as he staggers back, stopping when he hits a tree. He looks winded. Wounded. There are genuine tears in his eyes. "What? August? For real?"

"Yeah," I say, unsure on how to elaborate on my name. His reaction reminds me of Steve Manke, who had a similar reaction to my name before dying.

But Mark isn't about to die. Far from it. Instead, he shoves off the tree and wraps his arm around me, weeping into my shoulder. Confused, I return the hug the way unclose relatives might, with a gentle pat and a sidelong glance that says, 'Are you really hugging me?'

"I thought they were crazy, man," he says. "I...it just didn't make any sense." He leans back. Looks me in the eyes. "But they weren't crazy, were they? They knew."

"Knew...what?"

"How to survive it." He lets go of me, hands on his head, and he starts pacing. "And man, holy shit, they knew about you."

"Me?"

"Yeah, dude." He stops pacing. "It was their final words. Well, not really their final words. They told me they loved me. But they left this." He digs inside his pocket and pulls out a long, yellow legal sized sheet of lined paper. He unfolds it with shaking hands and turns it around. There are two words written in bold marker, and they stagger me.

I take the page from him and read the two words again, hoping that they'll change, because it means that all of this is happening for a reason beyond our control. But the words haven't changed. I read them aloud.

"Find August."

"I found you man, I can't believe it, but I found you!"

"Yeah, you did," I say, despite the fact that *I* found *him*. "The question is, why?"

31

AUGUST

"What's his name? How did he survive? Where's he from? Did he get hurt?"

Poe's questions rattle against my eardrum faster than I could possibly reply. After telling her that I'd found the mystery survivor and confronted another Blur, she launched into the questions, most of which I can't remember. I cut in with, "I'm fine, thanks for asking." And that's not even the truth. The hole in my shoulder, which stopped bleeding strangely fast on its own, hurts like...well, it hurts like a hole in my shoulder.

"Sorry," she says. "I'm just excited."

"Me, too," I say, glancing at Mark, who is fast asleep, wrapped in a sleeping bag, head on his backpack. He's lit by the dull green glow of the sat phone's display. After recovering our gear, we returned to the cover of the woods, hiking a few miles east before settling down for the night.

"What's that sound?" she asks.

"Mark," I say. "That's his name, and he snores. Loudly." Mark's night-song isn't a solo, though. Scores of chirping insects and peeper frogs join in, making the night louder than the day. "He's fine. A bit freaked out, but fine."

"How did he survive?" she asks.

That's the second time she's asked that question, and she's trying to sound casual about it. During all the time we've talked, that's one story she hasn't told me. She knows all about how I survived, hidden below ground in a dark matter laboratory. But when I've asked her, she's deflected or claimed ignorance. Not wanting to make her uncomfortable, I haven't pushed. Partly because I don't care how she survived. I'm just happy she did.

However, her interest in Mark's survival story piques my interest anew.

When I don't answer right away, she says, "Did he tell you?"

During our hike through the dark, after explaining everything I knew about the Blur and Poe, Mark and I traded survival stories. How could we not? His ends with a note that reads, 'Find August.' Rather than tell her straight out, I fish for information, using Mark's story as bait. "Poe...did your parents know what was going to happen?"

I hear a quick intake of air on the other end, but she says nothing.

"Did they put you in something? Some kind of device?"

"Is that what happened to Mark?" she asks.

"His parents were a little off. UFO abductees. Drew schematics for strange devices on the walls. Stuff like that. They called him over in a panic and drugged him. He woke up in what he called an upright, padded coffin with a vent. It opened with a timed padlock. Sound familiar?"

She doesn't reply, but I can hear her crying.

"Poe." My voice is gentle, like I used to talk to Claire when she got hurt. "Is this what happened to you? To your parents?"

"Yes."

"Did they ever talk about being abducted by aliens?" The question sounds so ridiculous it makes me cringe, but here we are, fighting strange translucent beings at the end of the world—well, the human race at least. I think the rest of the world is going to be just fine. I wonder if apes will evolve to take our place. Or maybe dolphins.

"Yeah," she says, but she doesn't elaborate. "But I'm kind of relieved to know I'm not the only one. But what does that mean?"

"It means there's a plan."

"Whose?"

"I don't know. Poe?"

"Yeah?"

"Does my name mean anything to you? I mean, before we found each other?"

"Nothing more than the second most miserable month in the Northeast, after February. Why?"

"Did your parents leave you a message? Two words?"

She falls quiet again. I take that as a 'yes.' "What did it say?"

"It was inside the pod—that's what they called it—"

"The pod," I say. "Kind of like a human sized refrigerator?"

"Have you seen one?" she asks.

"Mark described it. Now, what was the message?"

"Two words. 'Stay home.' Did Mark get a message?"

"Yeah," I say, not really wanting to talk about it. The implications are disconcerting.

"*Well?*" Poe, I've learned, isn't the most patient person on the planet. Out of the three of us, she's definitely got the shortest fuse.

"Mark's note said, 'Find August.'"

"Geez."

"Yeah," I say, "and here's the kicker. I'm pretty sure that Steve Manke got the same message from whoever saved him. His last words were 'Find August. I found you.'"

"What does it mean?" she asks.

"Are we straight shooting tonight?" That she kept these kinds of details from me is frustrating. I can understand how she'd be worried about my impression of her. But we've built a familial trust, and after our first encounters with the otherworldly, she should have told me about her parents. "No more secrets? No more holding back details?"

"Okay."

"It means we're pawns. Someone—or the Blur—knew what was coming. They positioned us, or at least waited until we were in position, and then pulled the trigger, setting us down a path they are either directing without our knowledge or accurately predicted to some degree."

"But they're not in control of everything," she says. "Steve died."

"Not until he found me, like he was told to do. Our meeting and his death might all be manipulations designed to keep us on task. To move us in certain directions."

"Free will is an illusion," she says. "My father used to say that. About marketing. About laws. Religion. That our fates are predetermined by the world around us, that the external forces in the world are too great to surmount. I never thought he believed it. He was waxing eloquent. Trying to impress my mother. But maybe he was right? Maybe it wasn't a theory. Maybe he *knew*."

I wish this sounded like conspiracy. That I could dismiss it all with a wave of my hand, the way I might an errant radio signal from space. But the conspiracy theorists, crackpot abductees and UFO nuts were right. They didn't all see this coming, that's for sure. There would be more survivors if they had. But we're not alone in the universe. People have been abducted and the aliens are decidedly not friendly.

"What do we do?" she asks. "I don't know about you, but I've never been good at being told what to do. I don't want my life to be controlled."

Neither do I. Free will is a deeply ingrained human desire going back to the time when humans didn't have written languages. Agreeing to a plan is one thing. But manipulating people...only dictators and guilt tripping mothers can get away with it, and no one likes them for it. But there's a problem with not toeing the line this time.

"Not playing along means not coming to you," I point out.

Silence follows the revelation. Like me, she's torn between the despicable—being controlled—and the unthinkable. Remaining alone.

"I don't know about you," I say, "but I think I'd rather be a slave with company than a free man who dies alone. And I'm an introvert."

"If you reach me."

"What do you mean?"

"If Steve's role was always to die, we don't know what our roles really are. Maybe you'll never make it here."

"I will," I say with more confidence than I feel. "They're not infallible. They're not perfect. The Blur tonight, it was trying to kill Mark, and I don't think it had any intention of taking a bullet. Whatever their plan is, we can fight it, and them, and still find each other."

"Wow," she says with a laugh. "You're starting to sound..."

"What?" I ask, expecting one of Poe's humorous comparisons. Instead, she gets serious. "Strong. Capable."

My instinct is to joke at the compliments, but she's right. I'm not the man I used to be.

"You're going to make it, aren't you?"

It's not really a question, but I say, "Yes."

"I think that—oh!" She sounds surprised by something, and I'm about to ask what happened. If she's okay. But she beats me to it. "Squirt is kicking. I should probably go. I think I need to eat something. Time for breakfast. Just...don't stop, okay? I need you to get here. In one piece preferably."

"On my way," I say. "Hanging up now."

"Okay."

"See ya."

"Bye."

"That Poe?" Mark asks.

I've become so accustomed to having no one around that the question sounds like a thunderclap, and it nearly sends me sprawling to the ground. Mark laughs at my dramatic reaction. "Whoa, man. Chill."

"I'm chilling," I say. Mark is from Southern California. A real surfer dude type. At least in the way he talks. The stereotype ends there. When not surfing, he was a senior at Cal-Tech. An engineer. Would have had a good life, and given his good looks—tan skin and dark hair from his Hawaiian mother and bright blue eyes from a German father—there probably wouldn't be a woman out of his league. He also happens to be a relaxed, and kind, guy.

He stretches and yawns, and I realize I can see him clearly even with the phone off. I look to the East and find a purple sky. The sun is rising. Poe and I talked through what was left of the night.

"Said you wanted to get an early start, right?" Mark claps his knees and stands from his seated position without using his hands. He drops down into a stretch and flashes me a smile. "I'm good to go when you are."

I mentally explore my body. Aching from the long walk, swim and battle. My shoulder throbs with every movement. My feet...are bare. And I feel like I could pass out. "I hate you," I say with just enough smile to let him know I'm joking. Well, half joking. "First, breakfast. Then we need to find me boots and caffeine. And bikes for both of us."

He helps me up and looks worried when I grunt. Without asking permission, he tugs open the hole in my shirt. "Better add antibiotics to your list. This doesn't look so hot."

I pull my collar aside and look at the wound. It's swollen and deep purple in the center and still not bleeding, which is a bonus, but there is a centimeter-thick ring of black skin a half inch away from the wound's center, creating a bullseye.

"Looks like Lyme disease rash," Mark says.

"I'm pretty sure Lyme is transmitted by ticks," I say. "Not aliens."

"Yeah, dude," Mark says, "but I'm pretty sure that should scare you shitless. Cause if it's not Lyme, what is it?"

32

POE

Six weeks have passed since Leila slaughtered the animals and tried to kill me. I have rarely ventured out, except the one time. I thought I might be able to salvage some of the chickens, put them in the freezer, but I didn't have the stomach for it. I've avoided the barn, and the gore frozen inside it, since. It will be thawing soon, I think. Nights still bring the sharp bite of winter, but the days are warming into the mid-forties. A few more weeks and the temperature will rise into the sixties. When that happens... *I'm going to have to burn that barn down*, I think, but I have no idea how to do that without setting the forest ablaze. If I don't, the smell will draw carrion animals—racoons, turkey vultures, coyotes—to my door. Not the best environment in which to have a baby. I'm going to have to deal with it soon, before my rounding belly gets too big. And it's not just the animals. I still have the bags containing my parents' remains and Leila's, in a separate bag. I've always loved spring, with its delicious promises, but this time, I wish to remain in stasis. Forever winter. Squirt could just live inside me forever and I'd never have to bury my parents.

I decided to relinquish any blame, to just forgive Leila, my only human, physical companion for months now. I never found out her story, but I'm choosing to believe that before the event, she was happy. A lovely person to be around, with friends and family, a life equal to or greater than my own. A life anyone would envy, full of joy and compassion, lacking in psychosis. It's how I avoid feeling like *I'm* the crazy one. Whatever happened to her could have happened to me, but I was inexplicably hidden inside that tomb in the basement, riding out the storm, limbs intact with the rest of me.

But then there's August. In my mind, his name is spelled in all capital letters, written like a five year old's early script—that potent, careful and important. A significant mark, the crayon pressure squeaking along the paper. When a child first writes her name, with all the letters included, it personifies an important step in identity. She exists, and can write to tell about it. August maintains my existence. He preserves my identity. I have used all the crayons in my mental box to write his name across my brain.

The phone in my hand, this remnant of human ingenuity, feels heavy. The weight comes from its importance rather than its mass. It connects me to sanity, to August, who is once again, trying to talk logic and sense at me with mixed results.

"Just because you're all Ramboed out, doesn't mean I am," I say. "I feel like an out-of-shape potato. A misshapen potato, like one you'd find hidden at the bottom of the pantry. Wrinkled and old and neglected. And pregnant and alone and stuff."

"I think you're mixing your metaphors, now."

"What do you know, scientist? Go equate something."

I can tell he's laughing, because he's not making any noise. He's one of those silent laughers. I enjoy making him do this. It's usually followed by a sigh.

He sighs. "Well, how are you feeling? You mentioned feeling anemic. Do you think you need more iron?"

At times like this I realize I've forgotten whole aspects of his life— that he is old enough to be my father, that he lost a daughter only a few years younger than me, that he had a wife, with womanly issues. He can relate. I'm not used to this. My father was hands off when it came to feminine issues, including my birth. He waited in the lobby, reading Robert Frost. So when August, the astrophysicist, who has turned out to be more sensitive than my poet father, talks about birth and pregnancy and supplements, he's filling my mother's shoes.

"Probably," I say. "I don't know. It's just that I'm nearing the end of frozen meat, so I haven't been eating as much."

"And the canned meat still—"

"There's not much of that, either, but yeah, Squirt seems to disapprove of canned meats. Makes me hurl. Like vigorously hurl."

"And the grocery store is off limits, anyway."

I nod even though he can't see me. There's no way I'm going back there, and just about the only food still good will be the canned variety, which will do more harm than good.

"So you're going hunting, which makes sense. Both of us are going to have to learn to—"

"*Both* of us?" I ask. "What about Mark?"

"He seems to be a natural. Catches fish and rabbits like he was born to."

Mark is fun to talk to. His California accent and relaxed personality put me at ease, and he often gets me laughing. But I lack the connection with him that I have with August, and if I'm honest, I'm a little jealous of him. I can't wait to meet him, but August is the glue holding the fissure in my head closed. He's the one I *need* to get here.

August clears his throat the way he does before asking a question he fears will insult my intelligence, which is more often than I'd like to admit. My feelings of incapability make me defensive. "Do you know what to do with the animal, you know, once you've gotten it?"

"Oh, please. I'm from New Hampshire," I say, and I realize that might be too general an explanation. Not everyone in New Hampshire hunts. "My dad used to take me hunting. It was how he harnessed his inner Hemingway."

We're both quiet for a minute. This is how we talk, and we're both comfortable with the silences. We retreat into our brains for a bit, processing.

I break the silence first. "August?"

"Yeah."

"I'm scared." I hate admitting it, but he can't help me if I'm not honest.

"You're going to be fine. You haven't seen anyone else in a long time. And *they* have left you, and us, alone. Mark thinks they've gone."

He thinks that I mean I'm scared to leave the house, scared to go in the woods. It's where Leila had lurked for a while, before I ignored all my evolutionary instincts and allowed her into my home.

"No," I say. "It's not that. I'm scared...about giving birth. I start to think about it, and then I hyperventilate and have to lie down." He's quiet, just listening to me. He won't respond before he's ready to.

"I think that I can handle the intensity and the pain. Or maybe I can't. Ugh...I don't know. I just...what if I have to do it alone? You're not exactly speeding across the county. I'm going to have to do it alone." My voice in the living room feels large, animated, the words drawn in fat, cartoonish bubble letters, floating just below the ceiling. I lay down on the couch, my hand propped behind my head.

"We're making good time. And no matter what happens, you can handle it. I have no doubt about that." He says this with such tenderness, his voice quiet, almost a question. I like that he doesn't bullshit me and promise to be here. We have both seen too much at this point to not be honest, or realistic.

"Maybe," I say, which feels like the second prayer of my life.

"I was my wife's birth coach, you know. Before it was hip. I even cut the cord."

I laugh. "Really? Did you pass out?"

He's silent, the laughing again. "Only once. Listen, Mark is back and we're wasting daylight. I should go now, Poe. My girl needs me to keep moving."

I grin. His girl. Aside from my parents, why have I never allowed this vulnerability in my life before? I always discover things too late, a perpetual late bloomer. I'm the last to jump on any bandwagon, even when the trend is deeply and naturally human, like opening the door to devotion, or relaxing in tenderness. I could observe these positive conditions in others, could assign them value in my paintings, but kept them at arm's length for myself. Until now, with no one left on the planet. Figures.

"Hanging up now," he says.

"Okay."

"See ya."

"Bye."

Feeling bolstered, but more alone, I stand from the living room couch and shed the afghan. Luke looks up from his sprawl on the rug.

"Are you a good hunter, Lukey?" He thumps his tail on the carpet, still on his side. "Yeah, right, lazy boy. You would just run up and kiss the deer, huh?" I lean down and nuzzle him. He cranes his neck to reach my chin with his tongue, then jumps up to join me as I get dressed to find the rifle—in the barn.

It's warmer outside than I thought. Mid-fifties at least. Luke and I stand outside the closed barn door, staring at the handle. The gun is stored in a locked case in the hayloft, up a ladder. I think my dad should have stored it inside the house, I think that's a law or something. But, you know, it's New Hampshire, and our state motto is Live Free or Die. The older dudes take that freedom of expression and action to heart, and pretty much do whatever the hell they want, within reason. I once saw a neighbor across the street from my apartment building, an old Yankee with a long white beard, hurl a snow shovel at a passing car he thought was going too fast. And then he got on his motorcycle and went after him. Pretty typical stuff.

I can smell the dead. Inside. The rot is potent, even through the solidly built walls. *All you have to do is run past them and up the ladder, Poe. Just run as fast as your little pregnant legs can carry you. You can deal with them later. It's okay. The dead can wait.*

I glance down at Luke. He's watching the door with the same intensity I am. He doesn't know what's in there, not really. But his nose is twitching, taking in scents that he doesn't have any memory of, but are no doubt triggering some ancient instincts not yet fully bred out of canines. He cocks his head to the side, like he can hear something. Cocks it further. I listen, but hear nothing. *Rats,* I think. They're already here. But they won't bother with me. Short of an animal with rabies, anything that's found its way inside will run from Luke and me.

I put my hand on the painted red door. The wood is warm from the sun. With my other hand, I lift the black metal latch. I take a slow, deep breath, hold it and yank the door open.

The buzzing that explodes outward makes me think that the creatures are back, that they've finally come to take me, and I scream. But the scream is cut short when something light and crispy shoots into my mouth. I cough and spit, eyes closed as a flurry of gentle taps bounce over me. I squint my eyes open and see what's happening. Flies. Thousands of them. Nature is already taking care of the dead, and I realize that the best way to take care of this problem is to leave the doors wide open. Let the carrion do the job for me. In a few weeks, all I'll have to clean is bones.

As the cloud of manic black specks filters out and spreads over the yard, I step inside the barn. Sylvia's hulking carcass still oddly resembles her, the sweet cow she once was. Her baby, right by the door, mangled, rotting, looks like an alien mash of meat and bones, still living with globs of wriggling fly larva . I breathe through my mouth buried in the crook of my arm, afraid I might be able to taste the rank. The bodies get a wide berth as I skitter through the dirt and hay, to the ladder. My lips sealed tight, breath held, I scale the rungs up to the loft. At the top, I breathe hard, once more through the crook of my arm.

My father hid the gun case in the corner, behind a stack of hay bales. I drag it out, take the key from my pocket and shaking, I try it in the keyhole at the front of the large rifle case. My hands are fumbly, incompetent. I imagine Leila climbing the ladder behind me...can I hear footsteps? I drop the key. It strikes the slatted wooden floor, bounces and slides into the crack between boards. I gasp and reach, but I'm too late. I hear it clink on the concrete slab below, in one of the stalls where my dad used to keep gardening equipment. *I can't do it. I can't go back down there long enough to find it.*

I sit down in the hay for a minute, slowing my breathing.

Do I really need meat?

There are plenty of vegetarians and vegans who have perfectly healthy pregnancies. They also have access to fresh food and beans and any ingredients they want to combine together to form amino acids and whatever. I feel dizzy, and a wave of nausea.

I kind of lied to August. My dad took me hunting once, and I just watched. I didn't have the heart to pull the trigger. I also watched him take care of the deer afterward, so I think I can manage that, too. Maybe.

I need to get the key. Spring is here. The deer will be hungry and plentiful, especially with no other hunters for possibly miles, or forever. *We can do this, Squirt. Harness your inner Hemingway.*

I stand up, stick my chest and round belly out, and blunder down the ladder, around the dead animals, to the back of the barn, where the key rests. I know where it fell, because I heard it. After a few minutes of looking, I see its glint. And next to it, recognizable boxes. Rabbit traps!

A plan forms.

The smell and dead around me are momentarily forgotten. I retrieve the key, and then the old hunting rifle—a long black affair with a large scope mounted on top—along with a box of .308 ammunition. But it's the traps that give me hope. Even if I fail to shoot a deer, the stationary traps, with their wily ways, will snag a meal. Rifle over my shoulder, I drag the traps out of the barn and leave the door open. *Have at it,* I think to the scavengers. *Just leave the rabbits for me.*

My plan is simple. Step one, set the traps. Step two, my baby and I are going hunting.

33

POE

I stand at the precipice, before the woods where wild animals lurk, hunting and hunted. I feel like taking the next step will be like stepping back in time, to when distant hunter-gatherer ancestors eked out a life. That's who we will become. All the still-working technology around us will rot and fade. Fuel will run out. Parts will wear down. The fireplace has an unending source of fuel, if you can cut it and dry it, but food will become scarce in the great cold North. August once suggested we head south, where food can be grown year round. I balked at the idea, but not for any sensible reason. I just didn't want to leave this house...and my parents behind. But he's right. Canned food might sustain us for another winter, but we'll have to head south...and probably should after Squirt is born.

So this is it, my baptism into primal living. I snap my fingers at Luke, not wanting to make the transition on my own. He barrels into the woods, bounding through the melting, slushy leaves, full of joy and vigor, before plunging into a muddy puddle formed by the house's perimeter drain.

"You're not very sneaky," I say, and I whistle him over, giving him a few brisk pats before taking hold of his collar and leading him back to the house. I open the kitchen door, and he understands what I want. He goes in, tail and head down.

I lean into his big soft head, speaking into his ear. "I know, Luke. I'll be back soon. You guard the manor." I hesitate, remembering what happened the last time I left him alone. I returned to him frolicking in the front yard with Leila. *Nothing is going to happen. He's safe.*

Besides, I'm doing this for him, too. While I might be able to subsist on vegetables, he needs to eat meat, and his carnivorous ways have sent us plowing through most of the canned goods in the house. I have no typical dog food, and since the smell of canned meat makes me vomit, the chicken, tuna and soups have all gone to the dog.

I know there is always another option, the last resort known as the grocery store. Right now, that place frightens me too much. But I know that if I can't catch my food, I'm going to have to risk that trip again.

I return to the woods, alone now, and pick up the rabbit trap, which is designed to not hurt the rabbits when they are caught. I have mixed feelings about this, because I will have to kill the rabbit myself if we want to eat it. Rifle slung over my thin shoulder, I think, *Annie Oakley.* She is the only riflewoman I know of. Then, *Laura Ingalls Wilder,* who may or may not have ever shot a gun. I am trying to step into a role, give myself a little boost. *Ellen Ripley,* I think with a grin. Given the otherworldly nature of what happened to the world, and August's violent encounters, the alien-hunting Ripley is probably the most appropriate role model. If only she were real. I step forward, crossing the precipice, and stop. "Shit." I have no bait for the trap. I'm wasting too much time.

I'm out of fresh vegetables, and there won't be anything but sludge left in the grocery store, if that was an option yet. I've been eating my parents' canned and frozen vegetables, carefully harvested and squirreled away peas or rhubarb, the tanginess of which I've been craving. I head inside once more, resting the rifle on the kitchen table, and avoiding Luke's love. I go down into the basement and search through the icy chunks near the bottom of the big freezer. There isn't much food left. Miraculously, I find a bag of frozen, chopped carrots from my mother's garden. I chip away at the ice with the dust pan handle with which I attempted to sweep up my parents. The carrots are freezer burned but still smell strongly. *They'll work.*

Back in the kitchen, I douse the carrots in apple cider vinegar, something I remember my mother doing. When I catch a whiff of the stuff, I think it's to help the rabbits smell and find the bait.

I step into the woods again, *third time's a charm*, no looking back. My boots suck at the wet, slushy leaves, the bare earth now a sloppy mix. The snow left in the forest is patchy, but the smooth surface still tells a story. I see lots of tiny tracks, mice and squirrels, some deer prints—which is promising—and then the distinctive hopping track of a rabbit. I follow the tracks deeper into the woods.

It's so quiet out here, as always, but as my body reacts with the usual convention to a serene place—slowed pulse, deeper belly breathing, relaxed facial muscles—despondency encases me. I no longer need this escape, and I loathe the quiet. The emptiness and aloneness. I grieve for so much more than I first thought. The loss of tiny habits, frequent activities, comfortable needs and predictable emotions that defined my puny life. I haven't painted, drawn or even doodled since the end began. This brink scares me, the edge indefinable. A few more steps straight ahead and I could surrender, fall off some mental cliff, limbs limp. I want my old desires back. I'd even take my old neuroses.

Maybe even Todd.

Ten minutes in, I spot some scat on the snow, deer prints leading away from it, into thicker forest. I lay down the trap and crouch beside the mount. When I hunted with my father, we came across a similar pile and he picked it up like it was the most normal thing in the world. Told me the deer was close, because its scat was still warm. Luckily, I don't need to pick it up. Coils of rising steam tell me it's fresh. Very fresh.

As quietly as possible, I set the rabbit trap by a tree, placing the apple cider doused carrots inside. Then, rifle in hand, I head out, deeper into the woods, feeling adventurous, but also extremely pregnant. How long does it usually take a hunter to find and kill a deer? My energy is waning already. *How am I going to pull a dead deer back home?* My stomach rumbles. *In pieces if I have to.*

A light rain starts up, so I pull my hood over my hair and go slowly, enjoying the water pattering on the melting snow. Soon there will be torrents, rivers through our forest, streams burbling over with spring thaw. They've probably already started.

I allow my mind to daydream about beginning another art piece, a painting of water, with a figure reaching up from the current, arms extending. I did something purposeful today; I set a trap. I'm hunting. Maybe it's time to create.

My thoughts are on an embryonic painting idea when I hear a rustling in the woods. And then, a snapping of twigs and more rustling. Anxiety sears through my blood, *Leila, the shimmer from the store, another human.* I've got the rifle scope raised to my right shoulder before I even think to do it. I scan the woods with the scope, everything magnified.

A grayish-brown texture fills the scope's sight. Sixty feet away from me, on the path, stands an enormous white-tail buck, his backside to me. You've got to be kidding me. He's so beautiful, probably weighing at least two hundred pounds, his legs long against the white slush, the slope of his strong back big enough to ride on. He yanks and nibbles on something in the brush.

I focus on the animal, trying to place the crosshairs just above his legs. That's where the heart is, I think. I don't want to have to shoot him twice. He stops eating and stands erect, antlers high. Goodness, he's huge. New Hampshire Fish and Game suggest we have more than eighty thousand deer living here. Philosophy conundrums whirl through my brain. *Not now,* I think. Whose life is more meaningful, this large, beautiful buck's, or mine, Squirt and Luke's? It's so much easier to just eat the meat, rather than have to kill it. As usual, indecision will be my downfall. The buck takes a few steps. I hear my father's voice in my head, *press, don't pull the trigger. Be surprised by the gun going off, don't anticipate it.* I aim again.

My finger slides over the trigger. A moment of panic sets in when I think I haven't loaded the weapon, but I replay sliding the cartridge in and shoving the bolt forward. It's in there. Just don't miss. I breathe out and pull.

The shot goes wild as I shout in surprise and cover my ears. But it's not the cough of the rifle or its kick that has surprised me, it's the indistinct, deafening twang that is suddenly everywhere, an explosion of sound, like the breaking of one, loose guitar string. The deer darts away. *I should, too*, I think, but I have no idea which direction the sound is coming from.

Quiet returns as cold seeps into my backside. I've fallen backward into the gray slush. I stand up, lean the rifle against a tree and brush off the icy chunks clinging to my pants. I'm wet through and the gray sky unleashes a fresh surge of rain. *Was that thunder?*

I search the gray sky for flashes, but see nothing.

It was *them*. What else could have made that noise?

Fear rolls up my back to my neck. I need to get out of these woods.

As I pick up the rifle, the noise blasts again, so sudden I cry out and bend at the waist, one hand over my head, one across my belly. When the wail keeps going, the guitar string not breaking, not giving in, louder, longer, I run.

34

POE

Slushy mud clings to my boots, making them slick, adding to the chaos of my flight. Before getting pregnant, I ran marathons, and had planned on continuing to do so, one of those crazy women who keep running right through the ninth month. But now, what the hell was I thinking? Was my life so bland that I had to create painful experiences for myself? Pregnant running. So stupid. The bottom of my extended belly aches with each bounce of my body, the muscles stretching with Squirt's growing heaviness. I have to pee, and it might happen without my consent.

I'm running and tripping through the woods, confused and desperate and surrounded by horrible sounds, when I come across a slush and mud covered trail I know leads back to the house. The twanging resonance ceases, and I stop running, catching my pregnant breath for a second. *The hell was that sound?* You would think that the amount of weirdness I've experienced already might have prepared me for more, or made me immune to it, but that's not at all what happens. Mental numbness enters my brain, my body physically cold, rain dripping off the tip of my nose and running down my back. My hood fell back. Too late now. The cold will keep me sharp.

I start walking toward home, and then stop when I hear a metallic twang, distant this time. Maybe it is lightning? Maybe they did something to the air? Ellen Ripley returns to my mind. What do science fiction movies call it? Terraforming? Could they be changing the atmosphere to suit them? A soft hissing, like something hurtling through the air, follows the distant sound, growing louder. A red-tailed hawk screeches out of a pine tree above me, making me jump. The hissing increases, urgent. I scan the sky through the cross hatched lines of countless pine needles.

Lights flash in the clouds beyond. Silent. The gods awakening.

And then, waging war.

The voice of battle—what else could the electric explosions and bright lights above be—descends over the woods, sound chasing light. Stupefaction roots me to the spot. The hissing returns, from several different directions, a patchwork of layers intersecting. Fifty feet away, a projectile, trailing smoke, plows into the forest, chopping through branches before colliding with one of the tallest pines in the area, severing the top of the tree and sending splinters in every direction. Branches tumble and crash through the trees. The sharp crack of wood breaking startles me into movement, and I bolt.

I'm off the path, away from the falling tree. Roots still buried under the snow catch my boots and I stumble, off balance, and land on my hands and knees with a splash. I glance down. My belly hovers above the earth, untouched.

I squint through the downpour. A surprising mammalian instinct circulates through me. I am an animal. I protect my young and run from danger. The simplicity of this shift hyperfocuses my senses, bringing all things clearer. On my knees in the slush, I see the miniscule details—the small pock marks made by each raindrop, the contrast of green pine needles against white snow and the blink of my own dripping eyelashes.

All around, debris zips through the woods, hitting trees and ground. With a loud chop, like the sound of an axe blade sinking into wood, a bit of black, the size of a golf ball, embeds itself in a nearby pine's thick bark. That could have been me. The sounds grow sharper as I focus on them. This shit is coming down everywhere.

And then, I move.

I run, Squirt clutched in one arm.

Rain and energy spill over me. Branches creak through the forest, wind through leafless winter limbs. I stop, gasping for air, eyes darting. Which way? *Which way?*

Bright light flashes through the forest. It's followed quickly by a strange twanging explosion and the thunderous clap that rattles the ground beneath my feet. An unnatural blast of air, hot and sudden, bends the rain-pelted saplings around me. Another explosion, further away, sends more branches plummeting to the ground with a thunder-clap. And then another, closer this time. I smell smoke.

The forest is burning. Even with the rain.

The explosions burst quicker and lighter now, one on top of the other, firecrackers at a parade, and I plummet through the pouring rain deeper into the woods. Pine branches rake across my cheeks as I fight through the trees and undergrowth, pummeled by this battle, this attack, this fight.

Am I a part of this? Or just a casualty of it? It feels like the very forest is resisting my flight. Holding me back.

I pause in a clearing, out of breath, and try to get my bearings. The rain and the explosions slow like they're on cue, in syncopation with me. Smoke drifts through the air, and I can hear the crackle of nearby fire. My nose stings and my lungs burn from breathing smoky air.

A loud creaking to my right signals a tree about to fall. I can see it, a middle-aged pine, descending with more grace than I would have imagined possible. It snaps the branches of other trees as it goes, and lands with a squishy thud on the melting, muddy ground.

That final thud marks the end of the chaos. The rain falls, undaunted.

I wrap my arms around a sugar maple and place my cheek against its bark. I'm still alive, I think, and I note that I'm slightly disappointed by the realization. A part of me would like for this solitude, this nonsense, this terrible work, both boring and exhausting, to reach a limit. Apathy cycles through me. And then, after a time, when my breathing is normal, I feel my mind's emotional fracture present once more. Alive, but broken. It would be so simple to take the three necessary steps forward to plunge, free-fall, into despair. I think it would feel cool there, a soothing darkness, like a dry cave meant for long hibernation. These thoughts feel more real, and normal, than what I just experienced.

But then I feel a kick from inside, a reminder. She's wary, and reminds me that we both need to keep an eye out for danger, the interior peril. *I'm watching you,* Squirt says, and I imagine her doing that two-finger eye point thing, her miniscule fingers extended, crucial levity that obligates my retreat from the edge. If things are funny, I can endure.

A small crackling draws me away from the maple and my introspection—a low, quiet fire, almost sweet, soon to be extinguished by the rain and general sloppiness of the spring thaw, creeps bright against the gray snow and leafless scrubby twigs of the forest floor. Saplings are burning. I watch it, loving its aliveness; it's an indication of oxygen and normalcy, the planet still functioning, physics still somewhat intact. The flames smell wonderful.

A distant pop resonates through the woods, loud, and then a buzz, like when a transformer blows during a heavy storm in a suburban neighborhood, everyone wondering what that sound was, followed by a flash of light in the sky. Whole, not linear like lightning, but a sheet, a blast, covering the air above the trees. I've never seen anything like it.

Milliseconds later, a huge crash, shaving the forest. The snapping is so loud I know it's trees breaking, not branches. A pressure wave follows, knocking me back and bending the tall trees above, their great bodies leaning away, trying to flee. The ground ripples like water, chasing this pressure wave, knocking me off my feet again, back down into the slush.

Then, quiet. Again.

The drizzle dwindles to a mist. The freezing wet has reached my underwear, and I just let it, imagining myself as part of the ground. I could spread out, my cells mixing with all this slush and mud, a painless surrender.

Squirt, as usual, literally kicks my butt into gear, her squirms switching my brain back on, reminding me of my responsibility. For the first time, the word *mother* materializes.

I wait in the silent trees, and then curiosity gets the best of me. This most recent phenomenon, while loud, startling, and potentially life threatening, still feels less scary than everything else that I've experienced lately. Explosions and lights in the sky seem benign, almost commonplace compared to people turned to powder in seconds. I need to see what that was. It could be important. Could provide answers to any of a million different questions.

It's worth the risk.

Inside my thoughts, sloshing through the woods, I can almost see the house's windows through the tunnel of trees. As I walk, the slush and mud give way to surprising dryness, like autumn ground, crisp leaves under my boots.

A few more feet ahead, the trees are blackened, parched. The woods in this space seem dehydrated. I look down—the forest floor resembles a dry lake bed in Africa, undulating cracks in the packed dirt, all the snow and slush gone. Ahead of me, in a shallow crater, surrounded by toasted, broken trees, is the thing that crashed.

35

POE

My first thought is *UFO*, but I discount that with practiced efficiency. And then, with widening eyes, I reconsider the notion. My parents knew this would happen. They built a pod that protected me, that neither of them should have known how to build. What I always thought made my parents crazy and embarrassing was real. *It was all real.* The lights in the sky. The flashes of memories, of abductions, of operations, of dead-eyed captors.

I hesitate, crouching behind a parched tree, alternating between telling myself that's ridiculous and being convinced that what I'm seeing is real. I briefly wonder what a famous explorer would do in this situation. The only female adventurer I can conjure is Amelia Earhart, and look how things turned out for her.

With my fingertips, I brush at the bark of the tree I'm hiding behind and black ash flakes off like ancient paper, crumbling in my palm. My belly flips over with the thought that perhaps I am standing in the center of some radiation ring, or some weird, otherworldly, ghostly chemical floating through the air. But I haven't survived this long to turn my back on what's ahead. "I'll be quick," I tell Squirt, and I push forward, through the moisture-sapped forest.

I tiptoe to another tree, blackened and crispy, but closer to the crashed craft. It *is* a craft. What else could it be? I hesitate, listening, for another minute, and I hear nothing.

If I hadn't seen the light in the sky, the flash like a bright blanket, I wouldn't have considered the object before me to be some kind of vehicle. It's more like a modern art sculpture. Two huge rings, stainless steel looking, maybe thirty feet across, intersect each other, like the diagrammed rings of an atom around a nucleus. It reminds me of two Ferris wheels, one tucked inside the other at a jaunty angle, and where the seats would be, there are eye-shaped transparencies, like windows or portholes, lines of them circling the rings' circumferences.

Against the parched and dehydrated ground, colorful, stringy material, plastic or rubber in appearance, lies strewn through the trees. When I look up into the pine I'm hidden behind, I can see some of it, blue and red, stuck in the branches. I stand from my hiding, crouched position and reach up into the branches on my tiptoes. When I grab a low branch, it shakes the tree enough so that the colorful stuff tumbles down on top of me, disturbed and heavy from the higher branches, slippery. I let out a small squeal, just a gasp, as the unknown, ropey substance drapes over me. I stand stock still, heartbeat fast.

When I realize I'm still breathing and am unharmed, I gingerly grasp a bit of the bright cables, and pull it away from my body. The texture is rubbery, flexible. It bends only to bounce back to its original shape, hexagonal spaces between the colorful lines. Around the forest, clumps of this dangle from dry trees or lie in clumps like my mother's knitting, and the bizarre parallel gives me goose bumps.

From the heavy piece that landed on me I can see frayed edges, not frayed like yarn but like electrical wire. Another glance at the enormous rings of the craft, and I see that a large carpet of the blue and red rubbery mesh is underneath it all. Perhaps some kind of protective landing material? Like our car airbags? Reduced to smithereens upon impact?

A sudden bout of pregnancy nausea whirls through me, and my vision tunnels. The stress of...well, everything...doesn't help. I need to get home soon, but not before finding out what this is. I'll never forgive myself if I don't investigate. So far, I have been spared, for unknown reasons. The fact that right before Leila killed me, she was reduced to powder is not lost on me. My parents' protection of me, in the form of that pod, made just for me. The note, meant for me, written into the ceiling of it. The rose-scented Blur in the grocery store—it didn't hunt me down or follow me or harm me in any way. Perhaps I'm getting cocky, but a new sense of blessing, of protection, flickers in my periphery, the small flame of a new idea. How have I made it this far?

Mercy. That's how.

There's no other explanation. Aside from luck. But luck does not include a weird survival pod. August, being so far below ground. That was luck. But me? This all feels intentional, like Mark's note telling him to find August. Is there a mind behind all this? And if so, what does it want?

I think of wings, of Amelia Earhart, and step into the clearing, my boots thumping now, crackling nature to dust, instead of squishing. Everything is completely bereft of moisture.

In the middle of the massive rings, I notice a metallic silver sphere, like a nucleus, attached by a web of cables. Some have snapped. The sphere lolls to the side a bit, off balance. I go in for a closer look, trying to tiptoe, but with the arid ground, my feet still crunch, tiny sounds, like the feet of fairies.

Stepping over the lower three-foot-tall, three-foot-deep ring blade, I approach a hatch door that hangs open from the sphere in the center. Like in the grocery store, I press my body against the sphere and slide toward the opening, ready to peek with just one eye visible. I have no idea if I'm good at sneaking.

The sphere is empty. Nothing living, or dead. No seat. No machinery, either. Just empty darkness. The eight foot diameter looks like just enough space for one really large person, or maybe two people? People. Aliens? Beings? If something or someone occupied this before, they're gone now.

Or not.

I stand still, listening.

And then, sniffing.

No roses, but there are traces of something sharp and chemical, which I suppose makes sense for any kind of crash site.

It's gone, I think. Or was never here. We have drones, why can't they...whoever they are? The lack of seating and controls supports this theory. Standing on my tiptoes, clutching the metal rim with bent arms, I can almost see inside. I'd like to climb inside it, which I realize is a ridiculous idea, but I decide that I'm being watched out for, and head quietly back into the woods to find something to stand on.

I head past the dried out woods and trudge back into the slush. It's like walking out of a picture book about the desert and into one about snow, the illustrations side by side. I spend a few minutes searching before coming across a shattered pine, its trunk burst into large chunks. One of the logs is short, just three feet across, and while I can't lift it, I *can* roll it. It's slow going at first, the muck clinging to everything, but once I reach the parched earth, the log rolls as though on pavement.

When I reach the slight incline leading to the craft, gravity does the rest, pulling the log down until it clangs against the ring. The three foot tall ring. I'll never lift it over, but don't have to. The ring curls up and away. After circumventing the ring, I'm back at the sphere, log positioned below, sweating profusely and feeling even hungrier. I think of Squirt, but don't worry. Just because I'm hungry, doesn't mean she is.

I climb onto the log, balancing, and I end up at boob height in front of the sphere. I try to swing myself in, but I've forgotten my big pregnant belly, which seriously impedes my progress. If I didn't have a watermelon under my shirt, I could just land on my abdomen and crawl in, shimmying over the edge. I have always been able to lift my own tiny weight.

As I'm struggling, elbows and head and chest inside the dark sphere, my eyes adjust, and all I see are tendril-like appendages extending from the rounded walls. There really is no up or down, right or left, ceiling or floor. Just many ringlets or wires, rainbow-colored—and alive. The cables start to shift and wiggle. Several of the bright tendrils stretch toward my body. Something inside me tells me to climb down, but I don't, still convinced of that divine protective quality at work, which a part of me knows I am intellectually using to validate my stupidity.

When one of the tendrils brushes my arm, I remember petting a boa constrictor at one of those wildlife shows as a child, being surprised by how smooth and lovely it was. The tendril coils, fast, around my forearm. A soft blue light emanates from it, illuminating my face and hair. When another tendril touches my forehead, I yell and tumble backward out of the sphere, off the log. I land hard, tailbone first, on the dry ground.

The tendril remains coiled on my arm, severed from the sphere. It glows for another few seconds and then, blinking, extinguishes. I poke at it. It's soft and a bit squishy, like cooked noodles. The bright blue fades lighter. The texture hardens and becomes rubbery, just like the mesh netting strewn around the crash site and buried under the craft. Is this the same stuff?

I leave it braceleted around my forearm. Something about it emboldens me, makes me feel stronger, decorated like an Amazon, someone who's been through the initiation, the rites of passage. Never mind that it happened accidentally when I was poking my head where I shouldn't have been.

Walking around to the other side of the sphere, I stop short. A viscous liquid, dark and swirling, like oil, drips from the uppermost ring toward the ground, eventually plopping and sinking immediately into the parched soil. But on the path down, it arcs midair, and changes trajectory on its way to the ground. Over and over, a steady drip, straight down, beads up, arcs and slides, like it's moving over an unseen boulder. I think I am seeing a miracle of physics, or something related to the crashed craft, when I bend for a closer look.

A sharp, chemical, plastic smell invades my brain. The trees behind the arcing shape are blurred, shimmering. Just like the grocery store.

36

POE

The transparent shape shimmers faster as I stare, like it's being shaken, a quick change in vibration. It's low to the ground, not moving. *Is it injured?* The steady rippling, like water, is thrown into turmoil. *Is it quivering?* One more abrupt shake, and the movement stops. A long face, the texture of old wood, focuses on me, clear, solid. I freeze for a fraction of a second, but it's long enough to confirm August's physical description of the face—long, deep lined, gray-brown skin set in a permanent scowl, though the mouth...if there is one, never moves. And the nose—well, there isn't a nose. It's the eyes that hold my attention. The flesh around the eyes, which are shaped like oversized avocados, is perfectly still, but the actual eyes swirl with oily color, a mix of deep blue, turquoise, purple and black, full of unwavering loathing. In a strange way, they're beautiful, but in the way an H.R. Geiger painting is beautiful—horribly so.

Terrified, I back away. *Run,* I hear Squirt telling me. *Run, you fool!*

But I don't. I can't. My creative mind is taking in the details, exploring possibilities, and marveling at the fact that the thing in the grocery store is real. But I at least have the common sense to back-pedal, stepping over the lower ring and back. It watches me go, its thin neck turning ever so slightly, tracking me with the large, never blinking eyes.

And then I hear it. Crunching from the forest, all around, mixed with the distinct *shh* of heavy fabric being dragged over dry earth. It's everywhere, but not like the sounds from the sky. This is different. The mix of sounds have a source. Multiple sources. And I understand what they mean. I'm surrounded. I look back at the still watching creature. Surrounded.

A panicked glance in every direction reveals the same shimmering shapes, just like the grocery store, just like the one frozen next to the craft, oil dripping onto it. Dozens of them. The forest warbles, the motion of it twisting my stomach, a hallucination made real.

Tattooed on my right shoulder is the quote from Dante's Paradise, "My course is set for an uncharted sea." Here in the woods, ringed by unknown living things, the words seem whispered in my ear, nearly audible and mocking my pride.

With quavering tree limbs, patches of forest wrinkle wherever the beings move. They crush dried ferns and other low-lying plants. Branches, now brittle and dry, snap and fall to invisible limbs, reaching out to clear a path, the way any person might do.

One by one, the Blur stop, spaced out evenly around us like some transparent ancient Roman forum, waiting to proclaim judgment. The woods go quiet, the snapping and shushing drag to a stop. I wait, holding my breath, the woods warbling around, undulating contours. I try to count. There are at least fifteen of them, but there could be more. There could be hundreds.

My thoughts flicker to the man August found. Steve. He was brutally killed, stabbed through the heart just as August was later stabbed in his shoulder. And Mark nearly was, too. I wondered if it might be a gender thing. Sexist aliens. Willing to physically attack the guys, but leaving me alone. No, they didn't just leave me alone, they protected me. But why? Whatever the case, I'm starting to think like my luck might have run out, or whatever protection was over me is now gone.

But that's not how I *feel*. Here in the trees, with absolutely no way to escape, I feel a remarkable lack of tension. The newly arrived Blur hover, quietly, and I know instinctively that I am merely being observed.

With this knowledge comes the surprising scent of flowers—lilacs, I think—and other plant smells. Basil. Tomato leaves. The pungency of lilies. I turn in a circle, smelling, the shifting breeze carrying what I think are the varying scents of these beings. A tang of something acrid and chemical turns me around, back toward the ship and the lone, wooden-faced Blur, now hidden in its shimmer. They might all look the same, but they definitely don't smell the same.

The wind picks up and another wave of beautiful, natural smells wash over me, a garden in the middle of all this dry husk land, surrounded by slush and leafy decay.

A few of the Blur drag closer to me. I suck a breath through my clutched tight lips and I decide that's close enough. I turn to my left, where I think there is an opening, and run into the woods. Before I'm even clear of the parched ring of forest, I slam into something unseen, taking the blow on my shoulder, not my belly. I stagger backward, and it actually does the same.

I stand my ground, knees bent, ready to run.

A face resolves from the shimmer, identical to the Blur that crashed in every way, including the loathing, empty eyes. But it's not the same.

The fragrant scent released by the impact filters up my nose and triggers recognition.

Roses.

I know you.

The absolute stillness of its face reminds me of a mask, creepy because of its deadness. Tempted, like a naughty, impulsive child confronted with fire, or sharp objects, my hand extends without my assent. The rose scent disorients me, circling, and my breathing slows.

I'm not afraid of you.

I see the thing like Georgia O'Keefe's painting of the horse skull with the white rose on top of it. Bleak but lovely, a cold beauty, comforting in its stark preternaturalness.

You are the misunderstood one, my protector.

You won't hurt me.

A brief physical contact that feels no more meaningful or otherworldly than fingertips brushing against anything manmade and earthly—plastic, metal, you name it—and Squirt gives me a vigorous kick. She's always there to keep me on track, warning me, my responsibility. Use my brain.

The Blur doesn't move. It seems frozen with surprise, that I would reach out and touch it. With no real, rational reason to stay, I withdraw my hand and back away. The further I get from the still motionless Blur, the more I realize how big an idiot I am.

I *touched* it. For a moment, I *trusted* it.

These are killers of men, I remind myself, *of all mankind.* I turn and run into the woods, a steady sustainable pace. The monsters stay behind, not pursuing, not doing anything as far as I can tell. And then it's all behind me. I end up in my neighbor's yard, Luke's former home, and head for the road, following the now cleared pavement back to the house.

I arrive home, soaked, exhausted, and yet intact. Remarkable, really. My mind spins with possibilities. Of what did happen, what could have happened and what it all means. I need to call August.

Once in the front door, Luke leaps at me, front paws on my shoulders, tongue covering my face. I hug him tight around his broad furry middle while he balances on his back legs, like he's human. I head upstairs, quickly changing out of my wet clothing and into a pair of my mother's sweatpants, wool socks and one of my father's flannel shirts, ready to call August.

I head for the office and find the fully charged phone resting in its cradle. I sit down. My legs are shaking. Hands, too. A few deep breaths to steady myself, and I dial.

"What's wrong?" he says, worried because I'm calling outside of our regularly scheduled time.

"I'm okay," I say first, knowing that will be his primary concern. I hear him sigh with relief. "But, unlike you, I don't make unscheduled calls for nothing."

"Tell me," he says. "What happened?"

"You're never going to believe this," I say, and I explain the whirlwind of activity in the woods today, starting with the hunting, which he knew about, and ending with the downed...UFO...and my encounter with the Blur.

"I mean, whatever the heck that object was, with the wheel within the wheel and the tentacles, it was completely unearthly. Alien. I think my parents were right all along."

I still feel uncomfortable talking about my parents' pasts. We only discussed it once, when Mark revealed his story, which mostly corresponded with mine, except for the two word message.

"We can talk about that, you know," he says. "You don't need to keep it all bottled up. It's weird, I get it, but there isn't anything that's *not* weird anymore. It might be good for you to get it out."

"And maybe you'll tell me more about Claire, too," I say, and quickly regret it. I know what it feels like to lose a parent, all that history erased, a sucking void left behind. But what does it feel like to lose a child? All that hope. That potential? Parental death is a part of life. Of aging. But a child's? It goes against some kind of natural order. Squirt hasn't even been born yet, and she already feels like a part of my soul. What would losing her feel like? "Sorry," I say.

"Don't be," he says. "It's a good point. I'll tell you more about her. Tomorrow."

He gets a smile from me, but can't see it.

"For now, let's stay on task."

"Right," I say, "the spaceship...if that's what it is."

"Actually, I'm more interested in why you were allowed to leave. To live. It seems contrary to their nature."

He's right. The question of who lives and who dies is uncomfortable, yet tantamount. August and I appear to be immune to, or at least overlooked by, the Blur's aggressions. Mark, like me, was spared in a pod, but would have later been killed if not for August's interference. And even after that, the Blur did not kill August.

"I have a theory," I say, heading downstairs, phone to my ear, Luke by my side. "Maybe there are two sides to the Blur? I mean, just because we're all humans doesn't mean we don't have warring factions among us, right? We're a big, freaking mess. Or at least we used to be." I lay down on the braided rug in the living room, my head resting on Luke's broad side. His belly moves up and down, relaxed. "You know. *I'm* not a mess. Maybe you still are." I can feel normal if I can joke.

He ignores the joking, probably tired and not in the mood, but I can't help myself.

"Huh... What you experienced in the woods today certainly supports the idea. Just because there was a Blur architect behind your survival, and Mark's, and Steve's, and who knows what else, doesn't mean that there aren't Blur who oppose it. The best laid plans of mice and men..."

"And aliens," I say. "Often go awry."

"Right."

"Quoting poetry, now? August, they *were* fighting," I say, confident in my assessment until I realize I never actually saw a battle. "It *sounded* like a battle, at least."

August goes quiet again, both of us do, sorting our thoughts.

"The question," he says, "is why?"

"Why what?"

"Fight. There must be a reason, right? An instigating factor. Part of the opposing plans that intersect. Some action one side is taking that the other is trying to stop. Something both sides want..." The way his voice trails off tells me he's figured something out. Then I do, too.

I force a laugh. "Yeah, right. Maybe I'm their leader. All hail Overlord Poe."

He's silent.

"You're not laughing," I say. "Shit. You're not laughing."

"We have to consider that they were—"

"They were *not* fighting over me," I declare. "Don't even say it."

He doesn't.

Doesn't need to.

Luke lumbers to his feet to find his water dish in the kitchen, and I have to sit up. Uncomfortable with the conversation's track, I shift it.

"Did you notice how the Blur you encountered smelled?"

"What does that—"

"Just tell me."

He's quiet for a moment, and then, "Ammonia. Chemically. But what—"

"I think that's how we can tell them apart. The two sides. I've smelled Rose twice now. And the others...they smelled, I don't know, like nature. Pleasant. But the one at the crash site. It wasn't ammonia, but it wasn't good. It smelled industrial. Like you said, chemically. Isn't that what space smells like?"

He chuckles. "This is why I love you, Poe. I hadn't thought of that, either. You're right. There are several accounts of astronauts reporting that the outside of their spacesuits, after a moon or space walking, smell like something burnt, like spent gunpowder. A chemical, ashy smell. I can't say that I smelled that exactly, but I feel like I have a vague memory of it." He sighs, sounding like he's stretching. "You know, too busy kicking ass and stuff. Whatevs."

I laugh again, and then stop, remembering the smell of the first Blur at the crash site, the dead eyes and sense of foreboding I felt when I first smelled it. "So, nature scented good, chemical scented bad?"

"It might not be that simple," he says.

"Right, no odor profiling."

"But we can't discount it, either."

Luke trundles back into the room and I grab him as he goes by, pull him close to me. I hold fistfuls of his golden fur, shaking, comforting myself. I'm frightened by the detail I haven't told August, that I was stupid enough to make contact, that I am unsafe to myself, a threat to Squirt's security.

"Poe. I think you should go with your intuition. If there are actually two sides to what is happening, or maybe more, who knows, then you need to be ready to protect yourself and Squirt. It sounds like the Blur who have been protecting you, probably the same ones that took your parents, and Mark's parents, and gave them the knowledge to save you, won today, but I have seen the ruthless nature of the others. They killed Steve. Nearly killed Mark and me. You can't rely on these rose-scented Blur to always be there."

"Okay," I say, pressing my forehead against Luke's hard scalp, trying to stop my shaking. I take a deep breath. "What do you think I should do?"

"Get ready," he says.

"For what?"

"A fight."

37

AUGUST

Walking slowly, on bare feet, it took Mark and me a week to find shoes, and then bikes, my energy waning with each step. We'd argued about whether or not to pimp our rides, so to speak, with panniers, BOB trailers and other equipment which would have let us carry more. But Mark won in the end, making the point that we needed to be as mobile as possible. We might need to quickly ditch the bikes, or carry them through wreckage. Light and mobile was the key, and that meant keeping the backpack on my back, wearing me down.

And then, the rash around my now scarred wound knocked me on my ass. We lost three weeks of travel time, while I laid in a bed, sweating with fever. We tried antibiotics pillaged from a pharmacy, but they seemed to have no effect. The black ring spread wider, radiating pain through my body and out my fingers and toes, until, as though reaching its predetermined terminus, it stopped. The black rash remains, but once it stopped spreading, the symptoms subsided. It's now a reminder, like a black tattoo, of how dangerous a face-to-face encounter with a Blur can be. On occasion, the black ring will itch, severely. We tried anti-itch ointments, calamine lotion and Benadryl, but nothing helped. The dinner plate-sized ring has faded some, and the itching with it. I feel mostly healthy, but I wake most nights drenched in sweat, and often wake in the morning feeling like I've slept inside a pinball machine. Once I'm awake, fed and stretched, I'm back to normal, which is still improving every day.

Losing so much time irks me, but Poe, at least, has been left alone since her encounter with the Blur a few weeks ago. No more battles, or Blur or any sign of them. She has even ventured back out to the grocery store, for canned vegetables and beans for protein, when the rabbit traps failed to catch anything. She said the worst thing about it was the smell, but she took comfort that the smell of rot wasn't mixed with the scent of rose. She wants to believe that what happened over the woods that day was some kind of final battle, but I don't think we have that luxury. They must have been here for years, maybe decades before turning against us. When discussing this with Mark, he mentioned Foo Fighters from World War II, and the rash of UFO reports that have surfaced since. So at the very least, they've been around since the forties.

We're finally progressing again, though not nearly as much as I'd like. I tire quickly since the fever, and have to take lot of breaks. "It's the turtle who wins the race," Mark said to me once. "Slow and steady."

He's right, but we have a rough deadline to make. August—the month—is just two months away, and at our current lumbering pace, we're barely going to make it on time. We average about 14 miles a day, sometimes less if I'm not feeling well, or the road is blocked. Based on crude calculations and guesstimations, we have about one thousand miles to go. Seventy-one days. I suggested that he go ahead without me. He could get there in a fraction of the time. I nearly had him convinced, but Poe wouldn't hear of it.

I've been with Mark for forty-three days, and I'm now officially lean and on my way to a six pack. My arms are looking pretty good, too. But my legs? They look like someone else's. I have muscles in places I didn't know muscles existed. We've both got full beards, so we look like mountain men on mountain bikes, but there's no one around to judge us, so shaving isn't a priority. Though we've both agreed to clean up before meeting Poe in person.

While Poe and I continue our daily check-ins, she also talks to Mark. From what I can tell, their conversations are much different. Where Poe and I talk about future plans, survival, childbirth, aliens, the fate of the planet and all things serious, Mark does a lot of laughing on the phone. Which is good. Poe needs her spirits lifted. Poe, without meeting her, has become a daughter-figure in my life, and I love her dearly. But Mark...he might fill a different role for Poe, and for Squirt. So let them laugh. That bond needs to be forged and unshakable. I'm old enough to know that my life expectancy, without modern medicine, might be reduced significantly. Up until the industrial revolution, the average lifespan was just thirty years. Sure, some people made it to sixty, but just as many didn't get past age one. Unless we come across a doctor, I'm probably already well past the new average lifespan. Which also means that Poe and Mark are past middle age.

This line of thinking depresses me, so I focus on the road ahead. We're on Interstate 64 in Kentucky. In the suburbs outside Lexington, the roads were congested with rush hour traffic, but here the roads are mostly empty. We're crossing through the top most reach of what was once the Daniel Boone National Forest, and mankind's influence, which is already being assaulted by Mother Nature, is less evident here.

We ride in single file, using a bike riding technique Mark told me is called drafting. The rider in front takes the wind head on, reducing the strain on the next in line. It works better in larger groups, but is better than both of us taking the wind head on, all the time. I'm a fan of efficiency, so I've been on board since he brought it up, about five minutes after we raided a small downtown bike shop. In a perfect world, we'd be splitting the burden 50/50, but Mark takes the lead most often, allowing me to go just a little further each day.

Mark, who is currently riding in front of me, uses traditional hand signals mixed with a few of his own. So when he holds his arm straight out to the right, I know he intends to take the next exit off the Interstate. I look up and see a sign. Exit 133 to route 801. Sharkey Farmers. This is a deviation from the plan, and I want to argue the decision, but Mark's out-stretched hand becomes a thumbs-up, which translates the message to, 'Let's turn right, dude,' and I've become a sucker for his California charm. Besides, he's a smart guy and I trust him. If he wants to get off the road here, he's got a good reason.

I figure out the reason thirty seconds after we've turned right onto route 801, which is really a small country road leading deeper into the national forest. A small wooden sign on the side of the road reads, Cave Run Lake. I smile. Mark has deemed today a 'feast day.' This will be our third and Mark insists on them for 'morale and meaty protein.' We generally get by on protein bars, but Mark is a skilled fishermen and carries a collapsible rod and reel on his back, along with the rest of his gear.

We only make fires if it's still daylight, which is to say, not very often, because we try to keep moving during the day—emphasis on try—and sleep all night. So to have real meat, requires an early stop. It's 3pm now, so if Mark can haul some fish out of the lake in the next two hours, we'll still have plenty of time to cook them up, have our feast and put the fire out before nightfall, which is the time we both now hate—not because the Blur are more likely to attack then, because really, who knows... Poe's encounters have all happened during the day. We hate the night because *we* can see *them*, moving about in the sky high above, doing who knows what. We don't sleep under the stars anymore. The population is dense enough in this part of the world that there is always a home or business around, some with dust to sweep, others empty of their previous owners.

I struggled with the first few homes we cleaned of dust, but Mark seemed to have no trouble. When I asked him why, he explained that normal dust, the stuff that fills every home and is visible in shafts of daylight is, 'Like 80 percent skin cells, man.' I understood his perspective. We've been breathing in people dust since our first breath. It definitely helped me deal with the dust piles still lingering in sealed homes, but it also made me a little more wary of normal dust. I try not to look at sunlit air inside houses anymore.

I look up at the sound of Mark's squeaking brakes. He has his hand raised, signaling me to stop. Lost in thought, I didn't see it. I squeeze my hand brakes, but don't stop in time to miss bumping Mark's rear tire. When he doesn't notice or comment, I know something important has his attention.

After tumbling half way over my handlebars, propelled by the weight of my pack and the rifle slung over my back, I get my feet on the ground and ask, "What is it?"

When we're not biking or sleeping, Mark is talking, so when he simply points ahead, I look without further question. At first, I don't see it. But a subtle shift in the wind pulls the object across the road, making a dull scratching sound as it sails across the sea of cracked pavement. It's a piece of trash, like a hundred others we've seen along the roadsides, but with one glaring distinction.

I hop off my bike, shed my backpack and run toward the object. On my hands and knees, I pick up the foil wrapper. *It's shiny.* I hold it up to Mark. "It's new." Every other piece of trash floating around outside has one thing in common. They're old, dirty and faded. But this...it even has some melted chocolate still inside the wrapper.

We both know the significance of this.

Someone was here. Recently.

Mark squints at the wrapper. "I didn't know they still made Chunky bars."

"Well, they don't now," I point out.

"Yeah, but, there must be a lifetime supply of them out there somewhere, right?"

"Lifetime supply of everything, I suppose." I stand. "Any idea where our snack food friend headed?"

Neither of us are trackers. We tried hunting once and failed miserably. Never even got to take a shot, because despite knowing there are deer in the woods, we couldn't find a single sign of them.

"Unless they're on the move," he says, "The lake is the best place to set up shop. Fish, game trails, water."

"Sounds logical," I say, which gets a funny look from him. Despite our constant conversation for more than a month, we still speak like we're from different worlds.

"Good thinking, dude."

He chuckles while I gather my gear and return to my bike. "Let's keep going," I say. "But we can't get sidetracked. Whoever came through here might have gone the other way. We can't spend any more time than we were already planning.

"Right on," he says. "Squirt awaits."

Moving at half speed, we close the distance to the lake, the air becoming noticeably cooler, and sweeter. I'd never really noticed nature's varied scents, but I'm now able to smell water up to a mile away. We ride side by side, and slow together as a set of signs come into view. *Minor Clark State Fish Hatchery* and *Cave Run Cabins— Lodging, Boat Rentals, Pool.*

"A fish hatchery, with probably an unlimited amount of fish, easy to haul in, cabins to stay in, boats and a pool." Mark raises an eyebrow and turns toward me. "Have we seen a better place to live, post-apocalypse?"

I shake my head. Not by a long shot. Whoever dropped the wrapper has to be here.

Mark starts pedaling again, but I stop him, hissing, "Wait!"

He looks back at me caught off guard by my tone, but it's not me he has to worry about. He knows about Leila, aka Crazy Lady, so all I have to do is say, "Could be a Leila," and he gets it.

"Right," he says, and he climbs off his bike. "Let's scope it out first."

Leaving our bikes behind, hidden on the roadside, we enter the woods that separate the road from a clearing that leads to the long strips of artificial hatchery ponds, and the cabins beyond. Even without binoculars, I can see movement. Feeling excited, I tap Mark's shoulder and point to a short hill further to our right. "I'm going to get a look from up there."

He nods, already lifting his binoculars.

I move through the woods, doing my best not to be noisy, but failing. I'm breathing heavily, tired from the already long day, my shoulder itching, when I reach the hill's crest. But my heavy breathing isn't all from exertion. I'm excited. Beyond excited. I fumble with my binoculars as I lift them from my pack and put them against my eyes. I nearly laugh aloud. There are several people. Five. Seven. More! I can't see them clearly, but they're moving around the cabins, doing... chores? Everyone looks hard at work. *A good sign*, I decide. Crazy people probably don't coordinate like this.

I turn my view to the hatchery ponds and find three more people, hauling in a net full of fish.

I'm about to head back down to Mark, when I hear him shout in surprise, and then anger. "Dude, what the f-oof!"

I start toward him, shouting, "Mark!"

His reply stops me in my tracks. "Run, dude! Ru—"

The way his voice is cut short is ominous and reinforces the message. *Run*. So I listen, turning away from Mark and fleeing in the other direction. But I'm not alone. My pursuers crash through the woods behind me.

38

AUGUST

I now know what it feels like to be hunted. Not stalked in that slow predatory way, but the actual chase. The desperate weaving. The quick, instinctual decision making. But despite being in the best physical shape of my life, I'm slowed by the faded rash's side effect...and I still have the mind of an astrophysicist. I can navigate the night sky without opening my eyes, but charging my way through the tangling woods of Kentucky is a new experience.

My shoulder clips a tree as I run past. It's not large. A sapling really. But it's more rooted than I am, and the impact spins me. Nearly topples me. I remain upright and use the twisting motion to look behind me. Three shapes bound through the trees, moving with far more agility and speed. This is a race I cannot win. They're indistinct, fragmented by the vertical trunks and horizontal branches. A sloppy grid. But they're definitely human. Any relief that fact brings me is dulled by the violent intent I sense. That, combined with the fact that they are closing the distance in a coordinated way, suggests they've hunted together before.

The land drops down, and my speed increases as I follow the slope. But with the extra speed comes less control. Gravity increases my momentum beyond the top RPMs my legs can manage, and my top half overtakes the bottom. When the land at the bottom of the hill levels out, I slam into the ground like I've fallen the distance straight down, which is close to accurate. The air in my lungs coughs free and pain ruptures up and down my right side.

My intellect is momentarily blinded by the pain, but instinct keeps me moving. Unfortunately, there isn't much my body can do without oxygen, so I suck in one loud breath after another, filling my lungs and replenishing my body to the point where I can once again think clearly. That also happens to be the moment I notice the three sets of legs beside me.

Knowing I'm caught, that there is no action I can take to free myself, I focus on breathing. I flop onto my back, body slack, and I look up into the non-faces of the people around me. For a moment, I fear I was wrong about them. That they're not human. But then I pick out the bandanas, sunglasses and hats covering their faces. They look like bandits. Deep woods, Southern bandits.

Fight, some part of my mind shouts. *Become the silverback!*

I roll away from the bandits and get my feet beneath me. Before I'm standing fully, one of them has closed the distance between us. His pants are camouflaged in shades of green and brown. His shirt, a black long sleeve—too warm for the balmy June heat—hugs his muscular torso. Everything about him, except for his slight stature, screams military.

"Should'a stayed down, old timer," he says, and throws a punch. The swing is almost casual, but lacks enough force to drop me if it connects. Which it doesn't.

I lean away from the punch. The fist sails past my face, and strikes a tree. The man shouts in pain, clutching the hand. He's underestimated me, and overestimated his abilities. If he was actually in the military, he wasn't long out of boot camp. The hard lessons of battle haven't been instilled. Not that *I* know better. But a real soldier would have put me on my butt already.

Thinking I might actually have a chance, I kick the man between his legs. He drops to the ground, contorting into a position that suggests he'd like to return to his mother's womb. I nearly smile, but there isn't time. The biggest of the three, a man standing over six feet tall, struts toward me, arms by his side—not casual, but confident.

I take a step back, trying to find a weakness or escape route. But before I can, my knees are struck from behind. My legs pop forward, and I bend so fast, that I'm thrown to my back, wedged between the last two bandits and a tree. No rolling away this time.

Maybe they're reasonable, deep woods, Southern bandits? I think, and ask, "What do you want?"

The big man leans over me, and I see that he's holding a rifle—*my* rifle. I must have dropped it when I fell. Too bad I didn't think of standing my ground with it. He says, "First things first. We're going to teach you a lesson about spying."

"Jeb, don't," the third bandit, a woman, says. She reaches a hand toward him, but fails to prevent what happens next. Jeb lifts my rifle up and brings the butt of it down on my head. I hear the crack of it, but I'm spared the pain as unconsciousness whisks me away, before the pain sensors in my brain get a chance to fire.

I wake to the pain I thought I'd been spared. With consciousness comes an uptick in my heart rate, pushing blood into my injured head, harder and faster. Each beat brings a fresh wave of pain. After twenty beats, it begins to subside, or maybe I'm just getting used to it. Thirty beats later, I open my eyes.

The first thing I see is what I already knew. I'm bound to a chair, arms and legs. A gag fills my mouth, tasting and stinking of old engine oil. The scent contrasts the view. Cozy looking cabins. Green grass. A distant lake view. Before or after the apocalypse, this is a paradise. Of course, the masked group of people surrounding me kind of ruins the tranquility. My mind, quick with numbers, counts twenty-seven.

They stand there, arms crossed, looking angry, waiting. They're all masked in one way or another, hiding their identities, or perhaps hiding their emotions. Right now, they're all ominous, but if I could see their faces, maybe the story would be different. The woman tried to spare me, after all.

The lowering sun reaches my eyes, dilating the pupils and generating a fresh wave of pain. I turn toward the ground and notice a third foot, next to my right. I follow the leg up and find Mark seated next to me, similarly bound, but still unconscious.

"Mark!" I shout, but it comes out as a muffled, 'Muk!'

Movement pulls my eyes above Mark. The short bandit is there, sunglasses-covered eyes on me. Though his face is concealed, I sense a smile and imagine a horrible fate.

I struggle against my bonds, shouting a muffled and threatening tirade that is beyond comprehension. The short bandit just turns his eyes from me and starts pouring a bucket of water over Mark's head.

Mark sputters awake, confused and thrashing, blowing the water from his nose and gagged mouth. The bandit doesn't stop until the water runs dry. The short man drops the bucket and joins the others. Twenty-eight in all.

Mark and I look at each other. His eyes look as apologetic as I hope mine do. We failed each other. We failed Poe.

No, I decide. *That's not going to happen. These are people. They're survivors. Like Poe. Like Mark. Like...*

My head snaps toward the mob. I shout at them but it comes out garbled, "Lemah sayu fay!" When no one replies, I try again. "Peash! Lemah sayu fay!"

"What's he saying?" asks a familiar female voice. The woman bandit. She's the closest to me. Disapproving hands on her hips. Masks can't hide body language. She doesn't like this.

I turn to her. Calmly. "Peash."

"We haven't checked them for the rash," Jeb says with authority.

Rash? I try not to react to this. While mine has faded, it is still visible, and their need to check for it unnerves me. I get the sense that people with the rash will be treated unkindly. It also implies they've come across other people who'd survived violent encounters with the Blur. But why fear those people? Is anyone who's made contact now a pariah?

The woman bandit waves him off. He's not as in charge as he seems. "They're tied up. He can't kill us with words."

Kill *them*? They're afraid of *us*?

Before Jeb can complain further, the woman reaches up and frees the gag from my mouth. I spit to the side twice, trying to get the oil taste out. When that fails, I say, "Thank you," to the woman.

"Don't get the wrong idea," she says. "We're not pals. Now, what was so important?"

"I would like to see your faces," I say. "Please."

When no one replies, I add, "I'm tied up. We've already established that I can't hurt you with my words. And I get the distinct impression that if we don't pass some kind of test, you're going to feed us to the fish. Why are you hiding?"

"We don't know what they can do," the woman says. "If they can see us through you?"

"You mean, them?" I ask, looking up.

She nods.

"If they could see through me, don't you think they'd already be here?"

"They prefer the dark," Jeb says. "Use Rashes like you during the day."

"If that were true," I say, "I don't see how hiding your faces helps."

"He doesn't talk like one of them," someone says.

"I just want to see who I'm talking to," I say. "Then you can check us for rashes, or do whatever other tests you want to do."

I've never gambled. This might be the first time in my life. But it's at least an educated gamble. Not that I have a choice. If they check me for the rash and find it, I'm pretty sure I'm a dead man.

The woman complies with my request first, plucking her sunglasses from her face, revealing turquoise eyes and black skin. The mask goes next, and I see her face, which is distinctly sub-Saharan African, stunning—and young. Early twenties.

"Tanya," Jeb says, sounding annoyed. But he follows suit, pulling his mask and revealing an aquiline, white face framed by close cut blond hair and light brown eyes, the yang to Tanya's yin. The rest follow Jeb's lead, but since he follows Tanya, I think she's the one in charge.

I look at each and every face in the group and see exactly what I'd hoped to: youth. The youngest looks to be maybe eighteen. The oldest—Jeb—might be late twenties. It's far too small a range to be a random selection of survivors. These are people like Mark and Poe, who were spared because their parents had some kind of advanced knowledge.

Tanya leans in close. "Now you can see us. Anything else?"

"My...name," I say, trying not to smile.

"And that is...?"

"August," I say. "My name is August." I meet her eyes with my most confident gaze. "I think you've been looking for me."

39

AUGUST

Arms drop in unison with jaws. It's what I was hoping for. Even Jeb looks stunned, like he's woken from a dream only to find out it's real.

"How..." Tanya's lips move, but she can't find the words.

"Mark was looking for me, too." I motion my head to Mark, who is nodding, eyes wide, but not quite daring to show relief. Not yet. Not while we're still bound. "And before him, Steve. I seem to be a popular guy."

"Cut them loose," Tanya say.

"But—" Jeb's complaint is cut short by a sharp look from Tanya.

"Now," she says, confirming her leadership position.

Jeb draws a knife from a sheath on his belt. "I still think this is a bad idea. They could be lying." Despite his apprehension, Jeb slides the knife between my wrist and the chair's arm. I tense as the cold blade touches my skin, fearing I've been cut. But after just a moment of pressure, my hand is released.

After Jeb cuts the other hand free, I dig into my pants pocket and remove my wallet. I'm not sure why I've kept it all this time, the credit cards, cash and random receipts still tucked inside. Probably habit. But I'm glad for it now, because it contains something that will help put Jeb's mind at ease. I tug out my license and hold it out to Tanya while Jeb frees my legs.

She accepts the card, looks down at the details. The image. Whatever doubt still lingered fades away. A smile spreads. She looks at me, tears rolling down her cheeks. "We stopped thinking you were a person. Most of us believed we simply had to survive until August."

Before I can reply, she holds the license up in the air and turns to the unmasked community. It's a diverse group of men and women representing a wide swath of nationalities, having only their generation in common. "We found him!" she declares. "We found August!"

Instead of cheering, the group collectively sighs, unleashing months of pent up anxiety. Some sit and weep. Others hug. The rest step closer, eyes on mine, desperate to know me.

Tanya hands the ID back, and I pocket it, thinking I'll probably never need it again. Despite being freed, I remain seated. My body aches and my head throbs from Jeb's assault. I rub my wrists, which are sore from being tightly bound, and I turn to Mark. Jeb is cutting him loose, but hasn't bothered to remove the gag. I reach out and pull it from his mouth.

He coughs, winces and flicks his tongue a few times in a futile attempt to remove the flavor.

"You okay, kid?" I ask him.

"Fine," he says.

"Could we have some water?" I ask, and before the request can be relayed from Tanya to someone else, a girl, no more than twenty, sprints away toward one of the cabins.

I can see that Tanya is about to ask a question. It will no doubt be the first of many before I get a chance to really think. So I beat her to the punch, taking control of the conversation. "Before you ask, I don't know much more than any of you. I survived the...event, but not like any of you. I'm old enough to be a father to most of you, so I wasn't dragged into my basement and put inside a magic refrigerator."

The revelation that I know how they survived widens eyes even further. If anything, I'm accidentally elevating my status from mystery man to prophet, and that's not something I want. "I only know this because I've met three of you already."

Tanya straightens, looking into the distance. "Are the others nearby?"

How to answer that question?

Honestly, I decide. Secrets, in this new world, could be deadly.

"Poe is in New Hampshire."

"New Hampshire?" Tanya says.

"We found each other via ham radio," I explain. "We're on our way to her."

"She's preggers," Mark adds. "Can't travel."

He leaves out the fact that her two word message differed from everyone else's, which is good, because we only have theories about that and none of them are easy.

Tanya nods like this makes sense. "Where are you coming from?"

"New Mexico," I say.

"Pasadena," Mark says. "California."

When the young woman returns with two bottled waters, frigid and dripping with perspiration, the group settles down into sitting positions, surrounding Mark and me like eager kids waiting for story time. And that's not a far cry from what they're expecting.

"Tell us," Tanya says.

"Tell you...what?" I ask.

"Everything," she says. "Both of you."

So I do. I give them a rundown of who I was, and what I was doing so far beneath the ground. The blank stares when I talk about my work tells me that none of them have ever given thought to the nearly unobservable dark matter and dark energy that cumulatively makes up ninety percent of the universe. Probably a good thing, as most of the knowledge in my mind is now unusable, unhelpful and in no way increases the odds of survival.

There are tears when I tell them about Steve Manke's death and excited whispers when I tell them about the physical confrontation with the Blur.

"Good name," someone says.

"You've seen them?" I ask.

Tanya nods. "Some of us have seen them. Some of us lost people, too. Like Steve."

"But none of us fought them," Jeb confesses. He's seated on the grass along with the rest of them, looking a good ten years younger than he did before. In fact, he looks almost gentle, like the kind of guy who'd be incapable of knocking someone out with a rifle. "That took serious balls."

"I had no choice," I say, dismissing the idea that I'm a brave person. "As far as I knew, he was the only other person living aside from Poe and me."

"Dude," Mark says. "Seriously. You're like..." He shakes his head and smiles like I've just said something ridiculous. He turns to the group. "I met August—" He looks at me. "What? A month after you found Steve?" I nod. "A month later. He comes running out of the darkness, shouting at me. Total madman, right? I hadn't seen anyone else since, you know, and here's this guy... He shouts at me to put out my fire—"

There are nods in the group around us. They've learned this lesson, too.

"—and he *dives* on the flames. Puts them out with his fricken body, man."

Mark's dramatic retelling draws a few smiles from the group. He continues in this fashion, detailing our flight through the woods, and from his perspective, my quick thinking, decisive action and willing sacrifice. When he gets to the part where I shot the Blur, nearly everyone gasps and does something with their hands. While most hands are now covering mouths, a few people clap.

I should probably interrupt. Make it not seem like such a big deal. But looking back at it, and hearing the events from Mark's perspective for the first time, I can't really argue. Everything he said, while told excitedly, isn't inaccurate. I did those things, albeit, not all on purpose.

Maybe these people really were meant to find me?

The plan, I think. Whoever set all this in motion, knew what I had inside me, even if I didn't. But that is a revelation for another time.

"How's your shoulder?" Tanya asks.

"Huh?"

"It stabbed you, right?" she asks.

"It put him out of commission for a few weeks," Mark says. "Got infected. But he's a salty old man." He slaps my shoulder, right on the scar, and it hurts worse than I let on. "I'm telling you, this guy is a tank."

While Mark is a stranger to these people, I know him well. The excitement in his voice is forced now. He's covering for me. For the rash. Whatever these people have experienced with others who have rashes, I'm not the same. 'August' or not, they might not trust us if they learn about the rash.

"It's getting dark," I say, standing. The sun is a sliver on the horizon. When it disappears, the sky will get dark quick and the stars I used to adore will soon fill the sky. "Do you sleep in the cabins?"

"Yeah," Tanya says. "Is that okay?"

I'm taken aback by the question. Tanya is the leader of this group, but she's now asking for my approval.

That's when the full weight of what is happening here descends upon my shoulders. So far, I've only felt a personal responsibility for Mark, and at a greater distance, for Poe and Squirt. With all of these newcomers suddenly looking to me for guidance, for leadership, I feel like my own personal dark matter has been revealed, the burden of reality now ninety percent heavier. And ninety percent more meaningful. The human race now has a real chance, including a gene pool diverse enough that I'm even more convinced this has all been planned by a superior intellect—a superior intellect with enemies.

"How long have you been here?" I ask.

Tanya thinks for a moment. "Half of us arrived two weeks ago. The rest trickled in over the next three days, and then nothing until you two."

"Why did you stop?" I ask.

"No one knew where to go," she explains. "And this place seemed like a good place to hole up, you know?"

"Right on," Mark says. "But..." he turns to me, having been with me long enough to know what I'm going to say. Without ever meaning to, Mark has become my right hand man. My own personal Will Riker.

"But?" Tanya asks.

"We're leaving tomorrow," I say.

"Leaving?"

I nod. "At first light. First, because it's not safe to stay in one place. Second, because of Poe."

"She really can't come here?" Jeb asks. It's clear none of them are going to want to leave. They've found a good life here. But it won't last. And while I am thrilled to have met all of them, Poe claimed my heart a long time ago, and I will not, for anything, fail to reach her and Squirt.

"You ever been pregnant?" I ask Jeb. There's no argument after that.

"Now..." I say, but I'm interrupted by a hand gripping my shoulder. It's Mark.

"Dude," he says. "Sirius is usually the first star we see, yeah?"

Sirius, one of the nearest stars to our solar system and by far the brightest aside from the sun, has become our early warning system. As the brightest star in the sky—if you're not counting the planets, which can appear even brighter—its arrival tells us it's time to get off the road and under a roof. I'm usually the one to point it out, though. "Yeah," I say.

Mark turns back and looks at the lowering sun, speaking to himself. "Sirius rises in the morning before the sun, and sets after it. So it should be..." He glances up toward the sky where Sirius should be. I follow his gaze and see nothing, or maybe just the hint of something. I'm sure it would be visible with a telescope. But its absence isn't disconcerting. It means we still have plenty of time.

"So," he says, pointing south, "That's not Sirius."

My attention snaps south, scouring the sky until I find it. A faint pinpoint of light. I quickly scan through my knowledge of the night sky, recalling the position of Venus, which is really the only other object aside from the sun and moon that should be visible this early.

It's not Venus.

I do my best to stay calm and cool, turning to Tanya. "Get everyone inside. Now." I turn to Jeb. "I'm going to need my rifle."

40

AUGUST

The rifle in my hands provides little comfort. Sure, it increases my potential for lethal force, but we're facing the unknown. I have fought the Blur before. I even shot one of them. But did I kill it? Did I injure it in some significant way? I have no idea.

But here is what I do know: this time will be different.

This time I'm not going to run. I'm not going to hide.

Not out of fright. Or cowardice. While I'm feeling ample amounts of both, I'm determined to let the Blur know that I no longer fear them. That their intrusion will be met with force. That this scientist has overcome his previous limits. That these people are under my protection.

Flight has become fight.

Gatherer has become hunter.

I am the silverback now. But with an IQ one point shy of genius.

They might be the destroyers of worlds, but tonight, *I* become death. It's just a rifle in my hands. Not Oppenheimer's atomic bomb. But I intend to be an equally potent deterrent to future attacks.

I feel naked. Wild. And, for the first time, in charge. In the past, among a group of people such as this, I would have been unseen and unheard. A shadow. Tonight, I'm the one casting the light.

The group of survivors splits up into groups, performing a practiced exodus into the cabins that will provide no protection if the Blur decide to simply turn us into dust. But they haven't done that yet, aside from the attack on Crazy Lady, so I focus on preventing the only kind of attack we have any hope of repelling—the up close and personal kind.

"Do you have any weapons?" I ask Jeb, who has remained by my side with Tanya and Mark.

"Two hunting rifles," he says.

"Can you shoot?"

He nods. "I'm from the South and named Jeb. What do you think?"

I smile and turn to Mark and motion to one of the cabins not being used for shelter. "Both of you. In there. Defend the other cabins."

"We won't really be able to see it," Mark points out.

"You don't have to kill it," I say. "Just keep their attention off of the others. And once you have their attention...you'll see it just fine."

"Right," Mark says, frowning. He's as eager to see another Blur face as I am, which is to say, not at all.

"Uh." Jeb scratches his head. "You both keep saying 'it'. What if *it* is a *them*?"

"Then just try harder," I say and force a smile.

"C'mon," Jeb says, slapping Mark's arm with the back of his hand. The pair run to a cabin I assume contains the hunting rifles.

I turn to Tanya. "Go with the others."

She shakes her head, raising an eyebrow. "Uh-uh."

"It's not safe out—"

"You know how alpha females lead wolf packs? Or how lionesses do the real hunting? And fighting? And killing? Turns out human beings aren't all that different." She reaches behind her back and pulls out a handgun. I have no idea what kind it is, but its smooth black surface and hammerless body look lethal. Even more so when clutched in her confident hands. "I've kept this group alive for months. You might be the August we've been looking for, but these are *my* people, my responsibility, and I'll be damned before I let *you* die protecting them. Besides, given the universal theme of the notes our parents left us, you might be the most important person here. *You* should be hiding. Not me."

While I can't argue with her logic, I *can* stand my ground. "Not going to happen."

"Then we do this together," she says. "What's the plan?"

I cast an awkward grin in her direction. My plan felt bold and crafty when in my own head, but now that I have to explain it to a partner...

I cast an eye to the light on the horizon. It's larger. Growing closer, and fast. I tell her the plan, eliciting a groan. But there's no time to come up with an alternative. While Jeb and Mark sprint across the open space, rifles in hand, to one of the empty cabins, I get into position with Tanya by my side. All around the campground, cabins go silent and dark.

As darkness fully descends, I slip beneath my cover and listen. Aside from my own breathing, and Tanya's beside me, all I can hear are the awakening crickets, emboldened by the arrival of night.

After a few minutes of silence, Tanya whispers. "August."

"What?"

"So you were a scientist..."

"An astrophysicist, why?"

"What about before that?"

"Before?"

"Were you in the military? Maybe earned money for college?"

"No."

"Boy scouts?"

"I won a StarCraft tournament once."

"Is that like a competition for geniuses or something?"

"Or something. It's a video game."

Despite whispering, I can still hear her cursing.

"It's like chess," I say, hoping the cliché thinking man's game will help impress that I'm not a complete bonehead. "A game of strategy... against aliens."

"Sounds like the perfect preparation for fending off an actual alien attack." Her sarcasm isn't exactly biting, but my imaginary back feels a little less silver.

Distant but approaching light strikes my eye through my small peephole. "Quiet. They're here!"

The crickets continue their auditory domination of the night, until all at once, they fall silent, too. To them, the light of day has returned.

I hold my breath as the luminous craft, visible as nothing more than bright light, glides past overhead. I wait for it to do something. To attack. To turn me into dust. To send another translucent assassin. But it slides past, stopping beyond my range of vision.

I try to turn my head to continue watching, but a second light appears above me.

"There's more," Tanya whispers. Her voice is barely audible, but in the dead silence, it feels like an explosion. I reach out and pinch her arm, expressing my disapproval without making a sound.

A third light slips into view, the three craft forming a triangle above the field at the campground's center. Them, not it. *What are they waiting for?*

They don't know if we're here. They have limits. They're looking for us, visually. They can't see through walls. Can't even see heat. These aren't soldiers. If they were, they'd have military weapons beyond imagining. So what are they?

In the stillness, I decide to compare what I know about the Blur to what I know about the human race. What kind of person has the ability to destroy a civilization, yet lack the military might to win a conventional fight? What kind of person can kill a living thing without qualms, and without weapons? What are we to them in human terms? Ants? Apes?

Biology didn't come up much in the mathematical world of astrophysics. Conversations tended to avoid the physical realm. Subjects like sex, physical ailments and fitness were taboo. Not even more pressing subjects like an Ebola outbreak or the Hochman's illness came up at work. We couldn't be bothered with such things. The one time biology was discussed, and even hotly debated, was in relation to the idea of finding life on other planets. We might be focused on things like nebulas, dark matter and black holes, but life on other worlds sparks every child's mind and drew some of us toward space, even if we spent our lives in labs buried miles beneath the ground.

What kind of life was out there? And once we found it, assuming it was biological, what would we do with it? We were never able to agree on a Star Trek-like Prime Directive dictating how the human race *should* interact with alien life—advanced or not—but we all agreed on how humanity *would* react: greedily. We'd experiment on the living while plundering natural resources. It's what we do to our own planet, to which our future as a species is connected. Why treat alien life any better? The rich would hunt alien wildlife for sport, and science would collect, poke, prod and dissect any living thing, from megafauna to microfauna, in an effort to squeeze out every bit of knowledge. That is, assuming we were the dominant species.

I nearly gasp when I realize the truth.

We're the mice.

The lab rats.

Bacteria.

The human race *is* the lesser species, and the Earth is nothing more than a giant petri dish to these things. We few survivors are rogue cells, having survived a cull. Or perhaps this is simply the experiment? Wipe out the population and see how the survivors behave. When they become complacent, poke them. Give them some external motivation. Shake the cage. Throw in a snake.

"Oh my God," I whisper, but I'm silenced by three rapid-fire hums in unison with flickering lights. They've sent one of their killers. The flickering lights and hum repeats. Again. And again. Six times total. The craft Poe found appeared to be for a single Blur. The UFOs above us must be different. Larger. But I'll never be able to see them, or the interlocked rings, past the bright light.

What I can see is that they know we're here.

Hiding in the dark. Cowering.

Like rats.

Not tonight, I think. I kick away the soft plaid blanket I'd been lying beneath at the center of the field, hiding in plain sight. "Not tonight!" I scream, taking aim at the first patch of distorted light I see.

The rifle booms through the stillness, and its echo is interrupted by a shriek. Contact made. A face slips out of the light, becoming clear for an instant, as I'm spotted by oily eyes. Tanya sees it, too, sitting up beside me and pulling her trigger twice. The face snaps back, shattered, then gone. But the flattened grass beneath the still body is easy to see.

"We killed it," I say. I turn to Tanya with wide eyes that match her own. "We killed it!"

The night erupts. The silent Blur wail, high pitched, their alien voices unnerving. I can't tell if they're angry, terrified or confused. If they're scientists, it could be any of the above. Or a mix. Hollywood always depicts aliens as being of one mind, of one personality, but they're probably more like us than they'd ever admit, maybe arguing about what to do next. How to respond.

I aim and pull the trigger twice more before screams draw my attention. A cabin door flies into the air, wrenched free by some invisible force. Rifle fire from Jeb and Mark answer, pushing the Blur back with a shriek. But the people inside are now exposed.

"Protect the cabins!" I shout to Tanya, as I charge for the open door. A Blur fills the door's rectangular gap. I raise the rifle to shoot, but I can see people on the other side. If the round passes through the thing's body, I could kill one of the people inside. So I charge instead, turning the rifle around and wielding it like a bat. Before the Blur can fully enter the cabin, I launch myself up the stairs and bring the rifle down hard, connecting with something solid.

At the precise moment of contact, I'm flung back, repulsed by whatever technology that makes physical contact with the Blur nearly impossible. I land hard on my back and slide across the grass.

Gunfire surrounds me. Shouting and shrieking mixes. The sounds of battle. Then, above me, the night sky distorts, the light bent by the body of a Blur standing above me. I look for the rifle, but my hand is empty.

The Blur's face slips into view above me. The swirling oil in its eyes congeals for a moment, forming what appear to be pupils. For an instant, we make genuine eye contact. Its head cocks to one side, and I get a sense that it's evaluating me, inspecting the rat before putting it down.

The scent of ammonia stings my nostrils.

It's him. The one I shot.

A long gnarly hand with mottled gray skin rises from beneath the light-bending cloak.

This is how they do it. How they kill. A finger to the chest. If the Blur that had tried to kill Mark didn't miss and stab my shoulder, this is how I would have died a month ago. But it doesn't stab me with its one long digit. Instead, it opens its palm toward me. There's a flicker of light where its three fingers and thumb come together. And then, pain. It radiates out from the old, healed wound in my shoulder and explodes like a bomb.

All control of my body slips away and I fall back. I'm defenseless.

The Blur moves closer, and I sense humor in its alien eyes.

"It has August!" I don't recognize the feminine voice, but the mix of panic and rage is unmistakable.

What happens next is like some movie where the perfectly laid trap is sprung by the heroes and the tables are suddenly turned. Except this was not a trap, and it's just about exactly what I was hoping to avoid.

The cabin doors are flung open and the people hiding inside pour out. But they're not running away from the danger, they're charging headlong toward it, wielding shovels, branches, chains and anything they could find. The group of survivors, inspired by my impending doom, has become an army.

The Blur above me glances toward the ten people charging toward it, and then turns its attention back to me. It's just a momentary glance, but the expressionless face somehow conveys the look of a scientist on the verge of success. And despite the turned tables, this one is confident. It slips away, fully concealed once more, and then with a flickering flash of light and a pulse of hums, it's gone. And along with it, the paralyzing pain in my chest.

I sit up to greet my rescuers, clutching my shoulder. "It's gone," I tell them, and I take in the action taking place around me. Tanya is firing her weapon and doesn't stop until it runs empty. I can't tell if she hit anything, but she quickly replaces the empty clip with a fresh one and looks for more targets. Mark and Jeb hurry to her side, also looking for targets, but they find none. A group of five manages to tackle one of the Blur, but are then flung away, repulsed. The Blur disappears in a flash of light. Then all around us, the Blur retreat in a mass of strobing lights and sound. In seconds it's all over.

Tanya points her weapon skyward and unloads the clip toward one of the glowing craft. There's no visible effect, but the three craft buzz and shimmer before going silent and streaking into the sky. A second later, they're the size of stars, lost in the night sky.

The battle is won, but the confidence that Blur transmitted said otherwise. It said that the real battle, or war—or experiment— is already finished. We just can't see it yet. Rats in a maze.

41

AUGUST

"How many?" Poe is on the other end of the satellite phone. Aside from the limited description she's given me of herself, I don't really know what she looks like. But the image I've conjured of her is comically wide-eyed at the moment. Hand to her mouth. Seeking a chair to sit in.

"Twenty-seven," I say again. "Twenty nine if you count Mark and me."

"Oh my god," she says. "And no one was hurt?"

I remember the pain radiating out from the old wound. It's only been fifteen minutes since the attack, but I can still feel a lingering burn. I don't know if it's psychological pain or not, like still feeling a hat that's been removed. I haven't checked. If I'm honest, I'm afraid to look. So I focus on the positive.

"Everyone is safe," I say. "I wish you could have seen them. The way they charged out of these cabins. The way they fought. If these bastards had bothered with a more conventional war, they wouldn't have stood a chance. But that's probably also because they're not soldiers."

"You're sure about that now?" she asks.

"Aside from their apparent interest in Squirt, which is something a soldier would never bother with—not for any reason I can think of anyway—everything they do and have done screams scientist. To me, at least. I think I recognize them because their actions reflect those of more than a few of my colleagues. It's the results that matter. Not the equipment. Not the money spent. Certainly not the test subjects."

"The ends justify the means," she says.

"Exactly."

"Could they really see the human race as being so inferior that they'd conduct genocidal experiments with no regard to our lives?"

Tanya, Mark and Jeb take seats atop tree stump stools. They're here to talk business, having completed the tasks I set out for them—to pack up everyone and get ready to leave. Tonight. We're going to head out under the cover of darkness and continue on through the next day until dusk, moving closer to Poe and further from what is now our last known location.

I look at each of them as I speak. What I'm about to say is for more than just Poe. "We need to consider that these beings, these Blur, experience the world, the universe and maybe even time, differently than we do. Colonies of bacteria, grown in labs, thrive and multiply through countless generations, adapting to whatever medium they've been released into. We observe them. Test them. And in the end, destroy them."

"Dude," Mark says, "you really think the Earth is like a petri dish to these guys? We're like bacteria to them? And they're just cleaning up after an experiment?"

"Was that Mark?" Poe asks.

"Yeah," I tell her and put the phone on speaker. "You're on speaker now."

"Hey Napoleon," Mark says. Most times they talk, he tries to come up with a witty nickname for her, including the word, Poe.

"Hey Mark," she says, unimpressed. "Who else is there?"

"Tanya and Jeb," I say.

"Hi," Tanya says.

"Ma'am." Jeb chimes in.

"You sound like a good ol' boy, Jeb," Poe says.

"Yes, ma'am."

"You willing to come to the rescue of a pregnant Yankee?"

"Way I see it," Jeb says, "the only thing left that should define our loyalties is our humanity. You're my sister now, Poe. I'd do anything for you."

"We all would," Mark says.

"Back to what I was saying." I don't really want to tell them my thoughts, but they need to know, mostly because if I'm right, it will provide a clear window into the thought processes of the Blur, and perhaps present an opportunity to let them know we are more than they believe us to be. That we are worth saving. That we are *not* rats. "Take the laboratory, petri dish analogy to its logical conclusion. We're the bacteria, spreading through the medium, adapting through generations. They've observed, tested, theorized and postulated. Maybe the last six thousand years of a more civilized humanity has been a month to them. A day. Who knows."

Jeb chimes in. "'With the Lord a day is like a thousand years, and a thousand years are like a day.' Second Peter." He raises an eyebrow at me. "Sounds dangerously close to blasphemy."

"Except this higher power is present," I say, before holding up a placating hand. "I don't want to argue religion. I just want everyone to consider that if we're the bacteria in a cosmic petri dish—" I turn my eyes to the crystal clear night sky. "—it might be them who put us here."

Tanya gets to her feet. She looks angry. Ready to punch someone. "And that gives them the right to destroy us?"

"Maybe the bacteria think the same thing when we decide to incinerate the world we created for them?"

"We're not bacteria!" Tanya shouts.

"That's a matter of perspective," I say, but can see the theory is not being well received. It's offensive. I get it. But it could be the truth. The human race has advanced in unpredictable ways over the past hundred years. We're reaching out, past the moon. Past Mars. Voyager One is well on its way to explore the interstellar medium outside the confines of the heliosphere, at the outer fringe of our solar system. In biological terms, the bacteria is escaping the petri dish. It's a theoretical motivation, of course, based on limited data, but it rings truer than the Blur being cosmic environmentalists.

"Hey!" a distant voice shouts. "Over here. Check this out!"

I turn toward the voice and see dark shapes on the other side of the campground, aiming flashlights at the ground. The light appears to be illuminating nothing but the ground. That's when I notice the light is being bent on its way down. Distorted.

I take the phone off speaker, place it to my ear and stand up. "Poe, I need to go."

"What's happening?" she asks, sounding worried.

I'm not about to hang up on her like this, leaving her worried. I head for the distant lights. "I'm not certain yet, but I think there might be a body. I think we might have killed one of them."

"I hope you're wrong about that," she says, her voice serious.

I pause, realizing she's come to some kind of conclusion that I haven't. The idea that we can kill them, that we can fight back gives me a little bit of hope. "What do you mean?"

"When the bacteria gets out and kills someone in the lab, what's the typical response?"

My hope is dashed. "Clean slate. They'd sterilize the lab."

"Yeah."

"Well, if that's the case, it's already too late. But I think they already tried that. For whatever reason...maybe some ongoing experiment, they want the rest of us to live. Who knows, maybe the Blur aren't even the scientists. They could just be some kind of agitating medium."

"Like getting an electric shock if we pick the wrong food?"

"Yeah..." I stop walking. "Which means we're still being directed."

"To what?" she asks.

To you, I think, but I decide to keep that tidbit to myself for now. I don't want her doing something that would put Squirt in more jeopardy. "I don't know. Can I call you back in a little bit? I'm going to check this out, and then we're leaving. By tomorrow night, we'll be a lot closer to you, especially if we can find bikes for everyone."

"Sounds good to me. Be careful."

"Hanging up now."

"Okay."

"See ya."

"Bye."

The familiarity of that exchange grounds me and brings a smile to my face. In a world gone crazy, it's a steady reminder that some kind of normality can be reclaimed. *If* we survive long enough.

"Everyone get back," I say to the gathering group. Nearly everyone has formed a circle around the bent light. "You all have jobs to do. We're still leaving. This changes nothing."

"But—"

"Is anyone here qualified to examine a body?" I ask. I know I'm not, but my gear is already packed and my bike recovered. Mark and I are ready to go now. Since we don't know whether or not the Blur will return, the rest have no time to spare.

To my surprise, one person says, "Yes," and steps forward. She's a young woman, early twenties, with straight dark brown hair and matching eyes. "I was a Forensic Scientist Trainee."

There is no denying that her experience, even if limited, far exceeds my own. "You can stay. Everyone else, back to work." I point to Jeb and Tanya. "That includes you two. We're out of here in fifteen." Tanya looks unhappy about being told what to do, but complies with a nod.

Jeb tips an imaginary hat. "You got it, boss."

I point to Mark. "You stay put."

Mark doesn't look happy about it, but stands his ground. He's a smart kid. Knows that whatever we find here is probably going to haunt his dreams.

With everyone else back on task, I turn to the girl and offer my hand. "August."

She smiles and shakes my hand. "Megan."

"You know what's weird," Mark says, and I think he's noticed something about the light bending shape smoothing out the ground by our feet. "No one uses last names anymore."

"Huh," I say, finding the observation mildly interesting. Jeb is right. The things that separated us, that marked us as not united, including family names, might no longer have a place in the world. Of course, with only twenty-nine people around, the odds of people having the same name are slim. I crouch down without replying further and reach out. "Let's get this done."

"Wait," Megan says, her hand outstretched. "Shouldn't we be wearing gloves?"

"You have any?" I ask.

She shakes her head.

"Didn't think so. If you're uncomfortable, I can—"

"I can do it," she says, and reaches out, making contact. Light bends beneath her fingers as they slide over a surface. "Feels like thin plastic with a body beneath. Its frame is rigid. Stiff." She slides her fingers to the end and slips a digit beneath the fabric. It disappears. "Got a knife?"

I remove my knife from its sheath on my belt and hand it to her. She places the blade against the invisible fabric.

"Okay, August," she says, "hold this side. Mark, just keep that light steady."

Mark stands closer, aiming the flashlight over the top of my head, while I take hold of the fabric, watching my fingers disappear. She gives me a sidelong glance, and I nod. She draws the knife upward, slicing through the surprisingly tender material until the slight resistance slips away. She cuts clean through.

I take a deep breath, holding onto my side of the cut fabric, looking into Megan's eyes. We both know what comes next, but neither of us are ready for it. How could we be?

"My boss told me to pretend that the bodies I examined were just dummies. Organic parts assembled to resemble a body. Non-living material. It helped. Sometimes."

"This isn't a person," I point out.

"Just do it," Mark says, "before I puke."

I nod at Megan and say, "Now."

We both pull, and for a moment, I consider taking the cloak for myself, but then the invisible shroud parts to reveal what's very visible underneath, and I forget all about pillaging. The first thing I notice is the stench, like chlorine, chemical and sterile. *Like a lab,* I think, but I keep that to myself, not because I think the others can't handle the tidbit, but because that's when I see it.

The light from Mark's flashlight shakes as he steps back, hand to mouth. Megan has backed away, too, an arm over her mouth.

I stay rooted in place, my scientific mind running wild.

"Oh my god," Megan says. "Oh my god."

"The hell is it?" Mark asks.

"The enemy," I say, and I turn to Megan. "Still up for this?"

She hands the knife back to me. "How about I supervise and you cut?"

Without a word, I take the knife, turn to the exposed body and lower the blade toward its head.

42

AUGUST

The knife blade hovers over the body. The realization that I'm not sure if it's actually dead has stopped me. The three bullet holes I can see suggest a violent demise, but there's also no blood. And who's to say these things have hearts to stop. It's alien. The odds of its physiology being anything similar to human are slim to none. It didn't evolve on Earth. It might not have even evolved on an Earth-like planet.

No, I think, it *must have evolved in a similar environment.* The fact that it has arms, legs (four of them), eyes, a mouth (is it a mouth?) and is roughly six feet from head to toe—there are three toes on each of the four feet—suggests a similar evolutionary path. But the similarities end there. The body appears rigid and tubular. Pipe-like veins run up and down its limbs and torso, covered by taut brown flesh coated in gelatinous sludge.

Instead of cutting into the monster, I scrape some of the slime from its pipe-organ-like ribs.

"Dude," Mark says. "That's nasty."

I think back to my previous encounters with the Blur. The wooden faces. The long pointed fingers. "They didn't have this coating before."

Megan crouches next to me, sniffs the goo on the knife blade and winces. "Could be waste material. We don't know how they, for lack of a better word, shit. When people die, all their muscles go slack and—"

"I get it," I say, wiping the blade clean in the grass by my feet. "Sure you don't have any gloves around?"

"Tough man loses his nerves at the first sign of alien sweat-shit," Megan says with a hint of a smile. "I see how it is."

I turn the knife blade around and offer it to her.

She holds up her hands. "I know my way around human cadavers, not...this."

I spin the blade hilt back into my hand. "Then tell me where to start."

"We should confirm that the subject is actually dead."

I nod. "But how? It might not have a pulse. It might breathe through its skin. This slime could be some kind of regenerative coating. A full body scab, protecting the wounds from alien bacteria. We have zero idea what to expect here."

"Stab it in the eye, man."

Megan and I both turn to Mark. The idea is revolting, and I think Megan agrees with me until she nods and says, "That should work."

"You're serious?" I ask.

"Dude, if that doesn't wake it up, it's dead or so close to death that it can't react. Worst case scenario, it's alive and we blind it in one eye. If you're worried about that, just stab it in both eyes, so that it can't see us when it wakes up."

I turn back to the body and say, "I miss computers."

"I miss surfing," Mark chimes in.

"The Walking Dead," Megan says. "Now get it done or we're going to run out of time."

With my own tight schedule working against me, I clutch the knife in my fist and lean over the rectangular, line-etched face. I aim the blade at one of the oily eyes, imagining what it will feel like to stab it, then I draw the blade back and repeat. *No good*, I decide, and then I move past my fears, anxiety and revulsion.

The blade slams down, meets momentary resistance and then punches through. With a groan, I lift the blade up and stab down again. This time, the impact is different. Softer. I missed the eye and plunged the knife into the Blur's forehead. I lift the blade and stab again, hitting the second eye this time. I pull back, knife in hand, breathing hard.

"I think you could have stopped after you stabbed the thing in the forehead," Megan says.

"You're...assuming...that's where...its brain is," I manage to say between deep breaths.

"Geez," Mark says. "Check out its eyes."

Despite my hammering heart, I lean forward again and inspect the damage I've done. What I see takes a moment to make sense. "They...shattered."

The oily fluid seeps out of the broken eyes, leaking down over the expressionless face. My eyes track downward over the body. The flesh is taut. Uniform. Organic, but...flawless.

Almost flawless.

There's a horizontal line cutting across the Blur's forearm, which appears to be composed of four straight tubes arranged in a diamond shape and wrapped in tight skin. I lower the blade to the line. Without cutting, the blade slips between the folds of skin.

It's a seam.

The reality of what we're seeing comes out of my mouth even as I fully realize it. "It's a suit."

"A suit?" Mark asks.

Megan elaborates on my discovery. "A two stage bio suit. The outer layer protects against the elements, the outside world *and* discovery. The inner layer is more mobile. Tighter. Providing a second barrier of defense. That might be what the slime is for. Maybe the suit sensed a breach and secreted the gel to seal the suit and protect..."

Megan steps back.

"What?" Mark asks.

I know what Megan is thinking. The fear stamped on her face matches my own. I didn't stab it in the eyes. I simply broke the eye pieces of an alien hazmat suit. That's why they always seem so expressionless. The alien creature...the Blur...is *inside* the second suit. We haven't really seen it yet, and I don't know if it's dead— bullet holes or not.

I remain rooted in place, the knife blade still hugged by the seam, my need for knowledge outweighing the instinctual desire to flee. With a long slow breath, I steady my shaking hand and focus. *Ignore the others*, I tell myself. *Ignore the night. The urgency. The chemical stench.* I lay out a mental track. Information leads to discovery. Discovery to solutions. The Blur are a problem that needs solving.

"August," Mark says, sounding unsure.

"I have to," I tell him.

"Fire with fire," Megan says, understanding what's driving me.

"Science with science." Information, discovery, solutions. Ways to fight back. Ways to win, or at least, to survive.

"I have to," I say again, this time to myself. Then I apply pressure to the blade and draw its flat surface down the forearm, toward the hand. Clean, white sinewy flesh is revealed, still and motionless.

With a slurp, the hand, which is actually a glove, slips free of the arm, revealing three inches of flesh. There appears to be no skin at all. Only white sinews, tightly bunched together. Perhaps that's why the second suit is so important. Maybe the Blur have no natural defenses against external elements. But why would any creature, anywhere in the universe, evolve like that?

I turn my attention to the three-fingered hand. The long, pointed index finger retains its rigid form. *It's a tool*, I realize, *not an actual finger*. Or is it a weapon? *These are scientists*, I remind myself. While the Blur can certainly kill with the long sharp digit— Steve Manke was proof of that—it must serve some kind of other purpose. Perhaps several. The nearly invisible, needle-sharp tip suggests that it could be used for drawing blood samples...or injecting material into a subject.

My eyes flick toward my shoulder for a moment, but movement and a gasp pull me back to the gloved appendage.

"It's moving," Megan says.

She's right. The strands of exposed flesh are pulsing.

I draw the blade back, watching as the glove slips off the still rigid limb. Beneath are coils of the tight white strands arranged in what look like four round pipes.

The words, *not dead*, flit through my mind, but never make it out of my mouth. What happens next erases any doubt as to whether or not the creature still lives.

The glove falls free, propelled by some unseen force. The white, stringy flesh inside retains the hand's shape for a moment, but then unfurls with surprising explosive force. Loops of white tendrils wriggle in all directions.

Everyone human within eyeshot, including those some fifty feet away from the action, take a few steps back.

There you are, I think. The true Blur is revealed, and like science predicts, not even remotely human.

The entire alien suit twitches, its insides roiling about, no longer conforming to a rigid, tubular state.

Then, it changes again. The writhing loops pull back, slipping inside the suit while a single, long tendril slips skyward like a charmed snake.

It's all one creature, I realize. One, long worm-like creature. Its mind must be spread out across its mass. That would make it hard to kill. Maybe impossible to kill. Dividing its body might simply divide its mind into two separate entities. If the bullets severed the long creature inside the suit, how many of them are about to emerge?

And if that happens, how can we kill it? Bullet, blades, clubs and other conventional weapons will be useless.

Mark, who has apparently been debating the same issue, finds the solution. "Fight science with fire."

"Gasoline!" I shout to the distant observers. "We need gasoline!"

Several people sprint away.

I turn my attention back to the Blur. The long white strand is joined by a second. They lean toward me. I somehow sense their loathing. Their deadly intent. And then, for a moment, I *feel* it. In my shoulder. Pain radiates out from me. But the sensation is not alone. For a moment, I feel...pity.

And protective.

So much so that when Jeb arrives with a red gasoline tank, I hold out my hand and say, "Wait!"

But then I just stand there, useless and confused, watching the tendrils reach out for me.

I reach out to touch it, ignoring common sense, lost to a strange compulsion.

"Dude!" Mark shouts. "Just do it!"

Jeb sloshes the gasoline atop the writhing mass. I'm set free, my mind reclaimed. When Jeb finishes emptying the tank, I waste no time removing a small box of matches from my pocket and striking a flame. I toss the match onto the Blur and it erupts in flame.

"Fight science with fire," I say. "Good to know."

As the flames lick higher into the night sky, I turn to Jeb. "We're leaving. Now."

ARRIVAL

43

POE

I have boobs now. For the first time in my life, I consider what it would be like to go bra shopping. My new breasts even have names—that's how little company I currently keep. Ida and Ingrid. One of the many benefits of pregnancy, along with aching hips and the addition of an extra pillow between my knees for sleeping. When the ache starts, I fret over my pelvis size. Body parts are shifting around in there, but a tiny person usually equals a tiny pelvis. What if I can't push Squirt out? Her activity level borders on 'contained octopus'—she doesn't stir, she roams around, big luscious limbs slipping around my insides. Once, with thumb and forefinger, I caught her poking foot, to the left of my navel, a puny, vigorous stone, insistent and strong. She will be fine, it seems. But will I?

The two months since that chaotic day in the woods, when I found the crashed vehicle, and all those Blur, have been uneventful. If you don't count the continued news from August. His group—*twenty-nine* people—is on their way here. His revelations about the Blur, what they look like on the inside and what we might really be to them, is disturbing, but I try to focus on the impending arrival of August and his—*our*—people. They're still slowed by August's health, which varies from day-to-day, and by the logistics of feeding that many people while traveling, but they're making progress.

But no matter how boring my life has become, or the good news from August, my mind continues to wander back to the Blur, and why they are here. There isn't a single possibility that gives me any long term comfort. Even if I'm being protected by Rose, why? *My baby,* I think, but will they come for her? Will they come for me?

Is it delusional to think they're coming for you, when, in fact, they may be coming for you? Where does paranoia end and realism begin? Counter to my vigilance, many fractures run crisscrossing around my brain, so much so that I actually decide to venture back out to the grocery store, despite already having gathered most of what's left there. All I know now is that August and Mark were attacked, and we could be next.

My own ancient Volkswagen bug, long since freed of the snow that kept it rooted in place for several months, seems pathetic, too innocent and inadequate, not really something you'd take into battle. It's more of a burden in need of protection. Liabilities I don't need, especially the friendly and comfortable variety. I consider the massive propane truck, but if a quick getaway is required, that lumbering beast won't do. I give my lonely bug a pat on the hood and climb into my parents' red Chevy flatbed truck.

August and I discussed how to prepare the house against attack, ways to stumble intruders, early alarm systems. We devised easily rigged stuff, methods not needing an electrician or too much dangling of my pregnant self from ladders. Planning for the possibility that I might need to defend myself against aliens with unknown intent and technology, has forced those mental fissures open a bit more. It's just so other-worldly. Dreamlike. Like something a crazy person would do, like the way I thought my parents were turning out, ludicrous uselessness, spitting on a forest fire. But sometimes implausibility is all we have, and the dark, deep clefts opening up in my head force me to choose between complacent surrender or preposterous action. So I'm choosing.

I will be vigilant. I will hope for encounters with only the benevolent Blur, and that they will remain protective.

I say that I'm the one choosing, but really, Squirt has determined for me. And for that, for her, as I back my dead parents' truck out of the driveway, I'm grateful.

Abandoned cars still litter the streets of my town. I'm not sure why I thought anything would be different. Lawns are bright green and overgrown, weeds already reclaiming the flower gardens surrounding houses. Despite the humid heat of July, I keep the AC off and the windows down. This is the life I need to get used to. Eventually, cars won't work either, but I don't need to get used to that yet—not while I'm alone and very pregnant. My due date is next month, but that doesn't mean the baby can't come early.

It smells like nature outside. Like flowers and grass. Like *them*, I think, but I push the image away. These scents were wonderful and a part of the human experience long before the Blur arrived, hijacking nature's more pleasant odors.

I drive to the grocery store, there in minutes this time, and walk boldly in. I have brought bags from home, and expect to take more from the front counters—I'm craving chocolate. The smell sends me reeling. The contained, nearly airless environment has been a perfect petri dish for rotting meats, cheeses and old produce to host all manner of molds, fungus and bacteria. It smells like a landfill, toilet and a filled diaper, but stronger. Like I could be wearing the filled diaper on my face.

I've taken to wearing my father's T-shirts, due to my burgeoning belly, and I lift the neck of it over my nose, walking around that way, as briskly as possible, my own personal scent not nearly masking the stench. Slick juiciness coats the floor, sticky and nondescript. Water drops fall from the ceiling, remnants of yesterday's thunderstorm, dripping over rotted gunk, smearing it over the floor. I could contract something deadly in here, I'm sure of it. Salmonella. E. coli. *Ugh, what am I doing back here?* I remember the dog, and the very large, physical danger it presented. So obvious and bold. But now...I could bring a deadly bacteria home on my shoe soles, no doctors in sight. The silent invisible killer of mankind...before the Blur.

As fast as a large, pregnant woman walking through such dross possibly can, I decide to brave the stench and possible microscopic invaders for more than the cheap storefront chocolate. I get boxes of the good stuff. 70% cocoa, organic. No corn syrup or hydrogenation for Squirt. Hardcore chocolate. Growing accustomed to the smell, I move on, gathering bottles of juice, jars of peanut butter and canned goods. I'm just dumping everything non-perishable into my grocery carriage. I still have a lot of this at home, but the need to prepare for anything compels me, a squirrel before winter, hoarding food. Aside from the stench, the lack of people and the dark aisles, the trip is as uneventful as it might have been seven months ago. I push the over-full carriage out to the truck, unloading one bag at a time, careful to not lift too much, or push myself.

After looting groceries, I head to the pharmacy section and begin preparing for birth. August was helpful in this regard. I grab bottles of witch hazel and rubbing alcohol. Without an accurate prescription or a doctor or midwife to monitor me, the painkillers frighten me, so I decide against them. After a few minutes of fretting, I sweep the shelves' contents into the carriage with my arms, wanting to just get the hell out of there, and to never return. I'm going to take the whole pharmacy and sort it all out later, at home, where things aren't rotting. I may need all of it someday, and I have ceased feeling guilty about hoarding and over-preparing.

The looting takes me two hours. I've worked up a good sweat by the time I'm done, standing beside the now full truck. My blood is pumping. The sun shines on my face. I close my eyes and listen to the wind and the rustling leaves. Not a Blur in sight. Which, of course, doesn't mean they aren't present, but I decide that ignorance is bliss. That, and whether or not I'm home probably doesn't matter. If they want to turn me into dust, they can do it here or there. And August said the Blur he's encountered seem to prefer the cover of darkness.

Truck bed filled, I drive home, unload, feed Luke, let him out and then, feeling bolstered by my out and about achievement, I head back out, to the local farming supplies and hardware store, next to a popular yoga studio and a Goodwill. August and Mark seemed to enjoy tossing around ideas for how I could outfit the house with some early warning systems and other protection, but most of what they came up with seemed straight out of movies. Cans and bells on tripwires, boarded up windows, assorted booby traps.

The parking lot is empty. There isn't a car in sight.

The store must have closed due to the storm, before the event.

I slide out of the seat, wary of the emptiness around me, confidence fading. But I press forward and check the door. Locked. Of course.

I look at the mostly glass storefront, aisles of what I need on the other side. I consider breaking the window and climbing through, but I get visions of my belly being sliced open by an errant shard. Not going to happen. So how do I get in? I'm not exactly a locksmith.

I don't need to be, I think. In a world with no laws, rules or judgement, I can get as extreme as I want to and no one will ever care. I look back at the big truck and smile. "Sorry, Dad," I say, imagining what he would say about his pristine, shiny truck. Then I'm in the cab, swinging the vehicle around so the back end is facing the store. I put the truck in reverse and shove the gas pedal down. The wheels sputter and catch. The impact is jarring, but just for a moment, as the front door and windows on either side, give way to the truck. I pull forward again, hop out and grin at the gaping hole.

I feel bolstered by my ability to destroy. *I can do this*, I think. *I'm small, but I can fight if I have to.*

Inside the store, I gather several deadbolt kits, new bulbs for the burned-out, motion-sensitive flood lights at the house, fishing line and gardening poles for the tripwires, a bag of bells, nails and a new hammer. I'm sure my father has a hammer, but I don't want to waste time looking for it.

Before getting wood from the stacks behind the building, I have one more stop. Since this is a privately owned store, in New Hampshire, the back of the store is lined with guns. If there were anyone around to ask, I'm sure they'd say the weapons were for coons, coyotes and foxes, but people just like their guns. Not that the weapons did them any good in the end. They might not do me any good, either, but they'll make me feel better, at least. I have the one rifle at home, but I can position these around the house and the yard, so there's always one handy. I leave the handguns and take four rifles, mostly because I know how to shoot, reload and aim them.

I make several slow trips back and forth, carrying my goods out through the ruined storefront, loading up the truck. I'm acclimating to the endlessness of this type of life, which is interesting. Everything takes hours longer. But with nothing else to do, and no one else to deal with, I am hugely productive. I've even been doing some drawing, although the images that emerge are mostly terrifying, not meant for public consumption—if there were a public, which there isn't.

Back inside, as I reach for the last box of ammunition, I realize I'm still wearing the tentacle bracelet around my left wrist, the piece of the crash I took with me. I've been wearing it so long, this alien thing, that it feels like a part of me. It draws my awareness inward for a moment. I am barely recognizable to myself anymore. Huge, lumbering belly. I haven't plucked my eyebrows in months. The blue in my now wild hair is grown out and can be tucked behind my ears. It's been a while since I showered. Or shaved anything. I check my breath and wince. I need to remember to brush my teeth more often.

I look up at the gun display. The wall behind it is mirrored. The silhouette I see of myself is frighteningly wild, like I should be lumbering around the streets, naked, shouting obscenities at passing birds. I strain in the low light, to see my face, and I don't like what I find.

Such an abrupt morphing, both degrading and blossoming at once. I'm like a snake about to shed her skin, preparing for newness, or a hibernating bear, unsocial, fat and hunkering. In some ways I feel like a felled tree, only useful for the advancing of growth. Moss and insect homes. Felled trees and hibernating bears are unaware of their appearance, and just do their job. That's how they survive. So that's what I will do. Who cares what I look like?

Right now, nobody.

I make my way out of the hardware store and drive the truck through the chain link fence at the back. I consider the sheets of plywood first, but they're too big, so I settle for the easier to carry, easier to cut, pine planks. I take as many as I can, wipe the sweat from my brow and am assaulted by weariness. I did too much, but I decide to not be hard on myself. This stuff needed doing, and I've waited far too long to do it. Should have been done months ago. I'm not sure why I waited. I think preparing for a fight, somehow makes it feel more possible. Like setting a time and place for a schoolyard brawl. But now that I'm huge and swollen—in places beyond my belly—I feel less mobile and even more protective of the life inside me; the life that, if born today, would survive and grow outside of me. I'm going to turn the house into a fortress, a second womb for Squirt's safety.

Feeling lightheaded, I drive home, careful not to turn fast and lose the contents of my overfull truck bed. I sit in the driveway, watching Luke watch me through the window, his whole body moving back and forth from the vigorous wag of his tail. Then I lean my head back, watching him bounce side to side. The movement entrances me. My eyes slip shut.

I dream of August, whose face I can't see, although I know he is happy and smiling. In the dream, under a sunny sky, he hands me my bones, one by one. They are white, shiny and covered in scrawling, undecipherable, black script. Uninjured, I spread them out on the grass in an elegant, complicated pattern, and then take his warm, large hand in my small one. His fingers envelop mine, and I feel ready and satisfied.

When I wake to Luke's insistent barking, the pleasantness of the dream stays with me, although I swallow a throat lump over missing August, the man I've never met. Feeling slightly refreshed, I slide out of the truck cab and begin preparing our home for war.

44

POE

Ironically, boarding up my home, setting a tripwire perimeter with bells and stashing rifles in hides around the property are all activities that I manage well, but slowly. From beginning to end, my fortress-womb building takes two weeks. Sure, I need to take more than the usual amount of bathroom breaks, and once I'm down on my knees, standing is a slow, grunting affair. My skinny, muscular arms and equally slender legs are spindly sprigs framing a basketball, my belly button protruding like the air valve. I'm having mixed feelings about the stretch marks. If I lie on my back for too long, I can't breathe. In short, I'm huge. There is no denying I will be delivering a baby in a month. I just can't believe I'll get bigger.

Holding wood up while nailing it is a lot easier if you can hip check it into position. My sweaty, heavy body lacks grace and it frustrates me. The light in the house is diffused now, windows boarded up. The rooms around me are hot, airless and dusty. I sing quietly all day and talk to Luke and Squirt. And, if I'm honest, to myself. When I recognize the warm rumble approaching, those psyche scissor lines like earthquakes, mirror-shattering depression,

I enact embarrassing physical rituals. Activity I will have to cease doing if people ever find me.

It started the other day, after I thought I lost Luke. He went outside and took a good, long while to come back in. I called for him, quietly at first, wary of the unseen, and then loudly. I went outside and looked around for him, calling. After a few minutes, he came bounding back out of the woods, all muddy, but I was beside myself. I even yelled at him.

Trying to calm myself, I drew, and I got lost in it. Like driving a familiar road and suddenly being at your destination, the entire trip unnoticed, I saw the finished drawing on the floor in front of me. On several large sheets of paper, overlapping at the edges, I'd drawn an outline of my entire body. I was naked and holding a sharpie marker in my right hand. Upon inspecting my body, I saw black lines along one hip, one calf and both elbows, where I allowed the marker to glance off my sides as I traced.

Every day since then, Luke goes out into the woods for a while. I forgive him the freedom that I lack. Is he visiting the Blur? And also every day since then, dread burbles through my veins until I complete another body tracing. All of them I remember, now, though. I'm getting low on paper. The pages had gone askew when I stood up, fracturing my body, splitting the head in two, and I thought that it was a more accurate depiction of my breaking apart.

I fled from that state of mind by focusing on the house, and I'm done. I'm bored...and feeling like my mind is getting lost again. I talk to August twice a day, occasionally joking around with Mark, who may or may not have the depth required to keep up with my introspection. Perhaps before the event, he could have been one of my usual guy pals, someone to play video games with and we could eat macaroni and cheese. But now, as a mother and survivor, it's August who fuels my peace and my hope for the future. But that probably doesn't make me any different from the rest of them, all of whom had parents like mine: UFO abductees who built pods and shoved their children inside. They follow August, 'like I'm some kind of cult leader,' he said. It makes him uncomfortable, the responsibility, but can you blame them? Twenty eight people all with the same parting message from doomed parents—Find August—against incredible odds, manage to find him.

I keep busy with Luke and his daily routines, which are basically a cycle of sleeping, eating and pooping. The good life, though mine isn't too different now. I nap, make food and draw. I'm out of shape, which worries me, but walking around the neighborhood makes me feel too vulnerable and watched, with reason. There'll be no running away for me. I'm nesting, which seems very funny to me. A little blue-haired mama bird, my dead mama's sewing kit beside me on the living room couch, botching up infant-sized T-shirts made from my father's flannels. If only I had paid more attention to my mother's (and my father's, for that matter) domestic capabilities. This child would have been styling.

Theories tumble around in my head—the most potent one, currently, is that the Benevolent Blur, the naturey-smelling ones, are peaceable, at least now. It hasn't escaped my notice that they turned Leila to powder in the same way that my parents, and everyone else, died. The guys haven't dealt with that yet—not since the human race-ending attack anyway—and it's a good thing, because they'd be dead already, if they had.

Maybe the Blur have different jobs, wherever they're from? At times I want to extrapolate theories about who or what they are, but the anxiety of that intellectual effort leaves me breathless, hyperventilating, a reminder of my utter and alien aloneness, August still just not here, his three day car ride transformed into a six month migration. At least Squirt grows, steadily, on her own. I never thought that being pregnant would make me realize a human's true capacity for independence. She is truly her own little person, and I, am truly mine.

When the phone rings, I shout in surprise, which is common enough these days that Luke just raises an eyebrow at me. I look around and find myself sitting on the couch. When did I sit down? I can't remember. Nor do I remember picking up my sketch pad and charcoal. The image on the page draws a second shout from my mouth: it's a Blur, vague except for its wooden face. I've drawn it so well, that for a moment, I feel its presence, and I think I can smell roses. Inside the dead eyes, the oil swirls are in the shape of a baby, umbilical curling around the small body.

They're watching her, I think, and I shout a third time when the phone rings again. I take a deep breath and answer the phone. "Hi."

"You sound upset," he says.

"I drew another picture." I've told him about this, that I draw without remembering, without planning. He knows about the fissure. I thought that by bringing it into the light, I might help combat it, but I think I'm just making August worry.

"Anything you want to talk about?"

I look down at the craggy face, its child eyes, and then I smear my hand across the page, smudging it into oblivion. "No. I'm fine."

"How fine?"

"Perfectly," I say, sticking out my jaw with no one to see. The bravado and defiance is an act, but no one likes an emotional martyr.

"Then I think it's time."

"For what."

"To tell you about the Blur. To tell you what they really are."

I know all about his last encounter with the Blur. He called me that same night, and then again the following morning to tell me about the autopsy. He made it to the eye-stabbing when I stopped him. I nearly threw up. The detail was so disturbing, too perfectly conjured in my mind, that I couldn't handle it. But now...fortress made, weapons ready, perhaps he's right.

I should know my enemy.

"Just...go slow." The last thing I need is to crack up and greet them in the nude upon their final, triumphant arrival, covered in paint or something. The thought makes me snort with laughter.

"What's...so funny?" he asks.

I don't answer him. "Luke, no. No, boy, here!" He trots over to me, sock in mouth. I pry it from his jaws, roll it up and throw it for him.

"Sorry," I say, "throwing the balled up sock for Luke."

"Poe," he says, sounding a little sad. "You need to know what you're up against. How to hurt them. We've been lucky so f—"

"Or they left," I say.

"We can't even entertain that idea. Not until we're together and you're both safe."

Both. "I'm listening."

So, he explains, unveiling all the gory details; that they are actually endlessly long worms crammed inside two suits, the first like an invisibility cloak, the other to hold all their loose forms together and protect them.

"I see," I say, switching the satellite phone to my other hand.

He's quiet, too, for a minute. "You still there?" he asks.

I am, but I don't say so. Instead, I feel an uncultivated, feral shiver slowly push normal reasoning aside, like sliding a full bureau across a bedroom floor to a corner. The halting and skidding. A bit of shoving with one hip, and then a final positioning. Out of the way, in the room, but no longer the focus. I realize he's been talking to me.

"...laws of physics, but can definitely be injured and killed. How many guns do you have?" I wonder what else he's said that I've missed. I watch the new brain fuzziness with interest. It's quieter here, like being under a heavy blanket. With enormous effort, I mentally pull myself back to the conversation and mumble something to him.

"A few." The shiver hovers, wanting me back. This new development, combined with the ever-present fractures in need of constant monitoring, is rendering my psyche near unrecognizable. I imagine a brick building, only a few seconds into an earthquake, chunks of concrete foundation crumbling. The perfect image, combining both the fissures and this new shuddering. A beautiful metaphor. My father would have loved it.

"Poe, are you all right?" August doesn't wait for me to answer, unusual for him. "Listen. This is important. You can kill them with fire. Do you have some glass bottles around, like liquor bottles, maybe in the basement?"

A few more chunks fall from the foundation, tumble into the earthquake-created crack below. In my mind's eye, I watch the fragments tumble, down, down, into darkness, a deep too far to measure. "Why would I need glass bottles?"

"I was thinking you could make Molotov cocktails—you know, with rags and alcohol, or gasoline, stuff them in there. Poe, you need to focus. I...I just...if I'm not there in time and it's the baby they want..." I recognize that his voice sounds frantic, but it's also distant and muffled, the message unclear. I stand up and stretch, shake my head. I will pretend to still be here one hundred percent.

I try to deflect, but end up being honest. "I'm feeling a little funny."

Look at me, being vulnerable.

Bricks start to fall from the side of my mental building.

"Is the baby okay? Are you feeling her move around a lot?" His voice, so tender, a feather on my cheek. I put my free left hand to my cheek, pressing my palm against my skin. I run my fingers through the hair above my ear.

August, help me.

"She's fine. It's funny, she wiggled a bit when you said that," I say, managing a tiny chuckle. The pitch of my voice drops an octave. "I think it's my brain. I might be losing my mind." I start to cry. An entire brick wall crumbles, a pile of dust.

His voice is firm, immediate. "You are *not* losing your mind, Poe. You're my smart, brave girl. Do you hear me? You are *not* alone. I'm with you. I am right here with you. Together we're strong, okay? Poe? Sweetheart?"

A gentle jingle tickles my ears. I look toward Luke, on the floor, chewing a sock—what ever happened to his tennis ball? He still wears tags, so I can locate him easier, but right now, they're pinned beneath his furry neck, unmoving. Not making a sound.

From the front of the house, I hear the now distinct jingle of bells.

The tripwire.

My heart beats hard.

Vision tunnels.

Squirt goes suddenly still.

"August?" I whisper.

"You have to stay strong, Poe. I'm on my way."

"I think they're here."

45

AUGUST

My bike wobbles beneath me as I slip off the seat and let go of the single handlebar I'd been holding while speaking to Poe. The bike continues on without me for ten feet, slows and then tips, sprawling like a man whose limbs have just suddenly stopped working. I land on my feet, phone crushed to my ear.

"Poe," I say, my voice barely controlled. "What's going on?"

I hear shuffling. Breathing. Then a loud thud, and nothing. Silence. My phone beeps at me, and I pull it away. The screen reads, *connection lost*.

I frantically redial. It rings without stop.

Mark pulls up beside me. "What's up?"

"She's not answering."

"Could it be—"

The look in my eyes silences Mark. "She said they were there. She thought they were there. The Blur. Damn it!"

I want to smash the phone on the pavement. I want to scream. But I contain my anger and fear, disconnecting the call and putting the phone back in my pocket. Poe will call me back.

If she can.

I hate myself and my personal limits. If I was stronger, faster, younger and not fighting some kind of alien infection, I'd be there by now.

Fight them, Poe, I think. *Stay alive.*

The men and women biking with me, people I now consider my tribe, pull to a stop, looking at Mark and me. Their concern is evident. And appreciated, because I'm about to announce a doubling of our efforts, turning our cycling equivalent of a marathon pace into something closer to a sprint, knowing full well that I'm the one who will slow us down. But I'm fueled by desperation. My lips pucker to form the first sound in the word, "We," but it's not my voice that fills the air.

"Help!"

All eyes turn to the road ahead.

"What is it?" I ask Mark, who is taller than me and standing on the pedals of his perfectly balanced, motionless bike, looking over the heads of the people in front of us.

"Looks like Jon."

Before the end, Jon was a fitness freak. He's lean, but powerful, like a shaggy haired supermodel. Brook, his girlfriend, is like a female version of Jon, except she somehow keeps her wavy hair well brushed, despite wearing a helmet most of the day. Together, they are our point riders. They stay an hour ahead of us, watching for obstacles we might need to detour around, scoping out places to sleep at the end of every day. They're a pair of powerhouse introverts, but they're always together.

When I don't see Brook, the hair on my arms stands up.

Then the tone of Jon's voice settles in. I pick up my discarded bike, climb back on, and pedal hard, rounding the group to the front, where Tanya and Jeb have met Jon.

The world as I knew it is gone. My daughter along with it. But traveling with this group of fellow survivors, I have once again found community. More than that, really. Before humanity was wiped out, my community consisted almost completely of colleagues. Sure, I considered many of them to be friends, but we talked, almost exclusively, about work. But now? I'm leading a bicycle gang of twentysomethings who wear their feelings on their sleeves and aren't afraid to get their hands dirty with each other's problems. The result is a cohesive, healthy, thriving—and mobile—colony.

The future of mankind.

And I've become fiercely protective of them. Though if I'm honest, my heart belongs to Poe. She gave me hope when there was none. I love her like a daughter. I'll love her baby like my own grandchild. If they make it. If they survive. If we reach them in time.

The best guess for our arrival in New Hampshire—we're currently riding on Pennsylvania's Interstate 78—is two weeks, sometime in the first few days of August. That's also the best guess for when she's due. She hasn't complained about it much, but I know that child is weighing on her, both emotionally and physically. Strong as she is, she'll be waddling like a penguin, struggling to do anything more than survive.

My insides are tearing as I ride toward Jon, knowing in my gut that Poe will be on her own for a while longer, despite the desperation I feel. I want to scream, to pedal like a maniac and ride with the strength and speed of a demigod, but I can't abandon these people. Not only would it be wrong, but Poe wouldn't want me to. Even if this is something simple, like an injury, we're not...*I'm* not...going to get much faster. Exhaustion plagues me. At night, we hide, sleeping in locked basements or other easily defendable positions. But once that sun comes up, we haul ass, slowed mostly by the limitations of my age, and the rash-induced infection sapping my strength.

"They took her!" Jon says as I ride up, his words sealing Poe's fate in my mind. "Tried to kill me."

There's blood on his shirt, but I can't tell what kind of wound he received.

"I—I didn't want to run, but—" He shakes his head. He's abandoned the woman he loves.

"Doesn't sound like you had a choice," I say, but there is no more time to salve his emotional wounds, or even his physical ones. Poe needs us. Now. But if Brook needs us first, there is no time to waste. I take his face in my hand and speak in a tone that I hope will cut straight through the hundred horrible scenarios he's conjured about Brook's fate. "Who took her? The Blur?"

"H—human. Rashes. A gang of them."

"How many?"

"Thirty. Maybe more."

This is already looking grim. We're outnumbered.

"What else can you tell me about them?" I ask.

He blinks his eyes and wipes away the tears. Focusing. "They, ahh, they were crazy. Ambushed us. About ten miles up the road."

This doesn't sound entirely true. It's hard to believe anyone could catch Jon or Brook when they were on bikes.

"*How* did they catch you?" I ask.

A moment of shame is replaced by a set jaw. "We'd stopped to... We were..."

"I get it," I say, putting my hand on his shoulder. As fast as the pair is, they never seem to get as far as I think they could in a single day. Jon's perpetual smile, after a day of hard riding, always tells the truth. They stopped for some extracurricular activity and literally got caught with their pants down. "Were they armed?"

He nods his head. "Yeah, but with axes and swords. Shit like that. Some had bows and arrows. But not all of them had two arms. They were all shirtless. Even the women. They all had the rash on their chests, but it looked like their skin had been melted. Hanging from the stubs of their arms. From their faces. Like they had been melted, but not from fire. It was just loose, like..."

"Hochman's," I say, remembering the photos of people in the middle stages of the fast moving disease. Layers of fat and connective tissue holding skin in place would degrade, giving the infected the appearance of melting. Joints slipped free, and weakened flesh simply tore. Sometimes the fingers would go first. Then the arms. And eventually the legs. Life slipped away after that, as the internal organs turned to mush. The whole process took just days. But from Jon's description, the Rashes he encountered showed the *scars* of Hochman's, not the disease itself. If they'd been symptomatic, they would have been lying on the ground, slowly coming undone.

And that means they survived it somehow.

Saying the name of the disease that, prior to the end of civilization, threatened to end humanity in its own way, sends a hush through the group.

"Yeah," Jon says. "Like Hochman's."

"Could it be connected to the rash?" Jeb asks.

I glance at my shoulder, and Mark answers for me. "Naw, man. The rash isn't Hochman's."

We've talked about this before. All the people they encountered with the rash before meeting me had always been violent. Deranged. Like Crazy Lady. I have the same rash, even now, faded but present. Mark knows about it, but I've hidden it from the rest, mostly because I need them to trust me, to get me to Poe, but I've also never had a violent urge toward anyone in the group. Mark and I have never discussed it, but he's kept my secret. Knows what it could mean. For me. For Poe.

Jeb doesn't look convinced. And while I agree with Mark, there isn't time to get into how he knows that the rash isn't a Hochman's symptom. Brook is in trouble...and Poe is still too God-damned far away. "If they had Hochman's, they don't anymore, so let's worry about what we know for sure instead of getting worked up about what we don't." I motion to the wound on Jon's shoulder. "Is that okay?"

He looks at the bloody, but no longer bleeding, wound. "This was from a knife. Just a nick, but I couldn't get to my gear."

I try not to shake my head. Despite the casual air of the group, we have rules, one of which is to never be out of arm's reach from your weapon. If the Blur take another shot at us, we'll be ready. Apparently, it's other survivors we're not prepared for. The sun was up, so Jon let his guard down.

"Wouldn't be the apocalypse without some Mad Max assholes, right?" Jeb says. His attempt at humor is too accurate to be funny.

"Anything else?" I ask.

"They were on foot," he says, eyes up, thinking. "Dogs. They had dogs. Pitbulls mostly. Some chased me half the way here. And that rash... All of them. Dark black rings. Around their hearts." He taps his chest over his heart. "Just to the left of center."

I glance at my shoulder, where my rash is hidden. It's further to the left, originating from my shoulder. Could that be the difference? Whatever it is driving these people to kill their own doesn't work on me because the Blur missed my heart?

It occurs to me that this might be Brook's true fate. She'll be infected and come looking for Jon, who would be defenseless against her. He'd run right into her blade before ever considering she might turn it on him. But it's the Blur that do the infecting, with that long finger-needle organic suit. A memory of the Blur's stringy insides flits through my mind and sends a shiver through my body. I keep my thoughts on Brook, who I care for, and whose salvation puts us back on the path to Poe. "We need to find her before it gets dark."

"Find her?" Tanya asks. She's apparently decided that Brook's fate is sealed. "We need to protect the people here. Find a way around."

Part of me is tempted to agree. Abandoning Brook appeals to the part of me that is terrified about Poe's fate. But I couldn't leave Brook to that fate any more than I could leave Poe. There isn't time to argue, so I slide my backpack off, pull out my map and unfold it on the pavement. After finding our location on the map, I point to the off ramp we passed a mile back. "Here. Head back. Take this exit onto 309. Take Taylor Drive to Route 412 and then back up to the Interstate."

I follow the map up, ten miles. The 412 exit is fifteen miles ahead, beyond where Brook was taken, and hopefully beyond the gang's base of operations, if they have one. For all we know, they might be on their way here, or like us, they might be heading north. Either way, I'm going to reach them before the group does.

"We won't make it there before nightfall," Tanya points out.

I nod. "Find someplace to sleep. I'll meet you there in the morning."

"You're going after her?" she asks.

"I'd go after you, too." I fold up the map, stuff it back in my pack and hold the gear up. "One of our own has been taken. I'm going to get her back." The group around me, some of whom have heard the exchange, some of whom were out of earshot, stare at me. "I need someone to take my pack for the night."

Tanya takes the heavy backpack and places it on her handlebars.

"Thanks," I say. "Just get everyone to a safe house tonight. We'll meet up at the 412 junction at first light. We're going to ride hard from here on out."

"Is Poe in trouble?" she asks, and my tough front nearly cracks.

I manage a nod. "Brook first. Then Poe."

Mark holds his pack up. "Mine, too."

A volunteer quickly steps forward and takes the pack.

"Mark," I say. "You don't—"

"I'm coming."

"Me, too," Jeb says, and he hands his pack off to someone without asking.

Jon is coming, too. That's a given. And he doesn't have a backpack to give up. He lost everything, including his gun. "Jon needs a weapon," I say.

Tanya, who is now overloaded with two packs, happily hands over her sub machine gun and two extra clips. Jeb says it's an MP5. I have no idea, but the weapon came from the trunk of a police car along with a shotgun and two pistols. Whatever it is, it's deadly.

Deadly.

I try not to think about it, but I'm keenly aware as I ride away from my new family, that before this night is through, I will have killed again. But this time it won't be a Blur...

It will be people.

46

POE

Barefoot and pregnant, a living cliché, I stand and waddle to the wall, switching off the light. August is still on the phone, and Luke, hot on my heels, bounds around, thinking we're playing.

"Poe? What's going on?" August is saying.

I move to the kitchen, switching the lights off there. Why am I shutting off the lights? It's harder to see now. *Harder for them to see you, too*, I shout at myself, feeling serious and loopy at the same time.

Scrambling through the kitchen back to the living room, I trip on the threshold and land on my hands and knees, my heavy belly pendulous and tight under me. Some deep, interior abdomen muscle pulls, and I wince. The phone flies out of my hand and crashes against the piano. I scoot over on all fours, pick it up and place it against my ear.

"Hello? August?" I hear nothing. *Don't be broken, don't be broken.* I hit the power button but nothing happens. The phone is silent. Dead. He's gone.

Like Santa and his eight tiny reindeer, another jingling sounds from the front yard. I sit back on my haunches, wondering what to do. More jingling. The tripwires are nearly invisible; I did a great job hiding them, having worked on the placement for several days, doing nothing else. But now, here I am, crouched and voluptuous with child, alarmed by my own alarm. What good is this early warning going to do me if I just sit here?

Maybe it's just a deer, or a dog. I tiptoe to one of the boarded up living room windows and peer through the thin line between the boards. I left just enough space at the bottom of the windows to be able to open them three inches, or I would have started going crazy from staleness and the creeping quiet in here. The sunshine outside is bright and blinding, but low in the sky.

Daylight is safe, I tell myself, but I'm not convinced. Leila. The dog. The battle. In my experience, bad things happen while the sun is up.

My parents set the house fairly far back from the road, so an acre of land sits between me and the first tripwire, which runs along the line of trees at the road.

It keeps jingling, but I can't see anything.

I look for deer. For bears. For things that are visible. But what if it *is* the Blur? Part of me says, *hogwash*, that aliens capable of wiping out the human race wouldn't be tricked by tripwires. Or would they? It worked for Arnold Schwarzenegger in that movie. I should have rigged up some falling logs, or spiky traps, too.

And what if we're right, that there are two vying groups of Blur? How will I tell them apart without walking up and asking for a sniff test. I smell the air, but sense nothing beyond the hot dry dust of a window sill.

A more disturbing thought sneaks past what feeble defenses remain, *what if it doesn't matter?*

Maybe all of the Blur have just been biding their time? Maybe they did something to my parents, and now the aliens have come to collect me and Squirt. They'll pluck me from the house and my baby from my womb. And then what? More tests? On both of us? Or maybe they'll be done with me. Discarded, they'll keep my baby. Maybe raise her. The petri dish cleaned, maybe they'll start a new experiment. Name her Eve.

Seriously, my brain, evil disturber, will throw me under the bus way before my body gives in. I can't keep a sane thought in my head. I'm not even sure if the thoughts that sound insane, really are. Thinking positive thoughts might be what's crazy right now.

I run to a window on the side of the room, above the couch, and peer through the thin line. The forest on this side is filling in nicely, the rush of early summer growth, no wavering shapes in sight. What is hitting the wires?

Kneeling on the couch, I plunge my hand between the cushions and take hold of the rifle buried there. I spend a lot of time on the couch, and I pictured a Blur coming through the living room door, thinking me defenseless only to find a rifle quick at hand. It's not exactly what happens, but I still feel glad for the preparation. My father's rifle slides out from between the cushions, loaded and ready to go, covered in dust bunnies. With light fingers, I brush off the rifle, along with the surge of sadness that comes unbidden, with his possessions.

The second tripwire jingles, the bells a different size than the first. Without meaning to, I set up a musical early warning system, the sounds as lovely as a porch wind chime.

Any animal with a brain or instincts would have run from the first chimes. The identity of my visitor is down to two possibilities. Human or Blur.

They're coming, I think, but I'm afraid to commit to the idea. *It could be people. August has twenty-eight people with him. That could happen to me.*

The sky starts to darken and color. Dusk is upon us.

Night is coming. August's forbidden darkness. Maybe he was right.

I'm tempted to open the front door to the porch, demand whoever it is to show themselves. I imagine laughing at a shy deer, tangled in the wire, and freeing it, while Luke barks from the house. He would want to play with it.

Maybe that's all it is.

My eyes are slits, squinting through the planks over the window. I lean down. The window is open a crack. I turn and press my ear as close as I can, squishing my head against the plywood. After the second jingle, it's been silent.

Remembering the back door, I scoot back through the kitchen, lock the deadbolt and bump a long section of two-by four onto the hooks I attached to the frame. It will take a battering ram to get through it. Or whatever an advanced civilization might use.

Back door secure, I mentally run through the upstairs, everything tight and locked down. Basement, secure. The bulkhead lock is thick steel, and the door at the bottom is boarded up.

How will I know if it's the Bad Blur? August, where are you? How will I know?

His voice arrives in my head, my own personal Yoda, or the onset of schizophrenia. "You'll know, Poe. You'll know."

I'm panicking. Impending doom overwhelms me. I can't do this. I can't stand, on my own, against this. Not now.

I don't care who is out there.

Let it come. I don't care.

And then, I do. Because I can see it.

The backdrop of trees behind the cleared space of the front yard, where Leila threw the ball to Luke, a million years ago, warbles, as though seen through running water.

The shimmering quickens, and I know what comes next. The heavily lined face, like wood, materializes in a flash, like a light switch, somehow the black oiliness meeting my eyes, even through the board-ed window. The eyes promise suffering, and indifference to it.

I half expect to see anger and aggression seeping out of this thing, my enemy, but it looks as frozen-faced and uncaring as the first Blur I saw. *It's a mask*, I remind myself. *A biological suit.* The Blur don't have faces. Not really.

It's difficult to aim out the window, the opening so low and narrow. I hadn't thought of this. My preparations are those of a bored and broken woman. August was right. I'm out of time, and I didn't focus. Randomly, without aiming through the scope, I fire the rifle in the general direction of the Blur. A part of me just wanting to miss. Let them come.

The explosive shot reverberates through the living room, assault-ing my ears. Squirt flinches with a kick. But I don't slow. I pull the rifle back, and look through the window. The shimmering shape quavers. The tall grass beneath it flattens out. Did I hit it? Is it dead? *No*, I think, vaguely remembering something August said about fire.

I'm sorry, Squirt, I gave in too soon. You should have picked someone else. Someone mightier.

Be mighty now.

I chamber the next round, shove the rifle out the window and pull the trigger. I repeat the process again and again without checking for results, firing an aimless swath through the slender woods in the front yard.

You can all die, motherfuckers.

Descending darkness stops my barrage. I glance through the window. If there are any others, I can't see them. I *won't* see them. Fatigue settles into my core, weighing down my limbs. The pendulum that is my hormone-laden mind shifts. I don't want to figure anything out anymore. Don't want to fight. The loss of connection with August, and the coming night, plucked out my last thread of give-a-shit.

But I shot it, didn't I? It could be dead.

The third jingle, the bells' peal closest to the house, the highest note, agitates the sudden quiet from my ceased rifle. So alone, yet obviously not, I place my hands on my belly, feeling around with deep breaths for Squirt. Squirt, who in the absence of August, can give me strength for whatever is out there.

I feel nothing. My heart barrels over, thumping. Did the rifle firing affect her? The sound of it? The jolts? I rub my hands all over my belly, which is only smooth, round and motionless. Have I harmed her?

My worries are interrupted by the motion detector light illuminating the side of the house.

Not the front.

I don't want to look. I feel around for Squirt, and again, nothing.

I scurry into the kitchen, hands and knees, and peer through the small window.

The yard, cast in the triggered flood light, shimmers. For as far as I can see, past the edge of the light's influence, into the dark yard. The woods. Everything.

The air itself appears to be alive.

A horde of Blur, come to collect their prize.

47

POE

The yard, illuminated by the motion sensor light, looks like it's underwater. So many Blur, no separation between them. The visual distortion extends past the edge of the light into the now darkness of early evening, their bodies overlapping, crushed together in countless numbers. There could be twenty of them. There could be fifty.

What are they waiting for? What do they want?

My hands find my belly again, feel for Squirt, who is still, motionless.

I have lost August.

I have lost my reasoning.

I have lost my baby.

Let them come.

I'm done.

I lay down on the couch in the dark, quiet house, a shell. Luke, who had been hiding under an upstairs bed during the shooting, pads down the stairs and into the living room. He licks my hand, dangling off the couch. I stare at him, glassy eyed. I don't pet him. I notice each of his eyebrow hairs, lit up from the outside light, his soft, golden forehead, where I always kiss him.

Everything is quiet.

And then, assault.

The house rattles.

Doors first.

I should have listened to August. Should have focused past the fissures. Should have stayed sane.

They're trying to get in.

Luke barks at the front door and runs into the kitchen, barking at the window and the back door. Apparently we're surrounded. I seem to be floating somewhere outside of my body. In the room? Outside of the house? I don't know and I don't care. I watch Luke run around, barking, frantic, the sounds of actual, living aliens pulling siding and window frames off the exterior of my house.

They fly through the galaxy from who knows where and they can't make it into my house? Little old pregnant me? Can't they just blast their way in? Turn the walls to powder? The hell is taking them so long? A trickle of information finds its way from the depths: they have limits. August says. They're not soldiers. They're scientists. Just because they're an advanced civilization, doesn't mean they carry around alien bazookas.

They were fighting. In the sky. They must have some kind of weaponry...

You can't pluck a lone woman from a house with weapons designed for shooting down other UFOs.

They want us alive.

I sit up and lean against the back of the couch like a drugged person. Indifference lolls my head to the side, as I watch the second wall of my interior brick building crumble into the widening cracks. Then the picture goes blank, like the end of an old-fashioned movie reel, white space at the end of the show, the flap of the projection film, around and around.

I lose consciousness, slipping to the side, feeling gravity's tug.

Then nothing.

I awake when I hit the floor, one arm draped over my big belly. From my sideways visual, Luke faces the big living room window, his front paws up on the couch, barking and snarling. Slow motion barking, his sound deep and long. A long, thin, sharp object extends into the house, sneaking through the small opening where I had been firing the rifle into the yard, aimed toward Luke's chest.

Is that Luke?

The sweet, docile and passive pet is gone. It looks like Luke, but he's transformed into an enraged beast, finally finding the canine savagery he lacked when we first met. The sight of him shakes my apathy. He is going to protect me, or die trying.

A voice, actual, real and known, although not one I've ever heard before, speaks in thin, sprawling ink across the white space—the space where I used to produce art, the space where I used to care.

You were made for a purpose.

You were saved for a purpose.

Get up.

Get.

Up.

Fight!

I stand, dizzied. Get my feet beneath me.

The finger is inches from Luke's fluffy chest. He hasn't seen it. These are August's Blur. They kill with those fingers.

They're going to kill my dog!

Crystal clarity snaps into my mind, the pendulum of sanity no longer swinging.

"Not fucking happening," I say, and then I yell, "Luke!" He bounds off the couch to me, tail wagging, savagery gone. His eyes flit toward the window, but he stays with me, the alpha in charge once more.

From the kitchen I grab the largest knife, and chop at the needle-like finger now tugging at the wood covering the window.

The cleaved digit falls off and lands behind the couch, the arm withdrawing from the window. Wasting no time, I grab the rifle and aim out the window. I pull the trigger, reload and repeat using the rounds filling my pockets, balancing on my bare feet, a tiny woodland sprite gone bonkers.

Out of ammunition, I pull out the box waiting for me on a nearby shelf and reload. Shattering glass erupts into the kitchen, skittering through the gaps between the boards. They must be standing on the bulkhead, to reach the window. A rancid chemical smell, burnt plastic, roils into the house like thick clouds, causing me to gag. Luke runs to the kitchen, barking and snarling, ready to defend. But what else can I do, aside from spray bullets? I'm not even sure it's working.

"Come on, Poe," I say aloud, my words a croak. "You were raised better than this." I will not let them down.

What did August say?

A single word enters my thoughts.

Fire.

You can kill them with fire.

Molotov cocktail, I think, remembering his mention of glass bottles. I recall footage of the revolts in the Ukraine. The rebels used Molotov cocktails against the riot police, driving them back, their shields and numbers suddenly useless.

I run to the basement, even as I hear another window shatter, somewhere else on the first floor. In one corner, my parents' recycling still sits, never actually recycled after their deaths. They did so much of their own homemade cooking, canning and brewing, the recycling sat here forever, never quite full enough to bother with. I rifle through the glass and plastic and find a whiskey bottle. Then two more.

Quicker, Poe. They're coming.

I spin in a circle, looking for some kind of flammable fuel, and I spot a red gas can sitting by the bulkhead door. With the three bottles half full, I take rags from the workbench and stuff them into the bottles. I don't know if I'm doing this right—every move I perform is based on actors in movies I've watched with my guy friends, usually while doing drinking games or drawing.

Wood snaps upstairs, sharp and surprising. Three bottles in hand, I huff up the stairs, careful not to trip again, and I place them on the table. In the living room, I pick up my rifle, which I realize I should have never left. I aim it right into the undulating mass of warbling Blur, pressed against the cracking wood of the kitchen window above the sink. Then fire. The sound barely registers on my ears now, either toughened, or deafened. The bullet punches through wood and glass, and then body suit. The Blur falls away, which I see as a sudden clearing of the air.

I fire again and again, grunting, exhausted. Is this hurting Squirt? Am I hurting *them*? Their chemical pungency scorches the insides of my nose and mouth, making my eyes water. I reload, and fire into the crowd outside the kitchen windows, like some kind of crazed police officer at a protest, afraid and confused by the throng's intent. Then I run to the living room window and repeat.

A long, dull cramp climbs up the side of my abdomen and then tightens across the width of it. And then another, the tightness distracting me.

Oh my god, no.

Not labor. Not now. It's too early.

The mammalian instincts from months ago in the woods kick in hard and sudden, a whiplash, like stepping on the gas. I reload again and again, spending all my ammunition. I'm kicking ass. I've done enough damage to stagger some of them backward from the kitchen window, but many more climb up onto the bulkhead, their faces slipping in and out of view, my brain forming new ways to see their invisible outlines.

Time to push them back a little further, I decide.

I get a lighter from the junk drawer, lift the bottles from the table and head upstairs.

Way up in the attic, I didn't bother covering the two tiny windows. That's where I go now, with my matches and three small bombs. The windows are ancient, stuck shut, maybe even painted shut. I have to stand on a chest to reach them. Using an old, small club, like something you'd used to churn butter or grind grains, I pound against the window until it shatters. But I swing too hard. My arm slips through the broken glass.

I scream, my arm bloodied, glass splinters sticking out of it. I leave them in my arm, but clear the rest from the window.

Now or never, Poe.

From two stories up, I lean out just a bit, flick the lighter to life and place it against the rag. It smolders briefly, but nothing happens. What did I do—the rag is dry! I tip the bottle upside down, watching the gasoline inside soak quickly through the rag. The smell of gasoline blends in with the acrid odor of the Blur, but makes me smile. I try the lighter again.

The rag ignites immediately.

I hurl the bottle down and just far enough away to not set the house on fire.

I hope.

A beautiful explosion lights the night.

I will listen to everything you say from now on, August.

My left arm is seriously bleeding, but I know it will be worse if I pull the glass out. I hurl the second one down onto the crowd, enjoying the sight of them scattering, now ablaze, high pitched shrieking in the air, like I've just lit a bunch of cartoon chipmunks on fire. Another tight spasm ripples across my abdomen, the cramp stable and lasting.

You have to wait, honey, you have to wait.

God, not now.

On the opposite end of the attic, the other window waits, intact, Blur below it at the kitchen. This time, I see my old baseball bat in the corner, and a rush of youthful, pre-pregnancy energy fills me. I am still that person.

Two swings, hard. Even with the bleeding arm and the enormous middle, the small window shatters. In seconds I've thrown the third cocktail down onto the Blur.

I peer down. Chaos. And lots of fire.

A third cramp pulls my abdomen so taut I have to sit down and take deep breaths. When it subsides, I realize I may have just set my house on fire.

Distracted by this, I hustle down the stairs, sweaty, barefoot and bleeding from my arm. When I turn the corner into the living room, I run smack into an invisible wall.

The door hangs on hinges, deadbolt torn away, wood shattered.

They got through while I was upstairs. I don't even have time to wonder where Luke is, before invisible, shimmering limbs surround my legs and lift me into the air, flipping me upside down, my head inches from my parents' braided rug.

I still have the baseball bat in my hand and swing it, upside down, at all the warbling nothingness around me. It connects with alternating squishy and cracking sounds. It's quickly taken away from me.

Why did I leave the rifle? I suck at this!

Luke's name is in my throat, but I want him to be safe, so instead I think, *Hide, Luke, hide.* Limbs flailing, blood rushing to my face, coughing from the inescapable burning stench of the Blur, I scream at them.

"Bastards! Let me go!" I can't breathe. My own heavy belly is suffocating me, upside down like this. I get the sense they're laughing at me as I feel another texture hold my arms fast, and I'm tipped horizontally, like on a stretcher.

They're carrying me out of my house. This is it. The end of my one beautiful life: craziness in the woods, like my parents.

"Help," I cough. Just a whisper.

It's quiet as my captors carry me out onto the grass, the flames already gone, burned away with the gasoline.

A sudden but distant noise startles the Blur holding me to a standstill.

Grinding.

The noise should terrify me. It took my parents from me. It took everyone—including Leila. But when I hear it this time, I smile. The sound gives me hope.

The noise increases in volume, just like before, and the Blur spring into action, hurrying. I see a similar craft like the one in the woods, out past my driveway, around the corner, the two intersecting rings.

The Blur run now, moving my body bumping across the lawn, lugging me to their craft. And then what? Will they take Squirt? They would have already killed me if that was what they wanted.

"Help!" I shout.

The crushing grind increases, faster, louder, faster, and Luke comes tearing out onto the front yard, barking and snarling, biting at the Blur. One of them flings him aside, the shimmering warping his golden body as they fight him off.

We're at the street now. Luke shakes off the hit and runs back, biting and barking. He gets hold of the Blur carrying me, gripping the weird invisible cloak that the dog seems to know is there. I'm dropped. My head hits the street and I see stars. But I'm not free. The creature drags me by my naked ankles, the back of my head ripping along the pavement. I'm going to black out. My fingernails bleed, scratching the road.

Luke releases the strange fabric and disappears beneath it. A high-pitched alien shriek follows, and then a loud yelp. The grinding reaches fever pitch. The Blur drops me, stumbling a few feet away. Luke emerges from beneath the cloak, laying on the ground, burying his head under his paws. If he's badly hurt, I can't see where. Me on the other hand... I'm a bleeding mess, nearly unconscious, my uterus a series of cresting contractions. I crawl on all fours to Luke and rest my head on top of him. I cover my exposed ear with one arm.

The shape of my captor shimmers fast. It focuses its masked face on me, its intent malicious, despite the lack of expression. The grinding grows unbearably loud.

I look around. Luke and I are once again surrounded by the Blur. With some understanding of their physiology and the bodies beneath the cloaks, I see pain in their movements. The noise is twisting them.

The grinding stops, and the visible invisibility all around us crumples to the ground. White powder wafts out into the night air, barely visible in the now distant flood lights.

I hug Luke close to me, crying into his fur. He whines and twists around, trying to lick my face. I feel around on the back of my head. I'm missing a lot of hair, and pebbles are stuck in my scalp.

Squirt gives me a rambunctious kick.

I focus on my belly, searching for the twisting pain of contractions. But nothing happens.

False labor. Thank God.

Sitting there bleeding on the road, with Luke, a gentle breeze brings with it the smell of gardens. Basil. Lilacs. Tomato plant leaves.

And, roses.

I can't see anything, but even the darkness can't hide their invisible light.

I throw a clump of dirt at them, crying.

"Took you guys long enough."

The shhh-shhh of walking Blur fades along with the natural scents. Whatever these protective Blur want from me, they're not ready for it.

Yet.

48

AUGUST

"We're getting close," I say, ducking behind a large fallen tree. We rode to within a mile of where Jon encountered the Rashes, hid our bikes and ran the remaining mile, staying in the dark shadows of the Pennsylvania woods. The pain in my shoulder is intense. My whole body aches, but it's nothing compared to my concern for Poe. So close to our goal, I've shut the phone off. In the still quiet of night, even the phone's vibrate mode could give us away.

"How do you know?" Jeb asks.

I'm not sure how to answer this. I can't tell him that the rash hidden under my shirt has suddenly begun itching. The discussion that revelation would inspire might cost us precious time. With no clues about Brook's whereabouts at the actual abduction site, we followed what looked like a trail, but lost it ten minutes ago. An answer to Jeb's question presents itself. I tap my nose.

It's faint, but the scent of burning wood slips past on the breeze. My mind imagines the microscopic smoke particles making contact with the thick humidity in the air. The air in Pennsylvanian July is a swamp. It clings to my skin, to my clothing, and my nostrils. The scent grows stronger with each breath, and the others smell it, too.

Jon is the first to move, standing fast and charging forward.

I catch his shoulder and hold him back.

"What are you doing?" he snaps.

"We can't just run in, guns blazing." I lift my hand from his arm. "We need to be smart."

A sudden pain in my shoulder makes me wince.

"You okay?" Mark asks.

I make my face a mask. Wooden. Like the Blur, hiding the truth. "Fine. Now, let's go. Slow and quiet."

We creep through the darkening forest, ducked down like we're in a cave, closing in on the source of the smoke. We find it a half mile away, at the bottom of a valley. A small road cuts through the woods. There are two large houses, one on either side of the street, both with granite post fences, swimming pools, three car garages and wraparound decks. It's like two wealthy homeowners set up shop across the street from each other, kicking off a home improvement and upgrade war.

The Rashes are there, enjoying the fruits of the previous owners' labors. Generators buzz loudly. The homes glow with electricity. The pools are full of naked people, their ringed, black rashes visible from here. Some swim in awkward circles, like they're not aware that some of them are missing limbs. Or they just don't care. It's a party, after all. A celebration. The sound of drunken people fills the air. I was never part of a fraternity, but the sight below us is how I always pictured them.

With one exception. Unlike my group of survivors, these people vary in age. There are plenty of young people, but I also see some gray hair in the mix. There's also a lot of loose skin, like Jon said, but it's definitely not from age. Like most people, I could only look at photos of Hochman's victims for a moment before feeling nauseous, but I'll also never forget them. These people definitely had the disease. And survived. There are no kids, and for that, I am grateful. Evil or not, working with the Blur or not, I don't think I could kill a child.

"What's the plan?" Mark asks.

"Give me a minute," I say, taking in every inch of the compound that I can see. The long driveways are full. There're a variety of vehicles.

Cars. Trucks. A few RVs. Not one of them is decked out with spikes or machine guns. But there is a gasoline tanker truck parked on the side of the road. They're mobile. Unafraid of traveling in loud, easy to spot vehicles. Definitely collaborators. One of the cars, a blue sports car, is parked in the center of the road, twenty feet from what looks like a huge, unlit, bonfire. There's something odd about the hood.

I take the binoculars from my cargo pants pocket and take a look. Brook is tied to the hood. Naked. Arms and legs held open by thick ropes that are stretched out tight. "Godamnit."

"What?" Jon asks, nearly standing. Mark holds him back.

I hold out the binoculars, just out of reach. "Do *not* react."

He nods. "I get it."

I lean over so he can take the binoculars. "Sports car in the street."

Jon puts his eyes to the viewfinder, turns them toward the street and spasms. His body locks up tight. His fingers clutch the binoculars so hard that I think the glass might break. When he turns away from the view, his face is red. His veins stand out, twitching like worms trapped beneath his skin.

"I'm going to kill them," he says.

I shake my head. "We're here for Brook."

"What they did to her—"

"Is unforgivable," I say. "But there are only four of us. There are at least forty of them."

"They don't have guns," Jeb points out. He's just looked through his own binoculars.

"Look again," I say. "Look around Brook. What do you see?"

Jeb and Jon both look.

"Nothing," Jon says.

"What's your point," Jeb says. "No one is...oh."

It takes all of my self-control to not run down the hill and open fire on these savages, but I managed to pull it off and even use my brain a little, which is a good thing, since that's still my strongest muscle. "They've got it set up like some kind of ritual sacrifice. When it gets dark, they'll light the bonfire, summon the Blur, and let them have her. Maybe they'll take her. Maybe they'll make her one of them."

"You think they can do that?" Jon asks.

I scratch my itching shoulder. "Maybe. But when it gets dark and they go to light that fire, she's not going to be there."

Jon is nodding now. The idea of saving Brook outweighs his desire for revenge.

"So," Mark says. "We're going to just go down there, cut her free, and jet?"

"That's the plan," I say, starting down the slope, careful to stay low and behind the thick pines whenever possible.

Mark, Jon and Jeb follow me down to the road. We haven't been spotted, and the sound of laughter, debauchery and music rolling out of the two houses conceals any noise we might make.

I stop at the side of the road, hidden in the tree line. Once we step out into the street, we'll be exposed. No amount of sneaking will hide us.

The men line up next to me.

Poe...

Her name flits through my thoughts and makes my chest constrict. My hand grips the sat-phone in my pocket, my tenuous connection to her severed, feels like the loss of a limb. She could be calling right now. *No,* I tell myself. *Not yet. Brook needs you now.*

"Everyone have a knife?" I ask. I've got two, just in case, but all three of them nod. "Jon, you go first. Take her right arm. Let Brook know we're here for her, and to stay quiet. Mark, take the left arm. Jeb, you take left leg. I'll get the right leg. If we run, and cut fast, we can be out of there and back in the woods inside thirty seconds."

I have no idea if this is right, but we're only fifty feet from Brook now. If everyone's knives are as sharp as mine, and Brook is conscious, we should be pretty quick.

The first sign of stars shine in the deep purple sky. We don't have long. Even if we make it in and out without a hitch, we might only have a ten minute head start before night falls and someone goes to light that fire. But maybe we'll get lucky. Maybe they won't think to light it until midnight. Maybe they'll all be too drunk to even remember.

As the dark purple sky fades a bit more, giving way to more stars, any one of which could be a waiting Blur, I step into the road.

Nothing happens.

I wave to the others and run.

Despite my brief head start, the three younger men sprint past me, knives in hands, confident warriors. By the time I round the pile of stacked wood, Jon has already freed her right hand and is whispering to her. She's awake, wide eyed and smiling. "Thank God," I hear her say over and over as I reach her right foot.

My blade cuts through the rope like it was little more than a hot cooked sausage link.

Brook's naked body squeaks over the car's hood as she slides into Jon's arms. He quickly peels off his shirt and tugs it on over her head. Then, without a sound, we all turn to retreat.

And make it three steps.

An arrow—a friggin arrow, like we're living in a Robin Hood movie—tipped with something that's burning, strikes the bonfire. The wood must be doused in some kind of propellant, because the whole thing lights up, flames rocketing into the sky. The heat drives us back.

"The other way!" Jeb says, and we turn to run, but are stopped by an unholy sight.

A line of naked people, all with dark black rings encircling their hearts, some missing arms, some with warbling loose skin, stand across the road. A blockade of flesh. Armed with a variety of medieval weaponry. Swords. Axes. Crossbows. Just as Jon described.

We're armed with more modern weapons, and will no doubt kill a large number of these people, but we will need to reload at some point, and when we do... The look in these people's eyes tells me they're not going to slow down, even while they're being shot to bits. They might even reach us before we run out of ammo.

I'm running scenarios and probability equations faster than I ever have before, and I'm not finding a way out of this. I need more time.

"What do you want?" I ask, stepping in front of the others.

"Dude," Mark whispers. "There's a bunch behind us, too."

I don't look.

I just wait.

A man steps forward. He's at least fifty. Overweight. Balding. No way he's their leader. But maybe they don't have a leader. He squints at me. Cocks his head to the side.

"Brother," he says. "You belong with us." He reaches out with one arm and one stub of an arm. "Come."

The rest of the nude psychopaths reach their arms out to me, speaking in unison. "Come, brother."

The wound in my shoulder explodes with pain, sending waves of burning blood through my core, blossoming out to my extremities. I fall to my knees. I scream. Dark thoughts fill my head. It would be so easy to turn my gun around on Mark, Jeb, Jon and Brook. I could cut them down. It would delight me.

No! My inner voice screams.

"Argh!" I shout. "Get away from me!"

"August!" Mark's hand is on my shoulder. I slap it away.

"Get away!" With the last of my will power, I remove the rifle, intending to slide it away from me, but can't. I need it. To kill them. To kill Mark.

"Come, brother," the people repeat. "Come, brother."

I see Mark's face, dead eyes, blood dripping from his forehead, a bullet hole I put there. The vision feels orgasmic, like nothing else in the world would be better. The desire quivers through my body, extending from my torso. From my shoulder. From the rash. In a flash of clarity, I know that if the Blur had put its finger in my heart, the urge would be all consuming. Clarity fades beneath a tsunami of rage.

"I'm going to kill you!" I shout. I lift the rifle and pull the trigger.

The shot rips through the night, silencing everyone and everything, save for the crackling fire at my back.

I climb back to my feet, sweating and shaking. "I...am not...your brother."

I take aim with the rifle again. The naked fat man who spoke to me has a neat hole in his chest. A lone trail of blood runs down his hairy chest. But he is still alive. Still standing.

I pull the trigger again, sending a second round into the man's head. This time he drops hard and fast, striking the pavement with a damp thud. I'm not sure if the wetness is from blood or because he just vacated a pool, but it unnerves me, and weakens my resolve. I've just killed a man and doomed the others. We can't win this fight.

The line of people raise their eyes from the body, to me. The hatred within them is blinding and manic. They will run through our bullets. They will hack us to bits. The closest of them raises his axe toward us, wild eyes, and opens his smeared mouth, no doubt about to unleash a battle cry that will signify the beginning of our horrible end.

But he's interrupted by someone else.

"Attack!"

The distant voice is full of anger, but fails to fill me with dread. I expect to see the Rashes raise their angry arms up, cry out and charge, but they look just as confused as I am.

That's when the voice registers. I know it.

Tanya.

The first gunshot makes me flinch. A body drops.

One of theirs.

The second gunshot makes me smile, not because I delight in the taking of human lives, but because we might actually survive. *Fight, Poe, and we will too.*

Our people. Our tribe. They're here for us. All of them. They stream out of the woods, armed for battle and willing to use deadly force. This is not something I would have ever wished upon them. The last thing any of us wants to do is kill people. There are so few of us left. But these people are beyond redemption, and like Leila, they need to embrace the fate wrought on the rest of humanity.

And they do.

One by one, the men and women who kidnapped Brook and were about to do God knows what to the rest of us, are cut down. Some flee into the night, running down the street naked. Survivors, still. But I doubt we will see them again.

And while the carnage is horrible, it's also inspiring.

We're going to make it, I think. *The Blur can't stop us. And neither can these people.*

We're coming, Poe.

Like a freight train loose on the tracks, we're going to charge north and we're not going to stop until we reach the end of the line. Nothing, and I mean nothing, is going to stop us short of reaching Poe. I lift my rifle and take a single shot, dropping a man about to strike Jon with a mace. As the report from my rifle echoes and fades, the battle ends.

My eyes flit over the faces of my people, converging on the road. They're all here. All alive.

Thank God.

The fight has ended without Jeb, Mark or Jon firing a single shot. Silence returns as our group is reunited. Silence, except for the fire.

I turn toward the blaze, the pain and itching in my shoulder gone once more. The flames snap violently, releasing black smoke and bright light into the night. Easily seen from above. I'm about to order everyone back into the woods when Tanya approaches.

She looks grim. Like she's just fought a war and killed people. So I think nothing of the face until it turns into a sneer directed at me. "You son-of-a-bitch," she says, reaching out. "You lied to us!"

She catches my shirt in her hand and yanks hard, tearing buttons loose and exposing my skin. The rash, lit by the blaze, stands out starkly against my hidden-from-the-sun, gleaming white skin.

Some of the others gasp.

"You're one of them!" she shouts. "You *led* us here!"

She hasn't lifted her weapon yet, but she's holding it at the ready, index finger over the trigger.

"I'm not," I say. It sounds pitiful. A child's lie.

Jeb steps up beside Tanya. He looks at the rash, then my eyes. He's still deciding.

Mark, on the other hand, needs no convincing. He steps between Tanya and me, pushing her gun further down. "He's not one of them."

"He's got the rash," Jeb says. While he lacks the emotional kick Tanya wields, the coldness in his voice is worse.

"In his shoulder," Mark says. "Not his heart. And it's not as dark. You saw the others. His rash isn't the same." He waves his hand to a few of the nearby bodies, their rashes still visible, despite the blood. "He's not one of them. Never has been. They tried to control him, but he's too strong." He glances back at me, and then meets Tanya's eyes. "I've been watching him. He's cool."

"You *knew*?" Tanya nearly slugs him, but Mark raises his hands.

Mark points at the scar on my shoulder. "This happened to him the night he saved me. I owe him my life. Pretty sure most of us do. And while the rash has some kind of effect on him, he is *still* himself. Still *August*."

The way he says my name, as though it means something bigger than myself, is uncomfortable. Mostly they treat me like just one of the gang, but occasionally, someone reminds me that I'm not just August. I'm *the* August. Honestly, I'm looking forward to next month when there can at least be two Augusts in the world, if only for thirty-one days.

The bonfire's heat on my back and the darkness of night above weigh heavily. I lean around Mark. "Are you going to kill me?"

No reply.

"If you are, I would prefer you do it now and get moving. Poe will be giving birth in a few weeks. If I can't be there, at least you all can. But you have to leave now." I look up at the sky. They understand my tension. "Please, kill me and go, or let's all go together."

Tanya's shoulders drop. "You should have told us."

"I'm sorry," I say.

She places her hand on the center circle of the bull's eye rash. I know it's hot to the touch. "I'm sorry, too," she says, and for a second, I think she might actually shoot me. But then she steps back and adds, "It's still your show."

"Everyone!" I shout. "Back to the—"

A groan cuts me short. Laying amidst the bloody Rashes in the road, a body shifts. A survivor. A woman. Looks about my age. Asian descent. But one side of her face is stretched out. She's bleeding from two bullet wounds, one in her abdomen, one in her chest. She's wheezing. A lung punctured. No doubt bleeding internally, but she's still trying to get up.

When I step past Tanya and head for the woman, Mark says, "We can leave her. She won't last long."

"I'm not going to kill her," I say, and I stand above the woman.

She looks up at me, her body shaking from the effort. "Brother."

I crouch in front of her. "You can stop fighting now."

Her body sags, giving in to the weight of her brethren's dead limbs on her back.

"What's your name?" I ask.

Half her forehead scrunches up. I don't think she's thought about her name in a while. "M-Meiko."

"Meiko," I say, trying to sound calm yet commanding. "*Sister.* I have some questions for you." I decide to start with something simple. "Where are you from?"

"Pensacola." Her voice is a whisper between hard breaths.

"Did you have Hochman's?"

She nods. "Stage one."

"How did you survive?"

Her eyes turn toward the sky. "The owls...saved me. From Hochman's. From...the end. They kept us safe. Out there."

These people survived not just because they'd been abducted, but because they weren't even on the planet when the end came. The Blur took them, or already had, and when the rest of the world went poof, they weren't anywhere near the target.

"And they gave us the gift." Meiko reaches out a shaky hand. Puts it on my chest. On the rash. "Made us family." A lifelessness fills her eyes, but she's not dead. She looks past me, at *my* family. "But not them. They need to go. You *need* to make them go."

I feel a tingle in my shoulder, the connection to this woman and the others like her still active, but distant, like a radio wave from across the universe, detectible but spread out. Weak.

"Who are the owls?"

One half of her face grins, while the melted side remains flaccid. "Ask them...yourself."

And then she's gone, both sides of her face flattening out as the muscles go slack. My stomach sours as I stand, her final words landing in my gut like rotten meat.

Ask them yourself.

I turn around to the others, standing in silence, silhouetted by the bonfire, blazing brightness into the night sky.

"Everyone hide! The Blur are coming!" The group disperses quickly, some into the woods. Some into the houses. In seconds they're gone. Only Mark remains.

"August, let's—" His eyes move toward the sky, and I know they're here.

"Play dead!" I shout at him. "We're both dead!" And I dive to the ground, still holding my rifle, but lying awkwardly. Just another body. I don't see Mark move, but have no doubt he's following my lead. The question is, what do we do when they arrive?

The answer comes with a strange confidence.

We kill them.

Light floods the road, making the bonfire seem like a distant star in comparison. I keep my eyes locked on the woods, trying my best to not squint. Or blink. Or shift my vision. I probably should have closed them, but I need to see it.

The light flickers in time with three hums. Just once.

It came alone.

Why wouldn't it? These people were under its control. It had nothing to fear. A rancid odor washes over me. Chemical and sharp, like bleach. I nearly look toward a shuffle of movement, but then I don't have to. The woods in my field of view are suddenly distorted.

It stops, and though I can't really see it, I get the distinct impression that it knows something is up. Its acolytes are dead. It knew that before it came down. But I think it had somehow become aware of us, hiding in the shadows, behind trees, and amidst the deceased.

I can't let it leave.

If it makes it back inside the UFO, it will call for help, and how long will it take them to arrive? Seconds. We have fought these things before, and won, which is probably why they resorted to an army of Rashes, but I can't risk some kind of an assault from above. What could we do against that?

Mind made up, I turn my eyes toward the slowly retreating Blur. When it doesn't react, I sit up, lift the rifle and pull the trigger. The cacophonous report is followed by a shriek and then a pulse of energy. I'm lifted off the pavement and flung away alongside the bodies that had been littering the road. I slam into a granite post, but the impact is dulled thanks to Meiko's body, which strikes first. The dead land atop me in a naked, loose skinned and bloody jumble. But my painful and revolting position does nothing to diminish my hopes. Gun fire once again fills the air, drowning out the shriek of our enemy.

I shove the dead away in time to see the UFO pulse three times.

The gunfire ceases.

I look for a Blur's form in the road, but see nothing. It got away.

The UFO flickers and shifts to the side. It lacks the usual surprising speed and straight trajectory. It's out of control, slipping closer to the trees.

I push myself up off of Meiko and get to my feet, shouting, "Run!"

Mark rolls out from under the blue sports car as I sprint past, falling in beside me. I glance back over my shoulder as I reach a bend in the road. The UFO flashes like a slowing strobe light, each bright flicker interspersed with darkness. And that's when I see it. The rings. They're lit by the bonfire, and moving, but I can see them, both spinning, one inside the other. In the center of it all is an unmoving blurry shape.

One of the rings strikes a tree top, shearing wood and pine needles with a sharp crack. The craft drops, its rings chopping into the forest before the forest returns the favor. The halos fly apart, sending shards of alien metal in all directions. I'm tackled to the ground, landing on the side of the road. Debris punches into houses, vehicles and trees. I hear a buzz pass overhead. And then, the night explodes. A shockwave kicks the air from my lungs, and I feel a temperature shift, like the sun has just cleared a dense cloud. When I sit up and look back, the fuel truck is burning.

"Well, they're going to see that," Mark says.

"Thanks for the save," I say, and we get to our feet.

Mark shrugs. "It's what we do."

Before I can shout to our people still hiding, they begin to emerge from the woods, led by Jeb and Tanya.

"Everyone okay?" I ask.

"We're good," Tanya says. "Some injuries, but nothing life threatening. What now?"

She's still looking at me for leadership, despite the rash. Her trust means a lot, but there isn't time to tell her. "Where is your gear?"

"Back with yours on the side of the highway." she says.

"You followed us?" Mark asks.

"Couldn't let you all die alone."

"Let's get back to the bikes and find some place to spend the night. Tomorrow, we're going to ride like hell, no matter how much we hurt. Poe is facing this, too." I motion to the scene of destruction. "But she's doing it alone."

49

POE

My connection with August lost due to the broken satellite phone and my clumsiness, I wait for birth in animal stasis, days slipping by, in one hundred degree humidity. A typical New England summer. Rotting food from weeks of previous meals cover the kitchen table, flies buzzing around like they own the place. I recognize my state, now. Not crazy but not quite all there. Hanging on by a thread, my breath in and out every day, sweat rivulets pooling around my burgeoning body parts. It's so hot, and I am so big. Many days I languish in the tub for hours, pouring water over my enormity, watching it run down the sides. It's the most I can manage.

After the Blur attack, the summoning power to clean, nest and organize slipped away from me. I'm focused on my mental health, instead, doing my best to keep my thoughts neat and orderly. Even Luke won't touch the rotten piles of dirty dishes on the table. I walk up and down the stairs, counting, doing odd little math equations, the best I can manage to keep me at a minor level of physical and intellectual activity, the birth so imminent. The naked body tracings continue, one per day. I've doubled up on the paper, tracings on either side, now, sometimes fractured, sometimes whole, frequently completed without memory of the work. I keep eyeing the walls and the broad side of the barn. So much space on which to draw.

I talk to my parents a lot, and hear their voices. Mostly conversations from the past, but it's better than nothing. Sometimes a newness will emerge, and my mother will lecture me about my failure to sweep up all the dog hair. Or rather, any of the dog hair. Tumbleweeds of the stuff roll across the floors with the slightest breeze through the broken windows.

Occasionally, my father will send me a metaphor or simile, a perfect one.

'Silence like a star's core.'

Mmm, you're right, Dad.

Or a warning.

'Collect your marbles, Poe.'

Yes, Dad.

Other than the body tracings, I create no art. Too busy creating a baby...and sanity. Songs fill the house, though, music I remember and music I make up. My singing voice is terrible, and even worse than terrible after waking up.

One morning, I wake up and feel like I can't stand it another second—I need to get out of the house, and I need to get out now. Since my last, humungous trip to the grocery store, I've managed to eat through a lot of my provisions, but there's still quite enough to get by. My yearning is different. I need freshness. I need something alive.

The orchard, I think. How had I forgotten it?

Against my better judgment, Luke and I haul our sweating bodies into the truck and drive away like nothing unusual has ever happened. The closest local farm is less than three miles away. As we drive, Luke sticks his jolly head out the window, panting tongue and everything, the very image of a cliché retriever on a normal, summer day. I join him and trail my left hand against the wind.

Nostalgia nearly knocks me backward. I pull my arm in from the breeze and focus on driving. The things I miss: the radio, other drivers and people on bicycles, totally in the way on the road. Almost there, my uterus tightens in a walloping contraction that

I have to gasp through, my breath short. Must practice breathing, relaxing. We're getting close.

The truck's wheels crunch over the pebbled farm driveway, and I almost hit the farm dog, half-starved, who runs alongside us, barking with joy. I alternate between *oh no not another one*, and *oh look, another one!* She's a pretty little mix, maybe beagle and something dark and furry. I hope she's fixed, and will be more of a platonic friend for Luke, because if she's nice, I'll be taking her home with me. Luke could use the company as much as me.

We park the truck and the sweet dog puts her front paws up on me, barking and happy. Luke jumps out of the truck with a flourish. The two of them race off into the orchard together, immediately in love.

Good for you, luckies.

Another contraction and I need to lean against the truck. Maybe I'm not drinking enough water, in this heat? I've been having these false contractions for weeks now. August called them Braxton-Hicks contractions. Know it all. I call them a pain in the ass. Or rather, uterus. I've lost track of when I'm actually due, but I know it's within the next few weeks. Which I guess technically means now.

August.

My connection to him, in my heart, is still potent. But by now, I'm used to loneliness. I don't remember anything else, my emotional amnesia a protective device.

Will he ever arrive, I keep wondering.

The orchard smells wonderful, and as the two dogs circle back to me, tails wagging happily, I let myself relax a little bit. Perhaps August's sinister Blur have gone for good? I grab a wagon and the three of us venture out into the peach trees, still too early for apples here in northern New England. Crickets and other insect life thrives despite the lack of humans. Or because of.

The peach trees brim with fruit, rosy and fertile. They feel like a gift. I allow myself to feel safe and whole, while I reach up, again and again, twisting the peaches away from the branches into my hand. Sunlight through leaves, I want to cry, it's so beautiful and normal. The dogs join me on the grass, and I bite into a peach. Gratitude fills me.

In my periphery, a visual distortion. One of the trees looks a little different than the others. In my calm, I fail to recognize what I'm seeing. I chew, watching the bent tree, its leaves flickering light and dark in the wind.

But they're not just blowing. They're bending. Unnaturally.

A Blur.

I stand up as quick as I can, another contraction rippling over me, vice-like, and I grab the dogs by their collars. Luke pulls at my hand, barking. He senses it, too.

We wait together, my breath held, a breeze waving the branches around us. What will the scent be?

It's doesn't really matter. I have no fight left in me.

I thought I was done with this.

The scents of peaches, ripe on the branches, rotting on the ground, mingle with traces of rose.

Rose.

Interesting that my first thought is, *my old friend*, revealing the depth of my loneliness. Despite being invisible, the Blur is not trying to hide. It hovers nearby, quiet and unmoving.

Perhaps it's the beautiful day, or the new dog, or the intoxicating peaches, but I feel emboldened. I let go of the dogs, who run over to the Blur, sniffing, and then run away again into the orchard. Interesting. The first time Luke met this one, in the grocery store, he was terrified and immediately peed. The new dog must be following Luke's lead. Again, I sense acquiescence from this Blur, like in the woods that day. Not exactly submission, but a concession. Allowing us to be what we all are: dog, human, peach trees.

Like a philosopher.

Not a soldier, I tell myself. But maybe not a scientist, either.

"Are you following me?" I call to it. "Are you protecting me?"

I think back to all the events, the many times I've been spared, the demolition of any who would try to harm me. The plan, from the parent-made pod until this day and everything in between. Leila.

The Blur in my home, carrying me off.

"What do you want? Why are you here?" I take three steps closer to it. It doesn't move. I wonder, for a moment, if it can even understand English. Advanced, but not infallible, not without limits. An alien worm in a suit.

I decide to use my other language, my deeper language, the voice of my artist self. I've been ignoring it for weeks now, with only the robotic tracings as evidence of my talent. Looking at my materials around me, the leaves, the fruit, the grass, I begin forming a circle on the ground with fallen peaches. At first I feel ridiculous, like maybe I've cracked up for good, but the rhythm of making soothes me, and the Blur just remains there.

What symbol can I construct that would get through to it? Perhaps every move I make seems like the movements of an ant, or microscopic elements, meaningless and primal. To this Blur I might seem like primordial ooze, schlepping about without reason, just instincts for reproduction and survival.

I finish the circle of rotting peaches and start another, interior shape, fractals, with leaves I find on the ground, squatting like a tribal woman around the fire. What I imagine to be Squirt's skull presses hard and deep on my bladder. She's very low now, my walk just a waddle.

Crouched down, I pause and look up at the motionless Blur. What is it waiting for?

An invitation, I decide.

I walk close to the Blur and reach out my hand, filled with peach tree leaves. I think at it, *join me*. Doubting it can read my mind, but feeling like my intentions are obvious, I place the leaves on the ground at the bottom of the shimmer.

I turn back to my work, connecting lines with twigs, a mandala pattern of sorts, on all fours, my belly dangling beneath me, so heavy, contractions every once in a while. When I stand up, a real struggle, I stifle a scream. The Blur is right next to me, a tall, silent, fragrant presence.

It bends over, its invisibility warping the tree behind it. It holds the leaves I left plus many, many more in a dark hand, no pointy fingers.

And then, amazement. The Blur quickly arranges the leaves in a complicated pattern, weaving them throughout my lines and circles.

Stunning.

I turn toward it, shaking with relief. It shimmers fast, the mask emerging to gaze at me. The expressionless mask, same as the rest, feels different, the scent of roses surrounding me.

A long, white tendril rises up, emerging from the tip of the creature's finger. I take one step back, but then hold my ground. It hasn't hurt me yet. I glance down at the image it has created with me. It is an artist, like me. It understands life, and beauty, and it protects those things.

The tendril...the tip of the worm encased inside a four-legged biological suit, slips up toward my head. It hovers before my eyes, waiting. Patient. Its intentions are also clear. *Okay,* I think. August would probably stop me, but his experience is different from mine. I know I'm only here because these Blur arranged it, with my parents, and then protected me. I owe them my trust.

So I give it, and lean forward.

The tap on my forehead is so gentle, I barely feel it, but the words that careen into my mind are heard loud and clear.

IT IS TIME.

Time for what? I think, and the answer comes from within.

A scream erupts from my mouth as my whole body seizes, at the mercy of a contraction.

50

AUGUST

Trust is a tricky thing. It's earned over time. Through action, reaction and follow-through. In the two weeks since the revelation of my bull's eye rash, trust has been restored. I'm not doubted, avoided or excluded. To these people, I'm still August.

The August.

But I *am* watched.

I don't blame them. The rash has become a symbol for danger. The enemy. Anyone else bearing the black rings on their chest would be shot at a distance. The rings acting as judge and jury. One of these few, one of these innocents turned survivors, turned warriors, would be executioner.

Despite my apparent guilt, execution has been stayed. I live among them. I direct their path. And if the Blur somehow exerted control over me, the results could be disastrous. That's why I made arrangements with Jeb. If it becomes clear that I am no longer me, that my spirit has been lost, he will free me from this world and the potential burden that would come from harming my friends. He also promised, along with Mark and Tanya, to continue on to Poe should that horrible scenario present itself.

So far, it hasn't. And I'm grateful. Despite my willingness to die for these people. For Poe. I'd rather it wasn't them who had to take my life. The idea of taking one of theirs frightens me so much that I sleep separately from the others. I strap a string of jingle bells, taken from a home's front door, to my ankle at night. They will see and hear me coming.

It's a morbid way to live, but it eases the burden burning black on my shoulder and over my chest.

"Hold up," Mark says from ahead. I brake hard and pull up beside him. My body is grateful for the stop. We've been pushing beyond my breaking point, and then some—at my insistence. Poe's continued silence, never answering my calls, never reaching out to me, implies sinister outcomes I refuse to consider. So we've pushed, and made great time. We considered taking cars and just hauling ass for the remainder of the trip, which we could complete in a single day, but the further north we go, the more lights in the sky we see, day and night. We haven't witnessed anything as dramatic as the battle that Poe described, but there have been several occasions where it seemed like one UFO was chasing the other. Taking cars, while so very tempting, would expose us, and what kind of leader would I be if I risked revealing all these people to the Blur at the very end of our journey? As much as I'm worried about Poe, getting there later is better than never arriving...even if she is in trouble. Dying on the road won't help her.

"What's wrong?" I ask, face turned to the pavement, breath short. Rivulets of sweat roll over my forehead and drip from my nose. I've never been in New England during the summer before now, and strangely, it feels a lot like Florida. The air feels like steam. It saturates my clothes and merges with the sweat oozing from my pores to form rivers down my sides and my legs. I'm a sponge.

"Look," he says, while the group slows to a stop. No one is particularly worried. No alarm has been sounded.

I follow Mark's pointed finger up over the highway. The three lanes of Interstate 95 are all but free of vehicles. When the human race was turned to dust, New England was being buried by snow.

The only vehicles we see on the highway now are massive, orange snow plows still laden with heaps of brown sand and salt, and the occasional car or truck, many of them on the side of the road.

Ahead, I see a blue rectangle. It's a sign, but the sweat covering my sunglasses conceals the words. I remove the glasses and squint against the bright sun, while wiping the lenses against my equally sweat-soaked shirt. The rectangular blue sign, framed in white, reads, 'Welcome to New Hampshire.' And then below that, the words, 'Live Free or Die.'

Jeb rolls up beside me. "I might not be a Yankee, but that is a badass state slogan."

"That's what we're all about now, isn't it?" Mark says. He turns to me. "Maybe that's why we're here? In New England. The birthplace of freedom in America."

"Isn't that Boston?" Tanya asks. "Boston Tea Party and all that."

"What's the Massachusetts state motto?" Jeb asks.

We all shrug. Everyone in our group is from west of the Mississippi, or the Deep South.

"Ense petit placidam sub libertate quietem," a man from the group, says.

"What does that mean?" I ask without turning around.

"By the sword we seek peace, but peace only under liberty."

The last two words spoken by the man cause the hairs on my damp arms to break free and stand on end. He pronounced, 'under' as 'undah,' and 'liberty' as 'libahty.' It's a distinct Bostonian accent, mixed with a little something else. The speaker is *not* one of our group. And I'm not the only one to make this realization.

Moving as though of one mind, like a shoal of fish, our group dismounts from bikes, crouches behind the frames and takes aim at the newcomer. He's a young man, tan skin. If I had to guess, he's Puerto Rican. He wears a navy blue Red Sox cap—nearly identical to Claire's cap, which currently rests on my head, failing to absorb my sweat. His clean shaven face reveals a number of scars, but he looks friendly enough. He stands just twenty feet away, in the highway's median.

The man's hands launch to the sky in time with his eyelids and eyebrows. "Whoa!" He's armed, but the handgun remains tucked into his waist band. "Don't shoot!"

"Your chest," Jeb says.

The man looks down at his orange T-shirt, then back up to Jeb, uncomprehending.

"Lift your shirt," I tell him. "We need to see your chest."

"The hell for?" the man says, growing agitated, looking at us like we're a bunch of perverts.

"We've been attacked," I tell him, "by people with dark rings around their chest. It's like a rash, but black."

Recognition fills the man's eyes. He nods. "Seen a few of them, too." He lifts his shirt just long enough for us to see that he's built like Hercules and rash-free. "They're pretty much all assholes." He lifts his chin toward our group. "You all run into trouble or something? You're the first bunch I've seen roll in like you're expecting a war." He squints. Looks us over. "Or have already seen one."

I barely hear all this. As he speaks, I stand and lower my rifle. The shoal behavior continues, my group lowering weapons, growing more curious than afraid. But I'm only interested in a single detail the man let slip. I let my bike lie on the pavement, and head toward the lone man, stopping a few feet away.

Done speaking, he watches my approach.

"Nice hat," he says.

"It was my daughter's."

"Was," he says.

The detail breaks my heart, but I nod.

"Sorry."

"We're all sorry for something." I stare into his eyes. "Your name?"

"Luis," he says. "You?"

"I'll get to that in a minute." He looks annoyed by this, but I don't give him time to complain. "You said we were the *first* group you'd seen arrive expecting a war. How many other groups have there been?"

He looks my people over one more time and then answers, "Three. One came up the East Coast. Another from Canada. The last group arrived on a boat. Sailed into Rye Harbor like a ghost ship. Looked like no one was aboard until they reached land and slipped out into the woods. That was a week ago. I wasn't there, but that's how the story goes. And there is another group, one day behind you, coming across 495. From the West. Maybe Northwest. We haven't said, 'Hi,' yet. Being careful, you know?"

I can't help but smile. "What's your total number?"

"So," he says, avoiding the question. "You're the bossman."

"How do you know that?" I ask.

"Apart from the fact that you're the one talking to me now, I've been tracking you guys for a few days." He lets that sink in. Reaches behind his back and unclips a radio from his belt. "We have recon covering all major routes into the area. I've been following you since you passed through Danvers."

"Stopped us because we were getting close?"

He shakes his head. "Because you *arrived*."

I hold my breath.

"But you guys are different," he says.

"Dangerous?" I ask.

He nods. "Hell, yes."

"I hope so," I tell him. "For all our sakes."

He turns his head skyward. "Because of them?"

"Have you seen them?" I ask.

"Only in the sky. At first, just at night. Like they were looking for us. But they've come out in the day. I think they're fighting each other." He points northwest. "Over there."

I let my mind's eye slip into an overhead view of New Hampshire. I've studied the map and route to Poe's house so often that I could draw the map from memory.

Poe is northwest.

I know it's useless, but I turn away from Luis, take the SAT phone from my pocket and speed-dial Poe. When the speaker reaches my ear, it's not endless ringing I hear. It's screaming.

My heart pounds. Vision narrows. I'm about to scream her name when I realize the sound is digital. It's a hiss, like an old school

14k dial-up Internet connection. I pull the phone away from my ear, hang up and dial again. The sound returns.

Something is happening.

"When was the last time you saw evidence of a battle?" I ask.

"Today," he says, motioning to the distant sky with his head. "It's happening now, man. Look."

I turn northwest again, watching. The humid sky is hazy and full of towering, fluffy white cumulus clouds. I watch the giants shift through the atmosphere. And then, I see it. A flicker of light on the horizon, brightening the cloud's shadowed bottom for an instant. "There," I say, pointing. "Is that where Barrington is?"

Luis looks, "Yeah, I think so. Somewhere up there. Why?"

"We need to go there. Now."

"Uhh." He just looks at me. "No one goes up there. Before or now. It's too dangerous. They'll find us."

There isn't time to explain, so I unleash a strange power that I know, in my core, will shift the course of this conversation. "I'm August."

The man blinks. "What?"

"My *name* is August."

Eyes widen... "I thought.... But August is now. That's when people started showing up."

I take my wallet from my pocket, remove my ID and hold it in front of his face. "*I*. Am. August." I speak the words in a way that argues my point, that says I'm confident in my role. That I'm in charge. "Your parents left you a note. Well, here I am. You found me."

"Holy shit."

"And I need your help. Now."

"W—what do you need?"

"Everyone."

He still looks unsure, unwilling to give up his people. "For...what?"

"For Poe," I say, and I notice the name means nothing to him. "And her baby."

He perks up. "A baby?"

I point to the sky. "*They*...want to take her child." While they haven't come right out and said it, what else could it be? The first child born in this new world is important to them for some reason. There is nothing else odd or remarkable about Poe, at least not anything creatures from another world might care about. But a child, to scientists, could very well be the results of some cosmic experiment they've been waiting for.

"Why can't she just run? Meet us here?"

"Because the baby is being born..." I look up at the flickering sky, and make a guess that might turn out to be a lie. But I don't think so. "Right now."

"You're sure about this?"

"I have spent the last six months crossing this country to reach Poe on this day, and there isn't a God damned thing in this world that is going to keep me—" I point to my people, who are watching and nodding along. "—or them from reaching my girls in time." *Girls?* I think, and then I realize that somewhere along the way I began to think of Squirt as a girl, and both of them as my family. "This is why you're here, Luis. This is why your parents saved you and left you a note to find me. Find August. Two words. You can't find a month. You can only wait for it. But here I am, the only findable August on this planet. And you can either help me, or you can get the hell out of our way."

Luis looks at me for just a moment, then raises the radio to his mouth, presses the transmit button and speaks a brief command.

Both sides of the highway come to life as people emerge from the woods and climb up the sloped sides. Most, like us, stand astride bicycles. Fewer are armed in any obvious way, but they outnumber us five to one.

Despite this positive development, I can't find a smile. I turn to Luis and say, "I want everyone who can fight, and ride, in four lines. I'm setting the pace, and—"

"Barrington is at least thirty miles from here," Luis says. "We won't make it there until tomorrow."

While the string of curses running through my mind nearly comes out of my mouth, Luis smiles. "But I know where we can get some cars."

51

POE

The drive home, dogs in the truck, contractions squeezing me, is a haze, like when I draw now. But I'm home, in the kitchen, gripping the island for stability. What happened to the Blur? I have no memory of its departure.

The contractions are four minutes apart now. August coached me on a lot of this, as he and his wife had chosen natural childbirth, and she had Claire, his daughter, in a birthing tub at the hospital, a midwife attending. He told me that it's usually not what we see on TV, with the feet up in the stirrups, and to train my body to react to the pain and intensity with relaxation, rather than tightening, as that would open up everything for me and make an easier path for Squirt.

I'm terrified. As a marathoner, I understand training my body, so this I can do. I just should have been practicing more before now.

Go upstairs, Poe, I hear my mother tell me. *You can't do this in the kitchen.*

A glass of water is all I think to bring. The dogs run ahead of me upstairs, then double back as I place one foot in front of the other, clinging to the banister. They herd me up the stairs, the three of us mammals, in this thing together. Nothing is prepared.

Did I actually think this wasn't going to happen?

I make it to my parents' room, my first time in six months. It smells like them still, and comforts me. I lie on the bed, drenched, already exhausted. With difficulty, I pull off my wet, sweaty clothing and place my hands on my lower abdomen. Squirt is doing her thing in there, her body so low. I'm terrified that she'll be breeched, and I'll have to figure out how to retrieve her, legs first, all those limbs entangled up in there.

At that thought, my breathing shallows, and I climb out of bed to look out the window. He's not here. He's not coming. He could be dead. I can't believe I broke the stupid phone.

Lying back down on my side, I sip at the water, wishing I had a straw and someone other than dogs to attend to me. In between the contractions, I feel tired but almost normal, like I could just get up and do chores.

A deep intensity forces a gasp out of me.

It's happening.

It's happening, and I am all alone.

There is nothing to do but act, nothing to feel but purpose. Rolling out of bed to another profound sensation, only a few minutes away from the last, I shuffle to the bathroom and turn on the light. Too bright. I shut it off again and light a candle. Run the hot water while breathing through another contraction.

While the tub fills, Squirt nestles into a different position, her space quite cramped now, and warm liquid runs trickling down my legs. Have I peed myself? Is this what women in labor do? It wouldn't surprise me. But, no, more comes trickling out. I knock a towel onto the floor from the bathroom closet to sop it up. The liquid continues to trickle out, and I understand it. My water has broken. Maybe Squirt's head is preventing it from gushing?

Several points of acute pressure all over my body force me down into the tub, into the water. I can no longer stand.

Another profound sensation, both sharp and throbbing, roars over me. And then in one minute, another. The hot water holds me, a counterpoint to pain.

And then...a concussive force rolls over the whole house, shaking walls. The violence is matched by the sound, a twanging explosion.

Oh God, not now.

But now makes more sense than ever.

They're here for this. For her.

As a contraction fades, I stand from the water, dripping and shivering, but not wanting to get caught in this small bathroom, soaking wet and slippery. With just forty-five seconds before the next contraction drops me, I hobble down the hall, led by the dogs, naked and dripping, holding my belly. Ten seconds remain, as I roll up onto my parents' bed and sink into the down comforter. I'm wrapped in their warmth, and then unyielding pressure.

I cry out.

Alone...

The house rattles again, the sounds of some unseen battle in the skies above mirroring the turmoil within my body. The whole world is consumed by crackling, bursting, tension.

They're coming to get her.

What if one crashes into the house?

How long do I have? Can I run?

One on top of another, crests of energy jolt through me, rattling my teeth, erasing my thoughts. I bid my muscles relax, to embrace the intensity. *You were made for this, Poe. Breathe, girl.*

This is not pain.

This is lightning.

I beg my mighty artist heart to return to me, robust once again.

And it does, along with the realization that I will be a mother soon. I will feel alive again. I grind my teeth, and then, at the tail end of a contraction, I breathe deeply, through my nose.

Rose.

My eyes open to the Blur, sweet-smelling, filling the space, resplendent.

The dogs have retreated to the open closet, sitting still, wrapped in the hanging tendrils of my father's trousers, trusting the new arrival with my care.

A long thin strand of white is already stretching out through the space between us. It touches my forehead just as an explosion shakes the house and is followed by the sound of falling trees.

"Do not be afraid."

The words are powerful, deep and resonating. In that instant, the fissure is sealed, the crumbling walls rebuilt.

Compelled to take charge of this birth, I change positions, remembering August's insistence that while the missionary position might be the best for getting pregnant, it's not for giving birth.

I balance on my knees, my body cleaving and stretching past anything I ever thought possible. The scent of the Blur washes over me, earthy natural comfort. I lean forward on my hands, rocking. Sweat drips off the end of my nose, tapping the comforter.

Like the tumblers inside a lock, everything clicking into place, Squirt's body descends. A pinball, moving through the maze, all the layers. I can imagine her, my powers returned to me. She's ready to be with me, out here. The pressure and burning makes me scream.

An explosion, this one distant, is followed by a whooshing sound. I barely register it, but the Blur—Rose—is suddenly there, fully visible and leaning over my body, straddling my back with its arms. It lowers its head and a hum bursts out around us. I'm about to scream, but this isn't a betrayal. Debris punches through the bedroom wall. Much of it continues on into the next wall, but several chunks of who knows what deflect off of something unseen, and slam into the ceiling—instead of me.

Thank you, I think, and I reach under to feel Squirt's scalp. She's right there.

Rose steps back, under the cloak, invisible observer once more.

With both hands cupped beneath my body, I push, a fathomless groan.

The lightning my entire being.

And I push again.

Her body tumbles out, all her parts, a whole baby, and I catch her in my two strong hands, the sudden weight shift the most alarming aspect. Once inside me, now in my arms. A loss, then swift gain. She is pink, with a full head of dark hair. I knew she'd be a girl.

I scoop her up onto my chest and lie back into the pillows. She coughs twice and then cries, her small, frail voice like music.

And again, Rose is there, sudden and visible, reaching out, a sharp finger this time. I try to shout, to resist, but I can barely hold onto my baby.

And then, a prick. The needle tipped finger dips into my baby's skin, the back of her arm, and pulls free, a bead of blood on the end. Collected. The second arm comes up, like Rose is checking the time. But there is no watch. Instead, there is a flat oval patch on the forearm where the Blur taps the bead of blood out. The sphere of redness, shrinks down, absorbed.

In silence, I turn toward the empty eyes. "You had no right."

It turns the forearm in my direction. It's no longer empty flat space. Instead, I see an image. Of a baby. My baby.

Slowly, the image changes, the child aging from toddlerhood to adulthood in seconds. She's tall, and strong, and whole. The long pointed finger retracts and a slit opens. The worm emerges, and I fear it this time, but not enough to fend it off. I want to hear what it has to say.

I lean my forehead to it, the connection made.

The voice, deep and rushing like the wind, says, "She is pure. Like her mother."

And that's it. The wormy tendril snaps back inside the suit. The Blur turns its head to the outside wall, like it can see through it, like it has just become aware of something.

The pitch of the battle changes.

Mixing with the explosions, and otherworldly sounds, are the blaring coughs of something much more familiar. Gun shots. A lot of them. And among them, voices.

One of them is familiar and shouting a single word that trembles my lips.

"Poe!"

52

AUGUST

The man who once stared up at the night sky and wondered what lurked inside all that darkness, is dead. A forgotten relic. At least for the moment. All that remains is the long dormant silverback, the man my ex-wife would have appreciated. That overprotective beast rises up inside me, with all its chest-thumping fury, and propels me from the woods surrounding Poe's home.

After months of travel, of mending the deepest wounds imaginable, of believing against all odds, that the hope for mankind's future is represented by the child being born in this farm house, I arrive as a tidal wave. Energy built over time. Strength increased with each mile crossed.

Angry.

Vengeful.

Unstoppable.

And I have not come alone. There is a storm at my back.

After speeding past the remaining miles of highway, piled into five limousines, we make our final approach through the woods. While the sky above us blazes with battling lights, we sift out of the trees, announcing our presence the way armies of old might have as they raced into battle, or into oblivion. I take a deep breath and smell a mix of chemical odors: bleach, tar, ammonia. While the men and women around me, some old friends, others total strangers, simply scream, my battle cry is enunciated.

"Poe!"

It's the loudest I've ever screamed in my life, and the sound waves rising from within my chest tear at my throat. But if she's in there, and still living, she knows I'm here. Knows there is hope. That I am coming for her, as promised.

The house, which looks exactly as Poe described it—old, but sturdy barn in the back, a long rambling, farmhouse refinished with tan vinyl siding—is out of focus. The air hovering over the overgrown lawn is alive. The home's backdoor slams open as though on its own. Shimmering energy slides inside.

The home has been breached.

I stop in a sea of tall grass and raise my rifle. "Keep your aim low! Do *not* hit the house!"

Those who have come out of the woods alongside me—Jeb, Tanya, Mark, Luis and forty others, some familiar, some not—stop beside me and raise their weapons. Had this battle taken place two hundred years ago, our volley would have been forty rounds strong. But now, armed with rifles, shotguns and automatic weapons, we're going to unleash a torrent of modern humanity's wrath.

"Fire!"

The thunder that follows is shocking. I want to cover my ears and cringe. But I keep pulling the trigger and chambering a new round, taking a step closer to the house with each shot.

It's hard to tell if we're having any effect, but then one of the Blur turns on me, its face emerging from the light-bending cloak. The long, wooden mask is easy to target. I pull the trigger and the head snaps back. Compressed air and wriggling white bits burst from the exit wound, which pulls the cloak away and reveals the skinny, tubular form hidden beneath. Exposed, the monster becomes the group's focus. Bullets and buckshot tear into the Blur, into the long white worm filling the suit. It falls to the ground, immobilized, if not dead.

I turn to Jeb. "I need to get inside!"

He nods and turns to Charley, a man from our group. "Shotgun. Now!"

Charley and I trade weapons. I've never used a shotgun before, but I understand the concept. Point and shoot. Unlike the rifle, if I'm within ten feet of the target, it will be nearly impossible to miss.

"Here," Luis says, suddenly beside me. He's holding a belt with a sheathed sword. The weapon is exquisite, its white handle framed by swirls of gold and a Japanese style dragon.

I take the belt and strap it on, asking, "Where did you get this?"

"Museum of Fine Arts in Boston," he says. "Samurai exhibit. It belonged to a Shogun. A warrior. Like you."

A warrior. Like me. The words strike me as both ridiculous and accurate.

What was, is no longer.

What remains is less, but stronger. Simplified. Forged and beaten. Like the blade that hangs on my hip. How many lives did it take before being relegated to a glass case inside a stuffy museum? How many more will I add to its history?

I nod my thanks to Luis and shout over the continuing gunfire, "Clear the outside. Burn the bodies." He nods and moves down the line, comfortable issuing orders. I turn to my right and find Mark, Jeb and Tanya, waiting.

"We're with you," Tanya says.

Mark grins and says, "Lead the way, dude."

Jeb slaps a fresh magazine into his MP5. No words required. These people are my core, but my heart waits for me inside.

"Let's go," I say, and I take two steps toward the house.

The Blur counter-attack stops me in my tracks.

Arcs of blue electricity crackle through the air. Some strike the grass, setting small fires or dissipating harmlessly. Others streak high, hitting the trees at our backs, super heating the sap inside and shattering bark with loud snaps. The rest find their targets, flowing through human flesh before finding the ground. People spasm and fall.

More lightning splits the air as wits are regained and the barrage of bullets resumed.

Both sides attack.

Both sides die.

It's Luis who realizes that a change in tactics is necessary. Bullets, up close and personal, are still dangerous. Electricity on the other hand, would harm both sides. Armed with a pistol, Luis leads the charge into a wall of warbling air. "Let's go!"

The wall of humanity still pouring from the woods charges forward at his back, some still wielding firearms, others now raising swords, knives or clubs. For a moment, they appear as feral and mad as the rash-controlled collaborators. But we're not fighting people. We're fighting monsters.

With my friends at my back, I charge, shotgun raised and ready to blast any half-seen Blur that get in my way.

The arcing electricity drops a few more people, but ceases when the charge reaches the wall of bent light. Too close. If I'm right about the Blur, that they are like I once was—scientists rather than warriors—we might actually stand a chance. But the Blur, while lacking the physical savagery still available to the human race, are far from defenseless.

Luis is the first to be repelled by the invisible force that defends a Blur's body. He catapults overhead, landing in the grass behind me. I glance back, see that he's alive and continue forward.

Three people tackle the Blur that flung Luis away. Whatever technology protects them, it's limited. Needs to recharge. *The Blur, I remind myself, are not all powerful.* They are beings of limited capabilities and perhaps only slightly more advanced intellects. Just a few hundred years—maybe less—ahead of humanity.

The light-bending cloak is torn away from the Blur, revealing the slender, frail looking tubular body beneath. Exposed and undefended, the monster's head is crushed, its limbs cut open or cleaved away. The biological suit holding it together becomes useless. Immobilized. Writhing worm bodies slide out of the destroyed suits. All around me, similar scenes play out. People sail through the air. Blur are revealed. Slain. Then, desperate arcs of electricity spray in all directions, like a child's lawn sprinkler, striking both sides of the confrontation.

Clearing a path.

I try not to think about the people losing their lives because I brought them to this place, and I stomp forward, aiming for the back door, which is now in focus.

And then not.

A Blur, unseen except for its distortion, blocks my path.

Without thought, I pull my weapon's trigger. Accustomed to the fairly limited buck of my rifle, I'm unprepared for the sheer force unleashed by the shotgun.

So is the Blur.

The pellets hit the shimmering form like an oversized fist, lifting it off the ground and peeling the shroud of invisibility away. It lands on its back, exposed. Its swirling oily eyes show no emotion beyond frozen indifference. For a fraction of time, I wonder if it can truly see, the thing compressed within this suit. In even less time, I decide I don't care.

I pump the shotgun, place the stock against my shoulder and this time, lean into it. When I pull the trigger, I'm ready for the kick. The Blur, once again, is not.

There is no defense, human or alien, against the spray of buckshot. The organic mask shreds, peeling away. The writhing white tendrils beneath are hewn down, turned to mush. The body slumps back.

I continue past, headed for the home's back door.

Through the ringing in my ears, I hear screaming, human and inhuman, gunshots, the crackling of electricity and a cacophony of other sounds I don't recognize. But through it all, I hear a cry, muffled by walls, but striking my eardrums with nuclear force.

"August!"

53

AUGUST

"Poe!" I shout back, stepping into the kitchen through the back door. The interior of the house is both familiar as a standard farmhouse kitchen with all the Americana comfort I'd imagined, but also warped.

Occupied, I realize.

Without a word, I open fire. The stock punches into my shoulder, again and again. Tomorrow, there will be a bruise on top of the bullseye rash. The shotgun's explosive report is joined by the staccato pop of smaller weapons. My tribe has arrived, putting their weapons to the task of clearing the house.

"Poe!" I shout again.

I have a view of the living room and dining room, and while both spaces are full of light bending shapes, Poe is in neither.

The screamed reply doesn't come from Poe. It's high-pitched and frail. Raw and terrified. New to life.

Squirt.

She's above me. On the second floor.

"I'm coming!" I shout, hoping that Poe is alive and hearing me.

Fighting back tears of the deepest worry I have ever experienced, I fire into the hallway, where there's a warped set of old hardwood stairs leading up. The Blur falls back, its cloak flickering where the buckshot embedded.

I pump the shotgun.

Pull the trigger.

The empty click doesn't fully register.

I pump and pull again. Nothing. *Out of ammo*, I realize. With no shells to reload with, I drop the weapon and draw the sword. I've never held a sword. The closest thing to it would be a baseball bat, and I haven't held one of those since I was a kid. Still, I remember how my father told me to hold it. The lesson was lost on my younger self, but it comes back in a rush. My new primal self, understands, implements and adapts.

I raise the blade over my head and rush into the hallway while Mark, Tanya and Jeb hold off the other Blur still on the first floor. The sword comes down, cleaving the hallway light in two, its fogged glass raining down. Undeterred, the ancient blade of some forgotten Shogun strikes the light-bending cloak, slices it cleanly—and is repelled.

A wave of energy bowls into me, lifting me off the creaky, old plank floor and slamming me into the wall. Luckily, the old horse hair plaster wall covered in thick wallpaper caves in, diffusing some of the impact's energy.

But not all of it.

I fall out of the hole made by my body, coughing. Then I fall forward against the opposite wall. The Blur kicks free from its split cloak. Whatever it is that repelled me needs time to recharge, so I don't need to worry about that again, but the Blur is far from defenseless. All those tendrils, packed into the tight suit, are like muscles, tight, bunched and powerful. The dead, oily eyes betray nothing, but the bending knees and coiling fingers warn of attack.

Still breathless, I stagger to my feet.

Without a sound, the Blur lunges.

I step back and angle the katana forward, as its pommel strikes the wall behind me. The Blur can't avoid the blade, and takes it, center chest, sliding down the smooth metal until its ribbed chest strikes the guard.

But being impaled is nothing to a creature that lives inside this humanoid suit. Its hands reach up and find my neck.

"August!" Mark shouts. I turn to see him aiming at the Blur, but he doesn't take a shot, no doubt not trusting his aim. And then he's attacked, defending himself against a Blur of his own.

The alien fingers tighten around my neck.

With my face growing hot and red, my vision narrowing and my lungs burning, my resolve blossoms like some horrible flower. The silverback smiles at the Blur. And then shoves.

The Blur hits the wall on the opposite side of the hallway. The blade, still clutched in my hands impales deeply, striking wood.

With the last of my strength, nearly blind from oxygen deprivation, I twist and release the sword, reach beneath it and wrap my arms around the Blur. When my legs give out and I fall sideways, I pull the Blur with me.

The pressure on my neck bursts free.

I breathe long and hard, sucking in air. A fog horn in reverse. When my vision returns, I see the Blur, sliced nearly in half, its stringy insides wriggling, but beyond function.

Using the embedded sword handle as a handhold, I get back to my feet. I try pulling the blade free, but it's wedged deep inside the wall and the wood beyond.

Doesn't matter, I decide, and launch up the stairs. I take the first two steps in one stride, thinking I'll take them all two at a time, but my legs nearly give out with the second leap. I'm forced to jog up the flight, one step at a time, hand on the railing, the old, cherry banisters creaking and wobbling back and forth as I depend on them to support my weight.

The open hallway at the top wraps around to what I think must be the master bedroom. It's also the only door that appears bent and shimmering.

A baby's cry pierces the air.

I charge down the hallway, bend to leap and then slip to a stop, falling to one knee, several feet short of the Blur. Before it realizes I'm there, I duck into a side room and come face-to-face with a HAM radio. *The* HAM radio. A thing of legend. A glimmer of a smile appears on my face, but then I'm back on my feet and lifting the desk chair. I hurry back to the door and swing the chair out into open space, aiming for the Blur.

The chair sails free from my hands, and I duck back inside the HAM radio room. There's a pulse of energy and the chair explodes back through the upstairs hallway, crashing down the stairs.

Remembering my knife, I draw it and rush around the corner, colliding, head-on with the Blur, who has turned around. I fall back, but not before thrusting my blade up under the creature's chin. The razor sharp blade slices through the rubbery skin, unleashing a wriggling white beard of dripping white gore. The Blur spasms as I get back to my feet, clutch it in both hands, slam it into the hallway wall and then reverse directions. The hallway banister catches the thing at waist height and it spills over the side, toppling down the stairs.

I turn to rush into the bedroom beyond, where I believe Poe and Squirt are, but I'm blocked by a blurry wave of motion. And then, I'm struck. Hard. Energy flows through me, and then tosses me down the hall. I strike a door, knocking it from its hinges before landing on a hard tile floor and sliding until I strike the equally hard, tiled wall. *A bathroom*, I think, as my vision, once again, fades. This time, no amount of breathing can save me from oblivion.

But maybe my will can. I fight against it. Fight to stand. All I manage to do is stumble and bump my head again.

The Blur's face emerges.

Growing closer.

The sharp, stinging scent of ammonia fills the air.

It's him, I think. The Blur that killed Steve Manke, that tried to kill Mark and put a hole in my shoulder.

A long, pointed finger slips out from the cloak, zeroing in on my chest. On my heart. The unfinished job nearly complete.

Its sinister gaze leaves no doubt about my fate.

It's going to finish the job. It's going to control me. Use me. To kill the others. Poe. Squirt.

Adrenaline surges, chasing away unconsciousness, but failing to rouse me fully. I focus all my effort on my arms, lifting them slowly, urging my fingers to work.

The Blur's hand coils back, a snake about to strike, and then it stabs forward. I brace for the sharp pain of a puncture wound and then the burning agony of spreading infection, but neither occur. Instead, my hands ache. The pointed digit is clutched in my shaking hands, held back, but not stopped. The needle-tipped finger slides steadily toward my heart.

I scream out, terrified more about what I will become than by the idea of losing my life.

The needle slips through the fabric of my clothing like it was made of the loosest molecules, and then pricks my skin.

But only for a moment.

I look away from the sight as a scream, as primal and raw as anything I've managed, sounds out from behind the Blur. An axe, the wood deep brown from years of use, the head rusty and nicked, descends on the Blur, caving it in, folding the eyes upside down, and stopping in the thing's neck. The heavy blade comes up and down twice more, each with a powerful grunt.

And then...

Poe.

I see her face first, pale and sweaty, exhausted and glorious.

Then I see her body, naked and plastered in blood.

Her blood.

Something stronger than adrenaline bolsters me. I find my feet and stand.

Poe drops the axe. "You made it."

I reach for her. "I promised."

"Just a tad late," she says, and she falls into my arms. We collapse to the floor together, just outside the bathroom. I want to hold her like I used to hold Claire. I want to stroke her hair. Kiss her cheeks. Tell her I'm here. That I'll never leave her. But I can't. The creature behind her takes my breath away.

It's an uncloaked Blur.

But that's not what stops me. Clutched in its arms is a baby, bloody, kicking and...quiet. Consoled. Safe. A golden retriever that must be Luke and a smaller mutt peek around the creature at me, like I'm the one who shouldn't be here, though Luke can't seem to stop his tail from wagging.

The smell of roses wafts over me.

The Blur bends down as Mark races up the stairs, aiming his weapon at the creature's head. I hold up a hand, stopping him. He sees Poe, and then the baby. Eyes wide, he lowers the weapon and watches as the Blur extends its arms, offering Squirt to me.

The baby is deposited in the crook of my arm. I hold the child—a girl—and her mother, weeping freely. My new family is together at last. Hands occupied, energy sapped, I can do nothing to stop what happens next. The Blur lifts its hands away from Squirt and holds them out on either side of my head. In the periphery, I see thin white tendrils snake out. With gentle taps, they make contact.

In a flash of white, I'm no longer on Earth.

54

AUGUST

Whiteness engulfs me. But it's not bright, like light. More like I've been immersed in an ocean of endless, living fettuccini. The scientist in me says that all this material, loose, wet and writhing, should block out whatever light exists, that I shouldn't be able to see it at all. But I can see it. Or rather, experience it. I'm seeing myself from the outside, like a movie, but I'm still attached to my senses. I can feel the tightening mass worming closer.

Something tickles my eyes. I blink it back, but then it's inside my lowered eyelid, wriggling deeper. I try to scream, but my mouth fills. My nose, too. The undulating worms slip deeper, into lungs, gut and mind.

I am lost.

The white slips away, revealing a bedroom. My bedroom, thirty-five years previous. I'm in my childhood home, surrounded by long forgotten, but familiar and comforting sights—posters, toys, shelves of science fiction novels. Also familiar smells. Meatloaf. My mother is cooking downstairs.

I spent a lifetime in this room, mostly thinking, sometimes planning my future, willing my spirit to leave this world like a starship and explore the universe. While the dreams of my younger self return with a flood of nostalgia, I am still myself. A man. A warrior. Smarter, stronger, and not alone.

I turn to the presence in the room and find a Blur, exposed. There is no cloak hiding it. There is no biological containment suit. I see it. The long worm, coiled up in a formless pile. It's a single organism that must stretch for hundreds of feet when laid out straight. Its mass rivaling that of a human, its mind spread out along its length. *They evolved in water,* I think, *but longed for land, and then beyond.*

You are right, a voice says, and I know it's the Blur. The formless lump pulls tighter, finding form, wrapping around itself to form a rudimentary humanoid shape. Without a suit, the effort is continuous.

Images flit through my mind. A vast sea. Long white tendrils adrift. At the mercy of currents. Winds. Predators. Over time, they grow. Biological defenses emerge. Time grants intelligence. Community. Purpose. Dry land is viewed as precious, and bodies, like a fungus, are grown. Freedom granted. But it's just the beginning. In time, attention turns to the night sky. To worlds beyond. Countless experiments await. A society of scientists, hungry for knowledge.

It's a snapshot of otherworldly evolution. A glimpse into what drives the Blur. It's not resources, or greed, or bloodlust. It's knowledge. The simple act of discovery is addictive in a way I understand, but have never fully experienced. While humanity splits its longing between the mind and flesh, the Blur are purely cerebral. There is no mind-to-body ratio. They are living brains, contained in living suits, evolved to understand. To experiment.

The Earth *is* a laboratory, but not in the way that I thought.

While I had conjured theories of panspermia—the seeding of life on Earth by extraterrestrial beings—humanity was unknown to the Blur until seventy years ago. I see glimpses of Earth at the time, wrapped in multiple wars. Primitive and destructive to the observers. Silverbacks all. A lesser life form. Fit for experimentation.

A flurry of images flit through my mind. Abductions. Experiments, from subtle to overt. Subjects dying. Tortured. Wounded physically and emotionally. Wars influenced. Nature manipulated. A playground for learning. An oasis for beings composed of neurons.

Over time, a grand scheme. A meddling with the human genome. A created defect. A weakness. Made to spread. Generations carried it forward until nearly every human being on the planet was susceptible.

To what? I think.

A news report plays in front of my mind. The BBC. An update on Hochman's, the disease ravaging the human race, presenting with flu like symptoms.

We were made susceptible to Hochman's.

No.

The thought is not my own.

We were used to *create* Hochman's. That genetic flaw, bred into the human race, was by design. It made us vessels. Living incubators. How many modern plagues have actually been designed? And for what purpose? Are they just curious? Trying to cure their own ailments? Creating biological weapons? The Blur, like most science-minded people, are not very good at war. They have the capacity for it, but not the natural inclination. But if what we've seen here is any indication, there is a schism within Blur society.

Information is dumped into my mind. Images mixed with other senses made vague by a tightly confining suit. Memories.

'Schism' isn't a strong enough word to describe the divide between the divergent species of Blur. The simplest terms that come to mind are pure and impure. On the pure side are intellectual beings of infinite curiosity, tempered by respect for life, sentient or not, prizing wisdom above all else. The noodley Blur standing in the middle of my childhood bedroom, swaying back and forth, is one of these creatures. On the other side are the impure, driven by an addictive thirst for knowledge with no restrictions for how it is attained. Each discovery is a rush. Each advance an ego boost. I also detect a growing desire for conquest. Expansion.

Control.

I theorize aloud. "The bullseye rash. The control it allows. It only works on people with this genetic flaw. It's like a genetic backdoor, but instead of using it to hack a computer, they're hijacking humanity. They were going to enslave us. Build an empire on our backs. Hochman's was just the beginning."

The human race has done this a multitude of times throughout history. We understand how it works, and that it works well. It's why, to this day, people try to dominate each other. To the victors go the spoils.

But the impure, equal in might to the pure, and far too dispersed to wage a successful war, have come to create an army. But before they could control us, they had to change us. So they rewired the human race, making us slave-ready, but also weaponized. Plague carriers.

But not everyone. Some were immune to the change. Pure humanity still exists. Steve Manke. The name and his death replay in my mind. The Blur didn't try to infect him. It simply killed him. But me...they let me live. I was one of their children. Impure. *'Join us, brother.'* Not yet controlled, though. All of these people I've been shepherding. They are the literal future of mankind. Genetically free from manipulation.

But me...

I look down at my not-real self. At my chest. I tear open the shirt, revealing the dark bullseye rash emanating from my shoulder.

"I'm infected."

The Blur says nothing. Silent confirmation.

"But not controlled...because they missed my heart. But my DNA is corrupt... Like the other survivors with the rash. I'm susceptible to control. To Hochman's. Or anything else they've developed. And there is no cure, is there? Not even from you."

My thoughts drift to the men and women who attacked us. The savagery. They represent the human race's future. Or, at least, used to. Until...

"Oh my God." I stand and pace, wanting to attack the Blur across from me, but knowing it will do no good. This communication, while it feels real and physical, is neither. We are still in the hallway, in Poe's parent's house, and there is a baby—Squirt—held in my arms. I calm myself, fearing that my actions in this place might affect reality.

I thrust an accusing finger at the Blur. "*You* did it! *You* destroyed the human race! Not them. Not the impure. It was *you!*"

A single step in the Blur's direction is all the time it takes for me to feel its response. Overwhelming sadness. The human race was...corrupt. As a species we were on the verge of failure. Of being hijacked and lost.

My assault loses steam.

"You had no choice..." I say. The words taste sour, but feel true. "All those people..." All those lives, including Claire... There was no other way to save us. But is genocide ever acceptable? Could I even make that choice? Even if it was, technically, the right thing to do? As a member of the human race, with deep relationships, could I agree to mass extermination? To the murder of not just countless billions, but also my dearest friends and family? I doubt it. I probably would have fought it. But looking at this from the outside, with an analytical mind... If a population of endangered animals became infected with a disease that would wipe out the species, would the human race think twice about culling the infected to save the rest?

Unlikely.

Despite the loss of billions, the human race will survive, but not as slaves to the Blur. Poe and Squirt, Mark, Tanya, Jeb, Luis and the rest, will all live full lives, the first of a new humanity. A genetic restart, free of tinkering.

I look up at the Blur. It has no eyes, but I sense it can see me.

"But not me."

More silence. More confirmation. I need to come to this conclusion on my own. Or, at least, it's giving me the opportunity, a gift not granted to the rest of humanity.

"You have to kill me." It's not a question. I would never sacrifice Poe's future for my selfish desire to keep breathing. "As long as I'm alive, I'm a threat to all of them. And to you." Even if I don't have children and pass my DNA to a next generation, my body still contains all of the genetic code the more sinister Blur need to reproduce their work. Leaving me alive would be like ridding the world of nuclear weapons, but leaving just one, ready to be reverse engineered.

It nods slowly.

"But not yet."

The head tilts. A question.

Why?

"To say goodbye."

A second nod. I feel the connection drifting apart, but say, "Wait!" My bedroom flickers, but refocuses. "How did you know?"

About what?

"About me. You took all those people's parents, right? Implanted thoughts. Designs. Set them on a path that would lead them here, to Poe. To Squirt, who—" A tangential thought breaks in. "They were here for Squirt. They wanted to see if she would be born impure, right? To see if future generations would be susceptible to the same manipulation?"

She is not.

The statement answers the previous question and my next, so I shift back out of the tangent. "The parents of all those people. They all wrote notes. Two-word messages, all the same except for Poe's."

Find August.

"How did you know? About me?"

We did not. Your survival was unintentional.

"Then how did—"

Time is a dimension. With technology it can be seen, vaguely, in forward or reverse. The process is...difficult. As is the subtle directing of thought, without outright control. Years spent searching unveiled the path to success. The parents led us to the mother. The mother to the child. And the child...to the future, and a name.

My name, I think, and then I realize what I'm being told. "*Her* name?"

The child in your arms, August, will carry your legacy, in name.

Tears flow down my cheeks.

I sit on my old bed, the springs popping like they always did.

"These people...all this time...they weren't looking for me. They were looking for *Squirt*—the child who had not yet been born, but would be named August?"

The Blur steps toward me, places its wrapped tendril hands on the sides of my head.

I thank you for your part in the journey. Far more of your species survived than we projected. But I am afraid it is time...to say goodbye. Is there anything we can do for you, to ease your passage?"

I'm about to answer, but stop. I look around the room, full of moon posters, astronaut toys, and Time-Life book collections. The dreams of a child.

"Actually..."

55

POE

Three days. That's how long August waits to reveal his fate. He tells me all about it, his communication with the Blur I call 'Rose,' who disappeared in a flash of light. About Hochman's. About Rose and her faction of Blur being the ones who killed humanity, and my parents, and why. Genetic purity sounds a lot like the evils of mankind, except, August points out, that this purity has nothing to do with race or nationality. The now hundreds of people who have found their way here, come from around the country. Around the world. August thinks that there will eventually be thousands of us. And they're all here, for August.

Baby August.

He holds her in his big arms, forehead to forehead. He talks to her in a calm cooing voice, the way I speak to Luke. "You're a good baby. What a sweetheart." He kisses her head once, and then twice more. She gurgles and grabs his nose. "I know," he says, like they've just communicated. "I love you, too."

The importance of my child is not because she'll be a leader, or savior or anything so grand, it's that she is the beginning of the future. *Our* future. Purity achieved. And the Blur saw fit to bring a community to us, to me, the one of us unable to move and in need of support. We're still talking about heading south before winter arrives, but we'll wait for late arrivals. Since we no longer fear the more malevolent Blur, whose technological advances do not include the ability to reduce targeted species to dust, modern vehicles are available to us again. And August says that there are enough skilled workers that wherever we end up, we might still have power, though the rest of the world will crumble to dust long before our descendants repopulate the world.

It's all good news, but it doesn't feel that way.

For all of this to happen, to appease the strict standards of the human race's purifiers, August must die. In the meantime, the Blur have been scouring the Earth clean of the branded survivors, the people August calls Rashes. They survived by being off planet—so crazy—and were returned to kill those of us whose DNA was still fully human. Except in my case. I think Leila was here to watch over Squirt. Maybe even be·here to catch and abduct her at her birth. But her mind was too fragile to make it that long. The Blur who were turning the human race into a biological weapon have fled, abandoning Earth, their seventy years of experimentation eradicated.

August gently squeezes my child and holds her out to me. "I have to go now."

I ranted and raved against August's fate, until my tired, post-pregnancy body surrendered. There is no choice. His presence here, on this planet, threatens the Blur's plan to save us. Being scientists of the highest order, there is no margin for error. August explained it to me as a speck of dust in a clean room. It—he—could ruin everything.

And he is at peace with it.

So now, as the sun sets, on the third day, I stand at the cusp of my woods, August, and little August, in my arms, saying goodbye to the man I hoped would be her grandfather. He has said goodbye to the others. Only Mark remains, several feet behind me, trying his best not to weep, but failing. This goodbye is private. Family only. And while I haven't yet thought of Mark in that way, August does.

August stands, back to the woods, facing me, a smile on his face. He pets Luke, who has forced his way under his hand. The golden is here without his new friend, the less intuitive farm dog that I've dubbed Frida.

"Why are you smiling?" I ask August.

"You're alive," he says. "Both of you. It's all I've thought about for six months." He puts a hand on my cheek, then on the baby's. "Listen, this is going to sound horribly cheesy, but I want you to do it. It's going to be dark soon. Stay outside. Watch the sky."

"For what?" I ask.

"Their second promise."

The Blur, it seems, granted August two requests for his part in saving more people than was expected. The first was time to say goodbye. The second is a mystery to me, but will apparently be visible in the night sky.

August glances over his shoulder, to the woods, where a hundred yards back, there's a hill. My father made me a treasure map once. The path led me to the top of that hill, clear of trees, exposed to the sun. He'd hidden chocolate coins there, under a rock. It's a sacred place, reserved for the men I love. It's where he will leave me, for good.

"I have to go," he says again, and my body trembles.

Suddenly, Mark is there, shaking with silent sobs, arms around August once more. I break down when August kisses the man's forehead and tells him he loves him. I join the embrace, little August, safe between us.

"You are the strongest woman I've ever known, Poe," August whispers, before kissing my cheek, and then the baby's. "I love you, both."

He takes a step back, leaving Mark and me, still wrapped in each other's arms. He takes his Red Sox cap off, looks it over and places it on my head. I accept the offering, and the symbolism, like the greatest of awards.

"This is just the beginning for you," he says. "Enjoy this life. It will shape the world." With that, he turns and enters the woods, slipping into the shadows. Luke follows him, but turns back a moment after fading from view.

I stand at the edge of the woods, baby in my arms, Mark and Luke at my sides, willing August to change his mind. Defy the cold rose-scented bastards. Hide from them! Live!

We stay that way for ten minutes.

When a phone rings, I nearly shout.

"What is that?" Mark asks, looking at me.

The sound is coming from little August. I pull apart the blankets she's wrapped in and find a phone. My phone. Repaired and ringing.

I answer it.

"It's nice up here," he says, before I can speak. "I can see why your father liked it."

I try to reply, but just end up blubbering.

"I wanted to say goodbye like this," he says. "It's how I knew you. Too sappy?"

I manage a snotty, "Uh-uh."

"Good," he says. "I love you."

"Love you, too."

"Hanging up now."

"Okay."

"See ya."

"Bye."

The signal cuts out. "August?"

I lower the phone. "August!" I run into the woods, rounding trees like a wide receiver, baby clutched in my arms.

Luke bounds by my side, barking. Mark calls after me, running to catch up, to stop me, to tell me I'm being stupid, that I'm endangering the baby. I know all these things already, so I keep right on running until I reach the hill, out of breath, my body aching, not really ready to stand for very long, let alone to sprint. I start up the hill as Mark catches up. Instead of stopping me, he takes my arm and helps.

We crest the hill together, the night gathering above us, purple sky revealing non-threatening stars. I stop when I see his clothing, crumpled in the leaf litter.

I step closer, looking for something to bury. That last honor can still be bestowed on him, his remains next to my parents. But there's something wrong. Something missing. "Where is he?" I ask, looking down at the clean, powder-free clothing.

Mark crouches down and lifts August's shirt. It's clean. "I don't know."

We stand in silence, thinking about possibilities, but not voicing them.

When baby August stirs and cries to be fed, already aware enough to mouth at my shirt, night has arrived. Luke has settled down, tongue hanging as he lies in wait for us to move.

"We should head back," Mark says. "The others will be worried."

I turn my head up toward the dark sky. "He told us to watch."

Mark looks up. "He didn't say when, though. We can't stay out here all night."

I smile. "He wouldn't dare make me wait again."

Mark chuckles, and then, it happens.

A bright streak of light is followed by a second, and then, in a burst, a cloud of them. Beautiful. A promise of a better future.

"Dude..." Mark says, wonder in his voice. "How did he do that?"

"It's dust," I say, and I bark out a laugh that startles Luke, Mark and August. I look down to the clean clothing. "It's him."

A NOTE FROM JEREMY

I've written a lot of novels, most on my own and a good number with co-authors, but none quite so unique in terms of its story, its characters and how the manuscript was written. While *The Distance* was written with a co-author, there are a few things about the arrangement that set it apart. The first is that my co-author for this novel is my wife, Hilaree.

During the first fifteen years of my writing career (thirteen years of toiling without pay) Hilaree was essentially my writing coach. While I had no experience or schooling when it came to writing fiction, Hilaree was an English major before she dropped out to marry me. She'd spent most of her life writing, and reading novels, while I was focused more on comic books and movies. They're perfectly good creative outlets, but they're not novel writing. Without Stephen King's *On Writing*, Strunk and White's *The Elements of Style* and Hilaree's honest critiques, I would not be an author.

So writing a novel with Hilaree was very exciting, but also a little intimidating (for both of us). Hilaree has a high standard for literature, so I was afraid I wouldn't measure up to her more beautiful prose and deeper characters. At the same time, Hilaree was unpublished and writing with her husband, who had now written more than fifty books and was in a position to teach *her* a thing or two.

Despite our mutual fears, the combination of our voices, transformed into the voices of August and Poe, and we turned this book into one of the best books I've ever written. Hilaree's involvement elevated my writing and character development, while she benefitted from my plot development and penchant for action. I have rarely been so proud of how well a book came out, and I'm equally proud of Hilaree, for facing and overcoming her fears about writing a novel while being a full-time homeschooling mom of three kids. That alone is impressive, but the end result of our combined hard work is something special. Like our children, *The Distance* is something we created together, and I'm excited to see what it becomes when we set it loose on the world.

As always, if you enjoyed *The Distance*, and want to spread the word, reviews on Amazon remain one of the best ways to make that happen (in addition to sharing via social media). And as this is Hilaree's first novel, I'd personally love to see gobs of reviews. Thank you!

—Jeremy

ACKNOWLEDGMENTS

The Distance has been a long time coming. To make sure it was released right, I pulled it from its original 'Big Five' publisher, and then turned down an offer from another who wanted to publish it. Of all my novels, this is the one for which I feel most protective. After years of consideration, I decided the publisher best qualified to bring this novel out to the world, in the way I believe it should be, was my very own Breakneck Media. This meant giving up big store distribution, but it also meant the cover, design, formatting and cover price—good news for my readers—would be superior.

To Kane Gilmour for edits supreme, Roger Brodeur for line edits, and all of our proofreaders—Kelly Allenby, Lyn Askew, Sherry Bagley, Liz Cooper, Dustin Dreyling, Donna Fisher, Jamey Lynn Goodyear, Dee Haddrill, Becki Laurent, Jeff Sexton and John Shkor—I offer my kaiju-sized thanks. You guys help make all of my Breakneck releases primo. Couldn't do it without you.

And of course, massive thanks to my wife, Hilaree, who joined me on this crazy post-apocalyptic vision and took a chance writing something with her husband. That the book came out so amazing is a testament to our 21 years of marriage and the perfectly fit puzzle pieces that are our brains. Love you.

ABOUT THE AUTHORS

Jeremy Robinson is the international bestselling author of over fifty novels and novellas, including *Apocalypse Machine, Island 731,* and *SecondWorld,* as well as the Jack Sigler thriller series and *Project Nemesis,* the highest selling, original (non-licensed) kaiju novel of all time. He's known for mixing elements of science, history and mythology, which has earned him the #1 spot in Science Fiction and Action-Adventure, and secured him as the top creature feature author.

His series of Jack Sigler / Chess Team thrillers, starting with *Pulse,* is in development as a film series, helmed by Jabbar Raisani, who earned an Emmy Award for his design work on HBO's *Game of Thrones.* Robinson's novels *Project Nemesis* and *Island 731* have both been adapted into comic books through publisher American Gothic Press, in association with *Famous Monsters of Filmland.* Robinson's works have been translated into thirteen languages.

Robinson is also known as the bestselling horror writer, Jeremy Bishop, author of *The Sentinel* and the controversial novel, *Torment.* In 2015, he launched yet another pseudonym, Jeremiah Knight, now the best-selling post-apocalyptic author of the *Hunger* series of novels.

Born in Beverly, MA, Robinson now lives in New Hampshire with his wife and three children.

Visit Jeremy Robinson online at www.bewareofmonsters.com.

ABOUT THE AUTHORS

Hilaree Robinson is an artist, writer and homeschooling mother of three children. When she's not writing, painting or organizing an art show, she's working on poetry, conjuring adventures for the family or hiking the White Mountains in New Hampshire. *The Distance* is her debut novel.